KEYSTONE
A CROSSBREED NOVEL

USA TODAY BESTSELLING AUTHOR
DANNIKA DARK

All Rights Reserved
Copyright © 2017 Dannika Dark
First Edition: 2017

First Print Edition
ISBN-13: 978-1539818380
ISBN-10: 1539818381

Formatting: Streetlight Graphics

No part of this book may be reproduced, distributed, or transmitted in any form or by any means, or stored in a database retrieval system, without the prior written permission of the author. You must not circulate this book in any format. Thank you for respecting the rights of the author.

This is a work of fiction. Any resemblance of characters to actual persons, living or dead, is purely coincidental.

Professionally edited by Victory Editing and Red Adept.
Cover design by Dannika Dark. All stock purchased.

www.dannikadark.net
Fan page located on Facebook

Also By Dannika Dark:

THE MAGERI SERIES
Sterling
Twist
Impulse
Gravity
Shine
The Gift (Novella)

MAGERI WORLD
Risk

NOVELLAS
Closer

THE SEVEN SERIES
Seven Years
Six Months
Five Weeks
Four Days
Three Hours
Two Minutes
One Second
Winter Moon (Novella)

SEVEN WORLD
Charming

THE CROSSBREED SERIES
Keystone

Once upon a midnight dreary…
- Edgar Allan Poe

Chapter 1

"Mmm, just like my mom used to make," I said, choking on my disgust as I unlatched my mouth from the whiskery neck of a Mage. I hated relying on my Vampire nature, but sometimes it was a necessary evil to subdue my victims.

Not one to leave evidence, I wiped a drop of blood off the brown tile.

The paunchy man curled his lips where he lay on the floor, his face ashen.

I launched to my feet when someone outside the door jiggled the handle to get inside the private bathroom. The club had public ones farther down the hall, but there was always one joker who wanted a room to himself. The knocking finally ceased, and I listened as the footsteps grew distant. Taking down evildoers in human clubs was easier since there was less chance of someone calling the Breed authorities, especially since humans didn't have a clue about our existence.

I caught my reflection in the mirror as I turned—my black hair askew, burgundy lipstick smeared across my chin. Then I glared down at the man lying at my feet. "You shouldn't take advantage of humans. Stealing energy from a weaker species is just vile."

He didn't have any strength left to move. "Who are you?" he groaned weakly, his eyelids fluttering.

I knelt down and offered to shake his hand. "I'm Raven Black. Pleased to make your acquaintance, human killer." When he stared at my hand nonplussed, I flattened my palms against his and hovered over his face. "Maybe you're a high-five kind of guy." Before he could struggle, I proceeded to drain his energy.

This repugnant juicer was about to find out that I wasn't just a Vampire, I was a crossbreed—a one-of-a-kind combination of Vampire and Mage. Vampires have black eyes, and since mine were mismatched, it had confused him when I had to drain his blood to weaken him further. Now he was even more puzzled as to how it was possible I could pull his Mage light. It didn't matter to me. Only the dead knew my secret.

Breeds who can have children frown upon interbreeding. The magic between two different Breeds cancels each other out, creating a watered-down version of a species. Once in a blue moon, the powers weave together in a dangerous way.

After all, I was proof.

The difference being that I had once been an ordinary human who—like everyone else—didn't have a clue that the Breed world existed. Vampires can offer the gift of immortality to humans just as a Mage can, but a human body can't accept the power of both at once. You're either one or the other. Except in my case.

Magic will always find a way to bend the rules.

I glared into his beady little eyes, his dark light beginning to contaminate my own. "What did humans ever do to you? They're not disposable goods. You can't go around juicing their light and then throwing them away like an empty cup. I've been following you around for the past week, and I know all about your light addiction. You're littering the streets with their bodies like they're Popsicle sticks. I bet you didn't think anyone was watching, did you? *I see everything*," I hissed.

"What are you going to do?" he asked, choking on his own fear.

I squeezed his palms tightly. "You've had your opportunity for redemption. Sorry, human killer. Lights out."

"You can't kill me; it's against the law."

A smile touched my lips. "You're a declared outlaw. I asked around. That means you're wanted dead or alive."

"Then turn me in."

A little reward money would be nice, except for one tiny problem: I didn't exist in the Breed world. I'd been living as a rogue since the day I was illegally made.

Why couldn't this guy have been a Shifter? Or even a Relic? The only ways to kill a Mage involved decapitation, burning alive, and other gruesome methods I wasn't eager to entertain. We weren't magicians or sorcerers as humans believed, but immortals who manipulate energy as a weapon or source of power. Every Mage has core light, and even if you drain all their energy, that core will always replenish. That's what makes them immortal.

Unless someone has the ability to remove it.

The first time I discovered my rare gift to remove core light, I let my victim go. I thought it would be sweet revenge for him to live out a miserable human existence. Later I discovered that he'd located a Creator—a Mage with the rare gift to make another—and paid him good money to become immortal again.

Then I had to kill him for real.

"Hold still," I said, dreading what was to come. "This will only take a second."

His eyes hooded as he struggled to remain conscious. "Jesus, I'll pay you."

"Oh?"

Usually it was empty threats and cursing my immortal soul; this was the first time someone had actually offered me money. "How much?"

"I've heard about you," he grunted. "I've got money... *Lots*."

I rubbed my palms against his, considering the offer. Was I an easy sellout? I hadn't held a job in the years since I was human. Having a place to live would be nice. The Vampire part of me didn't need sleep, but the Mage side did, so I spent a lot of time napping in movie theaters or Laundromats. It saved on rent, but I missed having a bed of my own.

"How much is lots and lots? Or did you just say lots?"

His chin pressed against his chest. "In my pocket there's a bank card. I'll tell you the PIN—you can take it all."

"How many lives have you destroyed, can you count that? All

because you wanted to get high from their light. Does that card belong to one of your victims?" When he didn't answer, I sighed. Letting him go would mean issuing a death sentence to countless humans. "Sorry, Mage. The pity parade just left town."

With my hands still gripping his, I pulled every last drop of energy until his core light snuffed out. There was an audible snap that cracked like a whip, followed by a bright flash of light. His energy tasted bitter and cold, mixing with my own like poison. I'd retain it for another day before it naturally leaked out.

I'd once overheard a Mage talking about his gift as an Infuser. Supposedly, if someone like me pulled core light out of a Mage, an Infuser could permanently seal it to my own, meaning I'd get to keep their gifts. But if that meant their dark energy would stay with me forever, then no thanks.

The darker the light, the sicker I felt. My stomach turned, and I wasn't sure I was going to make it through the night.

The Mage gasped in disbelief, finally comprehending my full power when he felt his own mortality. Before he could protest, I lifted my blade, centered it over his heart, and drove it in to the hilt.

The best part about being a woman? I rarely paid for my own drinks in a Breed bar. Food, however, was another matter.

Vampires don't require food to survive. But I was only half Vampire, and my Mage half was starving. Especially after the showdown earlier in the human club down the street. I still had the vile taste of bad blood in my mouth.

I took a seat next to a burly man in a red shirt. "Hey, are those any good?"

He put away a large tortilla chip loaded with meat and gave me a skeptical appraisal.

Out on the streets, most people assumed I was a human since my energy was undetectable and I didn't look like a Vampire. In a Breed bar, it wasn't as easy to read people with so much energy pulsing in the room. Most assumed I was either a Mage concealing my light or a Relic, since they're genetically identical to humans. The only thing that separated them was a Relic's ability to retain information and genetically pass it down to their children.

I gazed longingly at his nachos, wishing I had the charming abilities of a Vampire, but once again, destiny screwed me over.

"They're not bad. I've had better," he grumbled, as if implying something else.

"Mind if I try one?"

When he licked his thumb and narrowed his eyes, I gave him my best come-hither look, making sure he could only see my brown eye, which was my left one.

He nudged his plate toward me, and I chose a cluster of chips tied together with cheese, guaranteeing me the biggest bite. Some of it fell onto my lap.

"Oh, sorry about that," I said, shoving them into my mouth. "I didn't mean to take so many at once." I wiped at the cheese stain, irritated since it was my only dress. "I love a real man who knows how to share. What's your name?"

"Murphy. What Breed are you?"

Talk about a guy who got right to the point.

I could sense he was a Mage, so I chose the best possible answer he'd want to hear since there weren't as many Mage women in the dating pool. "I'm a Mage. I'm just concealing my light for a little privacy."

When he pulled back his plate and resumed eating, I realized he wasn't interested. Most would have jumped at the chance to be with a female Mage, but I should have taken the time to feel him out. Every so often, I'd run into a guy who preferred Shifters, blondes, or sometimes men.

Strike one.

I searched the bar for someone else who had a plate of food in front of him. Chitahs didn't usually share with a non-Chitah female since they had a dim view on interbreeding, so I skipped over any tall man with golden eyes. A Mage was always a safe bet, which was why I scouted them out by seeking their energy flares.

"Take it easy on those nachos, Murphy. Thanks for the bite."

When I stood up, I spotted a man with a plate of mini burgers. I salivated, my stomach growling like a grizzly bear coming out of hibernation. I leisurely strolled toward his table, formulating a game plan. Only one man had ever offered to buy me dinner; the rest behaved like lions protecting their kill, but every so often, I found one who would share.

Muscle shirt, gold necklace, cologne wafting from a mile away... Yeah, this guy was here for a good time.

I hadn't eaten a proper meal in over three days, and stealing wasn't a standard I lowered myself to. Hustling, on the other hand, was a challenge and helped me brush up on my social skills. But tonight my body ached from exhaustion and dark light, so the sooner I could end this hunt the better.

"That's the way I like to see a man eat," I said, sidling up to his chair.

He lowered his eyes to my legs. They were long, elegant, and could lock around a man's neck and rob him of consciousness in ten seconds flat.

I hooked my finger on the corner of his plate and dragged it in my direction. "How about if I feed you, would you like that?"

His hand grazed my bare thigh and I playfully slapped it.

Before he lost interest, I spun a chair around and straddled it. He all but choked when my black dress left an opening in the front.

I gave him a coy smile, eyeing his juicy cheeseburger. "Why don't you feed me, big boy? I need something big and juicy in my mouth."

He pinched the bridge of his nose and looked me up and down, his expression switching from interest to disgust. "Get the fuck out of here, leech."

Leech. One of the colorful words Breeds used for scavengers like me who had no family, no job, and no dignity. I called it survival.

Strike two.

Discouraged, I kicked the chair in and relocated to the far side of the room where I spotted a Vampire at the end of the bar with the largest plate of golden onion rings I'd ever seen.

Now that's a sight to behold, I mused.

I assessed his black coat and lace-up boots, which were as worn as mine and told me he wasn't a man who flaunted his money—if he even had any. His dark brown hair was a little long on top, and despite the short beard that had recently graduated from a five-o'clock shadow, I could see his chiseled cheekbones. He was so unassuming that I almost hadn't noticed him sitting there.

Vampires often hung out in bars, eavesdropping on conversations with their heightened hearing ability. Some of them worked as secret-sellers and blackmailed people for money, which was probably what this guy was doing. I didn't trust them, but hunger makes you do desperate things.

"Hi, handsome. Would you like some company?"

He flicked his wrist, waving me away. "Shoo. I'm busy."

My words became tight, and I flashed him a baleful look. "Maybe you should order a clove of garlic on the side, *Vamp*."

As I turned away, he wrapped his fingers around my throat and yanked me against him, my back to his chest. The Vampire's grip was iron, and I couldn't escape if I tried.

His breath heated my neck just behind my ear, and he spoke with a dark Irish accent. "Careful who you rub up against, lass. I'm not into parasites, but I'm willing to let it slide for a little action."

"Keep dreaming."

He chuckled darkly. "Why don't you check out where my hand is?" Beneath my dress, he squeezed his fingers, which were resting on my bare hip. One of them slid beneath the thin strap of my panties. "Mmm, lace. I bet they're as black as your hair, aren't they?"

I tipped my head back, a smile in my voice. "Why don't you check out where *my* hand is?"

He released his hold, and I slowly turned, one of my push daggers pricking his family jewels. They were my favorite weapon to carry. Easy to conceal, they varied in size, I could wear one almost anywhere on my body, and the T-shaped handle provided a solid grip.

I tapped the three-inch blade against his crotch, careful not to look him in the eye so he couldn't charm me. "You're lucky you caught me on a good night."

His wolfish brows drew together. "Unusual set of winkers you've got there. Why don't you raise them up an inch and give me a better look?"

I'd learned early on that Vampires wouldn't hesitate to use their gifts of persuasion—all they had to do was hypnotize you with those black eyes. I hadn't inherited that gift, so I got out of dangerous situations by relying on clever tactics.

Like staring at his Adam's apple.

"You might be stronger than I am, but you're not as fast as a Mage."

He casually rested his elbow on the mahogany bar and leaned on it. "I'll give you a ring if you go away."

"I don't want your onion rings, nor do I want your hand up my dress. I'm going to back away, and you're going to keep your hands where they are. You know the rules about fighting in a Breed bar."

"Aye, but do I care?"

What incensed me wasn't his cocksure attitude or even that he'd put his hand up my dress. It was the unexpected thrill of how inviting and sensual his hand felt against my thigh, the slow and delicate way his finger slid beneath my panties, the familiarity of his touch—so much so that I had to calm my heart to a steady beat before he picked up on it.

The Vampire kept his black eyes on me, the intensity of his gaze molten. A shadow of rogue whiskers trailed beneath his jaw as if they were trying to escape the flock.

He looped one of the onion rings around his index finger and offered me a sardonic smile. "Perhaps another time, precious. Good luck with the scavenger hunt."

Chapter 2

I'M NOT SURE WHY I'D embraced the life of a nomad, but the novelty was wearing thin. It used to be liberating to go anywhere I wanted and not worry about bills, gas, or rent. Immortals didn't need to trouble themselves with health insurance or wrinkle creams. But living out of a green duffel bag wasn't a glamorous life, and neither was washing my clothes in a restroom sink because I didn't have enough coins to operate a washer.

My human life was ancient history, and without being able to use my real name or social security number, I couldn't get a job even if I tried. My options were limited to the Breed world, where most people held jobs specific to their skills, and I don't just mean running a business or managing finances. Most Chitahs I knew were trackers because of their acute sense of smell, and I'd heard that Sensors made their money in the business of sensory exchange—buying and selling emotions for cash. I really didn't know for certain. Despite our differences from humans, it seemed like most people wanted the same things. A secure future, a job, and—depending on your Breed—family. Even if I applied for a job, no one was going to hire a crossbreed. Most people didn't think someone like me existed. People are afraid of what they don't understand, so in order to keep a low profile, I lied about my Breed and didn't make friends.

Being part Mage posed an even greater threat. Each Breed has its own form of government or law, and the Mageri catalogues every Mage legally created. They also require that every new Mage live with his or her Creator until granted their independence. If they found out about me, I could wind up in serious trouble. And I had no idea how Vampire elders ran things, so fear kept me a rogue.

I sat on the back of the toilet tank, my shoes on the seat, staring at my wet dress that hung on the stall hook. Unfortunately, the only hand dryer in the bathroom was broken.

After leaving the Breed bar on an empty stomach, I'd found the nearest human club where I could wash the cheese stain off my dress and relax. Since there weren't many cars in the parking lot, I figured it would be a good spot to chill for a little while. I'd hidden my duffel bag nearby; most humans thought people carrying large bags into a public place were terrorists. Human clubs were safe places, and unless I instigated a fight, I never had trouble. I still brought one of my push daggers with me just in case; the leg holster was looped around the hook on the door, hidden behind the dress. Most of the weapons I owned were ones I'd taken from my victims—trophies from battle.

I tugged at the frayed threads surrounding the hole in my jeans.

I'd give anything to have a bed right now. To be able to curl up with a blanket over my head until the misery of the Mage's dark energy left my body, but I had no place to call home. In the summertime, I climbed onto rooftops to sleep under the stars. Any high place I could gain access to felt like home and separated me from the dangers of the city. But tonight the heavy rain would make it difficult to find a dry place to sleep, especially with the storm drains overflowing and flooding the streets.

I never thought I could feel so damn lonely, but the weight of it pressed down with each passing year. I sometimes thought about it in the daytime when people were having lunch with friends or shopping with their children, but the melancholy feeling often struck me in the late hours of the night.

Being a bounty hunter wouldn't be such a bad gig. But who would hire me? I had no credentials, and if the higher authority figured out who I was and arrested me, I'd have no one to come to my rescue.

Imagining this as my life for the next five centuries was

terrifying—no one had prepared me for immortality. But whenever I found myself wallowing in solitude, reality would intrude, reminding me that settling down would only make it easier for a certain someone to find me, and that someone was the reason why I had to keep moving and stay in the shadows.

I rubbed my eyes, staring down at the bathroom tile. The only thing I wanted was to get through the night without any more drama.

"Is it empty?" a man asked in a low register.

I cocked my head, wondering if I'd accidentally wandered into the men's bathroom. Wouldn't be the first time.

Someone's clothes rustled, and a second voice with a scratchy tone answered. "It's clear. The stalls are empty."

"I want you to take care of him. He's not cooperating, and I've given him plenty of time to change his mind." It was a commanding voice, smooth and controlled.

"Don't you think someone's going to make a connection?" the second guy asked. "Maybe we should space it apart like the others. Two human club owners in one week—if the higher authority gets wind of it, they're going to hire someone to investigate."

"I don't give a damn," the first man replied. "It'll send a message to these humans that I mean business. They can either pay for my protection or risk one of the local gangs torching their club."

The second guy chortled. "Yeah, but *we're* the gang. The new ones always want proof or else they think it's just a rumor. Why don't we have a couple of guys go in, rough up the patrons, make threats, and vandalize the place to make it look real?"

"Because we're dealing with humans, and humans like to involve the police. You'll end up with witnesses who will ID my men, and that's too much cleanup. Let me worry about the details. You just do as you're told."

"You got it, Darius."

"Make it clean. No witnesses, no fingerprints, no surveillance cameras. Torch the place."

"Whatever you say, boss. I need to go pick up some gasoline, but it'll be done by morning."

I heard a long, drawn-out sigh before Darius spoke. "They have no right to be here."

Hinges on the door squeaked, and then it grew quiet. What the hell were these guys doing, messing around with humans?

Footsteps strolled in my direction, and then I heard the sound of unzipping in the stall to my right. The door hadn't opened again, so I presumed one of the men stayed behind to drain his pipe.

I stayed absolutely silent.

Until my stomach growled like a mountain lion.

I grimaced, hoping he hadn't heard. But when the stream of urine abruptly stopped, I had only seconds to prepare.

His footsteps retreated, and my door kicked in with a crash.

I smirked at a man with a bad comb-over. "You're not all that scary."

Before he could open his mouth, I dove forward and slammed into him. The force of my attack caused him to stumble backward into the sink. He gripped my shoulders and threw a blast of energy into me.

I fell onto my back, energized. Mage energy only worked as a weapon against other Breeds, but throwing your energy into another Mage only juiced them up.

"Ah, shit," he said, realizing his folly. "You're supposed to flare in a public place, Mage."

"Don't you think that's an archaic tradition? Seems like I'm not the only one in here who forgot to flare and make their presence known."

The pungent smell of bathroom soap hung heavy in the air as I rose to my feet to face this idiot. He looked like an out-of-shape mobster in a cheap black suit.

The Mage chewed on his bottom lip as if he couldn't decide what to do with me. We were in a human club, and that complicated matters. There wasn't much of a crowd, but I'm sure in that walnut head of his he was wondering if someone might be able to ID him if he left a corpse in the bathroom. Breed didn't get involved with human law enforcement, and if he got arrested and his boss found out, he might leave him to rot in a human jail for the next twenty years before breaking him out.

With my shoulders squared, I stood with my weight forward, prepared to fight. "I don't care about you or your boss, but you're talking about killing humans, and that's where it gets personal."

He snorted. "You're not even human. What the hell do you care what happens to these termites?"

"Oh, I don't know. Maybe because I used to be one? Their lives are short enough; what gives you the right to take it away?"

He smoothed back his stringy hair. "Immortality gives me the right. They're nothing but parasites, destroying the planet and getting all the power. You're obviously not old enough to appreciate how insulting it is to live like a cockroach beneath a weaker species."

"Do you really want to start a war with a species that outnumbers us by the billions? We still haven't won the war against fire ants."

The door swung open and we both looked up as two girls breezed in with a jaunty step.

"Get out," the Mage said. "I'm about to fuck my woman."

Their eyes swung over to me in surprise.

I shrugged. "Don't worry, we won't be long. He never lasts for more than forty-five seconds."

"Ugh," one of them groaned as they turned to leave. "Let's go check out that other place up the street."

"You didn't have to say that," he growled.

Was this guy serious? "Didn't mean to deflate your ego. I was just under the impression that you didn't sleep with the parasites you were plotting to exterminate. But maybe you *like* sleeping with bedbugs."

I should have moved sooner and put my back against a wall, but faster than a heartbeat, he flashed behind me and shoved me against the sink.

Flashing was a Mage skill I hadn't acquired, and it made them impossible to catch. Once again, destiny screwed me over.

"Smartass," he hissed in my ear. "Aren't you going to beg for your life—for your virtue?"

"I'm just going to beg for you to eat a breath mint," I ground out.

He kicked my legs open. "Beg."

That was when I looked up at him in the mirror and flashed a smile, revealing my sharp fangs in the mirror's reflection. "You first."

When I caught his startled expression, I shoved back and spun around. His eyes were stupidly transfixed on my fangs, darting between them and my mismatched eyes. Before he could react, I kneed him in the groin.

No matter what his strengths were as a Mage, all men had balls.

He doubled over, grimacing and grunting out a few colorful words. He hunched his shoulders, making it impossible to get a good angle to bite his neck. Kneeing him in the head did the trick.

I dropped to my knees and drove my fangs into his jugular, but before I could draw blood, he punched me in the side three times and threw me off.

"I'm going to teach you some fucking manners," he snarled, mashing my face against the cold, dirty tile.

I glanced up, my heart banging against my chest as I realized my dagger was out of reach. When he kicked me in the back, it nudged me a little closer to the stall. I crawled on my forearms, pushing back the pain and gathering up my energy.

He gripped my ankle, so I flipped onto my back, twisting my leg out of his grasp. Small spaces limited a Mage from flashing around much, which leveled the playing field since they had to rely on their fighting skills. And as I'd come to find out, not every immortal knew how to fight.

When he came at me, I kicked him in the head, and he fell onto his left side. Once he was down, I executed a maneuver and scissored my legs around his neck, my knees bent, exerting as much force as possible. Before he could throw a punch, I gripped his left arm in a tight lock and then angled my body so my head was out of reach.

He thrashed as I delivered enough force to cut off the circulation above his neck. His knee jerked out a few times, but he couldn't see where my head was. Then he tried to get up, but he was losing strength with every passing second.

When his body went limp, I didn't hesitate. I released my hold and fell over him, puncturing into his artery with my fangs and drawing out the blood before he knew what had hit him. After enough swallows, I licked his wound. My Vampire gifts allowed me to change the chemistry in my saliva at will so that I could seal up bite marks left behind on my victims.

I rose to my feet and staggered around him, my stomach churning as his blood made its way down. The thought of having to consume his Mage energy made me tremble with revulsion.

A gust of fresh air blew in when the bathroom door swung open, and an older blonde halted in her tracks. "Oh... Oh my God."

I glimpsed myself in the mirror and saw blood trickling down my lip.

"He attacked me. Call the police," I said, panic rising in my voice. I reached in the stall for my dress, folding it over my dagger.

Holy crap, this was a hot mess.

The woman's fingers were tapping on her phone, dialing a number. A night in the slammer would keep this bozo out of trouble for now, but that meant letting him live another day to commit crimes. What choice did I have?

I bristled at the thought that people would die if I didn't finish him off, but I needed to get out of there. If the human police arrested me, I wouldn't have anyone to post my bail. The higher authority kept an eye on all arrests, matching them with Breed aliases and bailing them out within a certain time frame. As a rogue, I didn't have an alias.

"Hello? We need the police, and... Do you need an ambulance?" she asked me, her eyes brimming with concern.

"No, I'll drive myself to the hospital," I said in a hoarse voice, pushing past her. "He beat me up, and he's drunk. I can't believe this is happening." My voice broke as I pretended to cry, and I moved swiftly past her through the club.

Out the door.

Through the rain.

Down the alley.

I ran until I finally collapsed behind a Dumpster, sheltered from the rain by a one-foot overhang and a sympathetic breeze.

Chapter 3

IT TOOK ME TWO DAYS to get on my feet again. Not just from consuming vile blood from two thugs, but drinking up dark Mage light. The only place I could find to sleep was inside an abandoned Dumpster in an alley. Since no one was using it for trash disposal, it didn't smell, but I still had to throw out a few old boards. At least it kept the rain off my head.

In the evenings, rain hammered against the metal lid and kept me awake with only my thoughts to pass the time. When the bruises began to heal up on their own, I ventured out in search of a newspaper, but I didn't find any articles about a murdered club owner or a building fire.

That Darius guy must have realized that someone knew about his plan, and executing it meant putting himself at risk. His henchman knew what I looked like, so I wasn't taking any chances with walking the streets in the Breed district.

The rain eventually tapered off and the temperature cooled down, making it the kind of night when you could see a trail of frosty breath on a hurried walk home. I brushed the dirt off my coat and headed to a human diner called Ruby's. It stood out on the corner of the intersection with its red neon sign. I only came in on Tuesdays because that was when business was slow and Betty worked a double shift. Betty McGuire was seventy-eight, tough as nails, and still dyed her hair red. I had to admire a woman with six grandchildren, two great-grandchildren, and a soft spot for girls like me who didn't have a place to go.

There was a small parking lot in front and along the right

side of the building. The inside had an L-shaped layout since the kitchen was hidden in a room behind the counter. Rotating pie displays and old-fashioned décor added a nostalgic touch. You could either order something to go at the front counter or find a seat and have a waitress take your order. There were a few small tables and booths to the left of the door, but usually the only people who used them where those waiting for takeout. Chrome barstools with red vinyl seats ran along the counter, which went to the right and then stretched halfway to the back where the seating area was. Some people liked sitting at the small round tables in the middle, but I preferred the privacy of the booths alongside the windows. Ruby's was the kind of place you could peacefully sit and enjoy a cup of coffee on a rainy day.

I headed toward the back and chose my favorite booth, shoving my bag beneath the table and against the wall before dusting off the red vinyl seat. Despite how much I loved Ruby's, it was always a shameful walk to the back. I felt like a stray dog with its tail between its legs, coming in to beg for scraps.

Betty spotted me from behind the counter and waved. She deserved a gold star for heroism, and I hoped her children appreciated her half as much as I did. She always brought me a hot meal, whether I wanted it or not, and took it out of her own paycheck. Knowing that, I only came in as a last resort.

Fifteen minutes later, my stomach was doing a happy dance. Steam rose from my coffee cup as I finished off my last chicken strip, and I turned my attention out the window, watching two birds splashing around in a puddle.

When someone entered the diner, I glanced up at a silver-haired fox of a man walking through the door. He looked old enough to be my father. His hair, combed back in a soft wave, had dark grey undertones that gave him even more character. His beard was nicely groomed, longer around the chin and mouth area. I often wondered what I would have looked like as an older woman if I hadn't stopped aging at twenty-five.

The busboy collected the dishes off a nearby table and loaded them onto a cart. When he disappeared into the kitchen, the older gentleman headed in my direction—no detours, no rest stops.

I sensed his energy as he approached. I didn't know what Breed he was, but we had stronger energy than humans did.

Instead of going to the bathroom, he stopped at my table. "You're the Shadow, and I'm interested in hiring you."

I choked on my coffee as he sat across from me. "The what?" While I wiped my mouth with a napkin, I studied him closely. English wasn't this man's first language. "Do I know you?"

Amusement danced in his steel-grey eyes. The lines in his forehead and at the corners of his eyes showed he was an expressive man, and not quite as old as I first thought.

He laced his fingers together. "Let's not play around," he said, a thick Russian accent rolling off his tongue. While he spoke gruffly, there was a cadence to his voice that was like warm brandy. "You're the one they whisper about—the one who kills notorious men. Rumors of your existence have a lot of men pissing in their pants."

I warmed my hands on my coffee cup, trying to figure him out. Energy from Breed varied on many levels, and I couldn't ascertain what he was from that. "Why did you call me the Shadow?"

"You do not know?" His brows arched, deepening the grooves in his forehead. "I am looking at an urban legend who has taken down some of the most elusive outlaws that not even the authorities could catch. People call you the Shadow because no one has seen your face, just hair spun from midnight. Some call you the angel of death, others call you the Ferryman."

"Shadow is better," I said, swirling a fry in a pile of ketchup. "Ferryman sounds like we should be on a gondola in Italy."

His pale eyes ruled out a Vampire or Chitah. He still hadn't flared, so unless he was concealing his energy, I didn't think he was a Mage either.

"What are you?" I asked, sliding my plate aside and resting my forearms on the table.

"Shifter," he said, scrutinizing me with his eyes.

Shifters lived hundreds of years, maybe longer, and aged slowly. By the looks of him, he was probably a few hundred years old.

He pinched his chin. "You are rough around the edges, but I think with the right help you could be one of the best."

"The best what?"

"We do all kinds of jobs, and I only select people who stand out from all the rest. You have an impressive track record of kills. What motivates you?"

"Good fries."

Who was this guy? Coming in like the Soviet KGB, and I hadn't even had my pie yet.

"Let me make this clear: it is not important why you hunt these men, only that you do it well. I want to make you an offer, and you should carefully consider my proposal because this opportunity will only come once. You can refuse, but if you change your mind, the offer will be off the table."

Betty appeared to my right, warming my coffee with a refill. "Can I get you something?" she asked the gentleman.

"*Nyet*, thank you," he replied warmly with a brisk nod of his head.

She turned to me, concern brimming in her eyes. "Honey, do you want a second helping?"

"No, ma'am. But if it wouldn't be too much trouble, do you have any pie?"

Betty chuckled and patted my hand. "I have the apple pie all warmed up for you. I know it's your favorite. Let me finish up something and I'll bring it right over."

"Ice cream?"

"You betcha."

I smiled in gratitude. "You're a lifesaver. Anyone ever tell you that?"

She walked off, just a small pear-shape of a woman, but she was a godsend.

"You are generous to the humans," my companion noted absently. "My name is Viktor Kazan. Do you come with a name, or should I just keep calling you the Shadow?"

I bit into my last chicken finger and decided introductions weren't going to kill me. "Raven."

"And what are *you*, my dear?"

"Hungry, so if you'd wrap up this little ray of hope you're bleeding all over my table, I'd like to get back to waiting for my pie."

He sat back, shoulders straight. "I want you to listen to what I tell you. What we do is not different from what you do, only it's cleaner. But we do so much more than that. It is dangerous work, but you'll be one of us, and that means protection. You'll have food, shelter, and a paycheck."

"Maybe sweeping the streets isn't a job to me; maybe it's a mission I do for the love of it."

Viktor leaned forward, lacing his fingers together. "Forgive me. I did not know I was dining with Mother Teresa. The next time you're searching for a hot meal and don't have a place to stay, remember that you're wasting your talents."

I sipped my coffee and then set down the white cup. "So you created your own little organization of bounty hunters. What makes you so different from them or that HALO group of do-gooders?"

"Because we do what bounty hunters can't and what HALO won't."

A chill ran up my spine. HALO was a group of men who investigated crimes and brought down criminals, but they did everything by the book. The same applied for most bounty hunters, except that they did more extensive traveling. If what he said was true, that meant the higher authority was possibly paying them to do things in secret—breaking laws without repercussions. Breed didn't have an official form of government, but the higher authority was as close as it got. Elected members from each Breed sat on the panel, and one was located in every major city throughout the United States. From what I knew, they were the ones who imposed sentencing, whether it be serving time in Breed jail or the death sentence.

"How did you find me?"

"You can only catch a shadow when you stand very still. I have a tracker who is good at what he does."

I blanched at the idea this guy had been following me. Had I left behind clues? Bread crumbs? Evidence?

He slid a white card in my direction. "Keep it."

Betty set a white dish in front of me with a slice of apple pie and vanilla ice cream. She took my empty plate and went about her business, wiping down tables and refilling the napkin holders.

I flipped the card over.

"All it says is ZERO. Is that your phone number or how many times you've been laid?"

"Go to the bakery on the corner of Avenue B and 14th Street tomorrow. Do you know the place of which I speak? It has red lettering on the windows."

"I know it."

He pointed at the card. "Give that to the baker and ask for the daily special."

"Will he give me a loaf of bread with a microchip inside? That's almost as fun as finding baby Jesus in a king cake."

"Maybe this was a mistake," he muttered.

My whole life had been a mistake, so I didn't see the harm in making another. "Let's just say that I'm considering your offer. What if I join and then decide it's not the life for me?"

"Joining is not that easy, but should you decide to leave, you're free to go."

"Go where? Over a pier with cement blocks strapped to my feet?" I cut into my pie and ate a large apple slice. "I'm a lot of things, Mr. Kazan, but I'm not a fool. Do you really expect me to believe that you'd let me go, knowing who you are and privy to inside information? Something tells me that I'd wind up tied to the engine of a jumbo jet."

He smirked as if I'd told a joke.

But I was serious.

Dead serious.

"We've never had anyone leave, but should you choose to do so, it will be at your own risk. A Vampire will scrub your memory, and depending on how much you know and how long you've been with us, it could be messy. There is a chance you could wind up with a clean slate and new identity. Long-term memories are harder for Vampires to wipe, as you know."

I really didn't know much about Vampires. No one had taught me, and most people didn't sit around in bars talking about all their abilities. Most of what I knew I'd overheard or discovered on my own.

"I'll think about it," I said honestly, scooping up my ice cream before it melted.

He tapped his hand on the table. "I can offer you something you've never known: purpose. Do you think living on the edge makes you a rebel—a revolutionary who's fighting for the greater good? If you don't have ambition, you'll become just as bitter as the rogues who wander aimlessly, enveloped in their own hatred and jealousy. If you see yourself as a saint, remember this conversation ten years from now when you've grown resentful that you have nothing while others live comfortably. The line between good and evil is invisible, and if you cannot sense where it is, it won't take long to cross it. Aspire to be something greater than just a shadow of yourself."

He stood up and glanced at my attire, muttering something in Russian. "Do you have a place to sleep tonight?"

I took another forkful of pie and watched him counting money from his wallet. I didn't have plans to sleep, but I silently accepted the large sum of money he placed on the table.

After my pie, I enjoyed a third cup of coffee before gathering my things and heading out.

When I crossed the street, I had a perfect view of Betty picking up the biggest tip she'd ever received from my table.

It was a breezy night, and I spent most of it strolling through the city streets. But just after dawn, dark clouds rolled in, and punishing drops of rain drenched people on their way to work. The man selling umbrellas outside the apartment buildings picked a good day to make money. After a few hours of people-watching from my chair in the Laundromat, I headed north on 14th Street with the strap from my duffel bag weighing down my shoulder.

The heavy fragrance of fresh breads and pastries wafted through the open door as I entered the bakery. Water dripped from the plastic bag I'd put over my head as a makeshift hat, and I tossed it into a trash can.

A man who looked my age was sipping his coffee at a table ahead to my right, the chocolate éclair on his napkin half-eaten.

I studied the card Viktor had given me. What did I have to lose? It wasn't as if I had my life together, and maybe this was a chance to learn something. Our world was thick with criminals, and I didn't have a shred of guilt for the men I'd killed. Maybe getting paid for it wouldn't be so bad.

The woman behind the register greeted me with a warm smile. "Morning! Take your time and let me know when you're ready."

I eased up to the glass counter and admired all the sweet pastries lined up in neat little rows. The entire wall behind them was nothing but baskets of breads separated by grain and type.

Three workers were dashing back and forth behind the counter, filling orders and emptying breadbaskets. I tapped my fingernail against the glass, uncertain who was the baker. They were all dressed the same, so I looked around the room for an "employee of the month" plaque that might narrow it down.

"Young lady, is there something that I can help you with?" a dark-skinned man asked.

He had gentle eyes, and I took a chance that he was the owner and slipped him Viktor's card. "Um, the daily special please."

Without a word, he reached under the counter and then handed me a pink box. "Just as you ordered. Thank you for paying us in advance; we're more than happy to have it ready for you," he said with a wink. Seconds later, he disappeared into the back room.

A little mystified, I turned away with the small box and stood by the door.

"Excuse me," someone said.

I glanced up and stepped aside as the attractive man, who moments ago had been eating a chocolate éclair, was on his way out. I noticed his blond hair had dark roots, and he styled it in the disheveled manner that was the popular trend. When he smiled, it created grooves on both sides of his face.

"Don't get wet out there," I said with a chuckle.

"Says the girl without an umbrella." He turned around to open the door with his back. "Maybe I should wear a plastic bag over my head," he said playfully.

"Maybe."

His gaze lingered on my mismatched eyes and made me uncomfortable. People couldn't help themselves. I stared at his black ear studs in a half-assed attempt to find something wrong with him, but all he did was smile wider and then disappear into the rain.

Humans were becoming so peculiar to me, and it had only been five years since I'd been turned.

Now that I had privacy, I lifted the lid of my box, uncertain of what to expect. A key? A flash drive? A secret device? A pistol?

Beneath the wax paper was a lemon bar lightly dusted with powdered sugar.

I broke it into three pieces, searching inside for a folded-up piece of paper or… I don't know. What *was* I looking for? There wasn't anything underneath the bottom sheet of paper either. What the hell was I doing? Mr. Kazan must have been the kind of guy who sought amusement from messing with people's heads.

I threw the box into the trash and stormed out into the rain. As I crossed the street, my right boot landed in a deep puddle of water just before I stepped onto the curb.

"Swell," I muttered, my sock turning into a sponge.

A black Honda screeched to a halt, and the engine revved twice, as if screaming for my attention. When I approached the car, the window rolled down.

"Get in. I'll take you to Viktor."

I bent down and peered in at the profile of a man in a long black trench coat. The window rolled up, so I lifted the handle and opened the door.

He leaned over and looked up at me. "Your place or mine?"

"Well, my place is outside, so you decide."

I hugged my duffel and sank into the seat, squeaking against the leather as I reached to shut the door.

I felt him staring at me, so I peered over at him.

He pushed his dark shades farther up his nose. "If I'd known that I'd be picking up the ocean, I would have brought a sponge."

I suddenly recognized the lilt in his voice. The way he spoke had the lyrical swing that was typical of the Irish, but his voice was dark, gritty, and full of attitude.

He dropped his foot on the gas pedal, and my head flung back. I wrapped the seat belt around me and gave him an intolerant glare.

"I know you," I said, my mind working overtime trying to place him. It took me a minute because I ran into so many people on a daily basis. "Yes, I remember you now. You're the asshole with the onion rings."

He raised his sunglasses to the top of his head. "Aye. And you're the leech with the lacy knickers." His eyes flicked down to my lap. "Where's my lemon bar?"

I chortled. "So *that's* what the pink box was about. Sorry, but I don't like lemon bars. I threw it away."

He squeezed the steering wheel. "Jaysus wept. I think Viktor has finally lost his marbles."

I was having second thoughts when I realized that this guy worked for Viktor. Maybe he was just the chauffeur.

The scenery flew by—people rushing through the rain with newspapers covering their heads, a paper cup floating down the sewage drain, windows fogged over in most of the eateries. Cognito was quite a magnificent northeastern city, even at its ugliest.

The Vampire put on his turn signal and made a right. "There's a burger place just up the street. Viktor won't mind."

"I'm not hungry."

He turned his head all the way to face me. "It's eleven in the morning, scavenger, and your stomach is louder than my engine."

I chuckled. "A Vampire with a Honda. You made my day."

He snapped his attention back to the road, his voice clipped. "It's unassuming."

"Buy all the burgers you want, but I won't eat them." No way was I giving him the satisfaction.

"You must be a Shifter—stubborn and brassy."

With lightning speed, I whipped out a push dagger attached to my belt and held it against his whiskery jaw. "And you need a shave. Be sure to watch out for those speed bumps," I added, scraping the knife at an upward angle. "No more insults, or I'll cut you up into little pieces and ship you back to Ireland."

He slammed the brakes, and I flew forward, jerked to a stop by my seat belt. The Vampire disarmed me and clamped the back of my neck with an iron grip. "Let's keep the sharp weapons tucked away, shall we? Besides, a woman like you doesn't need a dagger. You have a tongue that could clip a hedge."

He reached for the blade that had fallen on the floorboard and released his hold. "And don't litter in my car. I never did like a litterbug."

I sat up and rubbed the back of my neck, my ego slightly deflated. The knife wouldn't have done him serious harm since stunners were designed to paralyze a Mage, not a Vampire, but sometimes a girl had to make a point.

We left the city and entered a wealthy area of town that I'd never seen before. The car slowed in front of a wrought iron gate that reached maybe fifteen or twenty feet high. Above it was a stone archway between two walls that stretched as far as I could see. On the keystone at the center of the arch was a carving of a Roman soldier's head staring down at me, his helmet on. The slope of his brows and pensive gaze made me shiver.

The Vampire veered to the left and swiped his card against a stand. While he waited for the gates to open, he switched off the windshield wipers when the downpour changed to a light sprinkle.

"I don't have to live here, do I?"

"Would that be too awful? Jaysus, will you fecking look at it?" He lifted his arm theatrically. "This isn't a mansion, it's a country.

If you'd rather live on the street than in here, you're a bigger fruit loop than I took you for."

"I'm not living on the street."

The car lurched to a stop. "I'll spare you the indignity of giving me an explanation since we both know that's a lie. Now why don't you cheer up, lass? You were so much more pleasant when you just wanted me for my onion rings."

"What's a Vampire doing eating in public anyhow?"

He scratched behind his ear. "I was trying to blend in."

I snorted. "Yeah. A Vampire eating food doesn't stand out."

We continued down the road that led to the mansion, which looked more like a castle. Once the car stopped in the circular driveway in front, I got out and soaked in my surroundings. Another road branched off to the right toward what looked like a garage door and a small building.

"What's that?" I asked.

"Underground parking," he said, lifting the collar of his coat to shield his neck from the rain.

I set my heavy duffel on the ground while I shut the car door. He collected my bag and swung it over his shoulder as if it weighed nothing.

I followed behind, studying the Vampire. His straight shoulders didn't slope down, and he must have been around six feet tall. He didn't walk with a heavy gait but glided forward with a purposeful stride. If he wasn't so cocksure and intimidating, he might actually be attractive. I didn't like Vampires, and the fact he was pleasant to look at made me hate him even more.

The stone archway above the front door had the same sculpture of a warrior's head on the keystone.

When we entered, it was nothing like I had expected. Instead of marble floors, crystal chandeliers, baroque furniture, and classic paintings, the interior looked like the inside of an old castle, just as it did on the outside. There was a nice open space, and farther up to the left was a curved staircase. Some of the candles on the walls were lit, but not many since the windows brought in sufficient light.

I recoiled at a statue on my right of a man wielding a sword in his right hand as if he were going to strike me down. A sharp wing extended behind that arm while the other wing curved around front to shield him.

"Viktor's a religious man, huh?" I asked, warily walking past the statue as if it might come alive.

"That's not an angel," the Vampire whispered in my ear, leading me to a hall on the right.

The gothic architecture was captivating. We headed toward a hall on the right, an archway at the entrance and a curved ceiling. These windows were tinted blue, and lanterns hung from the ceiling between every other window.

Our footsteps reverberated off the walls, and I tried to ignore the squishing sound coming from my right boot.

A woman with long brown hair was waiting at the end of the hall that branched off to the left. She possessed a natural beauty that wasn't overly feminine, and her features were distinctly Native American. The very first thing I noticed was her sapphire eyes—they sparkled against her dark features, making them the most striking thing about her. But there was nothing gentle about her rigid stance and serious demeanor.

"Set down her bag and open it up," she said. "I'll search her."

"I don't have any weapons on me," I assured her.

"It's routine. We thoroughly search everyone the first time. We're looking for weapons, recording devices, tracking mechanisms... Take off your shoes."

While the Vampire rummaged through my personal belongings, I unlaced my boots and pulled them off.

The Irishman tossed my clothes in a meaningless pile, searching the pockets and inspecting the hems.

She circled her hands around the waistband of my jeans and discovered a blade disguised as a belt buckle.

I shrugged. "Forgot I had that."

"Is that so?"

While she continued her search, I glanced up at a painting. It was a glum image of a dark moonlit river.

How very Breed, I thought.

She crouched down and found a push dagger hidden inside my pant leg. It was a small one infused with magic—one I only used in emergencies against another Mage. Stunners weren't easy to come by, so I hated losing one.

"I suppose you forgot you had this as well?" she asked, setting it on the floor next to the other.

"You could say that."

She held up my boots and felt inside, then looked closer at one and turned it over. I worried my lip, hoping she wouldn't find…

"And this?" She pulled out another blade tucked in the back heel.

"I made it myself. The handle folds out from the bottom and you can pull—"

"I see." It looked as though she was struggling to conceal a smile. "Maybe you should remove your socks."

The Vampire chuckled. "Careful, Blue. Those hooves might be the deadliest weapon she's concealing. Vile, to be sure."

I peered over my shoulder and gave him a cross look. I didn't rattle easily, but I was determined to find out what pushed his buttons so I could give him a taste of his own medicine. I lifted my foot and peeled off the wet sock. "If this is leading somewhere, I can tell you right now that I'm not stripping naked. If that's the deal breaker, you need to let me know." I hurled the black sock over my shoulder and heard it smack against the Vampire's face.

I didn't need to look to know that I'd hit my target. I could hear the revulsion in his whispered obscenities.

The woman named Blue stood up, and she was a couple of inches taller than me—maybe five foot ten if I had to guess.

Her eyes swept down to my chest, and when I noticed hers was bigger, I almost wanted to puff my girls out.

"I need to check your bra," she said.

This gal was all business, and I had a feeling I wasn't going to get special treatment because of my gender. I reached beneath my shirt and unlatched the hooks, executing a maneuver that all women know how to do when it comes to removing a bra through a shirtsleeve. She turned it in her hands and discovered a small piece of wood I'd concealed in the slot where the wire once was.

The Vampire snorted. "A toothpick for dinner?"

I glared over my shoulder. "I think we both know it doesn't take much of *that* kind of wood to paralyze a Vamp."

His eyes narrowed at my flagrant use of a derogatory word for Vampires.

My eyes narrowed at the red panties wrapped around his fingers.

When Blue's phone vibrated, she checked the message, her feather earrings brushing against the side of her face. "It's Viktor. I need to run. Can you finish this up?"

Horrified my strip search was transferring over to a man, I looked at the Vampire, expecting a gleeful expression. Instead, I saw a man sitting with his legs crossed, smelling a tube of my lipstick before swiping it across his wrist.

"I've got it covered," he said absently. "How is it that you can't afford to eat, but you seem to have plenty of face paint?"

I folded my arms as Blue hurried down the hall. "You'd be surprised what women leave behind in the bathroom."

He rose to his feet and approached me with an elegant stride, his head inclined. "I'm Christian Poe. Thought maybe you should at least know my name before I get close to those ample breasts of yours." He gave me a wolfish grin and brushed up beside me. "Come on, lass. I won't bite. Just up to the golden arches; I only need to see your midsection."

"I'm not lifting my shirt unless you carry large bills in your wallet."

"Suit yourself. Would you like me to drop you off in the puddle I found you in, or is there someone you can call?"

Blue hadn't seemed fazed at leaving me alone with him, so she must have gone through the process too.

"Just pat me down and get it over with."

"With absolute pleasure. Shall I get some baby oil before we begin? Sometimes a little lubrication helps with the process—makes it sufferable." He curved his arm around my waist and whispered in my ear, "My hands can be rough."

"You talk too much."

Christian leisurely ran his hands up the front of my shirt, just beneath the curve of my breasts. He was inches away, and I lifted my chin to look closely at his mouth, making sure he kept his fangs in check.

"Sorry, lass. I can see you're vexed, but it's my job to be thorough."

I gave him an indifferent look, which provoked him. He wrapped his arms behind my back as if he were hugging me, fingers splayed as he moved them upward. He watched my face for a reaction, undoubtedly using his keen hearing to see if my heart was doing a quickstep. I kept my breathing calm, my expression stoic, and my eyes on his lips.

Probably not the best place to look since he had an inviting mouth, but when the tips of his fangs peeked out, that was enough to rein in any sense of desire. I loathed Vampires and rejected that part of me. I used my Vampire gifts as a necessary evil, but evil it was.

His eyes tightened just a fraction when he ran his hand over a healing bruise, causing me to wince.

"If you're about done rifling through my panties and feeling me up, I'd like to speak with your boss."

"Raven. I'm so glad you came."

I stepped back as Viktor approached from the hall on the right.

"Come this way, and I'll show you to your room."

"I don't need a room, I just need some answers."

"Very well. Christian, take her things upstairs and then join us in the study."

Without a word, Christian collected my bag and weapons before swiftly heading back down the way we came.

After I put my boots back on, Viktor and I strode through the hall that Blue had gone down, passing several doors on the left.

I pointed at one made of steel. "What's up with the heavy door?"

"Everyone likes a little privacy, and some of our rooms are soundproof. I have a house full of different Breeds and temperaments; we've lost a lot of doors."

"That doesn't exactly make me feel safe."

"You need not worry," he said, his accent warming me like a strong drink. "They won't bother you once they learn what you are."

"And what exactly is that?"

Viktor didn't break stride. "A Breed killer."

Chapter 4

VIKTOR HANDED ME A GLASS of merlot and sat in a brown leather wingback chair across from me. Our chairs were angled slightly toward the fireplace, and I had a clear view of the door to my right. He had a quaint study with an unlit fireplace, bookshelves, and a statue of an archer aiming his arrow at my chair. I couldn't get over the antiquated use of lanterns instead of electricity, but the stone walls soaked up the light, lending a magnificent glow to the room.

"I have high connections," he began. "My group has some of the best information seekers with specific skills. We're given special assignments that no one else will do, and we're hired to bring down some of the most notorious criminals in the Breed world—the untouchables. Many of them are men and women who haven't been classified as outlaws by the higher authority, but we bring them to justice."

"So you gather evidence and make arrests?"

"*Nyet.*" After sipping his wine, he set the crystal goblet on a table to his right. "Lawmakers require written evidence, testimonies, photographs, computer files, that kind of thing to convict. In most cases, witnesses to a crime won't speak out. There is no witness protection program."

The bitter drink made me grimace. "I don't have any experience with investigative work."

His mouth turned down as if he were considering how to answer. "I choose open-minded individuals. Rumor is you've taken out twenty-one."

"Thirty-three," I corrected. "How did you trace all those murders back to me? I've been discreet. I'm not exactly leaving a letter of apology at the scene of the crime."

"It's a small world, and eventually all paths will cross. My inside contacts let me know when there's an unsolved murder, and occasionally one will match up with one of our cases. My Chitah couldn't pick up a scent that's uniquely yours, but he matched similar lotions or soaps. We knew you were a woman because some of the victims had lipstick smudges on their necks."

When I crossed my legs, his eyes skated to the hole in my jeans. "I must be an enigma to you then."

He lifted his glass and took another swallow. "You could say that. We suspected you were a Vampire, but it appears we were wrong. My tracker happened to be in the same location as your last crime and got a good look at you. Do you mind explaining why it is that some of your victims were drained of their blood? Do you work with a partner?"

I flicked my eyes at Christian, who was standing to my right near the door. "Does he have to be in here?"

Christian theatrically bowed his head.

Viktor cleared his throat, smoothing out his accent. "He's the one who found you. There are no secrets in my house," he said, wagging his finger. "That includes any special gifts that you may have. We'll assess your skills to determine what your strengths and weaknesses are, but for now, why don't you put on some dry clothes and rest?"

"I don't need rest. I'm a Vampire."

While Viktor's expression was unreadable, the reaction from the Vampire behind him was dramatic. Christian surged forward at an alarming speed.

I'd heard stories that female Vampires were highly sought after. There weren't that many to begin with, and their elders weren't looking to expand their population since the younglings were unpredictable and oftentimes dangerous. I'd also heard how wickedly beautiful those women were, but I'd never seen one myself.

Christian's obsidian gaze swallowed me up, and I shifted nervously in my seat. "Your eyes are not black and your skin isn't flawless."

"Gee, you really know how to charm the ladies," I said, twirling a lock of inky-black hair. "Before you get excited, I should tell you that I'm not entirely Vampire. I'm…" I hesitated. There was no reason to believe Viktor wasn't serious about his offer, and that meant coming clean. "I'm a crossbreed."

Viktor leaned forward, arms resting on his knees. "A cross between what?"

I'd never told anyone my secret outside of my victims. I could only guess how they were going to react based on my previous experiences.

"A Vampire and a Mage."

"Are you mental?" Christian exclaimed. "Viktor, you can't take her seriously. Such a thing doesn't exist. Once you're a Vampire, a Mage can't put his light into you and change you over. It doesn't work the other way either. She's touched in the head."

I uncrossed my legs and rested my hands on the armrests of the chair, smiling up at him with my eyes. I'd finally found the one thing that annoyed him.

Me.

"Are you telling me that you've never once heard of a crossbreed or met someone who doesn't fit the mold?" I asked.

He stroked his beard and averted his eyes, implying that he had. "Where's your maker?"

"My fangdaddy split the day I was born." I turned my attention back to Viktor. "I can sit in this room if you want me to, but I don't need sleep. I don't think I could go forever without it—maybe a week. The Mage side of me still likes to snooze. Anyhow, there's no point in my staying here. I'm sure there's a place up the road where I can get a room."

Viktor stood up, making a fist for emphasis. "Absolutely not. This isn't just a job, Raven. It's a way of life. We live together, and that's final. Until I've made up my mind whether or not you'll fit in with the group, you'll stay here. If you don't like it, I can show you the door."

Christian folded his arms and turned to Viktor. "She's bluffing. She's not a Vampire."

"Really, are you still stuck on that?" I rose to my feet and confronted him.

Christian's fangs slid down, and we faced off like two enemies. "I think you're confusing Vampires with Chitahs."

"I'm not a Chitah. Has anyone ever told you that you're a handful?"

His head tipped to the side, and he gave me a crooked smile. "Funny. Women seem to think that I'm more of a mouthful."

"I wouldn't be so cocky if I were you. Vampires have always been the easiest to kill, contrary to popular belief."

Viktor chuckled and clapped his hand on Christian's shoulder. "I'll let you two get better acquainted. I have business matters to attend to. Raven, we'll talk more later."

Neither Christian nor I took our eyes off each other as Viktor left the room.

When the door closed, I lowered my gaze. "Let's just get one thing straight: I don't care for Vampires. Don't get any ideas about knocking on my door in the middle of the night for some bonding time with my jugular."

He put his hands on his hips and retracted his fangs. "Don't flatter yourself. I'm a man with taste."

"B negative, I'm sure."

"I bet your maker will have second thoughts before making another female. Perhaps he should have waited until your cycle was over as you seem to be afflicted with *eternal* PMS."

"Get out."

He smirked, arching a sardonic brow as if he demanded the final word. "Unless you like cuddling with statues, follow me, lass."

I followed behind him, unruffled by his remarks. Vampires were often brash and spoke freely, a personality trait I'd grown accustomed to from an early age. Hopefully my room would have chairs made from the right kind of wood that would paralyze a

Vampire, often referred to as impalement wood. Nothing would give me greater pleasure than enjoying a meal in bed while he lay frozen on the floor, forced to listen to my every thought.

I chuckled at the idea.

"Something funny?" he asked, glancing over his shoulder at me.

Refrain, Raven. Refrain. "Nothing at all. I just had a tickle in my throat."

The study was located on the first floor, and we took a different flight of stairs from the grand one by the front door. I realized the place was so big that it must have several staircases for convenience. A small statue sat in the corner where the banisters joined. I marveled at the detailed artistry as we curved around it and ascended yet another flight. The house was breathtaking, with high ceilings and masterful carvings in the architecture. While the walls and floors were made from various kinds of stone, it wasn't doom and gloom. The house was regal, luxurious, something out of a fairy tale. Lanterns ran along the walls with unlit candles inside. I couldn't imagine someone tasked with lighting them all, but at least they wouldn't have to worry about burning the place down since almost everything was made from stone and iron.

When we reached the third floor, he led me to the end of the hall and then opened a heavy wooden door.

I gasped, branching away from him toward the stone railing to my right. A wide interior balcony overlooked the property out front. The balcony didn't protrude from the house but was built-in, covered, and yet completely open in the front. I could see everything from this vantage point: the front gate at the end of the driveway, the tops of the trees, how green the grounds were. A light breeze picked up the ends of my hair, and I leaned forward, taking it all in. Imagining how it must look moments before dawn simply stole my breath away.

"I didn't know places like this existed."

He half turned on his way to the opposite door, remaining quiet and watchful.

A series of stone arches ran along the railing, creating dividers between the openings.

"We have another that overlooks the courtyard," he said absently.

Courtyard? I almost had to pinch myself to make sure I wasn't dead. Maybe I hadn't survived the attack in the bathroom a few nights ago.

Thunder rolled, and the clouds opened up, rain falling like a heavy curtain and obscuring my view of the front gate.

"How many acres does he own?"

"Hundreds."

A gust of wind slapped me in the face with a spray of rain.

Christian chuckled and carried on, hands clasped behind his back.

We moved through the opposite door and then turned left down a narrow hall with windows along the left side. It confused me since it was the central part of the house.

"That's the courtyard," he said, catching the direction of my gaze.

We passed a quaint sitting room on the right, no more than six by six with a long bench on the back wall and two chairs that faced each other. Most of the doors in the hall were closed until we reached a large open room on the right. I caught a glimpse of one of those giant globes on a stand. This place probably had secret passageways and a labyrinth made from hedges.

After making another turn with more windows overlooking the courtyard, he fell back a step and entered a room on the right.

"Let me give you a piece of advice," he began as I moved past him. "Don't go exploring and sticking your nose where it doesn't belong. Viktor laid out the offer, but you're not an official member of the club until he says so. Some of these rooms are private, and the doors are closed for a reason."

I turned on my heel. "Afraid I'm going to discover your My Little Pony collection? Don't worry about me. Just go back to your coffin and let me settle in."

"You're an insufferable child," he grumbled, exiting the room in a swift movement. "And for feck's sake, put on a bra."

"It's not my fault you don't have a heater."

I wiggled my fingers in a farewell when the door slammed. Annoying Christian might actually be kind of fun. He seemed offended by my very existence. Most Vampires were loners, and women were merely a recreational pastime. They probably could have made more women among their kind, but they didn't. Their elders had laws that frowned upon making new younglings without approval—although I'm sure they made exceptions—but most Vampires didn't seem to want the responsibility. Younglings were impulsive and slaves to bloodlust, the insatiable desire to drink blood. Thankfully I'd never had that problem, and maybe that was why I didn't understand it. I'd targeted a few young Vampires who'd purchased slaves off the black market to feed on.

Sickos.

I stood with my back to the wooden door and took a moment to look at my room. The ceilings were high, the walls and floor made from grey stone, and there was a fireplace on the left with no mantel. This wasn't the penthouse suite by any means. The furniture was rustic and made of wood, from the armoire on my right to the end tables by the bed. Not a four-poster or even a sleigh bed, just a plain wooden headboard on a frame that was lower to the ground than modern ones. A small desk and chair filled the far right corner. I turned to my left and looked at the large floor mirror leaning against the corner wall.

"Do I really look like that?" I whispered, approaching my reflection.

A weary-eyed girl gazed back at me, her black hair unkempt and tangled from the rain. She looked haggard in her baggy shirt and ripped jeans. When I'd first turned, men found me attractive, but now I could see why it had become harder to lure some of them into private rooms. Most bathroom mirrors just showed the top half, so seeing the full scope of what I'd devolved into was rather depressing. I still had my long legs going for me, and I played up my features with dark lipstick and a little eyeliner. But I looked malnourished, my skin was pallid, my clothes stained, and there was even dirt beneath my fingernails.

Or was it blood?

"Disastrous," I muttered, wondering if I smelled as bad as I looked.

This was what street life had done to me.

I turned away and approached the window straight ahead, stepping onto a white rug. I traced my fingers along the metal lattice on the leaded windows. The arched window was wide, expressive, and each sash opened inward. I deduced by all the turns we'd made that my view was the back of the mansion.

The first thing I did was drag the rug in front of the fireplace. Then I set my bag on the bed and noticed my weapons were missing.

"Oh, you're kidding me," I said in disbelief.

Viktor wanted me to be part of his elite organization, and yet he didn't want me armed?

I turned in a circle and noticed there wasn't a lamp in the room. The rain outside had cast a dark shroud over the property, and all I had were lanterns affixed to the walls and candles on the tables. I peeked in a drawer and found fresh candles and a box of matches.

"Putting on my makeup should be fun," I mused.

To the right of the bed was an open doorway, so I went to investigate and discovered a bathroom behind the wall. The sink and oval mirror on the left were basic, and the standing shower straight ahead had a glass door that offered no privacy. But what caught my eye was the claw-foot tub within a recessed wall on the right.

"Hello, darling."

I ran the tub water and stripped out of my clothes. It was pure torture waiting for the tub to fill, and I turned away from the mirror after catching a glimpse of the bruise on my back—a reminder of my failure. The small window on the wall with the shower brought in enough light, but I retrieved some matches and lit the square lanterns on either side of the sink.

Most people would have found the room basic and uninviting, but those people hadn't spent the past two nights sleeping in a Dumpster.

Steam rose from the tub, and I slipped into the clean water, groaning at the blissful feel of that heat all around me. I took most of my showers in truck stop restrooms. Only on rare occasions after working odd jobs did I have money to spend on a motel room, and I'd forgotten the simple pleasure that a hot bath could bring.

I soaked.

And by soaked I mean I spent hours in that claw-foot tub, periodically draining the water and then turning it back on for more heat.

It was glorious, and I luxuriated in the exotic oils that were lined up on a small ledge in the wall.

Eventually I draped over the rim, resting my head in my arms. Maybe I'd wake up and this would have all been a dream. Or a setup. But for now it felt like heaven. Despite the balking I'd done earlier about sleep, I nodded off right inside that bathtub.

Clean. Warm. Safe.

And slightly mystified as to how I'd become so fortunate. Not that it would last.

Nothing good in my life ever lasted.

Chapter 5

WHEN I OPENED MY EYES, two things disturbed me. One, I had no idea where I was. And two, I was completely naked.

Disoriented, I looked about the dimly lit room, the candles burning low. Thunder rumbled in the distance, and rain drizzled onto the floor from an open window. I sat up and tried to recall how I'd gotten here. Sleeping hard will do that to anyone—especially when you're exhausted and wake up in a strange place.

Ah, yes. Viktor. It was all coming back.

I remembered the bath and touched my hair, the tousled strands now dry.

Had I really slept all day? A damp towel covered my pillow, and I rubbed my face, unable to remember even getting out of the tub. What if someone had carried me to the bed?

Perish the thought.

For all I knew, Viktor could have been a trader on the black market and—like the Pied Piper—this was how he lured people to his den of iniquity.

Hmm. No telephone.

I yanked on my black hoodie and a pair of jeans. Without central heating, an uncomfortable chill hung in the air, so I closed the window and spread a towel over the wet spot on the floor.

Staying cooped up was never my thing. Time to do a little exploring. I peered into the hallway, looking in both directions to figure out which way to go. The windows straight ahead overlooked the courtyard, but it was too dark to see anything. Every other lantern on the wall had a candle flickering inside, providing enough light to reflect off the glass and soak into the stone architecture.

Since it was raining, I opted against going in the direction we'd come, fearing I might lock myself outside on the balcony. I swung to the right instead, following the hall until it curved left. When the windows ended, I realized the house was bigger than I'd first thought and not at all shaped like a perfect rectangle. I passed a grand room on the right with tapestries spun from gold and exquisite furniture. That room had electricity, so I scurried past the opening in case someone was in there.

The stone floor chilled my bare feet, making me quicken my step until I found a staircase that led down. Remembering all the rooms, turns, and hallways seemed impossible.

I tugged on the drawstrings hanging from the collar of my hood, skulking in the shadows and searching for signs of life. The first floor was brightly lit, which led me to believe that people were down there.

A burst of laughter echoed from the end of a hall, and I quietly moved toward the sound of chatter. I entered a room through an archway and noticed a wall dividing that room from another. There were booths like you'd see at a restaurant, tucked against a series of arches on the short divider wall. Through the open arches, all I could make out in the dark room was a crackling fireplace.

As I turned left, I stopped dead in my tracks. Several people rose from a long wooden dining table filled with food.

I took a step back when one of them palmed a steak knife.

One man was a giant, and his upper and lower canines punched out in an aggressive display. His Chitah eyes were bright gold, and his predatory gaze made me flinch. It was like looking directly at a lion about to devour you for dinner. Aside from Christian, his was the only Breed I recognized.

I broke the silence. "I'm not sure if one of you was in my room earlier, but if anyone comes into my domain without explicit permission, I'm going to impale you in a way that will give you the very best idea of what it feels like to be a corn dog."

A violet-haired young woman bubbled with laughter and then covered her mouth when the others gave her scornful glances.

Viktor rose from the head of the table and closed the distance between us. "This is our newest inductee, Raven Black." He blocked my view and lowered his voice. "Come with me. You can't be in here."

"Can't I?"

He seized my upper arm and led me out. "You're not official yet. Until you've gone through our tests, you can't sit with us. Those are the rules."

The talking resumed in the dining room, and I wriggled out of his grasp. "What's with all the candles?"

"Immortals rely on modern conveniences far too much. I find them to be a distraction. I don't allow televisions, radios, or electricity in most rooms. This is a large house, and I'm a frugal man. I do not wish to pay thousands of dollars a month so you can leave a lamp on all night. I place electricity where it's needed."

We headed down a dark, narrow staircase, and he opened a door to an enormous gym filled with exercise equipment on one side and open space on the other. Unlike the rest of the mansion, there were overhead lights.

"Stay here while I get Niko."

"Who's Niko?"

But he was already gone. There were elliptical machines, treadmills, weights, and workout equipment I didn't recognize. A long rope hung from the ceiling, and I even spotted jump ropes. One section of the wall displayed various weapons and target boards.

Between the estate and everything within, these guys were loaded. Either that or some of them came from old money. Maybe I could work for them just long enough to get a substantial amount of cash and buy a place of my own.

Viktor returned with a man following behind him. He looked about six feet with an average build of lean muscle. Aside from his black hair, which was wispy and long, what stood out were his almond-shaped eyes. The blue was almost colorless—like crystal waters beneath sunlight. He appeared to be of mixed Asian descent with strikingly handsome features, chiseled cheekbones, and skin as pale brown as desert sand. By the looks of his tight biceps and broad shoulders, he was also a man who conditioned his body as though it were a weapon.

Without televisions or radios, I could understand why someone would spend hours down here.

He turned his head in my direction and suppressed a smile. "She's a girl."

"How you can tell that I'll never understand," Viktor said. "Raven, this is Niko. Niko, meet Raven Black. She's half Mage, and that's why I've called you down."

His brows knitted. "Half?"

"The better half," I said. "Are you a Mage?"

He gave a short grin and inclined his head.

Viktor gestured toward my bare feet and chuckled. "You came prepared. I like that."

"What's this all about?"

"I take it that since you're living on the streets, you've never had your gifts measured by the Mageri. Am I right?"

Measuring was something the Mageri did to document the gifts of a Mage brought in the legal way, which I hadn't been.

Viktor stroked his trimmed beard. "We're going to test your skills—both strengths and weaknesses. We don't keep secrets in this house, and it's important we know what your limitations are. Everything within these walls is kept secret, and that includes what you learn about others. Those who break the rules will suffer the consequences. Since you're a crossbreed, we'll start with your Mage skills and go from there."

I cupped my elbows, suddenly feeling vulnerable. "I'm not sure about this. How do I know you're not setting me up?"

"You know where the door is if you have second thoughts, but I'll need to scrub your memory of us before you go." He shook his finger at me. "We are as trustworthy as the Mageri, if not more so. What talents and weakness you choose to reveal to the public is your business, but under no circumstance will my men speak of them to anyone. The same goes for you. Do you understand?"

I nodded. "I have your word?"

"*Da*," he said, replying in Russian. Then he turned and placed his hand on Niko's shoulder. "Come see me afterward, Niko. *Spasibo*."

As he ascended the stairs, Niko moved like a panther, circling around me. The way he watched me was strange.

"Do you have a last name?" I asked.

"No," he replied, still moving. "In my time, we didn't have surnames. We were known by our clan."

My God, that meant this guy was one of the ancients. It didn't matter that he only looked to be in his twenties or thirties. In fact, I couldn't even place his age since there was something timeless and mysterious about his appearance.

"Is Raven Black your given name?"

"If you mean given to me by my Creator, then yes. Black is, anyhow. He let me keep my first name."

Learners traditionally take the surname of their Creator since that's how the Mageri tracks lineage. Creators are rare, and most of them are assigned their progeny from what I'd heard. Learner was one of those titles I'd always hated and never went by on the account it applied to a newly made Mage still living with their Creator and going through training. My education came from the school of hard knocks.

"You didn't have a good relationship with your Creator," he remarked, moving out of sight.

I spun around. "How do you know that?"

He smiled knowingly. "Your energy. It tells me all I need to know."

"I'm concealing."

"True, I can see that. But you have emotional and spiritual energy that you cannot conceal or control. I can tell when you're angry, when you are lying, when you're nervous… as you are now."

I backed up against the wall so he'd quit circling me like a predator. "How can you see that? I've never heard of a Mage being able to do that."

His eyes remained on me in an absent way. "I'm blind, but I'm not so blind that I can't see the truth."

Chills danced up my spine. We didn't retain injuries once immortal—not unless liquid fire was involved to seal the injury. Someone had chosen a blind human as their Learner. But why?

"This is a big house. How do you find the doors and get around?" I asked, noticing he didn't have a cane.

Niko kept his hands at his sides, his tone clear and pleasant. "Most blind people count steps and keep things in the same place. There's not much to trip on around here, and people don't move furniture without letting me know. I do rely on that at times, but my unique gift allows me to live in your world. Almost everything gives off energy. Plants, animals, rocks, light, stars, even fire. Even things that you touch retain an imprint, like there," he said, pointing to the floor. "I can still see your residual energy from where you've been. Enough about me. I want to learn more about you. Share your gifts with me."

Gifts? That was a laugh.

"My Creator didn't teach me anything." I pushed off the wall and walked around him. "I can't flash like a Mage, but I can sense energy. I haven't tried healing since the time I knocked myself out for two days after pulling in sunlight."

Niko rocked with laughter and then waved his hand. "Sorry, that was amusing. What about healing with another Mage's light?"

"I've never gotten close enough to a Mage I haven't killed."

"Well, that's reassuring. We'll test that later. What about rare gifts? We can all heal, sense time, move quickly… but every Mage receives at least one rare gift in their light that not many can do."

I flattened my back against the wall and reached overhead, gripping a pull-up bar just above me.

Niko tilted his head to the side. "Your energy is shifting colors. What are you hiding?"

"This is worse than getting naked."

His expression softened. "We're not here to expose your secrets to the world and make you vulnerable. How would that benefit us? The more we know about each other, the better we can help protect one another and improve our strengths."

"Is this required?"

"I'm afraid so."

"Then what's yours?"

Niko shook his head, strands of black hair floating in front of his face. "You already know one of my gifts, and I don't want to get sidetracked on conversations about me. Viktor has tasked me to learn what you can offer us."

He leaned against the wall to my left and remained quiet.

"I can pull energy from a Mage," I finally said.

"So can we all. That's called juicing."

"*All* the way out."

He turned on his right shoulder to face me. Niko didn't stare at me the way other men did. Perhaps I was just as exciting as one of those airport thermal detectors, but it made me self-conscious and I put distance between us.

"You can remove their core light until they're mortal again?"

"Yep. It's not always easy to take them down, but once I've gained the upper hand, it's lights out."

Niko rubbed his smooth chin. "An exceptional gift indeed. In early times, Stealers were hunted—feared because they had the power to remove immortality. It's a rare gift even among rare gifts. Do you keep their energy?"

"No, God no!" I exclaimed with a shudder. "It stays inside me for maybe a day and then leaks out."

"Does it make you stronger?"

"I've never played around with their gifts. It doesn't make *my* energy stronger, but I guess their power stays inside me for a short time."

"If you can't flash, are you able to use your energy to attack another Breed?"

"Yes, I can throw energy into other Breeds as a weapon." I took a seat on a weight bench. "I'm only half Mage, and I suppose mixing two species together diluted things. I guess that ruins the training session you had planned."

"Hardly," he said with a crafty smile. "I want to test how well you fight."

"This shouldn't take long then. I can't fight."

He belted out a laugh and moved toward me. Niko wore all black, except he wasn't wearing shoes on his feet. "Don't be so modest. I'm aware of your track record."

"I carry small weapons and have a few moves I rely on, but I'm not about to embarrass myself when you realize that I don't fight like a ninja. I have strong legs, so if I get into a tangle, I can hurt a man with these nutcrackers. I lure them into confined spaces, like bathrooms, and my opponents aren't exactly skilled fighters. I use other means to take them down."

"Other means?"

I shrugged even though he couldn't see the gesture. "Usually it's their stupidity I depend on the most."

"Are you really half Vampire, or is that just a rumor I'm hearing?"

I jumped when one of the lights above us began to buzz. "It's true."

A single brow arched. "So you bite your victims."

My tone grew defensive. "It works, but I never drink from Vampires; I just stake them up close. They're horny little bastards, so getting them alone has never been a difficult chore. Their overconfidence is what makes them weak, and most of them respond to a pair of tits and a little lipstick."

Niko's expression switched from a fierce warrior to that of a kid who just overheard his first sex story. Maybe I was too déclassé for polite society. I tugged at my drawstring, a little ashamed by how uncouth I'd become over the years.

Niko stretched out his arms. "You might have hidden gifts we have yet to uncover. I'm not convinced that you can't flash; I just think you must have had an incompetent Creator. We'll need to test your healing abilities before we begin any sparring. I don't want to hurt you if you can't heal. I'm going to run up and talk to

Viktor while someone else comes down to test your Vampire skills. Is there anything else you want to tell me regarding your Mage gifts?"

"No, but can you do me a favor?"

"Yes?"

"Don't bring up my Creator again. That's not something I want to talk about."

Emotions swirled within me. My Creator was the man I was hiding from—a monster who'd seized an opportunity to not only ruin my life but to make me nothing more than a commodity. I didn't want to revisit those memories; I wasn't ready. And if people knew about him, he might be able to find me.

I caught a look on Niko's face I couldn't peg, and his gaze darted around my body. "As you wish. As far as I'm concerned, you meet all my expectations for a candidate, but we still need to test your Vampire skills. Remain here. Round two is coming up. If you don't meet *his* expectations, Viktor might let you go, and this will be the last time we speak. Best of luck, Raven."

Chapter 6

I reclined on the bench and gripped the metal bar. The weights were set to 150 pounds. When I pushed on the bar, it took a Herculean effort to lift it. My muscles quivered, and I bent my leg, using the bottom of my foot to help push the bar up.

A sputter of laughter came from the doorway. I let go, peering at the entranceway to my left.

Christian was standing within the recessed wall by the door, leaning against the wall on his right shoulder, his arms folded. He was dressed casually in dark pants and a black Henley shirt that fit him too well. The first few buttons were undone, and he'd pushed the sleeves of the cotton shirt up to his elbows.

"Now that's just grand," he said. "I guess this means I can mark off physical strength from your checklist of Vampire skills."

I relaxed and stared up at the ceiling. "Tell me you're not the only Vampire in this house."

He clapped his hands together and strode in. "Let's begin, shall we?"

I sat up, straddling the bench, and watched as he crossed the room and made a sweeping bow, never taking his dark eyes from mine.

Christian reminded me of a cross between a handsome pirate and a serial killer.

"Don't you want to question me first?"

"I'm more of a hands-on kind of guy. Didn't you rough and tumble with Niko?" he asked in a velvety voice. "Smart as a whip, that one. But not very skilled with the ladies."

"At least he gets to the point. What do you want to know about me?"

He folded his arms. "I already know what I need to know. You're not strong like a Vampire, and you obviously don't have sensitive hearing or else you wouldn't have been startled when I walked in. As for your vision, I'd be curious to know if you see as well as I do. Shall we turn off the lights?"

"No need. I can see in the dark. And if you knock off a few of these weights, I can lift it. I'm not as strong as a Vampire, but I'm not as weak as a human. I've taken down men bigger than me, and sometimes it required a little elbow grease."

"Impressive," he said flatly. "Why don't you come up here and show me what you've got?"

"I can't fight."

When he smirked, I wanted to throw one of the weights at him.

"I'm curious how you've managed to take down Vampires."

"Got any wood on you?"

He grinned salaciously. "That's one request I'm *certain* I can accommodate."

"Forget I asked." I walked to the center of the room and kept a few feet between us. "I can't use my strength against you, but you're not so difficult to catch. You guys don't seem to care about public opinion when it comes to escorting a woman of another Breed to a private room. Taking down a Vampire is seduction followed by a little wood."

"Aye, most of the time a little wood does follow a good seduction," he said, his gaze making a reckless slant downward. "Now why don't you demonstrate for me, lass. I need to assess all your… *skills.*"

Christian didn't believe I had what it took to be part of this group. He also didn't seem to like me any better than a plate of onion rings.

Game on.

I stepped closer, my eyes centering on his neck. "I don't have trouble getting a Vampire alone. Usually it's a come-hither look, or

I just run my finger along the vein in his neck. That does the trick every time."

"Oh?"

I inched forward another step and softened my voice. "Vampires seem to like it when you stroke their arteries."

I could have sworn he released a shallow breath when his lips parted.

Christian's jaw slid to the side. "Is that what you learned in a book? I think we have a copy of *What Vampires Like* up in the study. You say you're half Vampire, Raven. You should know what turns us on based on your own experience."

I tucked my fingers in my jean pockets. "I only get in touch with my inner Vampire when I'm draining my victims to get them to relax."

He closed the distance between us, his voice rough and sexy. "I suppose you want to suck on my neck?"

"You're not my type."

He circled around me, whispering in my ear. "I'm O positive. I'm everyone's type."

"I don't drink from Vampires. Do you want to know how I take them down or not?"

He appeared on my right side, amusement in his voice. "Please… Continue."

"Once we're alone, I usually have impalement wood hidden on me. Something that's easy to conceal—about six inches."

Christian gave me a roguish grin. "Lass, I can personally promise you ten."

Okay. I asked for that one.

"Give me my weapons and I'll show you."

"Afraid I can't do that. Not until Viktor gives the word. We need to make sure we can trust you before we wake up with a knife at our throats."

I pressed my body close to his, and he sucked in a sharp breath. "Does Viktor make all the rules around here?" I asked in a husky voice, stroking my finger along the artery of his neck.

He stiffened, and I felt his pulse race at a wicked beat. Christian relaxed just like a baby kitten being licked by its mama. If I latched my mouth around that artery and began sucking, using my tongue to stroke his flesh, it would send him over the edge as it did all the others.

Instead of pulling out a real piece of wood, I mimicked the movement, which I would have never done so soon, and swung my arm at his chest.

He seized my wrist and spun me around, locking my arms in front. "And what happens if they catch on to your little scheme?" he asked between clenched teeth.

"No one has yet. I wouldn't have struck so soon. I make sure their defenses are down before making a move."

"Then why did you act so soon with me?"

I reclined my head, feeling his bristly whiskers against my temple. "Unless I can stake you for real, I'm not making out with you."

His breath heated my jaw. "Aye, and now you're trapped. Show me how you're going to escape."

"Let go of me."

"This is the real world, precious. How would you fight against a Vampire who's caught you—one who could crush every bone in your body? Are you scared? You should be. I've killed more men than I can count, and until you can say the same, there's nothing about you that intimidates me. You're just a wee child in my world, bragging about kills you can only count on your fingers and toes. You can't even escape from my hold. Do you really think you belong here?"

I bent my knees and dropped to the ground, sliding out of his grasp. As I crawled around him, he fell over my back, and I whimpered in pain.

Christian pushed off me and hovered. "What's wrong? I didn't land on you that hard."

Before I could answer, he held me down and lifted the back of my shirt.

"Get off me!"

"How did you get that bruise?" When he released his hold, I

crawled free. "If that's from one of your jobs, you're not as smooth as you think you are."

I rolled over and sat facing him.

He did the same, one knee bent and his arm draped over it. "You don't heal?"

"I don't heal as quickly as a Vampire, and drinking blood doesn't seem to help. Niko's going to find out if I can heal like a Mage. If not, then I guess you've found my biggest weakness of all."

"How did you get the bruise?"

"Don't pretend like you care. Let's just finish the test and get this over with."

When I started to get up, he caught my wrist.

"Neither of us is leaving this room until I know the truth. Now you can rabbit on and pretend to be a fairy princess with the *woe is me* routine, or you can answer my question."

"Three nights ago—"

"The night we met?"

"Yes. Can I finish? Three nights ago, I went to a human club to clean up in the bathroom. It's a new place, and business was slow. I'm sure I don't have to explain why I get more privacy there than in a Breed club. Anyhow, after I washed up and soaked my dress, I was sitting in a stall trying to figure out where I wanted to go. Two men came in, and I overheard a conversation I wasn't supposed to."

"They weren't human, were they?" he asked rhetorically. "Did they gang up on you?"

"No, just one of them. I would have finished him off, but someone walked in, so I had to cover my tracks and bail."

"And now you have someone who knows who you are."

I stood up and raked my fingers through my hair. "Yes, and I'm sure he's dreaming of all the different ways he wants to kill me if we ever run into each other again."

Christian surged to his feet. "Weren't you armed?"

"Lesson learned on letting my guard down. Thanks for the reminder."

He advanced, forcing me to step back. "How far did he go?"

I kept walking backward until my shoulder blades touched the wall.

When he zeroed in on my eyes, I looked down to avoid him charming me.

His voice became low and dangerous. "How far did he go?"

"It was a hell of a fight, but I can take care of myself. I knocked him out and lived to see another day. What more do you want? Life on the streets isn't easy, so I don't need your sympathy or chivalry."

"Darlin', you don't get my sympathy until you've spent a decade buried in a pine box."

I blinked in surprise. "That seriously happened to you?" I struggled to kill the laughter rising in my throat. "Sorry, I just thought that Vampire burials were an urban legend."

He flashed me a look of irritation and branched away. I'd heard stories that in the old days, Vampires were buried as a form of punishment.

"No, seriously," I said, following behind. "What did you do to entertain yourself? Sing songs? Recite Shakespeare?"

"I bet it's a big fecking joke," he said, waving his arms. "Go ahead and laugh it up. See if I have any remorse should it happen to you."

"I'll just pulse my Mage energy in Morse code for help."

He turned swiftly and pointed at me. "I thought you were lovely when I first saw you in the bar, but I don't think I can deal with a woman who has this many limitations."

"Don't be such a condescending ass. You don't have to deal with me at all. What you see as limitations, I see as advantages. I can pass for a Mage or almost any other Breed, so that makes it easy to trick people. Chitahs can't pick up my scent, and most of my Mage opponents rely on subduing me by force, not realizing I can drain them like a bathtub. I'll ask Viktor to have someone else take over. You're obviously not a man who can do a job without his emotions getting in the way."

He lifted a fifty-pound kettlebell and tossed it back and forth in his hands as if it were weightless. "You shouldn't be drinking blood from your victims for any reason. I'm sure you realize it can become an addiction."

"That's a last resort, not a first. Anyhow, blood isn't high on my list of things I like to drink, so that's not going to be a problem. I think the Mage half of me is repulsed by it."

He smiled wolfishly. "Mind if I see your fangs?"

"Mind if I see your cock?"

He dropped the ball onto his foot and then hopped back, grimacing.

"Sorry, Christian. That's a personal question."

He limped toward the door and grumbled, "I'll just be on my way."

"So that's it? You don't want to see what else I can do?"

He turned halfway around. "In my opinion, you're too green for this job. I'm guessing you don't even know if you can shadow walk. You're weak, can't heal, and haven't mentioned anything about picking up information in blood. You're like buying one of those worthless cars that require too much time and effort to figure out and repair. Viktor can find someone else who'll put up with your delightful personality… *if* you last that long." He gripped the doorknob and wrenched it open.

"Hey, Christian?"

He paused but didn't turn.

"Don't tell anyone else about my bruise. I screwed up, but I don't want everyone knowing about it. You Vampires are secret-stealers, but let's see if you can keep one."

"Why should I do you any favors?"

I didn't think this was a guy who wanted to take my side, but I spoke sincerely, hoping he'd understand where I was coming from. "Because you spent a decade in a pine box, and I'm guessing it wasn't voluntary. We all make mistakes."

He sighed. "Aye, lass. That we do."

Chapter 7

Shortly after Christian had left the training room, Niko returned to give me a demonstration on Mage healing. To minimize the amount of energy transferring between us, he made a small cut on his arm and then clasped his hand in mine. Threads of blue light weaved between our palms as he drew healing energy from me, which wasn't the same as drinking my light. The process worked like a filter and required pulling the right kind of energy.

We exchanged positions where I was the recipient, and I also made a tiny cut on my arm and watched the skin seal together like magic. It was exhilarating to discover that I could heal like other immortals. All this time, I'd thought I was incapable, but maybe all I needed was the right training. It wasn't near enough light to heal my bruised back, but that would be gone in another day since I still healed faster than a human.

After I recounted my sunlight fiasco, Niko laughed and said we'd save that lesson for another day. I still needed to practice to get the hang of it, but he cautioned me to use it only when needed. Mage light was addictive, so bruises, cuts, and the like should be left to heal on their own, while anything broken or punctured I could borrow energy to heal. Sunlight doesn't have an addictive quality like Mage light, so that was the preferred method.

When we ended the session and went our separate ways, I strolled through the dark halls of the mansion, although it was more of a castle. It felt like I'd stepped back in time, and it became easy to forget about living on the streets. Even though I wasn't sleepy, it was comforting to know that I had a bed waiting for me. Yet despite everything, I still felt like an interloper. Maybe that would change once I met everyone else in the group.

I paused by a window and furrowed my brow when I looked down at the courtyard. The pool had curved edges, the water lit with blue-green lights. But what made me step closer to the windowpane was a woman floating on top. I squinted, searching for signs of life.

I hurried toward the stairs and reached a crossway. A man burst out of nowhere and crashed into me, holding my arms as we spun around with his momentum.

He panted, his eyes wide, a slouchy beanie askew on his head. He looked to be a man in his twenties. Without introductions, he suddenly touched my face, mashing my cheeks up and down and lifting my eyelids. My heart thundered—I was completely startled that I hadn't seen him coming.

His shoulders sagged. Then he lowered his chin and pointed left. "Don't go that way."

Before I could open my mouth, he fled full speed down the hall to the left, looking back over his shoulder once.

Barefoot.

No wonder I hadn't heard him.

It made me peer down the direction he'd come, looking closely at the dark shadows that were climbing the walls. I couldn't even see the end of the hallway since the lanterns weren't lit.

A set of hands clapped down on my shoulders from behind, and I spun around, throwing my fist forward.

Niko caught the punch in his hand. "Viktor wants you in the dining room in ten minutes."

"There's a body in your pool," I said, my thoughts distracted by the lady in the water.

"That's just Gem." He turned away and kept a steady stride, acting as if nothing had just happened with my attempting to knock his lights out.

"Should I bring my bag?" I called out, wondering if my training sessions had been less than impressive.

I briefly returned to my bedroom to grab my sneakers. Walking around barefoot was a simple pleasure I hadn't indulged in for some time, and while it was a rare treat at first, the smooth stone floors held too much of a chill for my liking.

I reached the dining room, which was illuminated by the candles on the table and the round chandelier reflecting off the crystal glasses and bathing the walls in gold.

All eyes fell on me, and Viktor rose from his seat.

"Come in, Raven. Join us."

A breeze blew past me when a young woman in a kimono robe jogged by, a white towel wrapped around her head. "Sorry I'm late." She took a seat on the left side of the table next to the Chitah.

I claimed the only vacant chair on the right, next to Niko. No one sat at the left head of the table, and I sure wasn't going to be the first. But sitting across from a Chitah was making me uncomfortable. I didn't know these guys from Adam and was having second thoughts already.

I assessed the silverware on the table in case this conversation turned south.

"I have two rules in this house," Viktor began.

The girl with the towel on her head covered her grin, nudging the Chitah with her elbow as if sharing an inside joke. I had a feeling there were more rules than just two.

"The first rule is that we protect one another. Never turn your back on a brother or sister. You don't have to love these headstrong people. Piss in their coffee if you so choose; I am not your father and will not mediate fights. But when it comes to life and death, you're going to swallow that pride and protect their lives with your own. That also includes revealing our gifts or sharing information outside the house. By doing so, you put their lives in jeopardy."

I leaned forward so I could see him better.

Viktor plucked a red grape from a wooden bowl and popped it into his mouth. "The second rule is that we eat at the table. I'm a Shifter, and that's part of my culture. You might find it arbitrary, but there's a purpose behind it. It brings people closer together," he said, lacing his fingers. "It becomes easier to get over grudges when you break bread with that person, and it allows us to see each other as family and not just people passing by in the hall. There will be no eating meals in your room, in the hall, or outside. Fill up at the table, because that's all you get. We must stay united as a group. If your differences are so great that you cannot sit down at a table across from that person, then you have no place here."

"So if I have a date and want to go out to dinner, you all have to come?"

Niko barked out a laugh. It had a warm cadence to it that was genuine and friendly. It could make even the stoniest man smile.

"Tell her about the third rule," someone said with a snort.

Viktor plucked another grape from the plate and rolled it between his fingers. "What you do on your own time is your business, but you will still join us at mealtime when you are in this house. Even if he fattens you up on beef stroganoff and drops you off early, you'll sit at the table and be social."

"So that's it? I'm in?"

He bit the end of the grape. "This is a trial period. You meet all the requirements, but I need to test your loyalty and work ethic."

The woman to the right of the Chitah removed her towel and fluffed the ends of her wavy violet hair, which fell just past her shoulders and was parted off center. It wasn't a deep violet but a lovely, pale shade like raw amethyst.

Viktor gave her a scolding glance, and she blushed.

"Sorry, Viktor. I thought we already had dinner, so I was winding down before bedtime."

My brows arched as I looked at the food on the table. "How many times do you guys eat?"

The Chitah boomed with laughter. "If twice a night is a new tradition, let's keep her."

His curls of dark-blond hair covered his ears and nape of his neck. *Gorgeous* hair. It seemed to conflict with his brutish physique. He was tall, nicely built, and had a V-shaped torso with broad shoulders. Easy to see since he was wearing a white tank top. With all that he had going on, it was actually his mouth that stole the show. It had a perfect Cupid's bow and somehow softened his fierce features.

Viktor stood up and pointed at the Chitah. "Let us introduce ourselves. The Chitah across from you is Claude Valentine. He also runs a salon that caters to some of the most elite clients, who of course like to confide in their hairdresser."

Ah. That explained his wondrous locks.

"To his left is Gem Laroux. She's a Mage with unmatched knowledge—fluent in sixteen languages and is able to interpret many extinct languages that haven't been spoken in thousands of years. She knows about ancient artifacts and can also decipher codes."

I would have never guessed that from a pixie with purple hair.

Viktor gestured to the man on her left. He seemed the least friendly, and not because of the hard muscles and buzz cut that made him look ready for a cage fight. It was the cold stare he gave beneath those dark eyebrows. "And then we have Shepherd Moon, our resident Sensor. We obviously use him to investigate crime scenes and other jobs where he can use his gifts to read emotional imprints left behind. His skills are tactical combat and offending random people on the street."

Niko sputtered with laughter at the remark and tried to hide it. "Apologies. I had a glass of wine before you called the meeting."

Viktor clapped his hand on the shoulder of the man to his right—the same one who had slammed into me in the hallway earlier like a lunatic. "And then we have Wyatt."

Wyatt flashed a smile at Viktor, candlelight flickering in his olive-green eyes. He was slender but fit and appeared average height, although shorter than the other men. He seemed to be the one with the most gregarious personality. "Well?" he said, urging Viktor on.

"Sorry," Viktor replied. "I was trying to collect my thoughts on how to segue from a Sensor to a Gravewalker."

I furrowed my brow. "What's a Gravewalker?"

A few shoulders sagged, and Shepherd leaned back, tossing his fork on his plate.

"Here we go," Christian said.

Wyatt cocked his head to the side and then rose to his feet. "*What* is a Gravewalker? See, this is the problem I have, Viktor. Nobody ever takes what we do seriously. How is the world going to know about all we have to offer if you don't educate the young little minds?"

Gem peered up at him. "The only thing you have to offer, Wyatt, is the potato chips you leave all over the desk in the game room."

"There's a game room?" I asked.

Viktor heaved a sigh. "Now see what you've done? I have no wish to open that room to new members. It's a distraction."

Wyatt folded his arms. "I beg to differ. It sharpens my skills."

"Why don't you tell the truth," Christian said. "You're afraid to sit in a quiet room."

Wyatt pointed his finger on the table. "Hey, noise distracts them."

"Wait a minute," I interrupted. "What's a Gravewalker?"

Wyatt opened his arms dramatically. "Feast your eyes. I'm a Gravewalker. Born in 1803 to Nathaniel and Sarah Blessing. Raised in Tennessee and left home to leave my mark on the world when I was seventeen."

"Times were rough?" I asked.

He huffed out a laugh. "Nine older sisters. You tell me. And before you ask, I lost most of my Southern accent a century ago. Anyhow, back to Gravewalkers. We can communicate with ghosts who haven't moved on to where they're supposed to go."

I smirked. "And where are they supposed to go?"

He shrugged. "How should I know? Even they don't know. It's all part of the grand mystery," he said, wiggling his fingers.

"Why do they call you a Gravewalker?"

Candlelight flickered against his face, making this feel more like a campfire story. "In days of yore, Vampires were staked and buried alive for all kinds of reasons. Punishment, revenge, or even entertainment. Obviously they can't scream when paralyzed, and while Vampires have stupendous hearing, even they can't detect a heartbeat buried beneath six feet of earth. Nor can a Mage pick up on their energy. Gravewalkers know who does and doesn't belong in a cemetery. People paid us good money."

"Interesting. I guess that makes going to funerals super fun."

He dropped into his seat. "That's a negative. I don't like going where the freshies hang out. They tend to cling like socks out of the dryer when they find out I'm a link to the living world."

My gaze flicked down to his hands, and I noticed letters tattooed on his fingers. If he closed his hands into fists and pressed his knuckles together, it spelled out LOST SOUL.

"Moving along," Viktor said.

"You didn't mention my skills," Wyatt complained.

"Ah, yes. Wyatt here is masterful at washing dishes. He can perform a demonstration on polishing silverware after breakfast tomorrow."

"Forget I asked, forget I asked," Wyatt quickly said.

When Viktor turned to Christian, I said, "You can skip him."

Gem laughed. "I like her already."

"Might as well," Christian agreed. "She can't seem to help herself around all this sexual goodness."

Viktor grumbled something and then gestured to Blue—the woman who had searched me for weapons earlier that day. She leaned forward to meet my eyes.

"This is Blue. She's a Shifter, like me. Blue has a special gift that not many of us have. Most Shifters eventually black out when their animal takes over, except for alphas of any species. Most of us prefer not remembering; it's how we evolved, and it serves a purpose. But occasionally there are some who are aware throughout their shift and even control their animal."

"I wouldn't say I can control her," Blue added. "We understand each other and cohabitate."

I rested my arm on the table. "What's your animal?"

"It's impolite to ask, but maybe I'll show you sometime."

Blue didn't have the bright personality Gem had. She spoke frankly but didn't come across as rude. She seemed every bit as tough as the men, yet still displayed femininity in the regal manner in which she lifted her glass and took a sip.

Viktor sat down. "You already know Niko. He's older than my grandfather's socks and sees what we cannot."

My eyes settled on the Chitah's hands as he broke a loaf of bread. Those things looked better suited for crushing boulders, not cutting hair. I'd never seen such a diverse group of people working together, not just based on their Breeds but also their personalities.

"We're going to have to do something about this seating arrangement," Viktor said, refilling his glass.

Everyone resumed eating the fruit, bread, and cheeses on the table before us.

"Why's that?" Claude asked, chewing off a hunk of bread.

"Partners should sit together," he replied.

All eyes moved to one person who was sitting on the far right.

"Jaysus wept," Christian muttered. "You're not serious."

Viktor buttered a slice of bread, amusement dancing in his eyes. "Dead serious."

"What's he talking about?" I whispered to Niko, butterflies swirling in my stomach.

Niko leaned close. "We all work together, but we each have a partner. We sit beside them. Gem and Claude, Shepherd and Wyatt, and I'm with Blue. That just leaves you and—"

"Christian," I finished.

"She's a bright one," Christian mused.

I leaned back in my chair, narrowing my eyes. "Don't eavesdrop on my conversations."

"It can hardly be helped," he said, glaring back at me. "Your lyrical voice and eloquent use of vocabulary is *sublime*."

Viktor pointed his knife. "And that is why you must sit together. It's harder to bicker when there's nothing between you. See what wonders it's done for Wyatt and Shepherd?"

"I wouldn't go *that* far," Shepherd said gruffly.

Shepherd had a tattoo on his upper right arm that went beneath his short-sleeve shirt. I couldn't make out what it was, only that the design was elaborate and detailed. Maybe my eyes were deceiving me in the candlelight, but I could have sworn there were scars all over his arms. He lit up a cigarette and stared at me so coldly that I looked away.

"So what can Sensors do?" I asked.

Claude held a roll between his fingers, frozen. "Are you serious?"

I worried my lip, feeling the judgmental stares upon me. "I don't exactly hang out with Breed as much as you might think. I know that Sensors can pick up emotional energy and all that, but what are they doing in the back of the clubs when all that glowy red stuff is coming from their hands?"

Wyatt elbowed Shepherd. "Why don't you show her?"

Shepherd lifted a reluctant gaze to Viktor, who nodded in agreement. Shepherd stubbed out the cigarette on his plate and abruptly stood up, rounding the table with an angry stride.

When he neared me, I almost reached for a pointy fork.

He placed his rough hands on my shoulders and moved them down as if he were about to feel me up. I reactively gripped his wrists, ready to fly out of my chair, when suddenly…

"Oh my God," I whispered.

A faint red glow emanated from his palms, spilling magic into me. A sensation rushed through my body, so real that it felt as if someone were tickling me.

I couldn't control the laughter.

He let go and returned to his seat.

Gem giggled and raised her glass. "Wasn't that fun? Shepherd only ever gives us the tickles."

Viktor tapped his knife on the table to get my attention. "I don't allow sensory exchanges in my house. This is not a circus, and that also goes for sharing light. Unless you have a metal pin coming out of your skull and need to heal, I don't want you drawing light from anyone. Gifts become curses when they're not given their due respect."

I sat back in my chair. "Won't be a problem. I hate being tickled."

Viktor set down his knife. "Shepherd detects emotions, but

he can also pull them from people and store them. That's how Sensors make their money—sensory exchange. They sell emotional experiences, and in some cases, remove them. For customers it's temporary, addictive, and recreational. But it can also be used to gather information, and that's what he does best."

"I guess that makes going into public restrooms an unpleasant experience," I said with a snort.

Viktor ate two more grapes. "Sensors live for hundreds of years, like Shifters."

"Mileage may vary," Wyatt remarked, loading up his plate with cheese. "Gravewalkers live to a thousand."

"Good for you," Shepherd said. "More generations to annoy with your fashion."

Wyatt glanced down at his T-shirt, which said THE FUCK I GAVE WENT THAT WAY, with an arrow.

"I'm just here to educate," he replied, scrunching up his disheveled brown hair, absent of the knit cap I'd previously seen him wearing.

Claude's nostrils flared. He continued eating, but his eyes remained watchful as they analyzed me. "What are you?"

I only hesitated for a second. After coming out in front of Viktor, Christian, and Niko, it felt good to be open about what I was, even if no one understood it. "I'm a crossbreed."

You could have heard a pin drop.

"Is that why you've got them funky eyes?" Wyatt asked.

"Not exactly."

"Raven is half Mage and Vampire," Viktor added.

Gem's jaw unhinged. "That's impossible!" But her reaction wasn't as smarmy and bemused as Christian's had been. More of excitement and curiosity.

I looked past Blue, who stared at me wide-eyed. It seemed that Viktor hadn't told everyone, so Niko must have heard the rumor from Christian. "Viktor, can we get back to this whole 'partner' thing? I work alone."

"Not anymore," he replied nonchalantly. "Everyone is paired up based on their strengths and weaknesses. Although Gem is a

Mage, she is not physically strong, so I chose Claude. They protect each other in all ways. Blue is Niko's eyes and he is hers."

I touched the stem of my empty glass, spinning it. "It sounds like you put a lot of thought into it, except why do I feel like we're just getting thrown together because there's nobody left?"

He bit down on a piece of cheese, staring at it. "Sometimes we can't choose our fate, and it is fate that chooses us."

"Maybe we can rotate," I suggested. "Switch it up every so often."

"Uh-uh," Gem complained. "No way I'm getting paired up with Shepherd. He's a grump."

"Which brings me to my next rule," Viktor continued. "I hate to be blunt, but I make rules for a reason. Partners will not engage in—"

"Extracurricular sextivity," Wyatt finished, raising his glass to Christian in a toast. "*Sláinte*."

Christian rose to his feet and put his knuckles on the table, leaning toward Wyatt. "Put a cork in it before I drain you."

When Viktor cleared his throat, Christian sat back down. "I would highly recommend that you fulfill any urges outside this house."

Urges? I stood up, offended. "Do I look like a slut who can't keep her legs closed? You talk as if I'm a car that needs to be serviced at a gas station by a good pump. And just to clarify, I have no urge to fuel up with a Vampire."

Christian leaned back in his chair, his tone cool and dispassionate. "Worry not, lass. This gas station is self-service. Just the way you like it."

Niko must have seen a solar flare around me, because he couldn't stop looking.

"Everyone gets the same talk," Viktor assured me. "This has nothing to do with you personally. Please, sit."

When I did, Niko leaned in close and lowered his voice. "His intentions are in the right place, he just sucks at delivery."

Claude reached out his hand. "Give me your plate, female, and I'll put some food on it."

"No, thanks. I'm not hungry."

I'd heard Chitahs talk about their sisters or mates, and it sounded like they revered them—cared for them in a way I didn't understand.

"Don't you eat? Is it because you're half Vampire?"

"She's a scavenger," Christian said, lifting his glass of wine. "It's no fun unless she can hunt for her food."

I peered around Niko. "Why don't you shut up over there and find a wrist to sip on?"

Gem pointed at Christian. "Doesn't look like Raven plays on Team Christian."

"You better eat something," Christian sang. "The Chitah won't eat until the women at the table are fed."

This had to be a joke.

I looked up at Claude and realized there might be some truth to the remark. "Go on and eat, Claude. Ignore him."

Claude lifted his chin. "I can scent your hunger, female. Now give me your plate."

I still didn't feel part of this posse, and aside from that, even Betty had tried for three weeks before I'd accept her meals at the diner.

Claude leaned back in his chair and folded his arms.

"Rest up, little ones," Viktor said, rising to his feet. "We have important matters to discuss in the morning."

Chapter 8

"WHEN DO I GET MY weapons back?" I asked Viktor over a light breakfast.

Since no one had told me when the scheduled mealtimes were, I'd wandered into the kitchen early that morning before the house stirred with activity. Viktor invited me to sit with him and talk a little.

He set a plate in front of me with a sausage patty on it. "You'll get your weapons back today, just don't use them on anyone in the house."

"I can't make any promises with regards to my *partner*."

He chuckled and sat to my right. "If this works out, you'll learn to tolerate each other. It does not mean you'll work exclusively with him, only on certain jobs. It's also good to have someone you can confide in, someone who has your back above all others."

"I wouldn't bet on that," I muttered.

Viktor swallowed his orange juice. "Careful who you choose to provoke. Christian may come across as benign, but he is a dangerous man."

"Then why have someone like that in your group?"

He laughed quietly. "We are all dangerous, are we not? Some more than others. He and Shepherd are my newest inductees, so it will take a while for them to adjust. Don't push them over the edge. You're a willful woman, and sometimes that can be enough to drive a man insane."

"I can't argue with that. So how do I know when it's dinnertime if there aren't any clocks?"

"Most have a clock or watch in their bedroom. Can't you sense time? You're half Mage."

I stared at the uneaten sausage patty. "I haven't gotten around to that part in my training with Niko just yet. Where is everyone?"

"Claude went to work. Wyatt sleeps in."

Christian strolled into the kitchen wearing a pair of dark shades, his hair rumpled. He took a seat in one of the booths along the central wall, keeping his back to us. Filtered light trickled in from the arched window to my right. I had a nice view of a narrow doorway that led to the kitchen. I hadn't seen it, but that was where people were coming from with food or drinks in hand.

Shepherd swaggered in, and instead of taking his usual seat, he sat at the opposite end of the table, Blue claiming the chair to his right.

Gem floated in like a breeze, dressed and looking like a girl who didn't need coffee to start her day. Her locks were accented with subtle highlights so that her hair wasn't one solid color. In the light of day, she had arresting eyes just as violet as her hair. She also had a beauty mark high on her cheek, just below the outer corner of her left eye. Her chunky heels knocked on the floor as she approached the chair in front of me and bowed.

"Gem Laroux. It's so nice having another girl around. I was afraid Viktor would add more testosterone to the fire."

Gem gave Viktor a quick hug before she sat down. He looked uncomfortable with the display of affection, but not surprised.

"Are those your real eyes?" I asked.

She laughed and tucked her chin in her hand. "I bet you hear that more often than I do. They're real. What about yours?"

"Where is Niko?" Viktor spoke in a sonorous voice, one that must have echoed into the outer hall.

Niko strode into the room and found a chair next to Gem. "I'm here. Apologies, I was feeding the cat."

"How many times have I told you not to feed that stray?" Viktor chided. "You give them food, and then they hang around and poop all over my lawn."

While Niko and Viktor discussed felines, Gem leaned across the table, her voice low. "Was that you on the roof last night?"

I shook my head in a liar's denial. While the inside of the mansion was undeniably impressive, it was the roof that excited me the most. After everyone had gone to their rooms, I'd quietly stepped out of the window and walked the entire length of the mansion to get a better sense of the property. Heights gave me a sense of peace—a safe place where I could gather my thoughts and reflect.

"Oh. I could have sworn I saw someone on the roof. Maybe it was one of Wyatt's haunts," she said, widening her eyes and then snickering.

Viktor sipped his coffee and then set the mug down to address everyone in the room. "Claude's at work, and I don't have the patience to wake up Wyatt. I have business matters to discuss, and I'll fill them in later."

"Before we begin, can I ask a question?"

All eyes fell on me.

Viktor stroked his beard. "You may."

"Is the name of this group Zero?"

Everyone barked out a laugh, including Shepherd.

I glared at them. "What? It was on the business card."

"That would be a pathetic name for a group," Gem said. "I wouldn't want to be a zero."

Blue's voice softened with humor. "People would think that was our track record for captures."

"Or IQ," Shepherd added, talking with a cigarette in his mouth. He struck a match against the coarse strip on the matchbook and lit the end of his smoke.

I stole another glimpse of his scars, more noticeable now than the previous night. When he caught the direction of my gaze, I quickly looked away.

Viktor steepled his fingers. "Enough, enough. It's a fair question. No, Raven. Zero is just a way to communicate to our contacts when we need their assistance."

"Like getting Christian lemon bars?"

Gem played with a crystal necklace that hung from her neck.

"We do not advertise our group, so that's the first thing you must know," Viktor said, flattening his hands on the table. "It is possible with time that the public will figure this out, but for now, we choose to remain underground."

"I understand."

"Good. We are Keystone. There wasn't a need for a name when it was just me, but after picking up Niko, Blue, and Wyatt, everyone felt we needed something to call ourselves. The main rooms have archways with a keystone at the top. I like the meaning, because a keystone is the center stone that locks the arch together. It holds the pieces in place. Years ago, I wanted to do something with my life that had meaning. I had the right connections, so I decided to become a local bounty hunter. It evolved from there, and I sought out a partner. Soon the idea became bigger than me, so I looked around at all this space and thought, why not? It seemed a shame to let the mansion go to waste. Having the team live here makes it feel more like a home, and a team *should* be a family. Everyone here has an important role; we're not just warriors. I have assembled an equal balance of muscle and intelligence."

He took a sip from his water glass.

"Do you get assigned cases? Does everyone work on the same thing?"

Viktor set down his glass and waved his finger. "We never have just one open case, and *I* decide what jobs we take. Sometimes we open our own cases, and other times our services are requested. I've created a unique system that allows us to work independently and not answer to anyone. Since you are new, I'll fill you in on a case we're working on. Darius Bane has been high on the hit list for some time, and it doesn't look like anyone is close to arresting him due to lack of evidence. However, we have several tips from reliable sources. The most recent crime dates back two weeks."

"What's he done?"

"He's a human killer. Do you know why that is a deplorable crime? Because humans are the weaker species, and therefore deserve our mercy. Since his victims are human and not part of our world, we cannot call them to witness. But repeat offenders leave… how you say… fingerprints?" He looked to Shepherd for help.

Shepherd drew in a deep puff of the cigarette. "I think what you mean is that they follow a pattern."

Viktor nodded. "Thank you. Pattern is correct. You cannot allow immortals to kill humans. Empowerment is a dangerous thing and can lead to even greater crimes against humanity. It is true that humans would wage war against us if they knew we existed, but that is out of fear. Men like this bring more into their circle and plan murders in greater numbers. Soon they will want to rise up against humans in a rebellion. We will never be able to live peacefully and openly with humans, and that's why, centuries ago, Breed went underground and made ourselves into nothing but bedtime stories. It is far easier to live in peace, even if it means keeping ourselves secret. And we must always remember that they are the weaker species, even if they dominate us in numbers."

"I understand." And I did. After being around some of the older immortals, they had this sense of entitlement about them, as if they belonged in this world and humans didn't. Maybe that was why I tried a little harder to protect humans.

"This man, he is no good." Viktor began to spout off in Russian until Gem patted his hand.

"English," she said.

He sat back in his chair. "Forgive me. I think in Russian, I speak in English… It's too confusing."

Gem smiled and winked at me, as if implying this happened a lot when Viktor became emotional.

Then his gaze swung in my direction. "Our paths crossed a few months ago when you took out one of Mr. Bane's men. That's how we came to eventually track you down."

"Did you say his name was Darius?"

"*Da.*"

"The other night, I overheard some big shot talking to his lackey about killing a human club owner and making it look like a local gang. He wanted to torch the place, but I really didn't get what his motive was. The other man called him Darius. Do you think it could be the same guy?"

Viktor launched to his feet and kicked his chair over. "Son of bitch," he growled in broken English.

"I don't think he went through with it," I quickly added. "His partner got a good look at me and knows that I overheard their conversation."

"You didn't kill him? I was not aware you let anyone go."

I scraped my teeth against my bottom lip and folded my arms. "Believe me, it wasn't out of mercy. He got away, but maybe it's for the better. If he thinks someone knows what he's doing, maybe he'll stop. Why don't you just find out where he lives and burn the place to the ground?"

"He is well protected, and we must do this as discreetly as possible."

"There's nothing discreet about murder."

Viktor shook his finger at me, still pacing. "We cannot make ourselves out to be terrorists. If you want fireworks and a parade, you are in the wrong place. We have been unable to track him since he has many homes, and if we break into the wrong one, it could set us back years. It is impossible to know where he sleeps, and he does not make many public appearances."

Shepherd dropped his cigarette butt into a glass of water. "So what's the plan? We've been gathering evidence against this piece of shit for months, but it's not enough to turn him over to the authorities. We either need to catch him in the act or—"

"Cut his throat," Christian murmured from his booth. "I vote for plan B."

Viktor turned around, gazing up at the window when the room grew deceptively bright from thinning clouds. "I agree. He has too many friends in power, and without sufficient evidence, they would try to crush us."

"What else did you hear them say?" Niko asked, his pale eyes centered on the table.

I turned my small plate in slow circles. "It sounded like extortion, targeting new business owners in the neighborhood and making them think they needed his protection. But he said something weird before he left."

"Oh?" Viktor asked, turning around. He righted his chair and sat back down. "What did he say?"

I touched my lip, trying to recall the exact words. "He said that they have no right to be here. What did he mean by that?"

Gem waved her hand. "He was probably just making a general statement about humans."

"Those were his exact words?" Viktor asked, his stormy eyes lowering in thought. "Shepherd, do me a favor. After this meeting, I want you to have Wyatt pull up the list of victims and pinpoint the location of their businesses, even if their death was elsewhere."

Shepherd ran his hand over his bristly hair. "What are you looking for?"

"A connection. We've focused so much on the human aspect and the location of the murders that perhaps we're not seeing the bigger picture. If this is related to their place of business, we might have something to go on. Tell Wyatt to pull up old land records as far back as he can. See if he can trace any of those buildings or land to Breed."

"If you can't figure out where he's staying, then why don't you just charm one of his buddies?" I suggested.

"Oh, we tried that," Gem said. "Epic fail. Christian got staked, and Claude almost lost his pants chasing them down. Long story."

"They wear sunglasses," Shepherd said, his arms folded across the table, accenting muscles that made him look like a professional fighter. "They're smart bastards, always on alert, even when they're off the clock."

"Have you tried other methods?" I asked.

Viktor rubbed his hands together. "Like what?"

My eyes skated about the room. "Really? You have two pretty girls and you can't think of a single idea to get close enough to his men?"

"Absolutely not," Niko said. "If something goes wrong, they'll physically subdue them. It could be a death sentence if they don't have backup, and I won't have that on my conscience."

I raised my hand. "Then I'll be the guinea pig. That's what I do best."

Shepherd sat back, his arms draped over the back of his chair. "So you're offended when Viktor says there's no sex in the house, but you'll fuck a guard for information?"

Blue threw back her head and slowly whispered, "Shut up."

Now I knew what Viktor meant about Shepherd offending random people on the street. Shepherd had a crude way of speaking, even in polite conversation.

"First of all, Viktor didn't say no sex in the house. He just said no sex with partners. Secondly, I never said I was going to have sex." I laughed because the thought was too hilarious. "I just know how to lure them to—"

"Her spiderweb," Christian finished with a mirthless laugh. "Then the black widow can sink her fangs into her prey and spin him inside a little cocoon. Maybe we should have called you Black Widow instead of the Shadow."

Viktor regarded me for a moment. "I agree with Raven. Consider this a test."

Christian chimed in. "Think carefully, Viktor. If they catch her or Darius finds out about us, all your hard work is ruined in one night. She's too green to send in."

"Let's not be dramatic. She killed two men who were on our list. If she screws up, she's out."

I sat back, thinking this seemed too easy. "So all you want to know is where this guy Darius stays each night? That's all?"

"*Da*, but I don't want you killing his guards. He will panic and change his routine. I'll send Christian with you to charm him for information and then scrub his memory."

"Does he hire other Breeds?"

"As far as what we've seen, they are all Mage. He employs dangerous men, so keep that in mind. We know the pubs they frequent, but their schedule fluctuates." Viktor stroked his beard. "I need to see what you have to offer us before I can make decisions about your future with Keystone. Can you handle it?"

"If I can handle a shopping cart with a trick wheel on Black Friday, I can handle just about anything."

His brows furrowed, and I laughed.

"Never mind. Bad joke. Just take me to where they hang out, and I'll do the rest. Do I get paid for these jobs?"

"Your payment will be deposited into an account."

"Can I have an advance? I'm starving."

Gem eyed my sausage. "I'll fix you something better. We have a—"

"No, don't bother. I won't eat it."

Christian stood up and strode toward the table. "She only dines off other people's plates, so maybe you need to make yourself some breakfast and watch her in action."

I felt a flush in my cheeks and rubbed my eyes, hoping no one noticed. "If I can't earn my food, I take what people discard. I'm sorry if you have a problem with that, but it's not about me being stubborn. This is the only honor I have, so someone telling me that it's ridiculous is offensive. Eating isn't something I need to do as often as the rest of you, so it's usually not a big deal. I don't have things handed to me on a silver platter, and it's not easy to buy a meal when no one will hire you except to sweep up the kitchen as a one-time favor because they feel sorry for you. I'm not going to apologize for it. That'll change once I start working more jobs for you—*if* I'm hired. But as it stands, I feel like an outsider. If you give me an advance on the money, I'll buy my own meals until I'm officially hired."

"Very well," Viktor said, a hint of admiration in his voice. He took the sausage from my plate and bit into it. "Many centuries ago, there were warriors who lived by the same code. Sometimes when a man takes another man's life, even for the sake of good, he clings to the things that make him feel like there is still honor and goodness in him. I will give you an advance and leave the card in your room. I have my own account; we don't do business dealings through a separate institution."

"Sounds good."

Viktor stood up. "We begin tonight. Until then, feel free to go into any room with unlocked doors," he said to me. "We have many things to offer."

"Such as?"

Blue's brows arched, drawing attention to her sapphire eyes. "Did you see the pool in the courtyard? It's a little cold for swimming, but it's heated. There's also a rock-climbing room and billiard room."

"And a bar," Shepherd added, rising to his feet.

Christian patted him on the shoulder, and they swaggered out. "You read my mind."

I spent the full day exploring the mansion and got lost three times. I went outside and circled the grounds, but a dense wave of fog rolled in. Before it started to rain, I hurried back to the house.

Blue wasn't kidding about the rooms. I found one with billiard tables, dartboards, shuffleboard, and game tables, including one with a chessboard. I sat down and studied the chess pieces, wondering which one I was in the grand scheme of things. Steam rose from the heated pool outside, but I wasn't much of a swimmer, so I just admired it from inside. The courtyard wasn't a perfect rectangle and branched around as if it might be L-shaped.

The kid inside me wanted to skip down the halls and sing, but the pessimist kept reminding me that I was just a girl from the trailer park who had no business living this kind of lavish lifestyle. I'd grown up on the side of the tracks that even the cops didn't visit.

After my self-guided tour, I found a room with a large window, and sofas boxing in the fireplace.

Christian poked his head through the open door in the right-hand corner from where I was sitting. "Sounds like a little mouse scurrying up here with all that trampling you've been doing."

I ignored him, still curled up and staring at the empty fireplace on my left.

"Cat got your tongue?" Christian circled around the modern

grey sectional and sat on the opposite side, crossing his ankles on the ottoman. He made an L shape with his index finger and thumb, then rested his chin between them. "Think you can handle the big leagues?"

"Are you offended by my Breed, gender, or the fact you're no longer working solo? Something tells me you're not trying to save a young girl from a dangerous life of espionage, so which is it?"

Christian retrieved a small piece of candy from his pocket and tucked the wrapper away.

"How long have you been doing this?" I asked.

He crunched on the candy. "A few months."

I laughed. "That hardly makes you a pro. What did you do before this, stand-up comedy?"

"I was a guard."

"Who did you work for?"

He groaned and rubbed the side of his face. "Not that kind of guard. A bodyguard contracts his professional services; he's not an employee. Most people hire Vampires since we're not easily detected and don't require sleep. We protect their lives with our own until our services are no longer needed."

"Your last gig must have been a doozy if you ended up here instead. Did you rush through a hail of bullets and fling your body over his, only to find it was too late?"

Christian dodged my gaze. "He was a she, and she was no longer in need of my services."

There was a lot of implication wrapped up in that tidy little sentence. "And did you still need hers?"

He tipped his head to the side and tapped his fingers on the armrest. "You remind me of her in just one way. She always had to have the last word." Christian bit down on his candy and put his feet on the floor, widening his long legs. "Why so glum this afternoon? Where's that pocketful of sunshine you always carry around?"

I gave him the finger.

"Ah, there it is." He chuckled softly and reclined his head.

Christian looked like he'd taken a pair of scissors to the collar of his thin sweater to make it wider. It showed off his collarbones and drew attention to his dark features.

"Tell me, Raven, will it be the dress tonight or the sweats? Because I've seen your wardrobe, and it's astonishingly limited."

"The black dress hasn't failed me yet."

"I seem to recall a few failures on the night we met."

I put my feet flat on the floor. "Pickings were slim. Food is one thing, but I don't fail when I'm on the hunt for justice."

He leaned forward, resting his elbows on his knees. "Ah… justice. Tell me more about that."

I pulled my long hair around to one side. "What exactly is your job tonight, to keep an eye on me? Do you have a scorecard in your pocket to keep track of all my points?"

"I'm your guard, remember?"

"Be my backup if you want, but I don't need a guard. I never have."

When I stood up to leave, Christian sprang to his feet and blocked my exit.

"No need to get your knickers in a bunch. And for feck's sake, you can look me in the eye. I'm not going to charm you."

"Are you going to wear that?" I asked, pointing at the loose threads hanging from his neckline.

He flashed a dark smile. "Hasn't failed me yet."

"I guess if you're going to be a bad dresser, go for gold."

"You're a chirpy little bird." He lowered his head, looking down his nose at me. When he hooked his finger beneath my chin to tilt my head up, I looked away. "And a pretty one at that."

I stumbled backward, almost tripping over the edge of the sofa. "Stop trying to rattle me. I know what you're trying to do. You want me to fail."

"Is that so? My job is to make sure that you don't blow our cover tonight. You might think that's a swank little dress, but on the night we met, you smelled like the cheap soap they use in public toilets. So I hope this time around, you take a little more care with your appearance. Viktor didn't flesh out the details, but let me clarify a few things. If you're painted into a corner and start chatting about our group, you'll put us all in danger. Maybe you don't give a shite, but I do. No matter what happens—if they strap you to a train track or dangle you off an airplane wheel—don't mention names, locations, what we do, or how we like our eggs cooked. You need to develop total fecking amnesia."

"Don't let this body fool you, Vamp. I've also got brains."

Christian wasn't just trying to rattle me; he wanted to sabotage me. I could see in his eyes that he didn't trust me, and that made him a threat.

Even though Vampires didn't give off energy like other Breeds, I could have sworn that I felt a magnetic buzz that tingled across my skin. The hair on the back of my neck stood on end, and I didn't bother to slow down my heart, which was thumping a fraction harder than it had been just a moment before.

But he said nothing, and I left it at nothing.

Chapter 9

THAT NIGHT, I ARMED MYSELF with a push dagger strapped to my inner thigh. It was small enough that my black dress could conceal it, but there wasn't room for any other weapons. While daggers were convenient, my fangs and ability to pull energy were the tools I relied on most.

I knocked back the tequila, practically rinsing my mouth out with it. The scented oils from my bath earlier made my legs look spectacular, and I crossed them as I scanned the room.

Christian nodded toward the main entrance. "Now that's a door of a woman."

I furrowed my brow at the odd expression and glanced at a woman who could have been a linebacker. "Are you ever nice to people of the female persuasion?"

"Of course I am." He leaned toward me and pointed. "I was nice to that one, that one, and the bonnie one in the white dress was especially nice to me."

I blinked in surprise and he laughed, shaking his head and facing forward again.

A waitress appeared and placed a basket of food in front of Christian. "Are you the footlong?"

He slowly turned, undressing her with his eyes. "Ten, actually. But I've heard it feels like twelve."

"And hot dog number three," she said, setting a basket in front of me and strutting off.

Christian nearly spit out his drink as he looked over at my

meal. "Have you got worms? A parasite maybe? I don't see where you put it all."

I took a bite, careful not to smudge my lipstick. "I work better when I'm fed."

"I thought you were too good for bar hot dogs."

I licked my finger. "If I didn't have on lipstick, I would have ordered the Angus burger with extra cheese."

"You could just order the whole heifer."

We'd arrived early so as not to raise suspicion. It gave me time to hang out, have a few drinks, and mingle, which made me less anxious. Viktor wasn't sure if Darius's men would show up, but an hour earlier, Christian's eyes had slanted toward three men entering the bar. He gave me a subtle nod, and I spent my time assessing the group. I wanted the weak link in the chain, so I first had to figure out who that was and then how to lure him away from his group.

These guys had their sunglasses on, making it impossible for Christian to get close enough. Even if he could, a Vampire didn't have the ability to charm three people at once since they had to look them directly in the eye. Viktor warned us that outside the bar, they were always on alert, ready to stake or stab anything within a ten-foot radius.

This was the first time I'd sat down with Christian, so we pretended to be strangers who happened to be eating beside each other.

I'd watched him seducing beautiful women for an hour, and they were quite smitten with him. At one point, he'd backed a brunette up against a wall and placed his hand on her hip while whispering in her ear. He looked at her so differently than the way he looked at me, which was usually with cold indifference.

So much for having a guard.

Through process of elimination, I narrowed down the leader to the jerk who kept snapping his fingers at the waitress and pointing at their empty glasses. Out of the other two guys, the little one was my initial target, but he was so shy he'd look away when a woman walked past. Getting him alone would be as easy as bathing a cat.

That left contestant number three, who was tall, dark, and not so handsome. He had a face only a mother could love... after six shots of whiskey. Two missing teeth, a crooked nose, and sweaty.

Oh, how I *loathed* the sweaty guys. Not the ones with that fine sheen of what I liked to call "man mist" but the ones with fat drops of sweat rolling down their temples, even in a blizzard.

He was attentive with the waitress and admired the women who sauntered past their table. None had given him the green light, so he remained seated. It appeared this guy was searching for an opportunity but didn't want to take a chance with rejection.

Separating him from his buddies was going to be a challenge that required a little ingenuity.

I hopped off my barstool and slid my plate toward Christian. "You can finish my hot dog."

As I strutted across the bar, my peripheral caught my target's head turning in my direction. I made brief eye contact with him and smiled coyly, making sure he saw my interest. My destination was a jukebox just a few tables over. Breed bars loved jukeboxes, so I leaned over and gave him a nice view of my ass as I studied the song selection.

After counting to ten, I straightened up and pretended to fix my hair in the mirror, searching for an opportunity around me. When I saw a man on my right heading my way with a pint in hand, I sprang into action and crashed into him.

"Ah, shit!" he grumbled, the glass shattering on the floor.

Beer splashed all over my dress, and I gasped, stepping back with a horrified expression.

Darius's man rose from his chair and stalked in our direction. I could tell he was the kind of guy who wanted to be the badass in life, and maybe that suit made him feel more important than everyone else in a low-class bar.

"Why don't you apologize to the lady?" he said.

The man with the empty glass didn't look like he wanted trouble.

Especially after Darius's goon opened his jacket and showed him a gun and two daggers.

And now I knew what he was armed with.

The man nodded at me apologetically and backed away, his hands raised in a defensive gesture.

While Darius's man watched him with a sharp eye, I used the heel of my shoe to slice the top of my left foot.

"Thank you so much," I said, playing the damsel in distress.

I started to turn and stumbled so he'd catch me. We both looked down at my bleeding foot, but I made sure to keep our body contact nice and tight.

I lifted my gaze with an amorous look in my eyes. "Will you help me to the bathroom? My Creator is going to be furious if this beer stains my dress. And my shoe is covered in blood—he spent so much money."

This simple little statement conveyed two things. One, that I was a Mage—the main reason he'd find me attractive. Two, that I was still under the care of my Creator, which meant I was new in the Breed world and a little more naïve. Mage men didn't get excited over the prospect of sex so much as binding—the exchange of sexual energy through holding hands.

The man eagerly hooked his arm around my waist and led me to the bathroom. "You're a Mage?"

"Just last year," I said. "This is the first time he's let me out with no escort. He wants to see if I'm ready to be independent. If I go home like this, he'll never agree to it."

"Maybe I can lend you a little of my light."

I gave him my best doe-eyed look. "I've never taken light from a stranger. Do you think that's okay?"

I could practically hear him growling with anticipation.

Viktor had given me a brown contact lens for my blue eye so my mismatched gaze wouldn't become a distraction, but it was annoying the shit out of me. I kept winking as if I had some kind of facial tic.

"Do you live with your Creator?" he asked.

The crowd thinned in the hallway, and we chose the private bathroom instead of the public one.

"I'm in the same building, but I have my own apartment. He's slowly weaning me from being so dependent on him, but he still likes to lavish me with gifts," I said with a coquettish smile. "What's your name? I'm Bella."

The private bathroom door closed behind him, and without looking, I knew he was hard.

"Owen."

I lifted his sunglasses and tossed them into the sink. "Is that with a big *O* or a little one?"

I nestled my body against his and wrapped my arms around him in an embrace so that I could unlock the door for Christian, wherever he was.

"Your light's so strong," I moaned against his chest, silently turning the lock. "I like the way it feels on me. Do you have a car?"

"Uh…" He drew back.

"I don't care about this dress anymore, but I was hoping that maybe… Well, you know. I've never done anything spontaneous like this, but I can't do it when there's a toilet three feet away."

"What exactly do you want to do?" he asked, a bead of sweat rolling down his cheek.

Binding energy with another Mage was highly erotic, but I'd heard that doing it while having sex was otherworldly.

I rubbed up against him like a cat and whispered, "Everything."

Owen trembled, cursing under his breath as he leaned back. There was a peculiar look in his eyes that I couldn't discern. "Devon's going to kill me, but fuck it. He gets all the fun. Come on."

Before I knew it, we were moving out the back exit. He opened the rear door to a dark sedan, and I climbed in.

Owen slammed the door and got into the driver's seat.

"Don't you want to come back here?" I asked warily.

The plan was to get him out of the building so his friends wouldn't be able to corner us in a bathroom if they came looking. Usually men didn't go searching for one another, but since these guys worked together, it might be a habit, and we couldn't take any chances. Viktor had suggested either inside a car or in an alley near the building, just so long as we could make a quick getaway if caught.

When he started the car and backed out, my throat went dry. I crawled into the front seat and searched the parking lot for Christian as we sped away.

"Where are we going? My car is still back at the bar. Just pull over here; the alley is fine."

Ignoring me, he stepped on the gas even harder, and we sailed around the curve of the road. Buildings soon turned into trees.

Just a slight detour, I told myself.

What I didn't understand was why we were going so far out. Viktor had given both Christian and me a stern warning about causing a scene and tipping off his men. No bloodshed. Well, given my current situation, at least his friends were out of the picture.

Without Christian to charm him, I was going to have to work out another plan to get information. I was used to thinking on the fly, so I kept my cool. "I saw the guys you were with. I don't think you get half the respect you deserve."

There are two things that all men liked stroked: their cocks and their egos.

He veered off the road, and my heart finally slowed down.

Owen shut off the engine and turned to face me, his eyes dancing with mischief. "Ready to play?"

"If you have to drive all the way out here to have a little fun, maybe you need to find a new boss."

"That wasn't my boss," he ground out. "Hike up your skirt and show me what you've got."

"I'm not a prostitute."

"Do you think I'm a moron?" He gripped a fistful of my hair. "You're not the first person who's tried getting information out of me. My boss told us to keep an eye out for a rogue who has her nose in his business. I'm supposed to bring in any suspects."

"So why didn't you call your friends when you had me in the bathroom?"

"Maybe I'm sick of someone else getting all the credit. I've got plenty of time to take you in, *after* I get some information and have a little fun of my own."

"I didn't know you were into the rough stuff, but that's okay."

I traced my finger up my leg. "You want me to pull up my dress? You got it, daddy. I'll show you everything."

The automatic locks clicked on all four doors.

He knocked my hand out of the way and reached between my legs, searching for a weapon. I slapped his face repeatedly to get his hand away from my dagger.

Owen gripped my wrist, trying to subdue me. "Who do you work for?" he shouted.

I bit his arm and twisted out of his grasp. With my right hand free, I palmed the dagger and went for his throat, but he knocked the blade out of my hand before I made contact.

When I reached down to get it, he pulled a dagger from inside his jacket and plunged it into my thigh.

My scream filled the car like a nightmare.

Immortal or not, daggers hurt.

"What a shame to ruin those pretty legs," he said, his voice jovial. "Now tell me who the fuck you work for!"

"Take me to Darius and I'll deliver the message myself." My fangs punched out as I thrashed my head.

Owen panicked when he realized he was in the car with a Vampire. He went for something beneath the seat, and I knew he must have impalement wood.

I quickly pulled the knife out of my thigh and drove it into his leg. "How do you like *that*!"

He screamed louder than I had. Before he could react, I gripped his hand in mine and juiced all the Mage light I could.

"What the fuck?" he shrieked in bewilderment.

"Owen, you're not the brightest crayon in the box." I twisted the knife with my free hand, and he let out a guttural scream. "Why doesn't Darius issue you stunners? Just a plain old dagger?"

He tried to fight me with his free hand, but I'd drained his light to the point where all he could do was drape himself over the steering wheel.

"It's my turn to ask questions. Where does your boss hide? Better tell me, because you're not going to like some of my other talents." I pulled more of his energy out, already feeling nauseated from his dark light churning through my body like poison. "We're going to keep holding hands until you decide how loyal you want to be to that monster you work for. I can hold on for a long time, and you don't want to know how much I can take from you."

Owen struck me across the face in a surprise attack. "Can you take *that*?" He wasn't as weak as he'd led me to believe. "That's okay, bitch. I like it rough. Remember?"

When Christian's motorcycle sputtered around the corner, I was reclined against an oak tree, replaying the events in my head to figure out where it all went wrong.

Had Owen's friends discovered us in the parking lot, the situation could have escalated out of control. Three against one, and I couldn't be sure if Christian would have intervened. Maybe I should have packed my stunner instead of the regular dagger.

The headlamp on Christian's bike illuminated the fog, making it appear as if there was smoke rising from the earth. We were on a quiet stretch of road, surrounded by aging trees, moss, and croaking frogs.

His bike slid sideways, and the engine shut off. A cloud of fog and dirt eddied around the bike as Christian left it lying there and stalked toward me. All I could make out was a dark silhouette of a man, the tail of his coat floating behind him.

When he knelt down, I weakly swung my arm and slapped him. "You set me up."

"Pardon?"

"You were supposed to be there and you weren't."

"For your information, this wasn't an elaborate plan to sabotage you. If I wanted you gone, I'd drain you and bury you in the east cemetery. Now what happened?"

I lifted my eyelid and removed the contact lens from my blue eye. "This," I said, balancing it on the tip of my finger. "It jinxed me."

He scanned my body, which was covered with blood. "Is the dry shite dead?"

"I popped his cork."

He furrowed his brow, not understanding. "How many drinks did you have this evening? You really know how to pick 'em. I would have gone for the little guy."

I flicked the lens at him. "Then maybe *you* should have worn the dress."

He winked. "Afraid it's too short to accentuate all my curves."

I closed my eyes, a gentle breeze cooling my face. The air smelled of wet earth, pine, and my beer-stained dress. I'd never been in a predicament like this where I was so gravely wounded. Owen had put up a heck of a struggle, and I'd lost a lot of blood in the process. I had my legs stretched out in front of me—the holster still strapped to my right thigh but missing the dagger. My left leg was a mess since a lot of the blood had gushed down to my foot when I stumbled out of the car. I wasn't sure where my heels had gone.

Christian marched over to the vehicle, yanked out the dead body, and flung him into the open. It was almost comical to watch.

"Jaysus wept. It looks like you played pin the fang on the jugular in there."

"I ran into a snag."

Christian straddled the Mage, staring down at him. He could give a shadow a run for its money.

"A dagger in the heart was a nice touch," he offered.

I glanced at the handle poking out from the Mage's chest. "That one's his, so just leave it there."

"Exactly how did you manage to kill a Mage without cutting off his head? I thought you were draining your victims and juicing them to the point of death, but his wounds are still oozing."

"It's a family secret," I murmured, knowing he could still hear me.

After another moment, he stood up and kicked the body. "Viktor's going to have a conniption."

"Let him."

Christian turned a sharp eye toward me. "If we're not able to cover this up, we'll lose more than just a shot at Darius. It could be the downfall of Keystone."

"If I had to do it over again, I would have killed him in the bar and put him in your lap."

His jaw set.

"Don't look at me like that," I said, my voice weakening. "I had no choice. My guard was nowhere in sight."

"I thought you didn't need a guard?" Christian walked over and crouched before me. "You're an audacious creature."

Although his hair was a dark brown, his eyebrows were much darker and sloped down a little in the center. I'd never really stared at a man's eyebrows before, but I couldn't help but wonder why I found it so attractive that some of the hairs in the center weren't cooperating. It made him seem less like a Vampire and more like the Big Bad Wolf.

Something dark flickered in his eyes when he noticed my bleeding wound.

Probably hunger.

"Looks like he stabbed you in the leg. Where else?"

"My back. Did you go off with that woman? What kind of bodyguard are you?"

"Are you daft? The plan was to lure him into the parking lot, not take a sightseeing tour of the city. When I heard you two in the bathroom, I kept my distance so his men wouldn't get suspicious. They were eyeing the hall, and I suspect they're probably searching for him as we speak."

Christian looked over his shoulder and scraped his teeth against his bottom lip. "There's too much evidence. I'm either going to have to call in for help or put gasoline on the car and torch it, and I'm fresh out of matches. I knew I shouldn't have brought the damn bike," he muttered. "I'm going to have to rope you to my back."

A wave of terror swept through me when I thought about riding on the back of his motorcycle. It wouldn't be the first time

I'd ridden a bike, but I was too weak to hold on and didn't have any desire to end up as roadkill.

His fangs punched out and he used them to slice a hole in his shirt. After he tore off most of the bottom, he used the material as a tourniquet on my leg.

"So much for your lucky dress," he said.

I flicked another glance at his bike. "Don't even think about putting me on that piece of junk."

"Junk?" he exclaimed. "This old Ducati is more reliable than anyone I've ever met. Maybe she's not as flashy as your Harley-Davidsons, but I'll have you know she's gotten me out of many a jam."

Personally I was a Harley girl. Christian's Ducati Scrambler reminded me of a Bonneville Triumph, only less flashy.

The rain suddenly unleashed, as if punishing me for what I'd done. I began to laugh at the insanity of my life. What kind of monster had I become? All I'd ever wanted as a child was a normal life, and here I was, sitting in the pouring rain, bleeding profusely from stab wounds, and having an argument with a Vampire about his mode of transportation.

"You've gone mad," he said with a shake of his head.

"We're all mad here."

Christian launched to his feet and stalked toward the Mage. In a swift movement, he pulled out the knife and then punched him in the face.

The laughter died in my throat, and I stared up into a canopy of darkness. "This wasn't in the brochure."

Chapter 10

After Christian admonished me about the mess I'd made in the Mage's car, he tossed the body into the trunk and then hefted his motorcycle before busting it through the back windshield.

I passed out, and when I awoke, I was in the passenger seat of the Mage's car with a black coat tucked around me.

I smirked when I noticed the Vampire behind the wheel.

"Something funny?" Christian asked.

"You're naked."

"Not entirely, but the night is still young."

He'd removed the rest of his shirt and only had on a pair of black trousers. The next thing I knew, I was staring at the back of my eyelids again.

"Don't ask inane questions. Just get Niko," he said in clipped words.

Bewildered, I opened my eyes and realized how much time had passed. We were no longer in the car—Christian was carrying me through a hall in the mansion. A bone-deep chill made it difficult to move, and every muscle tightened as I shivered uncontrollably. My neck hurt, my back hurt, and my legs were numb. All I wanted was a warm pair of socks on my feet.

The lanterns were making me dizzy, so I rested my cheek against Christian's bare chest. Who would have thought that a Vampire could feel so warm to the touch? Christian's body felt like a blanket that had just come out of the dryer, and all I wanted to do was wrap him around me.

"I see someone's awake," he murmured against my hair.

"How did you know?"

"Your lashes are tickling my chest."

Wyatt peered down at me as we passed by him. "You really screwed this one up. Where's the Mage?"

Christian snapped his head around, his tone sharp. "In the trunk of the car. Why don't you go outside and say hello?"

"Shepherd! I need you down here. Hurry up before the freshy gets in!" Wyatt's voice grew distant.

"Set her down here," Viktor said.

The next thing I knew, I was on a metal table with sterile instruments all around. I shivered uncontrollably when the cold surface touched my back.

Viktor pulled Christian's coat away from my body. "This is unacceptable."

Christian leaned against the table on my right, blood smeared across his chest. "I called in our cleaner to take care of the scene. There was blood and emotional imprints left behind, but nothing he can't clean up."

"And the body you decided to bring home with you as a souvenir? How did this happen? I thought we had an understanding."

"Apparently the shitebag who put a dagger in her back and leg didn't get the memo. He drove her over the county line and into the woods. Maybe we've underestimated how many times this has happened to them before. She put up a hell of a fight. I'm guessing he was the sort of man who got his jollies by roughing the girls up."

Viktor pointed his finger in Christian's face. "Why did you let her get into the car? All this for nothing. If Darius's men saw Raven with the victim, they'll be able to ID her."

"I had on my brown contact," I mumbled.

Christian's lips twitched.

"Let me paint you a picture," Viktor began. "Darius discovers who we are, and instead of taking matters into his own hands, he reports us to the higher authority. They will strip away everything we have worked for because they will have no choice, even if they have backed our previous cases. Only a chosen few are delegated to use funds for such things; they don't *all* know what we are doing for them."

"They can't ignore what you've done for them already," Christian retorted. "And I don't think we have to worry about this dolt going to the higher authority if he's busy going after humans."

"You cannot take such risks. We're not bound by the laws, but I do not operate a casino," Viktor argued, his voice reverberating off the walls. "You're gambling with the life of this organization when you break my rules."

"I know where he lives!" I cried and then rattled off the address.

The bickering ceased.

I swallowed, my throat parched. "Do you think I went through all that and didn't get what you needed? Darius knows about me, and he warned his men to be on the lookout. He thinks I'm working for someone, and Owen tried to get me to talk."

"You summoned me?" Niko called out from across the room. He paused at the foot of the table. "Who is that?"

Viktor turned away. "Raven is injured, and we cannot stop the bleeding. Normally there is some clotting. Can she last until dawn?"

"Move aside," Niko said, entering my line of vision. He hovered over the left side of the table, looking at me but not really looking at me. "Three stab wounds."

"Two," Christian corrected.

"Did you miss the one behind her neck or on her back?"

"What time is it?" Viktor asked.

Niko shook his head. "It won't matter. She doesn't know how to use sunlight to heal; it's not something we've tested yet. Aside from that, it's raining."

"She's Vampire and Mage," Christian stressed. "I don't think she's on the brink of making a trip to the pearly gates just yet."

Niko's expression tightened. "And if that were Blue lying there and she wasn't able to shift to heal, would you just walk away? I can't say if she'll die—we have not yet learned enough about her. It's inhumane to allow someone to suffer a slow healing that could take days or even weeks."

"Don't turn this around and make me look like the bad guy. I'm just making an observation."

Niko turned his head in my direction. "Raven, do you heal naturally fast?"

"I've never been this banged up. I heal as fast as a Mage without healing light. Maybe you should just stitch me up."

"Nyet, nyet," Viktor grumbled. "You will be no good to us lying in a sickbed. Do not give her too much light, Niko. I may need to question her further, and I don't want her knocked out for days."

"I'm not going to use Mage healing light."

My brows popped up. "Exactly what are you going to use?" Fears of metal instruments without anesthesia popped in my head.

His hair tickled my neck when he leaned over me. "I'm a Healer. That's my Mage gift. Have you ever heard of one?"

I shook my head, focusing on his eyes, which glimmered like pale blue crystals. I'd never seen eyes like his.

"It means I can heal any Breed except for humans. I don't transfer energy through our hands like we normally do. It's a more concentrated energy exchange, and I go straight to the wound."

Anxious, I peered down as he held his hands over my body until he stopped where my leg was sliced open.

Viktor shook his head, giving me an incensed look. "I'll leave you alone. I have a bloody car and a dead Mage to dispose of."

If that didn't make me feel guilty, nothing would.

Christian rested his forearms on the table to my right, his face close to mine. "He's not as vexed as all that."

"I didn't follow orders."

Christian touched my cheek with his finger. "Sometimes you have to break rules. He knows that better than anyone. What do you think Keystone is founded on?"

I turned my head away from his touch. "Better stop that. People might think you like me."

When Niko placed his hands on my leg, my body jerked and I reflexively scooted back.

"Keep her still," Niko said. "Raven, I promise this won't hurt.

Christian, you didn't tell me there was a bandage on the wound. It's better if you remove it."

Christian moved away, and when I felt a pressure release on my thigh, Niko whispered something in another language.

"Is it bleeding?" I asked.

Christian reappeared with a dark smirk. "Have you ever visited Yellowstone? There's this grand geyser—"

"In other words, I look like a drinking fountain for Vampires."

"If you want to know the truth, I don't think it was the contact lens that cursed you. I'm willing to wager my immortal soul it was the third hot dog."

A quick burst of light filled the room, and my leg flooded with heat.

"What are you doing?" I exclaimed.

Niko raised both hands. "Turn her over and I'll do the others."

"Niko?" I leaned up and gripped his wrist. "Before you finish, can you do me a favor? Take some of his light out of me."

He shook his head. "It's better if I don't."

"You don't know what it's like. I need to get it out of me. Just take a little."

Christian flicked a hard gaze up at Niko. "What's she asking you to do?"

"She can pull core light all the way out of a Mage. It's a rare gift indeed. Any Mage can drain the light of another Mage, but core light is what replenishes our strength. It's the very essence of immortality. Raven has the ability to make them human again."

"Jaysus."

Niko withdrew his arm and stepped back. "It remains in her for a day or two, and she wants me to take some of it out."

Christian stood up. "And?"

"It makes no sense to do it. Whatever I take will weaken her, and no matter what, it won't be enough to remove it all. Viktor expressed his concern about sharing—"

"Then don't. Finish up your magic show. I have to pull my bike out of the back windshield of that fecking car before Viktor drives it to the junkyard."

I gripped Christian's pinky finger, pulling it toward me. "I'm not asking for a lobotomy. Maybe it doesn't make sense, but neither of you are the ones walking around with this poisonous light. *Please*."

Christian stepped back and folded his arms.

I turned to Niko, my eyes pleading in vain to a blind man who couldn't see my pained expression. "Can't you see his dark light? I'm sick with it. I shouldn't have taken it all; I made a mistake. His light is so spoiled that it's crawling through my flesh like a nightmare. Normally I'm strong enough to tolerate it, but my own light is weak and he's all that I feel. You won't have to do this again, I swear." I covered my face, tears battling against my lashes.

"Yes, Raven. I see him. Let me heal you first and then I'll draw some of it out."

Moments after Niko had removed as much energy as my body would allow, I blacked out. He couldn't specifically select one light over the other since they were mixed together, but at least it was just a little bit less than it was before.

I awoke in a dark room, my surroundings unfamiliar. The simple décor and arrangement told me this wasn't my bedroom. The bed was in the same place with the door to my left, but the bathroom was on the opposite wall. I could make out the dark entrance to the left. A few flickering candles in the fireplace to my right drew my attention. I sat up, my fingers smoothing over a fur blanket, and noticed there weren't any windows.

Light spilled beneath the door to my left, and I spotted a shadow leaning against the wall.

"Who's there?"

"A Vampire," he whispered back.

When I recognized Christian's voice, I swung my feet onto the floor and waited for my Vampire eyes to adjust to the dim light. As he came into view, I noticed blood smeared across his chest.

My blood.

Not much time had passed.

"Whose room is this?"

"Mine," he replied in a velvety voice.

I reached behind my neck, searching for a wound that wasn't there. "And why am I not in my room?"

He folded his arms. "I gave it some consideration, but when you made the rule forbidding us to enter without your permission, that left me with few options."

"Why am I not surprised?" I touched my bare leg and felt no pain. My smooth skin didn't even have a hint of a scar. Niko had a miraculous gift.

Christian pushed off the wall and swaggered toward me. "Don't flatter yourself. I only took you in because the others didn't want you."

I stood up. "You're the biggest fanghole I've ever met."

He caught me when I made a misstep, then set me back on the bed. "If you want to go to the toilet, I'll drag you along. But Viktor wants you healed and back to your perky self by morning. That means bed rest."

"I'm not an invalid."

His gaze hardened. "Can you see as well as I can in the dark?"

"I don't know. How well can you see?"

"I can count all your freckles."

I laughed. "I don't have any freckles."

"Next time you're in Bed, Bath, & Beyond, locate one of those magnification mirrors and a black light."

"Okay, okay. I don't see *that* well. But I did inherit some of that gift." I shook my head. "Now I know why you guys are mostly loners."

"Oh?" He ambled over and sat in a chair near the bed, dramatically crossing his legs. "Enlighten me."

"Vampires are about as cuddly as barbed wire. It's no wonder that women haven't been lining up to become one of you."

He reached over to the table near his bed and lifted the lid of a crystal candy dish. The sweets inside looked like toffee or caramel, and he popped one into his mouth. "What you know about Vampires could fill a thimble."

I glanced at the dark entrance to the bathroom and slowly got up. "I need to wash off the blood. It's probably all over your sheets."

"Doesn't bother me, lass. Gem will just think it's my time of the month."

When I entered the bathroom, Christian followed behind with a candle. The room looked identical to mine except there wasn't a window by the shower. He also had a claw-foot tub, but I couldn't imagine a Vampire, one who wore menace like a cloak, soaking in bubbles.

Hell, he barely shaved.

"Does Gem do your laundry? Way to go on embracing women's liberation."

He handed me a towel and sat on the floor, arms draped over his bent knees. "We rotate the chores."

"Remind me when it's your week so I can wash my own panties."

After running the towel under hot water, I took a seat on the floor next to the sink, crossed my ankles, and began wiping the dried blood off my leg and hands. It left stains on his white towel, but he watched with mild interest, not raising a complaint. My blood-soaked hair would have to wait until morning.

I looked up at Christian. "So impart some of your wisdom to me about Vampires."

"Ah, yes. Your better half."

"Why is it a man's world?"

He laced his fingers together. "There aren't as many female Vampires for the simple reason that centuries ago, men built armies of men, not women."

"Nothing sexist about that."

"They were different times. Vampires were demonized and hunted, and some found security in making younglings who would protect them—strong, loyal men. Women didn't go to battle. They were the caregivers of the family, groomed to be mothers and wives, not warriors. Do you think they wanted to go to war? I knew grown men who didn't want to fight. A woman born in this century will never understand what life was like in a time when speaking out could get you killed."

"So why not make more female Vampires now that you're not busy making little fang warriors?"

He shrugged. "Nowadays not many want to embark on the task of a maker. We're governed by laws and no longer at war with humans. Most of us are old and set in our ways. Younglings are a handful, to be sure. It takes a long while for them to control the bloodlust. Aside from that, they're more dependent on their makers than a Learner is with their Creator. The blood connects us."

"So you didn't want to be connected to a woman?"

He sputtered out a laugh and then wiped his eye with the heel of his hand. "Vampires relied on each other for protection and information. Not for a cuddle."

"And a woman can't protect you?"

"Will you put a cork in it and let me finish? If you're going to pluck a rose from the garden, you're going to choose the finest-looking flower. Not many women in those days wanted to leave behind their families to become creatures of the night."

"You're not exactly Bela Lugosi."

"We didn't have sunglasses, and black eyes get noticed fairly quickly in the daylight. That's how we got the reputation for being night creatures."

"Ah. That makes more sense." I continued cleaning off my arms and neck.

"And it didn't take long for Vampires to figure out that bringing a woman over by force wasn't going to make her a loyal subject, blood or not. When time wore away the feeling of submission, they'd hunt their maker down. Finding a wickedly handsome woman who was willing to give up her mortality wasn't as easy as all that. Men are easier to convince. They thirst for power, war, and revenge."

"Is that why you decided to take the plunge?"

He pulled at the whiskers on his chin. "After the Mageri was formed, some of the older Vampires got together to put rules in place. It was a big fecking mess back then. There were too many who were making bloodslaves, so the elders put a stop to it and set them to burn."

"Do I have blood on my face?"

He pointed at his lip. "Just a little there. And there," he added, pointing at his eyebrow, ear, cheek, and neck.

I stared at him blank-faced.

"Here, let me." He scooted forward and took the towel, using it to wipe my temple. "And what about your maker? Clearly he's a bastard if you can't stand the sight of me."

I smirked, and he wiped my humor away with the towel. "You think highly of yourself."

He leaned in. "Did you get any blood on your breasts? I'm willing to go the extra mile."

When I snatched the towel from his hand, he scooted back and leaned against the wall again. Christian was treading dangerous ground by asking about my maker. That wasn't a topic I wanted to discuss with anyone, let alone a smarmy Vampire who was champing at the bit to make an offensive wisecrack.

Christian's voice was deep and growly, like someone who had just woken up. "If you're more than just sex on legs, then why is that *all* you offer to get a job done?"

"Because as handsome as you are, Christian, your hairy legs would have never gotten that man out of his chair."

He raised his pant leg just an inch or two. "They're not that hairy. See?"

"How am I supposed to trust you have my back when you're busy dry-humping women in a dark corner somewhere? You should have been close enough that when he started the engine, it would have only taken you seconds to come out. What if he'd pulled out his gun and shot me in the head?"

He picked at a dried piece of blood on his chest. "Are you trying to blame this on me? Don't bother preparing a speech for tomorrow with Viktor; I'm not taking the fall for this one."

"I should have killed him as soon as I got into the car."

Christian shook his head very slightly. "You're digging your own grave and don't even give a shite. Say that tomorrow and see what happens."

"You still should have been there."

He pointed his finger lazily at me. "You were armed, and you knew he might have a stunner on him."

"Stunners don't affect me. But a bullet might."

He cocked his head to the side. "Say again?"

"When I've been stabbed, I can usually tell a stunner from a regular dagger. It just feels different. Plus a lot of the men acted really surprised when they put it in me and I was still moving around. It didn't take long for me to figure it out."

"Are you telling me that you don't succumb to the paralyzed state that a dagger infused with magic brings to a Mage?"

"Pretty much."

I decided not to tell him about impalement wood not affecting me either. I didn't know how much people in the house talked to each other, but if I was on my way out the door because of tonight's stunt, then maybe I needed to keep a few things to myself.

He ran his fingers through his hair forward and then back, which I found to be a peculiar gesture.

"Dazzled?" I asked.

"Perplexed… would be a better word."

I leaned forward, giving him a good look at my mismatched eyes. "Don't you know who I am? I'm the Shadow. Legend has it that if a man loses his shadow, it means that I ate it, and I'm coming for the rest of him."

When his eyes flicked down at the floor, I laughed.

"Made you look."

His jaw set, and he straightened his legs. "You're a peculiar woman. Next time go for the handsome man of the group, you hear? How often do you think that sweaty little troll got singled out by a beautiful woman? From the moment you batted your lashes at him, his fantasies were peppered with doubt and suspicion, so when you asked him to go to the car, it's no wonder he pulled a

Ted Bundy. Instinct always tells you to pick the weaker one, so you need to go for the leader... or the most handsome."

"None of them were handsome, and I don't think I could have drawn him away from that table."

One eyebrow arched. "Good-looking men will always do foolish things for a woman."

I grabbed the sink and pulled myself up.

Christian gathered me up in his arms, and everything spun for a moment. "Take me, for instance."

He swiftly moved through the doorway and flung me onto the clean side of the mattress. After stripping the sheets out from beneath me, he tossed them in a pile in the corner.

"I didn't tell him about Keystone," I said. "But I can't prove it since he's dead. Do you think Viktor will believe me?"

He gripped the ends of a pillowcase and gave it a hard yank, forcing the pillow out. "Why are you really here?"

"I'm not here for the pool, I can tell you that much. It seemed like a way to make a few bucks so I could tuck it away for a rainy day, but once again, destiny screwed me over."

"Ah. So it's about the dollar signs."

"How easy do you think it is for me to get a steady job? Think about it. I can't get a job in the human world since I'm legally dead, and none of the Breed places will hire me since I have a sketchy background and no alias that's been registered with the higher authority. I'm an illegal creation, and I can't risk someone turning me over to the Mageri. I've worked a few odd jobs, but someone like you wouldn't understand what it's like to have everyone turn you away."

Christian circled around the bed and lifted the mattress, causing me to roll over to the opposite end.

"This is *my* side," he said.

"You're not going to sleep with me."

He bounced onto the mattress and locked his fingers behind his head. "No, I'm going to sleep next to you."

"Vampires don't sleep."

When Christian spoke, it sounded like he was musing aloud.

"If Viktor brings you into this group, I'll have no choice about it. We'll be partners, and he doesn't change his mind about such things."

I crossed my feet at the ankles. "He might if one of us turns up dead."

"Maybe I'm just a tangle of barbed wire to you, but you're a jellyfish."

"Are you saying I'm out of shape?"

He peered over at me. "Beautiful and deadly. Can't get too close or she'll latch on and sting you to death."

"Keep that in mind if you're going to lie next to me," I said playfully.

I turned on my side to face him. Shadows leaped across the walls like dancers in a ballet. Christian's room had a different smell than mine. Musky and familiar—a space that had been lived in for a while.

"Have you ever tasted a Vampire other than your maker?" he asked.

I stared daggers at him. "I'm warning you."

Christian rolled onto his side. "I'm serious."

"No. And that's not an invitation to ask me."

"I'm only thinking that if you've never tasted Vampire blood, then you don't know how it affects you."

"And I suppose you want to be the sacrificial lamb?"

"Feck, no. I don't give my blood freely to just anyone. But you won't know the extent of your strengths and weaknesses unless you test everything."

"I don't have any desire to be turned into a marionette. I've heard rumors about the influence it can have."

"Vampire blood is powerful, to be sure. But it's not what you think, and everyone's affected differently by it. It's a sacred act that's revered because of the power and pleasure within the blood. The blood is dark and sweet, like nothing you've ever tasted. When your maker feeds you his blood, you're not yet a full Vampire, so you can't appreciate the complexities."

"It's not fine wine. I'm sure it tastes like everyone else's."

He snorted and placed his head in his hand. "It's not nearly the same, lass. Not by a mile. Maybe Viktor can get a sample of blood off the black market," he said absently.

"Don't bother adding that one to the grocery list."

His dark brows drew together. "You really don't have any cravings for blood, even after drinking so much of it?"

"No, and I've tasted more than I care to. It doesn't heal me, it doesn't excite me, and it sure as hell doesn't taste like a margarita."

"Does it taste like a Bloody Mary?"

I brushed a strand of hair away from my face, stealing a glimpse of his bottomless eyes. They reminded me of a line in a poem that went: *And his eyes have all the seeming of a demon's that is dreaming.*

I shivered and looked away. "Blood does nothing for me."

"It's a shame you can't enjoy the full-bodied taste, but I can't complain, because your lack of taste will come in handy. Blood is what makes even the best Vampires weak with want, so at least you have that going for you. Can you glean information from it?"

I turned away, showing him my back. "You're nosy."

The bed didn't move, but somehow Christian had eased up behind me, his words nothing but dark whispers in my ear. "Know thyself. You'll never learn who you are by watching others or reading about it in a textbook. You'll never know what you're capable of by avoiding what you fear. Who are you, Raven Black?"

When I rolled over, Christian was gone.

Chapter 11

THE NEXT MORNING, I SLIPPED out of Christian's bedroom and took a quick shower before collecting my things. I had a feeling this might be my last day, so I wanted to leave on my terms. The halls with windows were humid and smelled of rain, so I put on my lace-up boots, which were good for treading water.

Keystone had become a temporary reprieve, and I was going to miss its winding halls, grand staircases, majestic rooms, and sumptuous views. It had offered me protection, where I didn't have to sleep with one eye closed, and the quiet rooms allowed me space to gather my thoughts.

When I reached the lower level, energetic conversation filled the dining room down the hall, but I continued moving toward the front door.

"Where do you think you're going?" Wyatt yanked the green duffel bag out of my hands from behind.

I whirled around. "Wyatt, give me the bag."

He held it high in a game of keep-away, so I snatched the grey beanie off his head.

"That's all right, buttercup. I've got plenty more where that came from. It's time for breakfast, so follow me." Wyatt turned on his heel and headed toward the dining room.

"Give me the bag!" With a flying leap, I hooked my arm around his neck in a death grip.

He choked, running down the hall with me draped over his back. "C-c-c-an't bree-breathe," he stammered, gasping for air.

"Drop the bag and I'll give you oxygen."

We flew into the dining room, making a dramatic entrance. The chatter ceased as everyone at the table stared at us like frozen statues.

Wyatt heaved the bag across the room and shook me off his back. He gasped, coughing several times before regaining his composure. A lick of embarrassment rattled me when he gave me a cold stare.

He snagged his hat out of my hands and gave it a light shake before sliding it back onto his head, covering most—but not all—of his light-brown hair. "A gentleman can't even carry a lady's bag."

When I moved to retrieve it, he got ahead of me and kicked it next to Viktor's chair, right before taking his seat with an impish grin on his face.

It felt like the walk of shame, and it infuriated me to think they had the audacity to sit there smiling in a show of mockery. Then again, I wasn't sure why I expected compassion from a group of bandits. Sneaking out had nothing to do with saving face—I was hoping to avoid getting my memory scrubbed.

Claude rose to his feet, his nose twitching. "What's wrong, female?"

"I just want my bag."

Gem stood up as if trying to get a better look. "Where are you going?"

Claude wrapped his arm around my shoulders and led me to the table. "To her chair, that's where she's going."

As we neared the vacant chair, I dug my heels in. "Hold on, wait. Just stop."

Viktor laced his fingers together in a prayerlike gesture, watching us in rapt silence.

Gem plopped back in her seat and scooped out a spoonful of jelly from a jar, carefully spreading it on a strip of bacon.

The chair to Viktor's left was vacant.

"Where's Christian? You didn't fire him, did you? If so, you made a mistake. He didn't have anything to do with what happened last night."

Viktor flipped a linen napkin across his lap, his voice edged with disappointment. "I like to see that kind of camaraderie. It gives me hope."

"I didn't say that I liked him, only that I take full blame for everything that happened last night. The way I see it, Darius is now a man short, and that's one less evil Mage in this world we have to worry about. So keep that in mind while you escort me to the door."

"Last night I gave you specific instructions. One of which was not to behave impulsively and commit murder. But life does not always go as planned, and we obtained the information we needed. That said, I have spent all evening making arrangements to cover up your mistakes, especially the two men you left behind at the bar."

"What did you do?"

"The bartender is a loyal supporter of Keystone, and he fabricated a story and told the men that their partner was apprehended by Regulators of the Security Force for attempting to purchase a child on the black market. In order to explain the car's disappearance, he had to tell them the Regulators confiscated it as evidence."

"And they believed it? But Darius—"

Viktor rubbed his eye. "Darius will not find out. These men will turn their backs on their friend. To inquire about him or ask questions will put a target on their back as someone who supports child molesters. Everyone knows that the higher authority does not make arrests without sufficient proof, and no one wants to be associated with a pedophile. The last thing these men will want is a Regulator knocking on their door. Should they tell Darius, he will wash his hands of it. A man who breaks the law does not get involved with the law, even where his men are concerned. It calls attention to him."

"You don't think he'll suspect anything?"

"I can promise he is not going to check on a lowly guard arrested for slave trading. This buys us some time."

Claude gripped my shoulders and forced me into my seat.

I stared blank-faced at a plate of sausages, hash browns, and strawberries.

"You eat today," he said.

Viktor sliced a banana into several pieces. "I am not going to sit here and praise your actions. Loyalty is essential, and you have failed to impress me, even if the result was a good one. I can't award you credit for chance. I am placing you on probation."

I shook my head. "What does that mean?"

He ate a slice of banana from the blade of the knife. "It means you will not go on any assignments in the near future. We need to measure your skills and make sure you are able to acclimate to the team. This is not a club. Every person I bring in, I watch before they're ready to move to the next level. You can still help with planning and theories, but jeopardize this case or any of my men's lives, and you're out."

My heart sank. At least I still had another shot, but why couldn't he be proud of what I'd done, even if it wasn't by the book?

"Understood," I said, dodging the stares from everyone at the table.

Viktor brought his knife up to his mouth and ate another slice. "Before we make a move, I need to confirm something."

"I'm working on it," Wyatt said, shoveling eggs into his mouth.

Niko lowered his voice. "How do you feel?"

"Better, thanks," I whispered back.

His eyes skated around me, as if looking at something. "Your light isn't back to normal."

How could he see energy that didn't belong to me? Unless it was an educated guess. I was usually in a cantankerous mood after pulling core light from a criminal.

Blue offered me a basket of bread, and I waved it away. Watching everyone eat was making me nauseous. I still hadn't gained their respect and didn't yet belong. Being reprimanded in front of them also didn't help my mood.

"I need to take a walk."

Claude reached across the table and gripped my wrist. "Why won't you eat?"

"You're making the Chitah nervous," Gem said, leaning her head on his bicep. "He's a softy when it comes to looking after us girls."

I pulled gently out of his grasp. "I can't eat—not after last night. I'll just get sick. Sometimes it takes a couple of days before I can keep anything down. Go on without me; I'm not feeling good."

When I got up to leave, my steps quickened as the distance between us grew. A feeling of suffocation overwhelmed me, making it hard to breathe. The dark light, the newness of my situation, the uncertainty of my future—I needed fresh air. I emerged through the back door, drifting into a blanket of fog that rolled across the estate and into the surrounding woods. It had an ethereal glow, making it seem as if I were lost in a dream. Morning light filtered through a veil of dark clouds, but there was no thunder or smell of rain. The blades of grass below my feet glittered with tiny prisms of dew, and I left tracks of flattened grass behind me as I moved toward a grove of trees.

I wiped some of the moisture off an iron bench before taking a seat. The Keystone estate was another world. No trains, cars, airplanes, voices, or even dogs barking. The only sounds were drops of water dripping off the leaves and into puddles, a woodpecker tapping against a tree in the distance, and the occasional rustling of leaves.

In a burst of movement, Gem flashed by me and jumped onto the rope swing. She stood on the wooden plank and used her arms to swing back and forth. "Mind if I hang out with you?"

"Once my heart starts beating again, sure."

The rush of air from her movement stirred up some of the leaves below. "You can't flash? I thought you were half Mage."

I glanced up at the creaking branch as she swung back and forth. Gem had on a knit duster that was so thin the wind lifted it like a floating shadow. Her black shorts made her legs seem long, and I realized Gem had a style all her own. Tousled violet hair touched her shoulders in pretty waves, making her seem like a fairy who lived in the forest.

"I can't do everything you can do."

She leaned back, gripping the ropes and looking up at the tree as sprinkles of water shook from the leaves. "I think that's why Viktor chooses us."

"What do you mean?"

"Well... I think we all have something in common. We're different from everyone else in some way. And we also had nowhere left to go—nothing left to live for. Am I right?"

She was definitely right about me, but I wasn't so sure that applied to everyone else. "Most of those guys don't look like they're at the end of their rope. Claude runs a salon, right? And Blue seems to have her stuff together."

Gem hopped off the swing and approached me with an exaggerated step due to her heavy shoes. She eyed the wet bench and then squatted down on the concrete area before my feet, her arms wrapped around her knees. "Everyone who comes into the house has the same melancholy look in their eyes. But you don't have to worry; that goes away after a little while. Not all the way, but Viktor fills in a lot of those empty spaces by giving meaning to our lives."

Gem's skin glowed with the humidity, so pale and lovely that it made me envious.

"Did your Creator name you?"

A smile brightened her angelic face. "She sure did. I could have kept my first name, but Gem was her idea because of my love for gemstones. See?" She held the quartz crystal necklace between two fingers. It was a beautiful raw cut with several sides and a point on the end.

I didn't know everything about the Breed world, but Learners took on the surnames of their Creator in order to create a lineage. It was also a practice put in place to help humans sever their ties with the human world—probably more psychological than anything. I knew that some Creators didn't have last names because they were ancients, but I wasn't sure how they handled naming their progeny. It was frustrating to have so many questions about my own kind and no one to give me those answers without making me feel ignorant.

"I've always been fascinated by gemstones," she continued. "I wish my last name was Stone. How spectacular would that be? But alas…"

"Did you like your Creator?"

She looked wistfully at something in the distance. "I loved her like a mother." After a moment, Gem tilted her head, holding me in her rapt attention as if she were an otherworldly bird just seconds from flying away. "Are you strong like a Vampire?"

"No."

"What's it like to be half Vampire? What's it feel like?"

My answer came out as a trembling whisper. "Terrifying."

"That's okay. You don't have to talk about it. Is Raven your real name or what your Creator gave to you?"

"It's my given name."

She rocked on her heels. "I bet your mother loved you a lot to give you such a special name."

My eyes dragged downward, and Gem gripped my hand.

"Look, I'm sorry if I brought up a touchy subject. I'm just so curious about you and don't know how to start a conversation that might not be a land mine of trauma."

I threw my head back and laughed. "That's one way to put it. What's the deal with Christian?"

She stepped on the bench to my right. "Tell me you're not—"

"No. God, no."

Gem blew out a breath and crouched next to me. "Good. He's trouble, and if this job means anything to you, then you won't hook up with anyone in the house. It won't take long for any temptations to vanish, especially when you learn about their appalling habits. Wyatt never cleans up after himself, and Claude snores. I had to move to a different hall so I could sleep at night."

"And Niko? He seems pretty perfect."

She wagged a finger at me. "Just remember what I told you. Your curiosity will pass, but if you start up anything, it's going to make working together a nightmare. Imagine a nasty breakup where they start seeing other people and telling you all the ways that you don't compare. You'll have to see each other in the halls, eat at the same table, and go on assignments together. Someone's going to wind up dead."

Gem and I were going to get along just fine.

"You don't get tempted by Claude? He's a looker as far as Chitahs go."

She snorted. "Why would you think that?"

"He's your partner. I'm guessing you spend a lot of quality time with him."

"When we first started working together, I got hurt on the job. Nothing serious, but I guess I took it hard because I didn't want to look weak in front of the group. Someone as tough as you probably can't relate, but I fell asleep in a puddle of tears. When I woke up in the middle of the night, Claude was stretched out across my legs, warming them the way his kind does when they're trying to be compassionate. Trust me, if anything was going to happen between us, it would have happened that night."

"Is he gay?"

"No, he's definitely not gay. But he does great hair. Women just love him. You know how Chitahs worship their females? Well, just imagine all the clients he has lined up who want a big guy like Claude doting all over them for an hour or two."

"I'm guessing he gets a lot of information. Women talk a lot when they're nervous or want to impress someone."

"Bingo. He overhears a lot of stuff too. Unless he's forced to give his word that he won't share the information, he relays anything of importance to us."

I flicked an ant off my jeans that was attempting to crawl inside a hole. "Does he date his clients?"

"Chitahs like their own kind. I think he wants a girl who will purr for him. Have you ever heard a Chitah purr?"

"Um, no."

She gripped my arm. "It's wonderful, like walking into a house and smelling homemade cookies. He doesn't do it a lot, but every so often he'll be in one of his moods, and I'll just snuggle up next to him the moment he starts up his motor. He also does my hair. I'm sure Claude wouldn't mind if you asked him to cut or dye yours, although I think it's pretty just the way it is. Maybe a few inches to clean up the split ends."

"Thanks, Gem. I don't mean about my hair, but for making me feel better."

"I didn't want you to come out here and sulk alone. It's not easy being the new kid on the block. It's lonely. Blue's more reserved, and our personalities don't blend. We get along okay, but we don't hang out a whole lot. Her experience is a lot different than mine since she's a Shifter. I feel more comfortable talking to you, so I've decided we're going to be best friends."

It almost made me want to look around to see if this was a practical joke. I'd never met anyone so forthright and vibrantly positive. She also seemed a touch nosy, so I decided to make it a point to sit on a different area of the roof at night so she wouldn't be wondering what I was doing up there.

"You have really tall shoes," I said, staring at her chunky boots.

Gem stood up and hopped to the ground, hands on her hips. "A girl my size needs all the boost she can get."

"What's your Mage gift?"

She kicked an acorn, and it tumbled across the concrete and disappeared into the grass. "I'm a Blocker."

"Blocker…"

Her brows rose. "You really don't know much, do you? I don't mean that in a bad way, but most Creators teach their Learners the basics. It's a rare gift, and it just means I can block other gifts, kind of like I have a big ol' force field around me or something. A Mentalist can't read my mind, a Charmer can't seduce me—it's a form of protection."

I wondered if I could pull core light from her. Did she know all her limitations? In any case, that was a useful gift for a Mage to have.

She snapped her fingers a few times, light sparking between her fingertips as she looked around. "We better go inside. I feel a storm coming. I'll race you!"

"Only if you run regular speed."

Gem took off, her duster flapping in the wind behind her. I couldn't help myself; I raced behind her, and although she might have used a little flashing to keep my pace, I still beat her by an inch.

"I don't see what's wrong with the clothes I have," I complained, holding up a black shirt.

Gem replaced it with a red one. "There's nothing wrong with your clothes; you just don't have enough of them. Viktor pays us good money, so treat yourself. Ooh, this one's pretty."

"I don't do pretty."

"Look at the sheen on it. You have to get a few nice things in case he sends us to a party or something."

"It doesn't sound like he's going to be sending me anywhere in the near future, let alone a party." I looked around at row after row in the consignment shop and realized if I didn't start filling my basket, we were going to be here until the next ice age. "Fine. I'll get the shirt, but I draw the line at sequins."

Gem added the blouse to the basket and veered off toward the handbags. When she held up one that had a purple butterfly in rhinestones, I knew I probably wouldn't see her for another thirty minutes.

"Enjoying yourself?" Niko asked.

"I guess. I've decided to let Gem pick out my clothes so when Viktor decides to give me the boot, I can just leave them with her. My bag won't fit all this."

A woman across from me flashed her eyes up at Niko for the second time, as if she were mentally chanting for him to make eye contact with her. I hooked my arm in his and led him away.

"Do you always wear black?" I asked him.

Even Christian had color in his wardrobe, and I only knew that because I'd peeked in his drawers before leaving his room that morning and spied a few beige shirts and other muted colors. I'd been curious what Vampires kept in their rooms, and it was his fault for having left me alone in there.

"It makes it easier to dress myself," he said matter-of-factly, resting his hand against a nude mannequin. "I don't have to worry about looking like a fool in public."

"No, you don't," I said, pulling his grip away from the mannequin's boob. "Let's go outside. I'll buy you an ice cream cone."

"What about Gem?"

I glanced back, spotting her in front of a mirror with three scarves around her neck. "She can finish shopping for me. I gave her most of my money."

As we headed toward the front, the brunette with the cropped hair gave Niko a regretful glance before she continued shopping for tube tops on clearance.

Niko kept his gaze downcast. Unless you were speaking directly to him, it wasn't easy to tell that he was blind. He got around quite well, didn't use a cane or guide dog, and had a confident air about him.

Before we stepped outside, he pulled his black hood over his head so that it obscured his eyes.

No one paid any attention. For one, it was gloomy weather. Aside from that, we were on the Breed side of town. People dressed all kinds of ways in this area, especially with so many immortals who held fast to their historical attire. That might explain why Cognito has always been known as an eccentric city and, because of its reputation, wound up attracting humans who were artists and free spirits. I'd heard many immortals in the bars talking about the good old days when Cognito was inhabited only by Breed, and human settlers lived on the outskirts of town or in isolated pockets. Immortals had been claiming and purchasing real estate over the past few centuries, and that made it easier to sell businesses and houses exclusively to supernaturals. In time, the human population grew and so did their form of law and government, and Breed had to relinquish some of the property so they wouldn't get noticed. Sometimes humans wandered into our shops and cafes, but most of the clubs and restaurants embraced the reservation system to keep them out.

Viktor had given me cash in addition to the credit card, so I paid the street vendor a few bills and handed Niko a vanilla cone with a hard chocolate shell.

He licked it and then jerked his head back. "What kind of ice cream is this?"

I laughed and walked toward the corner of the building near the alley. "Bite into it and you'll see."

When he did, a giant piece of the shell clung to his cheek and then fell onto the sidewalk. His lips were covered with vanilla. "You're an amusing woman."

When I noticed the sarcasm in his voice, I took a moment to pick off all the chocolate from his cone.

"I'm sorry. I didn't realize."

He wiped his mouth. "It isn't the end of the world. I just wasn't expecting it."

Niko closed his lips over the ice cream and looked content again, leaving a small dollop on the tip of his nose.

I studied him for a moment, curious about something. "Why did you want to come shopping with the girls? Men usually flee in the opposite direction."

A strong gust of wind blew his hood back, and his hair tangled around him. He swept it to one side, drawing attention to his carved cheekbones.

"Did you ride along to babysit me? Was Viktor afraid I'd start a world war on my shopping spree?"

"On the contrary. I enjoy your company, Raven. Besides, someone needs to keep an eye on Gem, and Claude is at work. She's impulsive and sometimes gets into trouble. She might spend all your money." He leaned in close with a playful look on his face, his voice falling to a whisper. "Gem likes to sho—"

A shadow crashed into Niko, and then he was gone. I watched his cone fall to the ground as if it were all happening in slow motion. One minute I was talking to him, and the next I was staring at thin air.

Two seconds later, someone slammed into me from the right—knocking the wind out of my lungs.

Chapter 12

THE ENTRANCE TO THE ALLEY disappeared into a thin veil of fog. My body jerked to the right as someone carried me around a corner—probably a Mage based on how fast he was running. I prayed it was a Mage and not a Chitah, who could run just as fast, if not faster. The force of speed kept me from reaching behind my back for my push dagger.

We abruptly stopped, and my head spun like a Ferris wheel out of control.

Before I could reach around, someone grabbed my wrists in a tight hold. The familiar sound of duct tape ripping came seconds before the sticky adhesive was wrapped around my mouth and head, covering up my two best weapons inside my mouth.

Still dizzy, I writhed despite being stretched between two men who were subduing me with an iron grip on each arm. I couldn't reach for my weapons, I couldn't fight them, and I couldn't escape.

I erupted with anger, kicking at their legs and trying to pull out of their grasp. Someone punched me in the back, and I crumpled to the ground long enough for them to tape up my ankles. They lifted me back to my feet, still gripping my arms. I sensed their Mage energy, and that meant I couldn't even use my energy to blast them.

"Let her go. She has nothing to do with us," I heard Niko say.

When I shook some of my hair away from my eyes, I got the full scope of our situation. Niko was in a position of genuflection, but I had my doubts that he was worshipping these men.

I hoped.

Two flanked him, joined by a third man, who tossed a giant roll of duct tape to the ground. The others looked to him, waiting for his command.

"Nikodemos… did you think I wouldn't find you? I almost didn't recognize you with the long hair."

Niko's arms tightened around his stomach as if he was going to be sick.

I grimaced, bending my knee and trying to loosen the tape around my ankles. The dark-haired men were also Asian, but not the same ethnicity. Sometimes older immortals had different physical features than modern people—carrying genetic traits that had phased out or changed through new generations. But in this case, I was certain they weren't of the same origin. The leader appeared Samoan with a broad nose, dark hair and eyes, and skin like bronze. He had ink on his biceps that looked like sleeves of armor disappearing beneath his blue shirt.

"Let the woman go, Cyrus," Niko repeated.

Cyrus advanced and flipped Niko's hood back. "Still the same weak man I remember. I've spent five centuries searching for a blind Mage. I finally gave up in Europe and came here. You were always so much trouble." He briefly glanced over his shoulder at me. "So, did this white woman take pity on you and make you her servant? You fool. You can't even see the people you don't belong with."

Niko's crystalline eyes rose, and when I saw a flicker of light within them, I fought harder against the men restraining me. The man on my left was the weaker of the two, so I buried my nails into his arm until he almost lost his grip. He wrenched my arm, nearly pulling it out of its socket.

"I am not the weak boy you remember," Niko said, his voice cold and defiant.

Cyrus laughed haughtily.

That laugh galvanized Niko into action. He withdrew his hands from inside his open jacket, brandishing two katanas, one in each hand.

My eyes widened as he expertly sliced the air around him, forcing the men to retreat.

Cyrus stared him down, unflinching. "Let us see what the *boy* has learned." He stepped back and nodded at the two men, who reached behind their backs for their own swords.

Energy flooded my veins, and without being able to use it, I was forced to keep it tempered so that it wouldn't consume me.

The swords weren't long, which was how Niko had managed to keep them concealed underneath his long jacket.

Niko extended his left arm and glanced over his right shoulder, his gaze skating about as the men advanced. Steel clashed together, clanging as they exploded into action with expert moves I'd never seen before. These men didn't fight with savagery but with precision.

Cyrus's men attacked from different directions, and Niko spun around, blocking each strike and dodging their swings with impossible speed before countering with his own attack.

One man swiped his sword in a lateral move, and Niko bent backward, his long hair cascading behind him. Before righting himself, he swept his arm along the ground in an arc and sliced the legs of the man behind him.

A guttural scream poured from his opponent, blood streaking across the air and splattering on the wet asphalt.

When Niko was upright again, he lunged at the uninjured man with a vengeance, wielding both swords in a whirling blur and driving the man back, who could barely keep up his defenses. This wasn't a typical skirmish between men; these were warriors.

The man with the injured legs looked up, cursing the clouds for shielding the sun and preventing him from healing. He staggered forward, holding his sword like a baseball bat, ready to swing at Niko from behind.

I screamed through the tape, trying to warn Niko.

My heart clenched as the man raised his sword over his right shoulder, his eyes wide. He was aiming for Niko's neck, and beheading was certain death for a Mage.

Cyrus's men could barely restrain my arms as I writhed in an attempt to break free. My eyes widened with horror as a glint of light on the blade caught my eye.

Niko was too distracted—unaware of what was unfolding behind him as he struck his opponent, slicing his arm, his side, and leaving a gash across his face. It looked as if he took pleasure in delaying the kill, and the man weakened—finally taking a step back and conceding defeat.

The Mage standing behind him swung, and all that I saw was a flash of silver.

Niko dropped to his knees, reversed his sword, and drove it into the man's stomach. He quickly withdrew his blade and backed away from them—his hair askew, his lips peeled back.

"What's going on down there?" someone shouted.

In the distance, a woman leaned out of her apartment window, searching through the layers of fog that moved like smoke.

"Someone's going to call the Mageri," one of the men hissed at Cyrus.

Niko raised his bloody sword, aiming it at Cyrus. "Tell your men to release her."

Cyrus stepped forward and narrowed his eyes to slivers. "We'll finish this another day, Nikodemos. It's been a long time, and we have catching up to do. I'd like to know who taught a blind fool to handle a sword." He stalked toward the injured man and grabbed the cuff of his jacket, yanking him up. Their hands discreetly touched as healing light moved between them. "I've waited five hundred years, and I've learned how to be a patient man. We'll see each other again, because you know what I've come for."

The men flashed out of sight, leaving behind nothing but bloodstains and a roll of tape. Niko used the end of his coat to wipe his blades clean before returning them to their scabbards.

Meanwhile, I fell to the ground like a slug, tugging at the tape that was constricting my ankles.

Niko approached and drew his sword. He carefully lowered it until it tapped against the tape, and then he sliced it apart with a gentle stroke. "They didn't hurt you," he said, relief in his voice.

I peeled the tape off my mouth, pulling as hard as I could to try to stretch it since they had wrapped it around my head. Niko looked nervous about his sword near my face, so I handled the tip and cut the tape in the front. He touched my head and then paced around me, feeling the large strip of tape still stuck to my hair and making downward slices with his blade.

"Who the hell carries around duct tape?" I exclaimed. "What kind of people do you hang out with?" I stood up and kicked off the last remaining strip that was clinging to my ankle.

Red marks blotted my arms, but luckily nothing had been broken.

Niko put his hand on my back and led me away from the scene. "We must go before someone calls the authorities."

I snorted. "No crime was committed. Since when are you a master swordsman?"

"Perhaps you should have paid closer attention to the way I handled my butter knife at breakfast."

As we neared the end of the alley, he pulled the hood over his head.

"Wait," I said, gripping his sleeve. "Who were those guys?"

Niko turned. "How many enemies have you acquired in your short years as an immortal? Consider that I'm over a thousand years old. In time, you'll see that this world is much smaller than you imagined. Your enemies will become shadows around every corner."

"Who would want to come after you?"

That was a thought to ponder. Niko was one of the most sincere people I'd met, and aside from that, he was blind. How could anyone be enemies with a disabled person?

Then I had to laugh at myself when I remembered how Niko handled two swords like a man who was born with them attached to his wrists. This guy was an enigma.

"Is there blood on my face?" he asked, wiping at it again.

"On the left side."

He cleaned it with his sleeve.

"Hey, what are you two doing in the alley? I've been looking everywhere, and my arms are killing me."

I peered around Niko when I heard Gem's bright voice and the crinkling sound of shopping bags. Niko must have heard them too, because he hefted the bags and collected them all before walking away.

Gem anchored her hands on her hips and gave me a teasing glance. "What did I say earlier about romance in the house?" She hooked her arm in mine, and we followed behind Niko.

"Does he know where he's going?" I asked.

Her tall shoes clomped on the pavement. "He's okay until he reaches the street. Cars make him nervous, but he can dodge people pretty well. Not so much fire hydrants or steps."

"I just want to take a hot bath," I murmured.

"Not yet. We have to make a detour for french fries."

"Explain?"

Gem skipped a few paces ahead of me and turned around, walking backward. "Wyatt has an addiction. You'll see. Did you know you have tape in your hair?"

After we arrived at the mansion, Niko branched away from us and disappeared. Gem had tried interrogating him in the car, but he was evasive and said we simply ran into a little trouble. It wasn't uncommon on the Breed side of town since juicers were rampant and someone was always looking for a fight. I'd been in my fair share of rumbles, and most of them weren't even worth mentioning.

"Delivery girl!" Gem announced, dropping two sacks of fries onto Wyatt's desk.

The dark room had a desk alongside the right wall, which held multiple computer screens, a laptop, keyboards, snacks, pens, toys, and gadgets. Straight ahead was a massive television and several beanbag chairs in front of it. To the left, an L-shaped black sofa with colorful pillows. The floor was a smooth stone, but the grey walls were like something you'd find in an ordinary house.

Wyatt spun around in his leather chair and unrolled the paper sack. He drew in a deep breath, his smile turning orgasmic.

Gem headed toward the television. "Want to play video games?" she asked me.

I was busy watching Wyatt empty the sacks onto his desk, creating a mountain of fries.

He flicked a gaze at me and grinned. "Don't bother educating me about germs. Gravewalkers don't get sick."

"No, but now your desk is covered in grease, and you're getting salt all over the floor. Isn't this a shared room? Or do you just share it with the critters who live in the cracks of the walls?"

"This is Wyatt's World," he said with a mouthful of fries. "It's supposed to be *my* domain, but I can't seem to keep them out."

I clapped my hand on his shoulder as I walked past him. "Are you sure two sacks are enough?"

"Hmm, probably not. Be right back."

"Wyatt!" Gem shouted. "*Great.*"

I sat down on a roller stool with a round leather seat. "What's the big deal? His fries will just get cold."

She plopped down in a beanbag chair. "The last time that happened, he borrowed my hair dryer and left it on low to warm them up in the bag. My hair smelled like french fries for a week."

I rested my elbows on the desk and put my head in my hands. I was still feeling sick from having consumed Mage light the night before, and the kung fu scene in the alley earlier had left my head spinning. I thought *my* life before was full of drama, but these people ate it for breakfast.

Claude swaggered in, looking like some kind of Adonis with those big beautiful curls, and grabbed a handful of Wyatt's fries. After tilting his head back and shoving them into his mouth, he stared at me, chewing silently. Despite his handsome features, there was raw power in his eyes—an animalistic ferocity that flickered in their golden depths. You felt his presence in a room, especially being that he was six and a half feet tall.

He suddenly gripped my arm and rolled my stool out, spinning me around to face him. I jerked back when he touched the pieces of tape in my hair, making me turn my head left and right.

"I'm going to have to cut it out," I said.

He held up a section of my hair and examined the ends. "That's okay. You needed layering anyhow. I'll take care of it." When he reached the doorway, he pointed his finger at me. "Don't move."

Gem crossed her legs. "Looks like you're his new favorite toy."

"Is this where everyone hangs out?"

"Sometimes. It's mostly Wyatt's playroom, but since Viktor detests electricity and Wyatt needs it for his work, we just happened to notice this great big wall in dire need of a television to plug into that beautiful socket." She gestured behind her like a female model on a game show.

I tugged at a piece of tape. "No one's heard from Christian? Seems strange."

Gem played with her hair. "Christian marches to the beat of his own drum, so nothing surprises me. Unless Viktor sends us on assignment, we can come and go as we like. Planned vacations are fine, but who needs a vacation with all this house? Everything you could want is right here."

I spun around and rolled up to the desk. The touch screen blinked to life when my finger grazed over it.

"Wouldn't do that," Wyatt warned me, out of breath. "I have it rigged so if the password isn't entered correctly, a small country blows up."

"Sounds like fun."

"You're a dark soul." He rolled me out of the way and sat in his chair, flourishing a can of cheese dip and setting it on the desk. He peeled back the metal lid and dipped his fry.

"Ugh." Gem wrinkled her nose in disgust. "You've ruined them."

"Speak for yourself," he said around a mouthful of fries. "If I'd known back in the eighteen hundreds that one day there would be food you could prepare in less than thirty seconds or cheese in a can, I would have time-traveled my ass to the future."

"Did you drink milk straight from the udder?" she quipped.

He waved a fry at her. "You modern kids are spoiled. You don't know what it was like to wash your clothes on a washboard, sleep with heated stones in your bed because there wasn't a heater or fireplace in every room, or have ink stains on your hand because ballpoint pens weren't invented. As soon as the fifties hit, I felt like I was born again. Microwaves, television, washing machines, Twinkies, James Dean… it was magical."

"I think TVs were invented long before that," I said.

"Yeah, but not everybody had one. Let me enjoy this century before it changes and they have us wearing fedoras and eating wheat grass because fast-food places have become outlawed."

Gem giggled. "You're so dramatic."

"You sound like Viktor."

I jumped at the sound of metal blades slicing together. Instead of katanas, it was Claude holding a pair of scissors, a comb, and a spray bottle.

"I changed my mind," I blurted out.

Claude winked. "Don't worry, I have magic fingers."

Wyatt watched with avid interest while Claude began snipping at the tape. "You know, I bet a blow-dryer would loosen some of that adhesive."

Gem stood up. "Stay away from my hair dryer."

She stood beside me and watched pieces of my hair float to the floor. "Isn't Claude gentle with his hands? You'd never believe he could crush a man's skull with them."

He gripped my head and turned it left.

"Oh, I believe you, Gem."

"Who cut this last?" he asked, the horror in his voice thinly veiled.

"Me."

He moved in front of me, spritzing and combing. "Using what?"

"One of those pink razors."

Claude dropped the scissors on the floor.

Gem sputtered with laughter. "Poor Claude is going to have nightmares."

Wyatt switched on his dual monitors, and a wall of text scrolled up while he clicked on different windows.

I blew a strand of hair out of my eyes before Claude resumed his shearing. "How does a man go from hanging around in cemeteries to computer hacking?"

Wyatt peered over his shoulder. "A misspent thirty years in the arcade."

"So *you* were the guy who was always hogging the machines and making kids cry."

"Gauntlet was an awesome game. And I'm not a hacker. That's a human subculture that speaks their own language. They sit around playing Magic, watch reruns of *Doctor Who*, and wear clever little T-shirts that tell the world that they're hackers. There's nothing glamorous about what I do. I'm shut up in this hole for hours, my vision blurring, searching for vulnerabilities in a system. There's no fancy holographic images beaming onto the wall like you see in the movies. Half the time, I've already got access, and I just have to sift through a bunch of records. Like I'm doing now."

"Can't you just perform a search?"

He snorted. "You should see how they decided to archive the Breed land titles for the past few centuries."

Claude shoved my head so my chin was touching my chest. "Keep your head down. I'm a hair genius, not a magician."

"I thought you had magic fingers?"

He chuckled. "Maybe I do, but they don't perform miracles."

Gem circled around him. "I bet I know a few women who would disagree with that," she said with mischief in her voice.

I peered up and smiled at the remark.

Blue walked gracefully into the room and sat on the edge of the desk, lifting one of the fries and tossing it into the wastebasket. She had on jeans and a pair of black boots that reached her knees. "What's going on in here, besides a french fry massacre?"

Wyatt sighed, still staring at his screen. "Research."

"Viktor's getting impatient," she said, her shoulders hunched.

Loose hairs tickled my nose. "Why do all this research? By the time you finish, he'll have bought a house somewhere in Paris and you'll never find him."

"That's why we need Wyatt to expedite the process," Blue said, giving him a verbal nudge. "Human witnesses aren't enough to pin the murders on him; they're only a lead. The information you gave us will help, but we can't act impulsively. You didn't actually see him in the bathroom, so you couldn't even be a witness if something went wrong and the higher authority interrogated us. Viktor is searching for a motive."

"And I just fell into a steaming pile of it," Wyatt said. "Take a look at this."

Claude stepped away, and everyone swarmed over Wyatt, transfixed by something on the screen.

I flipped my damp hair back and stood up. "What is all that?"

He scrolled through scanned copies of documents. "It took a while to gather up all the data on the suspected victims to trace where they worked. Most were business owners. These here"—he pointed out the names, tapping his screen—"are old Breed records that show Darius owned that land up until last century. I still need to map out the area and make sure the businesses fall within it, but I think that gives us all the motive we're looking for."

Blue hopped off the desk. "That little weasel. If Darius used to own the land, how did humans get their hands on it?"

Wyatt licked salt off his finger. "Maybe he lost it in a bet. I don't know. I still need to dig."

Claude patted him on the head. "Good work, Spooky. Find out if he owns any other land… now or then."

Wyatt gave him a peevish look. "Any volunteer helpers?"

Gem flashed out of the room.

Claude turned to look at me and held out his hands. "Your hair is perfection." In a burst of action, he ran at Chitah speed out of the room.

"I'm serious!" Wyatt called out. "Aren't we a team?"

Blue casually strolled toward the door. "I'll give Viktor an update."

Wyatt dunked some fries into the cheese dip and spun around to face me. "When the going gets tough, they leave skid marks on their way out the door. There's no way I can get this done as fast as Viktor wants it."

"Don't you have enough evidence?"

He tossed a fry back onto his desk. "It could backfire on Viktor if we can't at least provide a solid motive. We're not allowed to ignore any new evidence, even if it slows down the case. We still have to follow protocol before we move in."

Wyatt's monitors suddenly went black.

"Son of a ghost. That's the second time today." He leaned back in his chair.

"I don't believe in ghosts."

His eyes skated off to my left as if he were looking at someone. "That's okay, buttercup. They don't really care."

"What if you just have a mental condition, like schizophrenia? I mean, I believe you can locate people buried alive, but the rest is probably just self-induced fears from spending so much time in graveyards."

Wyatt laughed and ended it on a snort. "Who do you think keeps shutting down my computers? They get mad when I don't talk to them."

I shook my head. "Power failure."

He pointed his finger at the lamp. "But the lights are still on."

Wyatt held the can of cheese dip and swirled two fries around. "It's a crazy world when a half Mage, half Vampire doesn't believe in the afterlife. How did you get tape in your hair?"

I paused in the doorway, turning to answer in a playful tone. "Gem tied me to the clearance rack."

"I always knew she was kinky."

Chapter 13

"Mr. Bane, you have a phone call in your office." Darius threw five more punches at the bag and then stepped back, wiping the sweat from his brow. He caught the reflection of his secretary in the wall mirror. Darius didn't really need a secretary. He'd only hired Camille because it was nice to have a woman in a skirt around the house. He didn't get out much, and the only people who kept him company were a bunch of male guards. But lately Camille had been wearing slacks and a lot less makeup.

"Who is it?" he asked, removing one of his wrist wraps. "And why aren't they calling my cell?"

Darius had a landline for routine calls, not for business. And routine calls were not important enough to interrupt his workout session.

Camille shifted her hips, and somehow her perfume managed to fight its way through the musky air. "He says he's your Creator."

Darius unwound the second wrap. "Tell him I'll be just a moment."

After she closed the door, he gulped down a bottle of imported water and then wet his curly black hair with a second bottle. He had a modest gym no bigger than the average living room, equipped with a punching bag and weights. It would have been nice to have something larger with high ceilings, but there wasn't enough room on the floor.

He tossed the empty bottle into a wastebasket. He didn't tolerate anyone disturbing his private time, but a man didn't ignore a call from his Creator, especially when his Creator was a member of the higher authority.

Darius took long strides down the narrow hall toward his office. Most of the rooms in the building were closed off, leaving long hallways like one might see in an office building. It gave him another level of security knowing his guards wouldn't have anything to distract them from their duties.

When he entered the tiny room, he shut the door and took a seat in the leather chair behind his desk. A short towel hung from his neck, and his thin T-shirt was drenched with sweat and water. He braced himself as he watched the blinking red dot on the phone.

Darius was a low-key individual who spoke in a modulated voice and preferred people who kept the excitement level down. Patrick, on the other hand, was an extrovert who had a politician's knack for steering the conversation and talking over people.

"This is Darius."

"Have you been hiding from me?" Patrick asked. He possessed a pleasant Irish accent that was light and lyrical, making everything he said sound wonderful. "I had a little trouble when your number was no longer in service, but I had a good friend of mine look you up. Staying out of trouble?"

Darius leaned back in his leather chair, his gaze shifting to an old photograph on the wall of him standing in front of a building. His face was obscured with a fedora, but he remembered that day like it was yesterday. "I was in the middle of negotiating a contract for a piece of property."

"Is that so? I'd love to hear the details."

Darius shifted uncomfortably in his seat. True, he bought and sold properties for profit, but not recently. "I'm stretched for time. What can I help you with?"

"You're not my financial advisor, Darius, so don't bother with addressing me so formally. I have every right to see what my progeny is up to, especially after what I've heard."

Darius stood up and flipped the towel away from his neck. "And what have you heard?"

"That a certain employee of yours was recently incarcerated for assault and attempted rape."

"And what does that have to do with me? I have no control over what my employees do any more than you do."

"True, true. We can't put a leash on them. But I happen to know a fella who knows a fella. Humans love surveillance cameras, and it seems that your partner was arrested in a human establishment. What intrigues me is how the video shows *your* car in the parking lot. What were you doing on that side of town?"

"You can't fault me for having a beer. What is this leading to, Patrick? My time is valuable."

Patrick's voice lost all humor. "As is mine. You're not even bothering to clean up your messes. Why didn't your man call the Mageri? It's standard protocol when arrested by humans to notify the Mageri so they can send in a team to perform a thorough cleanup."

"And what consequence is it if Salvator's fingerprints belong with human authorities? These are just humans we're talking about."

"*Just*, he says. You're my progeny, and what you do reflects on me. That's the way it is, and it's my right as your Creator to find out if you're involved in any illegal activities that could jeopardize my position. If you need money or help, I'm always here. Tell me, Darius, do you need money or help?"

Darius was far too proud to ask for help, especially after he'd lost everything his Creator had given him when he'd become independent. Ever since Darius's incarceration, Patrick meddled in his affairs, which was why Darius had put distance between them. But he couldn't afford to get on Patrick's bad side. "I've already bailed him out, and if you wouldn't mind taking care of the records at the police station, I'd appreciate it," he said reluctantly.

"Already taken care of, but I'd still like to know what it is I'm protecting you from. It's been years since we've seen each other. Let's get together. There's someone I'd like you to meet, and it would mean a great deal to catch up with my progeny. I won't take no for an answer."

A knock sounded at the door, and when Salvator poked his head in and started to back out, Darius snapped his fingers and pointed at a chair next to the door.

"Very well," Darius agreed. "Name the time and place and I'll rework my schedule."

Patrick laughed quietly. "You were always such an eager entrepreneur. I'm so glad to see you on the straight and narrow with your real estate dealings. Let's meet for lunch tomorrow at Angelo's. Noon. See you soon. Oh! And one more thing before I forget. Let me know if you have any prime real estate on the north side of the city. A colleague of mine is looking for a new place, and it wouldn't hurt for me to offer him the expertise of my progeny. It could be a good move for you. We'll talk about it more over lunch. See you then."

Darius hung up and rounded his desk before sitting on the edge, his arms folded, and glaring at Salvator. "I have a mind to throw you to a pack of Shifter wolves. All you had to do was take care of one puny human, and you couldn't even do that."

"Like I said before, some nosy bitch in the bathroom heard everything. I had no choice but to take care of her."

"And yet you didn't."

"She wasn't normal."

Darius put his palms on the edge of the desk and tried to release the tension in his shoulders. Whoever this woman was, she posed a threat to Darius and could undo everything. "What did you come in here for?"

Salvator released a breath and rubbed the side of his nose. "I came to talk about the woman. I still don't know who she is, but a tracker owed me a favor and found out where she's staying." He ran his fingers through his stringy black hair, one section falling out of place. Salvator looked like a balding Mafioso in his suit, with bushy eyebrows and a small mouth.

"And?"

The chair creaked when Salvator scooted to the edge as if he wanted to bolt. "In a mansion. A big fucking mansion with so much red tape around it that I can't find out who the hell lives there."

Darius frowned. "It should be public record."

"Should be, but I searched the records and couldn't find it listed. I'd need your permission to hack into—"

"No," Darius interjected. "I don't want my fingerprints all over the place. You've already proven your ineptitude."

Salvator wiped his nose with the cuff of his sleeve. "You haven't heard the best part. Want to know where it's located? Remember that piece of land you were looking at last week? It's next door."

Darius thought Salvator was exaggerating when he'd said it was a mansion, but that neighborhood? If this woman was staying in one of those homes, she was well protected, and that meant big problems if he wanted to take her out. Even if she had no interest in who Darius was, it wouldn't be long before she might see an opportunity to blackmail him.

Darius took a slow stroll around his desk and sat down in the chair, his thoughts scattered. He'd been saving his money in hopes of buying a magnificent piece of real estate to live on—something that would impress Patrick and make him forget about how Darius had lost everything. He'd never be able to acquire the land Patrick had given him now that humans controlled it, but he was going to milk those greedy little humans for every red cent until he accumulated enough to show everyone how successful he was.

Salvator tapped a small pendulum on the table beside him, initiating the swinging action. "Another five grand was deposited into your account. The new guy is cooperating."

"Yes," he murmured, thinking about how difficult all this was becoming. He had to be careful about how much he took because of their tax laws and how closely they were watched.

Extortion wasn't the business it used to be back in the forties. In those days, men were easily bought off, and the law was equally corrupt. Times had changed. Now humans had wiretaps, could snap pictures and record conversations with cell phones, and had information at their fingertips thanks to the Internet. It wouldn't take long to discover that Darius wasn't listed on any business pages or social profiles. He only used his alias with humans, but it had become increasingly difficult to intimidate business owners.

"Well, if you don't need me anymore…." Salvator said, rising from his chair.

Darius opened a drawer. "Hold on. I want you to finish off Mr. Bassett. He still hasn't paid. Don't go through with the original plan—we need to be more careful. Make it look like an accident. Once you finish the job, we're going to find out how protected this woman is. I want her dead."

"You and me both. That's one thing you can count on, boss."

Darius stood up and handed Salvator a file. "These are the signed documents. Give them to my secretary, and tell her I want them sent off tonight. Have her contact my architect."

Salvator's caterpillar eyebrows rose. "For?"

Darius glanced up at the photograph on his wall, feeling a sense of nostalgia in owning things instead of turning them over for profit. "I think I've outgrown this house. Don't you?"

Salvator shook his head. "You're one crazy son of a bitch."

Chapter 14

After putting away all my new clothes, I changed into a pair of grey shorts and a long-sleeved violet shirt, courtesy of Gem, who'd tried to fill my wardrobe with as much color as she could. I ventured down to the gym, hoping to get in a little exercise since I was used to walking all day and climbing buildings. I could have paced the halls, but it felt intrusive since my footsteps would continually draw attention, and my housemates might start wondering if I was neurotic.

As I reached the stairway to the basement, someone gripped my arm.

"I wouldn't go down there," Blue said.

"Why not?"

She coaxed me in another direction. "Shepherd's working out, and he likes to be left alone."

"The room is huge; he'll never know I'm in there."

"He wouldn't like that."

"Not a very friendly guy."

Blue's eyes skated off to the side. "Shepherd's a reticent man when it comes to his personal life. He likes his alone time. It's just his way."

I could relate since there were times I liked my privacy, but part of me still craved the companionship of others. Life on the streets had been a lonely experience.

Blue noticed a lock of hair that fell in front of my face. "He cut off a lot."

I touched the ends. "It's cleaned up now, that's for sure."

She gave me an impish grin. "You can't imagine how badly he wants to get his hands on my hair and how I torture him by trimming the ends with a blunt pair of scissors."

"You're a cruel woman."

Blue's locks fell past her breasts—the kind of hair most hairdressers dream about.

She held her index finger in front of her lips. "Shhh. Don't let him know how much I enjoy it. Besides, they always take off too much, and I love my hair long. Have you seen the courtyard?"

"From the windows."

Blue placed her hand on my back and led me away. "Come on and I'll show you."

We moved through a magnificent room with high ceilings and a fragrant array of flower arrangements. I could only imagine how beautiful the mansion looked when the sun was shining. Nothing about it was garish or showy, and every room was pleasant and homey in its own way.

Blue opened the french doors, and we entered a veranda with beautiful stone archways that ran in both directions. She drifted through an opening that led to the courtyard. The walkway expanded in some places and narrowed in others, curving around and creating space for the lush landscaping. Some areas had grass while others were covered in ivy or moss. There were a couple of trees, but not a lot as they would have obscured the scenic view and prevented sunlight from getting in.

The house that enclosed us seemed imposing, as if it were somehow a living entity that was watching us. Or maybe it was the voyeuristic reality that there was no privacy out here, and anyone within the house could see us through the windows.

A breeze picked up the ends of Blue's long hair, and it floated like ribbons of silk. Her tall black boots clicked on the path, and nearly every time I'd seen her, she was wearing a hood of some kind. While one was attached to her shirt, she didn't bother to cover her head, even when a little drizzle began to fall.

"How much did all this cost him?" I asked.

She found shelter beneath a tree and approached an old statue.

"This estate has been in his family for over three hundred years—long before humans colonized this area. Viktor comes from a line of wolves, so his pack once lived here."

I wondered if Blue was also a wolf. She didn't seem to have the same mannerisms I'd seen in Shifter wolves. "Where are they now?"

She circled the statue while I sat on the bench, the air chilly against my legs. "Who knows? People move on. Shifters wage private wars and slaughter families for land. Viktor doesn't talk about it, so I haven't asked. Sometimes it's better to let a scab heal than to keep picking at it."

"That would be a pretty tragic story. This house could easily fit a hundred."

"You have unusual eyes," she said absently, not looking directly at them.

"Kids teased me with all kinds of names, but eventually I hit high school and liked standing out. People thought they were cool. Most adults don't say anything, but they stare. I never wanted to hide them behind sunglasses until I became a Mage. It was like reliving elementary school all over again. I learned how to avert my eyes or show someone my profile so they don't notice them right away. I didn't realize how prejudiced immortals could be over something so superficial. It's not like I have a nose growing on my forehead."

"Some of the ancients are superstitious, but most are looking for anything that makes you inferior to them." Blue looked up thoughtfully. "My tribe believes that people born with mismatched eyes were meant to be someone else—that their body was given one soul, which was quickly replaced with another."

"So I wasn't supposed to be here? That's uplifting."

"It means you were chosen for a reason—to serve the fates. Anyhow, that's just what my tribe believed. Everyone has a different story."

Blue draped herself over the back of the kneeling statue—another winged man, only this one had his face in his hand, as if grieving. "Isn't he handsome?" She pressed the side of her face against the back of his head, her arms spread out as if she were embracing him from behind. "I think this is my favorite thing about this place."

"He looks broken."

Blue slowly stood up. "Maybe that's why I like him the most." She circled around it and sat to my right. "Is it true what Viktor says, that you're a killer?"

I wasn't sure how to answer that. While it was true, I was finally coming to terms with how other people saw me because of it. "He speaks highly of me."

She turned to face me, bending her left knee. "Do you think the blade on my axe has never been stained?"

When she lifted her shirt on the right side, I noticed a short handle and a black sheath against her belt.

Blue covered it up and sat back, crossing her legs and putting her arms over the back of the bench. "You either carry the guilt for your sins or you don't. I do whatever I can to avoid bloodshed, but I still know how to protect myself. Just be sure you're not doing it for pleasure, or you've crossed a line you might never return from."

This conversation was treading into uncomfortable territory, so I quickly stood up and folded my arms. "Does your family know where you are?"

She uncrossed her legs and looked skyward. "If any of us had family, would we really be here?"

"Has anyone ever left Keystone?"

"We're the originals," she said. "I suppose someday, if we live that long, we'll eventually want to leave. I can't imagine that far off—this is the only future I see when I dream at night."

"Why?"

She stood up and reached for a low branch. "For the same reason you're still here. Viktor has a way of channeling our talents into something that's helping people. Every criminal we take down is saving future lives." Blue's feet lifted off the ground as she swung. She laughed, looking up. "This old tree puts up with me, but one day he's going to drop his limb on my head for tugging on him so much."

"It might if you put enough weight on it."

She set her feet on the ground. "Our cultures are so different. My tribe believes everything has an awareness of its surroundings. Has Niko told you that he can see most living things because of the energy?"

"Yeah, so?"

We strolled toward the veranda.

"Energy is a real thing. Plants don't think the way we do because they obviously don't have a brain, but on some level, they're aware of positive and negative energy. They react to it. People who talk to their plants aren't crazy. Some believe the extreme weather in this city is driven by all the Breed energy."

"So if we all start singing happy songs, the sun will come out?"

She laughed and touched my shoulder. "You first. My voice could shatter windows. Do you want to hang out with me in the rock-climbing room?"

"Sure."

Blue closed the doors behind us. "It's one of my favorite things to do."

Blue had a smooth, matter-of-fact way of speaking. I could sense the wisdom she must have acquired from her tribe, but she seemed to blend really well with the modern world considering she was a transplant. From what I knew, Shifter tribes were steeped in tradition and culture, often separating themselves from other Breeds. Where was her tribe now, and why wasn't she with them?

"I need to speak with you," Viktor said, approaching Blue and putting his arm around her. "It's about a job."

She peered over her shoulder and nodded at me as they walked off. The axe handle subtly bobbed against the side of her jacket, something I'd never paid attention to before. I couldn't imagine why Blue would arm herself in the house, but it made me consider going upstairs and retrieving my weapons.

Despite all the amenities, I was confined to the property. Without a car or the city nearby, I couldn't leave like everyone else. They all had something to do—assignments. Not that my status diminished what I'd already done for them, but it still left me wandering the halls aimlessly.

I jumped when a shirtless Shepherd emerged from the adjoining room, his body encased in sweat. He moved past me without a word, his muscles taut like a thoroughbred just after a race. I flicked a glance at a few scars on his chest.

Only two people in the house gave me nervous butterflies: Shepherd and Christian. Shepherd looked like a hardened man just released from prison. His dark eyes carried a haunting emptiness that I'd seen in my own reflection, except that his was too far gone, as if every sense of innocence and goodness had been stripped away from him. His buzz cut showed off rich, dark hair that matched his pensive eyebrows. He was over six feet of ripped muscle, with a warrior's face and a penetrating gaze that could strike fear in anyone unfortunate enough to cross his path. Even the tattoo of a phoenix on his right arm and across his shoulder was intimidating. It spread across his chest and looked like it stretched to his back, but I didn't turn around to watch him going.

Christian, on the other hand, was a Vampire. That alone earned him a spot on my "Do not trust" list. Most immortals spoke without a filter, but Vampires were cunning at masking their emotions with humor and indifference, when in truth they were plotting your demise. How does a man go from being a killer, to a bodyguard, and then back to hunting killers? Clearly Christian hadn't quite figured his shit out.

Viktor pairing me up with a Vampire was like the universe giving me the finger.

As I turned down another hall, I overheard voices coming from behind one of the closed doors. I didn't have exceptional hearing like a pureblood Vampire, so I tiptoed over to the door. Viktor had mentioned that some of the rooms were soundproof, but not this one. I recognized Viktor speaking.

"Are you familiar with this area?"

"I think so," Blue said, her voice more distant. "Do you think he'll have poachers?"

"Nyet. He does not come from the Old World. In my time,

men were always prepared for spies. Get as close as you can without putting yourself in danger."

"Are you sure your source is reliable?"

"Whether Darius changes his mind is another matter, but we cannot dismiss an opportunity."

"And if he moves?"

"Follow," Viktor said tersely.

"If he leaves the property, do you want me to call in for backup?"

I could tell Viktor was pacing around the room by the way his voice shifted direction and volume. "He has reservations at a Breed restaurant. I cannot initiate an execution in such a public place. We have an end goal, but you must always consider how you choose to reach that goal."

I pressed my ear closer to the door.

"Do we have enough evidence?" she asked.

"Sufficient. Wyatt gave me an update and linked all the businesses to an area of land that once belonged to Darius. His motive for extortion is evident. It was no secret to me that Darius was arrested many years ago, but after Wyatt's discovery, I called a close friend of mine. He knows this area well and said it was commonplace that those who served time in Breed jail had to relinquish their land. The higher authority must have noticed the growing human population and wanted to create more division since many locations were a mixture of the two."

I heard Blue's boot heels as she trod across the room. "Wow. So the authorities stripped away his land, and once free, he couldn't get it back because they sold it to humans. What was he in jail for?"

Viktor laughed, and it was a warm, sonorous sound. "What do you think? The very thing he is doing now. Extorting people for money. That is how I received the tip to open his case. Darius was acquiring money too quickly, and it caught the attention of the higher authority when he was buying and selling expensive properties. They suspected he was back to his old habits but had no proof. There were rumors of wealthy humans turning up dead, but the higher authority couldn't question the victims' families because it goes against our laws."

"What do you want me to do if he moves to a more private location? There's always that possibility."

It sounded like someone was tapping their foot on the floor.

"Nyet. It will be daylight. Too much risk," he said, his accent heavier.

"Too much opportunity," she suggested.

"If we're caught and endanger the reputation of the higher authority—who is paying us—we will be cut off like a necrotic limb. Just follow. We need to confirm if the information Raven gave us is correct—that he's staying in this house. Follow the vehicle and identify him. When you get to the restaurant, shift back and call me with an update."

"Are you sure, Viktor? We could surround him and—"

"I cannot take the chance," he stressed in slow words. "Christian is not here, and we would have no one to take care of witnesses. You would have a body to deal with—blood and emotional imprints. You are smarter than that. Leave early in the morning, and keep your phone charged. Put it on vibrate so it doesn't draw attention."

She laughed softly. "You must think I'm an amateur. I keep my clothes well hidden when I shift."

I scurried down the hall and ascended the stairs. When I reached the top floor, I slammed right into Wyatt.

"Well, it looks like we meet again. Does something have you… spooked?"

Once my heart stopped hammering against my chest, I put my hands on my hips, still out of breath. "Feel up to some covert spy stuff?"

Wyatt put his arm around me, and we strolled toward his game room. "Now you're speaking my language."

Chapter 15

THE CAR LURCHED TO A stop, and I gripped the driver's seat in front of me, which happened to be on the right side of the car and not the left. "I thought we were going to be covert?"

Wyatt shifted to park and turned off the engine. He jerked his thumb at Shepherd. "He's my partner. If I keep anything from him, he'll move my bed into a graveyard while I'm sleeping."

"I meant the car."

Wyatt's expression twisted comically. "Leave my girl alone. This is a vintage 1971 classic Mini Cooper."

"Yeah, nothing conspicuous about that," I said with a snort.

Shepherd opened his door, looking like a sardine trying to climb out of a can. "Stay here while I circulate the blood in my legs."

We waited in the car for a minute while Shepherd scouted the area. I'd only filled them in on part of the conversation I'd overheard, leaving out all the warnings that Viktor had given Blue. What this organization needed was new blood to shake things up.

"Are you sure this is the place?" I asked.

Wyatt checked the map on his phone. "I put a tracker on her cell last night, and the signal is coming from right here, so my bet is that her stuff is up yonder," he said, pointing at the roof of the pastry shop.

We didn't have trouble figuring out where Darius was supposed to show up. Viktor said something about reservations, and the only place in the immediate area besides the movie theater was a restaurant named Angelo's.

Wyatt tilted his mirror. "It hasn't even been a week and you're already going behind Viktor's back. You are a *bad* girl."

"Viktor's too worried about visibility."

"He likes to keep a low profile. Don't hold your breath on us getting uniforms with name tags anytime soon."

I pulled off his hat. "Open the door. If I have to sit in this cramped car for another minute, I'm going to scream."

Wyatt got out and pushed the seat forward. I stumbled onto the curb, and he snatched his beanie out of my hand and put it back on his head. It was more stylish than practical, with the fabric loosely flopped over in the back as if it were meant for a larger head.

I raised an eyebrow at his T-shirt that said YOU'RE DEAD TO ME. It was partially tucked in, revealing a belt buckle with a skull.

"I bet you're a real hit with the ladies."

All he did was pucker his lips and give me an invisible smooch in return.

There was nothing subtle about the way Wyatt walked. He had the swagger of a fashion model who'd just discovered his calling. I scanned the streets, hurrying toward the pastry shop where Shepherd was holding open the door.

Once inside, Shepherd stole a seat next to the window and slanted his eyes, signaling for us to buy something.

"Holy Toledo!" Wyatt exclaimed, flattening his palms on the counter, gazing upon row after row of mouthwatering pastries. "Is it possible for me to just work my way from left to right and you can send me the bill?"

The girl behind the counter smiled coyly. "You can have whatever you want and as much as you want."

He folded his arms on the high counter and rested his chin on his wrist. "Is that so?"

I nudged him and cleared my throat.

"Tell you what, buttercup. My friends will have two brownies, and I'll take the biggest cinnamon bun you make."

"Coming right up," she said, using a singsong voice.

Wyatt turned, scoping out the empty room.

I glared at him. "Is it possible for you to *not* draw attention?"

"You do things your way, and I'll do them mine," he said coolly.

"Says the man who drives a red car with a blue door."

He leaned in. "Says the woman who has one brown eye and one blue. Sometimes things that are different have more personality."

Wyatt was too adorable to hate, so I just shook my head and wandered toward a table in the back. Shepherd kept a close eye on the restaurant across the street. The valet parking allowed us to see people coming and going, and although I didn't have a clue what Darius looked like, Shepherd did.

Wyatt set a plate in front of Shepherd and then headed toward me. He didn't wear the lace-up boots most men wore, or even sneakers. Wyatt lived in a pair of old black cowboy boots. I wondered what he looked like in the century he was born—if he'd worn spurs on his boots or had dressed more like a city boy.

"The way you're staring at my boots is making me blush," he teased in an exaggerated Southern accent. "Why, I *do* believe I just might feel one of my fainting spells coming on."

"You do that accent so well it scares me."

He winked, his voice back to normal when he said, "I used to be a Southern boy, but when you live in different places, you start losing pieces of yourself."

I gaped at the size of his cinnamon bun. "That thing's bigger than your head."

He peeled off a strip around the outer edge. "I hear that a lot. So what's the big plan if we see Darius?"

"It depends on how many goons are protecting him. There's one I wouldn't mind taking out myself."

"Just don't do it around me," he said, chewing on a wad of the sticky bun. "The last thing I need is some freshy who wants to haunt me because I hang out with the girl who snuffed out his light."

"Your life must be miserable if all that's true."

He straightened his shoulders. "Hey, maybe my Breed isn't

as glamorous as shifting into animals or draining people with your teeth, but we do something else that no one else can, and sometimes it has its rewards. Like identifying the soul of a missing person. It's not always a happy ending, but at least it's closure for the family. I don't engage in that kind of help very often, but they can be persistent."

"Where's Christian? I haven't seen him."

Wyatt mumbled an unintelligible answer, his lips coated with flaky icing. After five tremendous chews and a swallow, he said, "Why do people always ask you a question the second after you take a bite of something?" He wiped his mouth with a paper napkin and smiled at the girl behind the counter. "No idea what Christian's up to. Viktor might have sent him on a job, or maybe he's taking a break. We don't keep tabs on anyone except our partners."

I tilted my head to the side and gave him a cold stare.

Wyatt chuckled. "Oh, yeah. Well, that's for you two to figure out. When Viktor first paired us up, Shepherd wanted to kill me."

"By the menacing look on his face, I'd say nothing's changed."

Wyatt wagged his sticky finger at me. "Yeah, but at least he doesn't try anymore. You develop a bond with your partner that defies all logic. You'll see. It's always an adjustment period when someone new comes in. I thought you two would get along since you're kind of the same."

I poked at my brownie. "I don't trust Vampires."

"That's a therapy session I ain't got time for," he said around a mouthful of cinnamon bun.

"We're so busted." I slouched in my chair and shielded my eyes. "Cover your face. It's Blue."

When Blue entered the shop and glanced at the back of Shepherd's head, her eyes went glacial. Maybe it was the way the stubble leaned or a freckle on his ear, but she knew exactly who was sitting in that chair.

"Hey, Blue!" Wyatt boomed. He turned around in his chair and blithely waved his sticky fingers at her. "The cinnamon buns are out of sight."

She had a thin hood pulled over her head, but I recognized her remarkably long hair.

"What are you doing here?" she hissed, gripping the ends of the table. "Viktor will—"

"Start rambling on in Russian and put us on video game restriction. Blah-blah. Did you really think we were going to let you have all the fun? Take a seat; you're making a scene and drawing attention to us."

I gave him a cross look as she pulled up a chair and sat to my right. "How did you know that was Shepherd?"

Blue tucked her hair behind her ear. "The Celtic tattoo on the back of his neck."

I craned my neck and looked across the room. "I never noticed. What did you find out about Darius?"

Blue pulled out her phone and checked her messages. "He's across the street. They've been in there for about an hour, but the information you got from that Mage was right. He's definitely staying at that house. Are you going to eat that?" She dragged my plate in front of her when I shrugged indifferently.

Wyatt chuckled. "Is that your Shifter craving?"

She shoved half the brownie into her mouth. "No, but it'll distract me."

These were questions I'd always wanted to ask before but didn't. The last thing you wanted to do in a bar or club was stand out for not knowing anything about the Breed world, especially when you were illegally made. "What's a Shifter craving?"

Blue wedged the remaining half into her mouth, giving me a guarded look.

Wyatt pulled more of his hair out from beneath his hat, playing with the ends. "Since she's busy eating half the bakery, I'll tell you. When they shift back from animal form, they each have a craving. It's different for everyone, and nobody knows why. At least, that's what they've told me. I once knew a guy who craved peas and gravy."

I laughed when he shuddered dramatically.

Wyatt smeared his finger around his plate, gathering up flecks of icing. "Blue won't tell us what hers is. I don't know why all the secrecy."

"Because not all my business is *your* business," she said, glancing back at the window. "Oh, no. He's coming this way. Raven, does he know what you look like?"

"I don't think…" I glanced past her, searching for the Mage I'd fought in the bathroom. "His partner should have my face memorized, but I don't see him."

Blue stripped off her thin jacket and wrapped it around me, drawing the hood over my eyes. "It doesn't matter," she said in a hushed voice. "We can't take the chance since your eyes stand out. Keep your head down, and go sit with Shepherd. It looks suspicious to have him sitting there by himself. Hurry!"

I launched to my feet and scuttled over to the table in front, taking a seat so I was facing the door.

Shepherd discreetly slid his brownie in front of me and held my hand as if we were dating. I felt myself blush with the weight of his touch. He seemed to be a contradiction in so many ways. I always thought Sensors would be more empathetic and compassionate, but Shepherd was hard and raw. Maybe that was why it caught me off guard to have an affectionate moment with him, even a staged one.

I glimpsed an entourage crossing the street, and Shepherd lifted my knuckles and kissed them with expert timing as the door opened.

"Hurry up and finish. We'll be late for the movie," he said in a soft voice.

I'd never heard Shepherd speak so tenderly. If he ever decided to quit Keystone, he could either be a street fighter or an award-winning actor.

I lifted the fresh brownie with two fingers and hunched over my plate, peering through the opening in my hood at the two men approaching the counter.

"Pick out whatever you like," a gentleman said in an Irish accent. His tone was pleasant, not dark and disdainful like Christian's, but lyrical.

When I saw a little boy in a Zorro mask pressing his hands against the glass casing, my heart sank. I'd secretly been working out a plan to lock the doors and take out Darius once and for all. The man with the Irish accent didn't appear to be one of his bodyguards, who were all waiting outside with their suits and sunglasses. But the child threw a monkey wrench into the plan; I couldn't risk accidentally hurting him in the melee.

The Irishman tapped his ring against the counter. "We should do this more often."

"I'm a busy man, Patrick. But I can always make room for you," Darius remarked.

I couldn't see anything but his legs because of my hood, but I immediately recognized his voice. My fangs descended, and I quickly snapped my mouth closed before anyone saw them.

Patrick lifted the boy into his arms. "We'll take the small cupcake. Which color, boy?"

"I want the green one," the little guy said, pointing his finger. I guessed him to be about four.

Shepherd's green eyes locked on my plate, but his full attention was on the two men standing just five feet behind him.

What the heck were we doing? Our enemy was standing in the open, and our response was to casually eat brownies and pretend to be invisible?

I lifted my head to get a better look. I deduced that the lanky man on the right with the faded red hair was Patrick, which made the Italian-looking man with the black curls Darius. I didn't find anything remarkable about him. He had a small mouth, tall forehead, sideburns, and a clean-shaven jaw. Beneath his dress shirt and slacks, I could tell he was a fit man. Some guys had that look about them. You could put a suit on Shepherd, and he'd still look like a bulldog in clothes.

When Darius settled his soulless eyes on mine, he didn't blink. If his bathroom buddy had told him anything about me, he would have mentioned my mismatched eyes.

When I smiled at him, he made a tight fist.

Patrick looked between us and strode over. "You two look like old acquaintances. I don't believe I've had the pleasure."

Shepherd twisted his body around to look up at the man.

When the little boy reached out for Shepherd, Patrick gripped his arm. "That's impolite. What did I say about doing that? Go stand outside."

The black-haired boy quickly looked over the man's shoulder. "But my cupcake…"

"When you learn the rules, you get rewards. Stand outside like a good boy and we'll see."

Patrick opened the door and snapped his fingers at a big guy in a black turtleneck. The guard moved in close and kept his attention on the boy.

Whoever this guy was, he was big-time. Darius's men looked like amateurs compared to Patrick's bodyguard.

"Such a precocious child," Patrick said.

"Is he yours?" I asked, having sensed Patrick was a Mage.

Aside from not being able to reproduce, a Mage had no business with a child. If Patrick was recently turned and this was his human child, the Mageri would have made him sever the relationship. But something in his eyes told me he was very old.

Patrick cupped an elbow with one hand and pinched his chin, looking at the child. "Sadly, no. I have many people in my employment, one of whom was my Relic. Helen was an exceptionally bright woman, and I was quite fond of her in some ways. A year ago, she was walking to a restaurant when a Mage juiced her energy to the point where it killed her." Sadness brimmed in his eyes and he shook his head. "Terrible tragedy. The boy was hers. As is the custom, he would have been in my employment after his mother retired, so it just made sense to raise him. It's not the ideal situation, but what can you do?"

My heart sank. Tragedies like that occurred far too often—I'd seen them. So many rogues developed an addiction to energy. If they couldn't find another Mage to juice from, they'd choose any Breed. Their light was dimmer, so it wasn't uncommon that it resulted in their death.

Blue and Wyatt were hunched over in private conversation, making themselves barely noticeable.

Patrick glanced back at Darius. "You two look as though you want time alone to catch up. I'm going to run across the street and visit with the owner to schedule another reservation. You were right about the linguini. Wait for me outside; that wasn't enough time for us to get reacquainted, so I'm inviting you to my place for drinks. No arguments." He turned on his heel and bowed to me. "It was a pleasure, Miss…"

"Black," I answered.

"Patrick Bane, at your service. Perhaps we'll meet again. Good day to you."

He left the shop and walked briskly across the street, leaving Darius staring daggers at me.

I stood up and approached him, hands in my pockets.

"At last we meet," he said, his tone layered with irritation and contempt. "One of my men told me that you roughed him up in the bathroom and had him arrested. You fabricated lies about him and risked exposing our secrets to humans. I could have you arrested for slander."

I lifted a toothpick with a cookie sample on the end and took a bite. "Something tells me you won't. Even if you did, you can't prove anything. I didn't make any statements, and your man is less than reliable."

"Is there something you want?"

I shrugged nonchalantly and set the toothpick on the counter. "I just happened to be sitting over there when I recognized your voice. Thought I'd say hello. There's nothing I want; your friend in the bathroom just caught me on a bad day when I wanted to be left alone."

His expression went rigid.

I wasn't sure what to expect, but I certainly didn't expect what happened next.

Darius leaned in close, his voice a cold whisper. "I'm going to kill you."

With a mirthless smile, I lifted another sample from the tray and ate it. "You're a funny guy, Darius. Chances are you'll send one of your goons after me. If that's the case, can I put in a request for your bathroom buddy? I have a score to settle with him."

"If you couldn't finish off Salvator, what makes you think I'm quaking in my boots?"

I poked him in the chest with the toothpick, and he flinched. "Did one of your guards go missing recently?"

He stared for a frozen moment, unblinking.

I tucked my dirty toothpick in his coat pocket and patted it with my hand. "Don't make empty threats you don't mean to carry out yourself."

Darius slowly inclined his head, moving around me. Before he passed, he bent down and whispered in my ear. "Did one of your Vampires go missing lately?"

I blanched and quickly looked up.

His dark eyes sparkled with interest. "I wasn't sure at first. Thanks for the confirmation. Shame," he added, implying the Vampire was dead.

I turned on my heel as he went out the door.

A bluff. It *had* to be.

Wyatt all but flew out of his seat, his chair knocking over. "You're Dirty Harry! The whole toothpick in the pocket... *man*." He threw his head back. "That was *classic*."

Darius and his men drifted out of sight, leaving behind Patrick's guard and the little boy.

I approached the window and peered out. "Should we go after him?"

"Not in the daylight," Shepherd cautioned. "Take a seat until the rest of the party leaves."

I sat across from him, Wyatt and Blue joining us and facing the window.

Wyatt hooked his arms over the back of his chair. "Do you know who that guy is?"

"Darius," I said, unimpressed.

"No," he said, lazily lifting his hand to point at the restaurant. "*That* guy. His last name is Bane."

"One of Darius's Mage brothers. So?"

Wyatt shook his head. "I discovered a record this morning that lists the original owner of that land. It was Patrick Bane, Mr. Irish Wonderful over there. He's Darius's Creator and also happens to be a member of the higher authority."

Blue touched one of her earlobes as if searching for the feather earring she wasn't wearing. "Do you think he knows what Darius is up to?"

"Bet he doesn't have a clue," Shepherd said. "That poor bastard is in for a rude awakening if this thing blows up."

Wyatt pulled his hat down so that it covered his ears. His brows angled. "Do you think Darius is a Creator?"

Shepherd scratched his jaw. "There's always the chance. So what if he is?"

"Because the last thing we need is a legion of Learners coming after our ass for killing their father. Didn't you see *The Princess Bride*?"

Blue smacked his arm with the back of her hand. "Don't be ridiculous."

Wyatt rubbed his nose. "Even still, now his Creator's in the picture. Going after Darius is like going after Patrick, and you know how the Mageri protects its own."

"Fuck me," Shepherd grumbled, glaring at Wyatt. "Don't you have anything positive to say?"

"I bought you a brownie."

The boy outside slapped his hand against the glass, holding it there. He did it again, a pout on his face and blue eyes glittering behind the black Zorro mask.

"Poor kid," Shepherd said. "Bet that bastard doesn't give him the cupcake."

Wyatt chortled. "Careful, Shepherd. People might actually think the Tin Man has a heart."

Shepherd placed his palm on the window, eclipsing the tiny hand. The boy smiled wide, his cheeks ruddy.

"Look, he likes you," Wyatt teased. "Little does he know you eat wishes and dreams for breakfast."

Wyatt touched his thumb to his nose, wiggling all his fingers. The boy stuck out his tongue in response, making Wyatt laugh.

Shepherd lowered his hand and turned away, giving me a pensive look. "What did Darius whisper in your ear before he left?"

I swallowed thickly, my eyes skating between them. "Christian's dead."

Chapter 16

"WHAT DO YOU MEAN, HE'S dead?" Viktor bellowed, his voice reverberating off the stone walls of the gathering room. The news was a grievous blow to the team, and most of them sat in quiet disbelief.

The gathering room was separated from the dining area by a stone wall with small archways down the center. The ceiling was high, and the stained glass window on the left side of the room was exquisite—images of people, flowers, and wolves tangled together. With the window behind me and the crackling fireplace to my left, I had a direct view of a grand bookcase on the opposite side of the room that was filled from top to bottom. Viktor had been pacing since learning about Christian's fate. The lines on his forehead were pensive, his hair unkempt.

Blue kept talking, trying to placate him. "Can you give us any information on where we can start looking? What was the last thing Christian said to you?"

He stroked his beard repeatedly, speaking in words I didn't understand.

"English," Gem said gently.

Viktor took a detour to the other side of the room and stopped in front of a liquor cabinet below two stained glass windows alongside the fireplace wall. They overlooked the courtyard, colorful glass creating a mosaic masterpiece of light across the stone floor. He lifted a decanter and filled a short glass with a clear drink, then swallowed half. "I sent him to dispose of the body and vehicle."

"But that was two nights ago," Blue said cautiously. "If you had mentioned this to us, we would have searched for him."

He refilled his glass and then ponderously crossed the room. His accusatory glare made me shift in my seat. The girls sat on the couch to my right, with most of the men standing, except for Niko, who sat on the armrest of the sofa.

Viktor raised his glass, using one of his fingers to point at Blue. "Do you know why I said nothing? It would take the full night to complete the job, so I did not expect his return so soon. In our last conversation, Christian agreed to do this one thing for me and then he was temporarily stepping away. He was conflicted about the recent changes in the house and expressed doubt that he could trust a crossbreed who has devoted her immortal life to killing the very Breeds she's made from."

A hush fell over the room.

"So that is why I have said nothing," he continued. "I just assumed he was taking an immediate vacation. Christian was very upset. It is not the most convenient time, but I would rather he step away and gather his thoughts than make an impulsive decision. I am not negligent; I was simply misinformed."

Blue put her head in her hands. "Now what?" she said to herself.

Viktor leveled me with his eyes. "How did Darius connect you to Christian? Even if he somehow captured him, Christian would have never talked. Why did he say this to you?"

I uncrossed my legs. "I asked him if he was missing a guard—to make him paranoid. Before he left, he asked if I was missing a Vampire. Darius said he wasn't sure if I knew anything about it until he saw my reaction. He threatened my life, and I didn't want him to think he was talking to an amateur."

"You *are* an amateur," Viktor ground out. "Now he'll know us all."

Blue spoke up. "Darius only noticed her with Shepherd. He's not a very astute man, from what I could tell."

Viktor waved his hand dismissively. "Raven is a baneful influence. I thought I could trust you."

"You can!" she argued. "I did what you asked."

Viktor approached the couch and cradled her head in his hands. "I do not know what I would have done had I lost you. The goal was to follow him for information; you were not prepared to fight against him in broad daylight, cornered in a shop with all his men and so many witnesses. I believe you when you say you had no part in confronting him, but maybe you should have called me or led the team away before Darius showed up. I care for each of you like family. You must never go against my wishes."

She placed her brown hands over his. "I would never do anything to jeopardize Keystone."

He stood upright and glared at Wyatt and Shepherd. "I thought you were leaders and not followers. I've always been fair to each of you, and I care for you as one of my own. There are moments when you have to make quick decisions, and I try to support you where I can and teach you the right way. Raven killing the Mage was a decision forced upon her by circumstance, and for that reason, I had to accept it, just as I've accepted many of your actions. But this… this was premeditated," he said, turning on his heel to face me. "It is not easy to have so many lives dependent on me, and now one is lost. If you deceived me once, you'll do it again and again. I gave you a probationary period as a second opportunity to prove to me that you were willing to change, but you did not. For that reason, you must leave."

I waited for the punch line that never came.

"But nothing happened. We just confronted him."

"Nyet. You turned my men against me and devised a plan without my knowledge. How is that nothing?"

"If I hadn't done it, you would have never known what happened to Christian. You would have just assumed he took off and left Keystone. Darius should know I'm watching his every move; sometimes that's enough to make a man play by the rules. He'll be too afraid of getting caught."

Viktor folded his arms, never removing his eyes from mine. "Without a Vampire on site, I cannot scrub your memories of what little you know. I'm certain you won't be waiting voluntarily for that to happen, and I do not wish to hold you by force and hurt you. I will reach out to an associate, and he will complete the task by nightfall."

"Aren't you afraid I'll tell someone your secrets before then?"

"To whom? You do not have friends."

Niko rose to his feet. "You can't do this, Viktor. He'll kill her. She doesn't have protection, and without her memory, she'll be a target."

"She's no longer my responsibility. I have opened my home to her and given her more opportunities than I gave to any one of you. I took a chance because of her uniqueness, but I am not willing to sacrifice this organization or any of your lives for an impetuous rogue. You are all gifted, but when it comes to choosing people for Keystone, I only want those who are willing to die for their brethren, not be the cause of their death."

"Give it time," Niko pleaded.

Viktor shook his head. "We have lost a good man. I'm out of time."

I stood up, the welcome mat having been ripped out from beneath me. "No hard feelings, Viktor. Obviously I wasn't cut out for this kind of work, but just so you know, if you send a Vampire to scrub my memories, don't be surprised if he turns up missing. I don't voluntarily give up anything that's mine."

No one tried to stop me, and while I packed my bag with the things I came with, my only regret was having let Darius walk out of that shop. Killing him could have led to my arrest, but how bad could Breed jail be? At least I'd have a warm bed.

―――

Damn if I didn't cry while Blue was driving me back to the city. I turned my head so she couldn't see the doleful look in my eyes as I watched my future drifting farther away. Life had taught me to be cynical, and even though I'd been skeptical about Keystone from the start, I couldn't deny that I'd become attached to the idea. Gem and Niko had grown on me—a reminder of how much I missed having friends. Even something as simple as sitting at a table filled with laughter and conversation had given me a glimpse of a life I'd never had. Some of them might have thought I had set my sights on living in a big mansion, but I was happy just to have had a bath. Most of all, I was going to miss the view from the rooftop.

Once again, destiny screwed me over.

"Do you have a place to go?" Blue asked.

"There's a diner up the road called Ruby's. That would be great."

After a few more turns, she pulled up to the diner and parked in a fire lane. We watched a young boy standing outside, washing one of the windows with a squeegee.

"Viktor's not a bad guy," she said. "I can't imagine the kind of decisions he has to make and the pressure he feels having our lives in his hands, so I trust his judgment. I'm a Shifter like he is, so maybe I understand his ways a little better. Loyalty is everything to our kind, so we have to respect him as a leader. I haven't gotten to know you very well, but you seem like a strong woman. Maybe too strong an influence."

I gripped the door handle. "Yeah, but what did Viktor say earlier to Wyatt and Shepherd? That he wanted leaders, not followers. Take care, Blue. Maybe we'll run into each other again someday."

"Yes, but you won't remember me. So long, Raven."

A light drizzle fell, but it wasn't the rain that made me cover my head with the hood of my black sweatshirt. I entered the diner and walked to the back, taking a seat in my usual booth. Betty wasn't on duty, so no one asked if I needed anything.

No one fussed.

No one cared.

It made me miss my dad. My real one, not the immortals who'd made me into the monster I'd become. We'd never had the most conventional relationship, but he'd looked out for me. Maybe it was time to pay him a visit. Not to see him; he thought I was dead, so knocking on his door would give him a heart attack. Just to be near him and feel a fleeting sense of comfort. My dad was the umbilical cord that connected me to my past, to the girl I once was.

After my mom died, it was just my dad and me. He taught me how to think for myself. He couldn't afford to buy me things, so instead he gave me advice. I had a good head on my shoulders until high school ended. Then I grew wild, stubborn, and a little resentful when I realized that affluent kids had more advantages in life than I ever would. Unfortunately, I turned that resentment on my father and began distancing myself from him. I didn't let him know it, but I suppose it was one of those awful phases that kids go through, only mine happened a little later than most.

But before all that, I was just a little girl with big dreams. I had a white music box, and when you lifted the lid, a beautiful princess turned in a circle to a whimsical melody. I used to curl up in bed with it and imagine myself becoming her someday. There weren't a lot of kids my age living in the trailer park, so I spent a lot of time alone. It wasn't a deprived childhood by any means. I had a huge imagination, pretending that the trailer was really a secret castle and all the ladybugs were fairies in disguise. My father was the king and protected me from the evils of the world. But once his princess grew up, there was one evil he couldn't save her from. He raised a strong daughter, and maybe that was what got me through living on the streets for the past few years. I imagined myself as a dark queen, vanquishing all the evils from the city.

Sitting in that diner and smelling the food around me wouldn't have been a big deal had Viktor never come along and given me a glimpse of an alternate life. It wasn't the absence of a plate that bothered me anymore, but I missed the companionship of having someone sitting across from me to fill the silence. The Keystone mansion not only offered me solitude, but moments of sanity where just a brief conversation in the courtyard made me feel like a real person—not some low-life rogue who was searching for my next meal and killing immortals so I could feel better about myself. Perhaps the fates were trying to tap me on the shoulder, and I needed to start thinking about doing something else with my life.

Get a job.

Save money.

Buy a house.

Kill the bastard who'd just entered my line of vision.

My breath caught when a man strode in—the jerkface I'd wrestled in the club bathroom. The one Darius referred to as Salvator, his right-hand man. I stared for a frozen moment, wondering if it was a hallucination. Cognito could feel like a small city sometimes, but his timing was impeccable.

He glanced up at the menu. "I'll have the burger and onion rings to go."

While he rattled off how he wanted his burger, I discreetly tucked my hair back and pulled my hood farther down. There weren't many customers, so it was easy to spot his car out the window since it hadn't been there when Blue had circled around the side parking lot to drop me off out front. I'd be willing to bet anything he hadn't locked his doors. Most Breeds didn't.

When he started fiddling with a napkin dispenser on the counter, I quietly got up with my bag and went out the side entrance. I stood by a red car, pretending to search for my keys, but I kept my focus inside the diner. As soon as he sat down on one of the stools, I sprinted across the parking lot to his car. The windows were nice and tinted, so I tested the back door, and like magic, it opened.

I needed to act fast, so I got in and wedged myself behind the driver's seat, flattening my bag against the floorboard on the opposite side so it wouldn't be noticeable. I was a chameleon against the black leather interior. The headrest was pulled up and would allow me access to the back of his neck. I withdrew a push dagger and gripped it in my left hand while holding a longer blade in my right.

It was a good thing I wasn't wearing perfume, because after I'd spent ten minutes in the back of his car, he would have smelled me the moment he opened the door.

Heavy footsteps approached the car, and a sack rustled.

"Don't see me, don't see me," I whispered, gripping my weapons, ready to spring into action.

The car rocked as Salvator sat down and slammed the door. He was munching on something and growling like some kind of starved raccoon.

Knees, don't fail me now, I thought to myself. If he was starting up the car, that meant he might be bending forward. I needed to wait until he was reclined all the way back in case my reflexes weren't fast enough.

The engine purred, and Frank Sinatra crooned about having some woman under his skin.

"You never can win," Salvator sang out of key.

I rose up and circled the dagger around his neck. He made a strangled sound, and the singing died in his throat when I pricked his nape with the smaller push dagger.

"Peekaboo." I exerted pressure on both blades. "I have a little question for you," I said. "Go ahead and swallow those onion rings first before you choke."

I heard a loud gulp as he swallowed what was in his mouth.

"You've got some nerve getting in my car after calling the cops on me," he snarled.

"Did you make any new friends in jail?" I asked, some of his greasy black hair threatening to get in my mouth. "One move and I'll cut your neck two ways. I want to ask you something, and it's in your best interest to answer correctly. Don't bother going on about witnesses; we're in a tinted car and I don't really care. Do you understand?"

"Yeah," he bit out.

"Good. I need to know what happened to a certain Vampire."

I watched in the rearview mirror as he furrowed his brow. "What Vampire?"

Either Salvator was the best liar, or Darius had kept him in the dark.

"The one Darius got rid of. Think carefully before you answer."

I pressed the tip of the stunner into the back of his neck just enough to dull some of his senses and give him a taste of paralysis.

"I don't know what you're talking about," he grunted.

"Then maybe you're not that important in the chain of command."

His eyes flashed up in the rearview mirror. "Fuck you. He tells me everything."

Salvator carried out human murders, so it didn't make sense that Darius would have kept him in the dark and had one of his bumbling guards carry out the task. Either *Salvator* was lying, or Darius was lying.

"Tell me the truth. You have ten seconds to decide your fate. Ten… nine… eight…"

"Fuck, I'm telling you I don't know anything about a Vampire! You're just wasting your time."

"Seven… six…"

"Why don't you call Darius and ask him yourself? One of the other guards might know something."

"Five… four… three…"

"You're just going to have to cut me."

"Two… one. Time's up."

I pressed the push dagger halfway in, and he cried out, "Wait! I know."

I pulled out. "Excuse me? I didn't quite catch that."

A rivulet of blood trickled down the back of his neck, and he winced when the long blade dug into his flesh. "Darius wants me to find some guy who called him out of the blue and said he caught a Vampire driving around in one of our cars with the guard's body in the trunk. Said he'd take care of it if Darius held a favor in his pocket for him to collect on." Salvator tried to calm his panicked breaths. "The Vampire was buried in a cemetery, but that's all I know."

"Which one?"

"I don't know!" he shrieked. "What do you care about a corpse? I didn't have anything to do with it. Darius doesn't like being in anyone's debt, but he had no choice. I've told you everything I know."

Poor Salvator. I almost felt sorry for how easily he caved,

but not sorry enough when I thought about all the humans he'd murdered for money.

"You did real well, Salvator. Take a deep breath and relax. That's good. Lights out."

I drove the push dagger deep, and he slumped over to the passenger side, crushing his burger sack. The stunner had penetrated his spine, but he'd survive. It took a lot more than that to kill a Mage. At least for now he was under my control, so that bought me some time. Since the front windshield didn't have as much tinting as the other windows, I used a sunshade to give us privacy.

A phone peeked out of his back pocket, so I palmed it and stepped out of the car. As I sat on the trunk, a group of teenagers across the street caught my attention. Their boisterous laughs made me wistful, remembering what it was like to be that age when I had all the answers. Monsters didn't exist; life would get better; and someday I would die, so I needed to make every moment count. A cold chill ran down my spine when I realized that some of that humanity was slipping away from me. Was it inevitable with immortality, or was I allowing it to happen?

"Do I know you?" Wyatt said on the line.

"It's Raven."

He snorted. "That's a world record. I didn't think I'd hear from you for at least a hundred years. I thought maybe we'd bump into each other at a rodeo and reminisce over old times when you almost got me fired. Whose phone is this?"

"A man who works for Darius."

"Hmm. Should I ask where this man is?"

My tone became somber. "I just called to let you know that I have information on where Christian's remains are."

"Son of a ghost."

Chapter 17

TWO NIGHTS EARLIER

Christian cursed himself for having cozied up with Raven, imparting words of wisdom so she'd see the error of her ways. That lunatic wouldn't know what to do with a nugget of knowledge if it hit her in the noggin.

Still. A small part of him wanted to connect with her on some level, and he didn't know why. She had a way of looking at him with her mismatched eyes that made his heart quicken. He'd never seen eyes so enchanting. Maybe that was why he'd slipped out of his bedroom when she rolled over in his bed to face him. Christian had to remind himself that this woman couldn't be trusted, and if made a permanent member, he was going to be expected to put his life in her hands.

After leaving his bedroom, he descended the stairs to the second floor, inviting Viktor into one of the soundproof rooms. It was a quaint sitting room—absent of windows, a fireplace, or even a couch. It looked more like a medieval chamber used to hold hostages, except for the two gold chairs and resplendent white carpet with intricate details woven into the fabric.

Viktor struck a match and lit one of the lanterns on the table between two chairs.

"Are you angry?" Christian asked, pulling a clean shirt over his head while Viktor took a seat.

"Come sit, Christian. I cannot discuss anything when you're hovering."

Christian reluctantly strode across the room and took the opposite chair, his legs straight and ankles crossed. "She's a murderer. What other skills can she offer to Keystone? You can't just choose someone because they know how to kill a man."

The soft light flickered in Viktor's grey eyes, and he gave Christian a pensive look. "Do you think I make decisions in haste? She does not kill indiscriminately, and the evaluation period allows me to get a feel for her talents. I've never seen anyone like her before. She has potential. Raven is not as seasoned as the rest of you, but if I do not give her this opportunity, she may one day become the very person we end up hunting. Which side would you rather see her on?"

"You can't save them all."

"Nyet. But I was your last resort. You were each at a crossroads. What will hold someone to me if they have better options? I'm here to give each of you an opportunity to make a difference, and that means I need to be your only option. What we do is not glorious, and it requires a certain kind of… finesse that not everyone has."

Christian tapped his fingers on the armrest. "Like turning someone's car into a carnival of blood?"

"I need more men who have fighting skills, and you know it. I cannot continue putting Gem and Wyatt in dangerous situations. They were chosen for different reasons. And while Claude can fight, he's my tracker and inside man." Viktor wagged his finger. "You have expressed a desire to work alone, but you cannot be treated specially in a group of equals. You must learn to follow the same rules, and that means taking on a partner. It will do you more good than you realize. Vampires are loners by nature; I understand this, and you don't strike me as a man who has ever trusted anyone with his life. But it's time for you to step outside that comfortable place that limits your potential. I will not change my mind."

Christian shifted in his chair, unsettled by Viktor's resolve. In a perfect world, Viktor would skip the rules and pair her up with the next member of Keystone—*if* someone new joined their group. Viktor had never expressed how many people he wanted in Keystone, but Christian had secretly hoped that he'd be the last.

Christian tilted his head to the side, searching for the right words to reason with him. "She's a crossbreed. That's something you should consider before making a decision. You don't know what she's capable of because there's never been anyone like her. You're only seeing one side of the coin. She's dangerous and unpredictable."

"As are all of you."

"Aye, but we are not that to each other. She's been on her own too long without any guidance. If she's never had a positive influence in her life, she may be too far gone to save. Is it worth jeopardizing our lives for a rogue?"

Viktor laced his fingers together. "Tell me what this is really about, Christian. You are not a man who backs away from a challenge. Is it because she's a woman? Is it because she's a *beautiful* woman, and you somehow find that a distraction? What is the root of your fear? We are not angels."

Christian pinched at the whiskers of his short beard, attempting to feign indifference. Viktor's remark had unexpectedly struck a nerve. Misplaced affections weakened a man. And what was the point of partnering with a fetching woman he couldn't bed?

Torture, that's what.

He'd tried to ignore her cool confidence and dry humor that was much like his own, but the moment he spotted her vulnerable side, he wanted no part of it. Partners formed close relationships, even if they disliked each other. The last thing he needed was to grow attached to her, or even worse, watch her destroy everything they had built. Either way, this partnership had to end.

For feck's sake, he'd tucked her into his bed.

Viktor tapped his foot on the floor. "Do you have nothing to say?"

"I need to break away from here for a while and get my head together."

Viktor rose to his feet. "Nyet. I have a blood-soaked car in my driveway with a body in the trunk. No cleaner is going to touch that without reporting it to the higher authority. I do not trust those men with this much evidence. Cleaning a little blood off the street? Fine. That is not something they can report with much merit. I need you to take care of this for me."

Christian rubbed his face, realizing he couldn't hang Viktor out to dry. He rose to his feet and rocked on his heels. "Aye, I'll finish this job as you asked. But after that, I'm taking a holiday to think about what I want to do. If I stay here another night in my current state, I might leave for good."

Viktor sighed harshly, the lines in his face etched deep. "Very well. If you need to go away and think, I respect that. We'll work something out."

They didn't speak another word, and Christian left the house in the Mage's car. He wiped down the seat before getting in so he wouldn't have to sit in a pool of sticky blood.

Thank Jaysus they were leather seats.

"Raven Black. What kind of name is that?" he mused.

She kept herself guarded when it came to her creation, but without knowing those details, it left Christian uncertain about her stability. Who was her maker? Where was he now? Maybe she murdered them all and her heart was just as black as her name. After all, what kind of Vampire would abandon his youngling? Raven despised Vampires, and it wouldn't have offended him so much had she not been half.

Christian loved what he was. Eating was optional; blood wasn't necessary to sustain life, but it filled them with power and knowledge; and he was blessed with immortality. He was stronger, had exceptional hearing, and especially didn't mind how most Breeds avoided him. Had his maker not granted him this life, he'd be rotting away in a pine box alongside his brothers.

Although truth be told, Christian had no idea where his brothers had been laid to rest. His father and younger sister stayed behind in Ireland while the rest of them moved on in search of a better life. After many hardships, the brothers parted ways in pursuit of different opportunities. Christian remained behind in the big city, reduced to picking pockets because no one would hire the Irish. When he was around thirty-one, he met a Vampire who had offered him the unexpected opportunity of a better life. In those days, makers didn't need to obtain permission. Christian accepted without hesitation. His brothers would have said he was in league with the devil, but what else did he have going for him?

As the years went by, muddy roads and horse-drawn carriages transformed into paved streets and motorcars. As the cities became more populated, they came alive at night—more anonymous. Anyone could blend in.

Even a Vampire.

Christian wondered what his maker would think of him driving a stolen car with a dead body in the trunk. Not that Ronan was a pious man, but he believed everyone was born with a greater purpose.

"Is this what you have to look forward to?" Christian asked whimsically. He drove the car through the broken gates of the oldest cemetery in the city. "Meet your new partner, Christian. Isn't she a bonnie lass? Nothing to worry about. She's bright, gifted, and a murderous lunatic. You'll be spending the next century cleaning up her messes and dumping bodies. Every time she screws up, you'll have everyone judging you for her actions."

He slowed down, accidentally driving over an old gravestone that looked more like a rock.

"You're a fecking moron if you keep this job," he growled to himself. "She wouldn't bat an eyelash if you turned up missing or were burned at the stake. She'd probably bring the marshmallows. Viktor, you're such an eejit for trusting a woman like that."

When he reached a private mausoleum in the oldest part of the cemetery, he threw the car into park and shut off the engine. Christian knew this spot well. He'd not only filled some of these graves with notorious killers, but it was a peaceful place to come and think. Staring at the crypts and gravestones reminded him that he needed to do something valuable with his time. They say the dead don't speak, but they do if you listen hard enough.

Just ask Wyatt.

Christian popped the trunk and got out. An owl hooted in the distance, and animals scurried about in the underbrush of the surrounding woods. The smell of moss, decomposing leaves, and wet earth hung heavy in the air. He rubbed his nose with the sleeve of his shirt, squeezing his eyes shut and wishing for a miracle. Keystone was an exceptional group, and he'd had high hopes for a lasting career.

Now he wasn't so sure.

Christian suddenly lurched forward, pain lancing through his chest. Within seconds, his muscles seized from the unmistakable power of impalement wood. A black cloth covered his head before he slid off the trunk and fell onto his back, the wood pushing through the front of his chest.

Someone had managed to creep up on him, but he hadn't heard the sound of human heartbeats to tip him off. His attacker tightened the cloth on his head by wrapping something around his neck, likely a rope or cord.

Fecking hell!

He listened to their footsteps moving toward the mausoleum up ahead. The door opened, and then a stone slab made a gritty sound as it moved. The person returned and lifted Christian with ease. Whoever it was didn't seem particularly muscular, but they were certainly strong enough to move swiftly without a single muscle trembling. Unless she was flat chested, he had ruled out a woman.

Christian was immobile but still able to feel himself being placed inside a coffin with the dearly departed lying next to him. He waited for the man to speak but heard nothing.

That unnerved him more than anything. Men had a tendency to make a grand speech before committing murder or an act of revenge. Did he know this guy? God knows Christian had pissed off enough men in his time.

So it left him bemused when they laid him inside a crypt with a skeleton and covered it with the stone lid.

Then the door to the small mausoleum closed.

And a car drove away.

Christian was too stunned to even curse in his head. Whoever this shitebag was, he was a clever one. Christian cleared his mind, waiting for the car's return. After an hour, the permanence of his entombment became a grim reality.

Trapped in a tomb with Martha Cleavy.

He'd specifically chosen this grave to bury the body in because he thought Martha could use some company. This dried-up husk of a woman had once told Christian that he'd never meet a woman he deserved, that all he was good for was cleaning the horseshit from her boots. That was before he'd become a Vampire, back when he was just a young man trying to earn a few coins to better his life. Martha took pity and hired him to clean the muck and filth off her boots and horse's hooves. He soon realized that this spinster had an ulterior motive—to seduce him, promising a higher position in her house if he'd only put forth a little "appreciation" for her kindness.

That was what Martha did. She found strapping young men who were destitute—men who were desperate enough to prostitute themselves to a plain woman with a stern face. And from what he'd heard, none of it involved the act of sex. Perhaps it did for some, but he suspected she wanted to avoid the risk of pregnancy or disease. One man told him that Martha had asked him to scrub her bedroom floor in the nude, while another mentioned something about kissing her fanny whenever she walked by him and lifted the front of her skirt. And in Irish speak, a woman's fanny isn't her bum. Before anyone in good society would catch on, she'd quickly discard those men like yesterday's trash.

After he turned her down with an insult that she had a horse's fanny, Martha did everything in her power to ensure that no one else in the community hired him for any odd jobs. Christian went two weeks without food, eating stale bread that a baker had tossed out for the dogs. That was when he resorted to a life of crime.

Martha said with absolute confidence that he would eventually come to his senses and lie with her, to which Christian replied, "Over my rotting corpse."

Little had he known it would be hers.

Fecking Martha.

Even her coffin still bore the faint smell of her cheap perfume.

If he could move, he would have rolled his eyes in the back of his head.

Viktor wasn't going to call in a search party. Christian had led him to believe that he might not be returning as a member of Keystone, and Viktor wasn't the sort of man who would browbeat him into staying. Everyone had the option to leave, but it came at a price. Viktor would just assume that Christian had fled to avoid having his memory scrubbed of everything he knew about Keystone.

Instead, he was going to spend an eternity entombed alive. And in an almost comical way, all this was his fault. When they'd been on assignment at the bar and Raven was luring the Mage away, Christian had set her up. He'd wanted to test her quick thinking by stalling his appearance. After all, real life always came with a monkey wrench or two. What would she do without all the structure and safety nets, forced to make her own decisions?

And just as he'd sought to prove, his plans didn't go accordingly. When he'd tuned in to their conversation in the car and realized that the Mage was about to speed away, Christian launched to his feet to go after them. He might have made it in time had something not caused him to turn in the other direction.

Someone, to be exact.

Prior to joining Keystone, Christian had severed ties with old acquaintances. Nothing personal, but he'd needed to move on with his life, and that meant creating distance. He moved to an older section of the city and avoided his usual stomping grounds, but occasionally he'd glimpse a familiar face and dodge out of view. It wasn't difficult to keep a low profile in a big city like Cognito, but when he saw the familiar Chitah taking a seat near the hall, he slipped out the front door instead of the back.

Those few seconds had cost him precious time. When he reached the back of the building, Raven was gone. He turned in a circle, sharpening his Vampire hearing until he picked up her shouting. That was when he hopped on his bike and weaved through traffic, barely able to hold on to their dialogue long enough to sense which direction they were moving. It required concentration to block out the sound of his motor and all the cars around them, but once he reached a long stretch of road with few turnoffs, it was just a matter of catching up with them.

Christian had never believed in karma, but lying in the casket with old Martha Cleavy was giving him second thoughts about divine justice.

Chapter 18

WHEN I HUNG UP WITH Wyatt after telling him the news about Christian, I figured Viktor would reprimand him for speaking to me. It wasn't much information to go on. After all, there were dozens of cemeteries in Cognito, and it would be like searching for the proverbial needle in a haystack. Wyatt was going to relay the news to Viktor and leave it up to him.

I didn't think anything would come of it, so I started my own search. After all, I was partly the reason he was in the cemetery to begin with. I left the address with Wyatt in case one of them wanted to help out, but they probably had bigger concerns on their plate.

I could have just dumped Salvator in a junkyard and stayed out of it, and that might have been the smarter thing to do since Viktor now knew my location and would probably send a Vampire to scrub my memories, but I couldn't get Christian's last words about knowing myself out of my head. Keystone deserved to lay their man to rest in a dignified way, and turning my back was the wrong thing to do.

Two hours after driving Salvator's car to the cemetery, I'd only come across eight fresh graves. I pressed my ear to the earth, wondering if he might be down there. But I didn't have a shovel, it was daylight, and the local news would eat up a story like that. I stumbled upon a few structures that looked like community mailboxes, but instead of parcels, there were ashes behind each of the plaques. Since many families watched the caskets being lowered, I suspected that anyone hiding a body might have dug their own makeshift grave with no headstone, so I kept my eyes alert.

A vehicle rolled in my direction through the thinning fog. Keystone operated a black cargo van, used for transporting the entire group at one time. When it stopped, the rear doors popped open and a few familiar people poured out. I was surprised to see that everyone had come.

"Dead end," Wyatt said, approaching me. "Literally."

Gem elbowed him, and we closed the distance between us.

"There are three fresh graves that way," I said, pointing over my shoulder.

She sighed and spoke solemnly. "We searched there already. Wyatt can't locate dead bodies unless there's a ghost or other special circumstances. If Christian died angry, Wyatt thinks he might be lingering around. But chances are he's not, so we're looking for something else—like a fresh grave with no stone or something out of the ordinary. Claude can't pick up a Vampire's scent, and we can't detect his energy," she said, referring to herself and Niko. "It's a crapshoot."

Viktor remained behind the wheel, watching me with somber eyes but not getting out. Shepherd fell back a bit from the group, standing out among our foggy surroundings in a black leather jacket. Between the tall Chitah, Gem in her platform sneakers, Niko in all black, and Wyatt's slacker attitude, they looked like a group of misfit action heroes.

"What do you plan on doing?" I asked.

Shepherd folded his arms, his gaze fixed on something in the distance. "We don't leave a man behind."

We searched two more graveyards in the area before Wyatt suggested we try an old one on the outskirts of town. Breed had their own cemeteries, but chances were that they planted Christian in a human one. Less risk of a nosy immortal wondering what they were up to. Humans—even in the face of a crime unfolding before them—have a tendency to mind their own business.

We reached the cemetery by evening, and I turned on the high beams, unable to make out the unpaved road. The headstones were old—some of them near the entrance looked more like rocks than grave markers. We parked our cars halfway up the road, deciding to spread out.

"I didn't know places like this existed," I said, shivering when an owl hooted.

Wyatt held his flashlight against his temple and shone it on me. "It's a private cemetery—they don't bury people here anymore. Maybe we weren't looking in the right graveyards. If you wanted to hide a body, would you do it in a place with a lot of foot traffic and security guards?"

"Good point. What are all those buildings?"

"Mausoleums. People buried whole families in them, sealed up in the walls. They're different from place to place. Some are crypts that go partially underground, others are open to the public and look more like a post office." He approached one of the stone coffins and slapped his hand against it. "They don't bury people this way anymore—except for places that flood—because stone cracks. Not to mention all the vandalism. Plus I don't think humans like visual reminders that they're going to die. Most human cemeteries don't even like raised headstones anymore. They look more like a golf course. It offends the dead."

Everyone branched off, and I took a slow stroll with Wyatt between two rows of grandiose headstones.

"It doesn't bother you to be here?" I asked. "I thought all the spooks liked to chase you down."

"Just the freshies. Old specters do their own thing." He shone a light on a marble headstone. "See the date? Eighteen hundreds. Most of these folks have moved on to greener pastures. It's the newer cemeteries I don't like. There were a few at that first place who were eyeballing me."

I snorted. "Can they tell what you are?"

"Not unless I look at them." He lowered his voice to a whisper. "I try not to look at them."

"How close do you have to be to a Vampire to sense them?"

He shrugged. "It depends. The more obstacles between us, the harder it can be. When they're dead like Christian, I definitely can't sense them."

I turned around when I heard a thud—the last thing you want to hear in a quiet cemetery. Niko had tripped over a broken headstone. Blue stepped over a rotting branch and locked her arm in his, guiding the way, her flashlight creating a solid beam through the thin veil of fog. Dead branches littered the grounds, along with leaves, rocks, and holes.

Which got me to thinking. "Did you notice something at the front entrance?"

Wyatt's eyes rounded, and he turned in a circle.

"I'm not talking about ghosts. I didn't think twice about it until you just mentioned that people don't visit here. There were fresh tire marks on the road. It looked like they ran over one of the grave markers near the front gate."

Wyatt swung his light onto the road, and we hurried toward it.

I knelt down and touched the grooves in the soft dirt, which was still damp from the last rain. "These tire marks are recent. The rain and wind would have erased them if they were older than today."

"Holy Toledo. You're like the Breed version of Nancy Drew." He stuck two fingers in his mouth and whistled.

Everyone hustled back over, Viktor with his brows drawn together.

The excitement wore away from Wyatt's face, and he aimed his flashlight at the road. "Fresh tracks. We think it might be something."

We followed the tracks up a gradual incline that led to the back of the cemetery. A part of me dreaded finding Christian and seeing everyone's reaction. Would they cry for him, or was this just a professional relationship? Gem might have warned me about him, but she couldn't mask the obvious remorse she carried in her expression.

The tracks stopped, and it looked as if the car had moved several times to turn around. The right side of the road had nothing but old markers and rocks, and throughout the center of the cemetery were stone coffins and statues that littered the landscape. Straight ahead were rows of the stone houses that Wyatt called mausoleums.

Claude's nostrils flared—he appeared to be searching for a scent. "I can't tell. It's been too long."

Shepherd had his hands outstretched.

"What's he doing?" I whispered to Wyatt.

"Searching for emotional imprints."

I was staring at the ground, pacing in a circle, when I noticed impressions that might have been… bare feet? They led me to a modest structure made of stone with the word CLEAVY in bold letters above the door. Dead vines twisted around the building as if they had attempted in vain to strangle the life out of it. I tried pushing and pulling on the door.

"Find something?" Blue asked, coming up behind me.

I pointed at a shiny new lock. "You wouldn't happen to have any bolt cutters, would you?"

Blue reached in her pockets and fished out a couple of pins.

Wyatt sidled up beside me. "She's pretty nifty with picking locks."

After a long minute, Blue tossed the lock to the ground and tried to push open the door, but it was too heavy. Claude leaned his body against it and shouldered it open.

The room smelled musty, and I wrinkled my nose as we aimed our lights inside.

"What's all that?" I asked, noticing a pile of junk in the corner.

Wyatt entered and knelt down, wiping away some of the cobwebs. "Looks like someone wanted to take their silver to the afterlife."

A stone coffin claimed the center of the room, and what I noticed immediately were the fresh clumps of dirt on the floor.

Everyone backed up against the walls when Viktor came in.

He stepped up to the coffin and bowed his head respectfully. Butterflies circled in my stomach.

Viktor touched the coffin with his fingertips. "Christian did not deserve such a vulgar disposal. Death is inevitable for us all, even the immortals. But it should mean something. Let us give him a proper burial."

Wyatt's boots scraped against the dirty floor as he walked to the edge of the coffin, his head cocked to the side. "Hurry and open it up."

Shepherd and Claude gripped opposite ends, pushing with all their might to spin the lid open. Gem averted her eyes, and Wyatt leaned in like a little kid about to watch a firecracker explode.

"Someone was pissed," Shepherd muttered, looking at his palms.

Wyatt shone his light inside. "So we meet again. Déjà vu."

It seemed like a strange thing to say, but then again, Wyatt wasn't exactly the most normal guy I'd ever met. He untied the cloth wrapped around the corpse's head. When he snapped it away, glassy eyes stared up at us. Christian's face didn't look pallid and peaceful like most dead people, but eerily startled.

I expected a flood of tears, but instead, everyone behaved strangely.

"Move away," Shepherd ordered, reaching into the coffin. "This'll hurt like a bitch."

"What are you doing?" I asked in horror.

When Shepherd yanked his arm back, he was holding an impalement stake in his hand. Not the small ones I'd seen people use, but more like an arrow.

Christian flew up to a sitting position like a scene in a horror movie, his lip curled in a snarl. "Remind me never to do *that* again."

I blinked in surprise. The impalement wood must have missed his heart.

Viktor shouldered Wyatt aside and placed his hands on Christian's shoulders, his lip trembling. He waited a beat before finally speaking. "You need a shower."

Gem and Blue laughed, relief swimming in their eyes. The

tension in the room lifted, and the air circulated as everyone began to breathe easy.

Shepherd peered into the coffin. "Who's your girlfriend?"

A skull rolled to the side, and Christian shuddered. Without answering, he gripped the edge of the coffin and climbed out, stumbling when his feet touched the ground.

Gem reached out to help. "We're so glad you're not dead."

"You and me both," he murmured, dusting off his pants.

She worried her lip. "I'd hug you, but you have dead stuff all over you. Rain check." She skipped out the door, Claude shadowing behind her.

Christian lowered his voice and nodded at Wyatt. "I owe you one."

Wyatt shook his head. "Not this time. You can thank your ex-partner over there. After we kicked her out, she squeezed information from one of Darius's men. Then she spotted tire tracks on the road before anyone else. She's a keeper if you ask me," he said, giving Viktor a cursory glance as he walked out of the room with a brisk step, hands in his pockets.

Christian lowered his eyes, addressing those around him. "Can I have a moment?"

I turned to leave when he snapped my collar back.

"Not so fast."

When everyone had moved out of sight, I turned around to face Christian, my Vampire eyes adjusting to the darkness. His unblinking gaze unnerved me, so I stepped aside and put my back to the wall.

"Ex-partner, Wyatt says. Does that mean Viktor tossed you out?"

"Yep. Your dreams have come true."

Christian flattened his palm on the wall above my head, glaring down at me with obsidian eyes. His tousled hair was full of dust, and some of the particles floated around him. "So you did all this to get back in his good graces. Admirable."

"I don't want back in."

He tilted his head to the side, brows drawing together. "Are you langered? If he didn't trust you before, he certainly does now—regardless of your motives. Why would you turn him down?"

The way Christian looked at me gave me butterflies, and I couldn't tell if it was fear or something else. Maybe that was why I had reservations about joining up with Keystone. The second I saw Christian's body lying next to a skeleton, my heart squeezed.

Just a little bit.

I barely knew him, but I felt so responsible for what had happened.

He lifted the ends of my hair. "You cut it."

"Claude did. It's a long story."

Christian leaned in so close that I felt his breath on my cheek. He looked at me differently than he had before—touched me differently. Not as if he were playing with his food or amusing himself, but as if he were gazing upon something intriguing. His fingers grazed the side of my jaw, and my knees wobbled.

Just a little bit.

I scarcely breathed. "Why are you looking at me like that?"

"I'm curious about your motives."

"Even after I led your team here?"

He tilted his head. "Aye. Your decisions aren't pure. You might be fooling them, but you don't fool me."

"Saving your life isn't enough?" I'd met some imperious Vampires in my time, but this one took the cake.

"You did what you needed to do to get this job, no matter what you're telling yourself. Maybe I need a little reassurance that our partnership would supersede anything else, and that your actions tonight weren't just a stepping-stone to get on Viktor's good side. If *killing* me would have made Viktor happy, would you have shown up a few hours earlier with a can of gasoline and a match?"

Despite the animosity dripping from his tongue, the sensual caress of his fingers never stopped. Even without my looking into his dark Vampire eyes, he had me in his thrall. Maybe the truth kept my feet cemented in place. I wanted to make things right with Viktor, but it wasn't to get back into Keystone.

Or was it?

"I don't care if you trust me," I finally said.

"A man can't trust anyone, not even himself. But seeing as you've saved me from spending eternity with Martha, maybe I owe you a favor."

"Who's Martha?"

"I don't know what's transpired since yesterday, but I'm in your debt once over. If Viktor brings you back into the fold, don't ask me to trust you. My debt won't be paid in the form of loyalty; that's not something I'll do."

Debts in the Breed world were the most valuable asset a man could have. "You can't pick and choose what I ask."

He gave a mirthless smile, and his fangs descended. "Tread carefully. I'll pay my debt when you ask, and then we'll be square."

"You're nothing but an arrogant, poorly dressed, egotistical, sadistic Vamp who can't play nice in the sandbox. Did I step on your pride tonight? It's not my fault that you let your guard down and someone put you in that coffin. Maybe if you'd had a partner on the job with you, that wouldn't have happened. You can't even do your own laundry."

Christian's fangs retracted, and a slow chuckle settled in the back of his throat. He tilted my chin up until our eyes met. "Has anyone ever told you how fetching you are?"

"Oh, *Christian*," Wyatt sang from outside.

I weaved out of his clutches. "You smell like the dead."

He dusted off his clothes and strode outside. "So where's the little numpty who works for Darius? The one you squeezed for information."

"In the trunk of my car."

He pinched his beard, giving the mausoleum a thoughtful glance. "I think I have just the spot to put him. If the bastard who staked me returns, he'll be in for a surprise." Christian cupped his hand around his mouth, his voice loud and sonorous when he yelled, "Feck you, Martha Cleavy!"

"Shut the hell up," Wyatt snapped, jogging back down the hill. "Don't piss off the dead!"

I glanced up at Christian. "Did you see the guy who staked you?"

His jaw clenched, making his cheekbones appear taut. "No."

"Whoever it was knew Darius, but Darius didn't know him. At least, that's what Salvator said. The question is: did this guy know you, or was he just seizing an opportunity to get a favor out of Darius?"

"Hard to say. Men will do most anything to earn a favor. That might explain why he didn't say a word to me, unless the gobshite was a mute."

We reached the bottom of the incline to find Claude leaning over the trunk of Salvator's sedan.

"Look what we found," Claude said.

Christian clapped his hand on Claude's shoulder. "I've devised a plan for our hostage."

"Good. Because I don't like the scent he's putting out."

Chitahs had four canines—two on the top and two on the bottom. When provoked, the teeth slid into view, and a Chitah's fangs were deadly weapons against a Mage. They could tear flesh, but they also delivered toxic venom that could paralyze or kill a Mage, depending on how many teeth punctured the skin.

He peeled back his lips, tapping his hand on the trunk. Seeing those fangs gave me pause, and I took a step back.

Ahead of the car, the Keystone van sped off, leaving deep tire marks in the dirt.

"Where are they going?" I asked.

Claude stood up and ruffled his hair. "To wait for us at the club. Viktor wants to celebrate."

"Who's us?"

"You, me, and the witches three. I'm guessing he has something to discuss with you."

I arched my brows with a look of skepticism. "I thought he didn't want everyone to be seen together?"

"The only people who know we're connected—aside from trusted friends—are dead anyhow. Viktor's version of a party always involves business, and it sounds like he has a few ideas about what we're going to do about Darius."

I patted Christian's shoulder. "Well, with that new cologne you're wearing, if you go missing again, shouldn't be a problem tracking you down."

Chapter 19

Before leaving the cemetery, Christian placed Salvator in the stone coffin and closed the lid, certain that someone would discover him.

Eventually.

Christian had a dark sense of humor, but our dead jokes were clearly starting to penetrate his thick skin.

"You're a morose bunch," he finally said to Claude and me. "If the stench offends you, then we're going back home so I can shower."

"Everyone's waiting for us, and we're already late," Claude argued, his voice low so the cabdriver wouldn't hear. "It took an hour just to dump the car."

I suggested a truck stop by the highway that I'd frequented a time or two—one with showers in the bathroom. It was only a few blocks away from the club, so we paid the cabbie and got out.

"You want me to strip naked and wet my body down... in *there?*" Christian asked, pointing at the dilapidated porch where five truck drivers were chowing down on burgers.

I patted his shoulder. "Welcome to my world. They also sell T-shirts, and if you're lucky, you might find some pants. Have fun, and don't drop the soap."

Claude and I waited outside, laughing at the idea of a Vampire showering in a truck stop. Sometimes those doors didn't come with locks, and they definitely didn't have doors on the open showers.

When he returned all squeaky clean, it was hard to find something to tease him about. He'd groomed his hair back, and the grey V-neck T-shirt was a size too small, clinging to his wet body, and Christian didn't have an ounce of fat on him. I was used to seeing his hair disheveled. The way it looked now, it made him look almost debonair, and I wasn't sure how it was possible for hair to have that kind of power.

"Those aren't your jeans," I said, glancing down at the dark denims that fit his ass better than I should have noticed.

He gave me a dark smile. "I charmed a man who looked my size."

"You stole another man's pants?" I laughed, picking up stride. "You have no idea where those pants have been."

"I'm sure wherever they've been, it's a sight better than where mine spent the past twenty-four hours."

A damp chill hung in the air, and while there wasn't any fog, there were halos around the yellow lampposts along the street. We reached a Breed club called Flavors, and I glanced up at the sign. All the letters were green except for the *L*.

"I've never been here before." I warily searched the crowd inside. There were too many unfamiliar faces.

Breed faces.

I didn't spend a lot of time hanging out in Breed establishments unless I was looking for my next target or trying to hustle a meal. Humans didn't put up with that kind of thing; you couldn't just walk up to a table, sit down, and start up a conversation without them calling the manager. I preferred bars since they were open to the public, and that meant humans were allowed. Of course, in the Breed district the regulars always found a way to bully the humans out of there so they'd never return. Most clubs were exclusively Breed since they had the option to be a private establishment, and the doormen kept everyone out except for those on the guest list.

Only there *was* no guest list. It was just a legitimate reason to keep the humans standing in line.

Front and center was an oval-shaped bar, colorfully lit and busy with patrons. Music was playing, but not obnoxiously loud. Each side of the room had seating areas with boxy modern chairs that could fit two. They were arranged in groups of four surrounding a black table, and numerous pillars and short walls broke up the openness. The walls had colorful accent lights, and nothing about this place was uninteresting. I'd never been to Vegas, but this was how I'd imagined it.

Immortal roulette, anyone?

A crowd gathered near one of the bartenders, who tossed a bottle in the air and caught it behind his back. A few people erupted in applause, and he theatrically filled a row of shot glasses with a bright green liquid. We headed toward the rear of the club, and I made a quick scan of the place. The hall in the center appeared to lead to the restrooms, but Claude veered left through an open doorway that led to a game room.

I spotted a group of familiar faces near a dartboard on the far left wall.

"Someone looks spiffy," Wyatt said with a snort, noticing Christian's uncharacteristic attire. "All things considered."

Christian joined the group up ahead.

I sat down at a square table, Gem on my right. "Niko's playing darts?"

She glanced over at him, her radiant smile being the true gem about her features. "Just wait until you see him in action. Watch this."

Niko drew back his arm, his left hand extended in front of him. With a clean toss, the dart sailed through the air and struck the bull's-eye.

Shepherd slammed his fist on the table, tipping over a beer bottle. A cigarette was dangling from his mouth, and he looked like he wanted to beat someone senseless as he dug some bills out of his wallet.

"Pay up, buttercup," Wyatt said, collecting the money.

I gripped Gem's wrist. "How did he do that?"

She scooted her chair closer. "Your guess is as good as mine. Shepherd always bets against him. He thinks the odds are in his favor that Niko will eventually miss, but he never does. I never get tired of watching him do it." Her eyes sparkled with admiration when Niko turned his attention our way.

"Is that a can of apple juice?" I asked, pointing at her beverage.

She lifted it with two fingers and swished it. "I don't drink alcohol. Can I just say for the record that what you did back at the cemetery was epic?"

I peered over her shoulder to where Viktor was sitting. He clinked his glass against Christian's, and they fell into casual conversation.

Niko joined us, running his hands along the table until he reached the chair to my left. I noticed he had a few thin braids mixed into his hair.

"Be right back," Gem said. "I promised someone a hug."

She tiptoed behind Christian and wrapped her arms around him from behind. It amused me that Gem went through the motions of sneaking up on a Vampire. Christian patted her hand and quickly shrank out of her embrace. Undeterred, the violet-haired pixie took a seat next to Blue.

I turned to Niko, twirling a lock of my hair. "How can you tell the difference between men and women? Or can you?"

He rested his forearms on the table, eyes downcast. "Their energy is different. I can't explain it."

"How do you decide which woman you want to hit on if you can't see them and haven't spoken to them?"

Niko sat back in his chair and changed the subject. "You should talk to Viktor while everything's copacetic. He's in good spirits, and we still have a job to complete."

I glanced at Viktor's table and lowered my voice. "Do you know what he'll say?"

"No, but you made a strong impression tonight."

I chuckled and rapped my knuckles against the table. "It's been one hell of a day."

"Invite him to speak with you privately before the moment's lost," Niko suggested. "You seem to be waiting for fate to choose its moment."

Inspired, I stood up and approached Viktor's table. The laughter died down, and Christian half turned, showing his profile as he watched me saunter up next to him. I lifted my chin and ignored the smirk on his face.

"Viktor, do you have a moment to speak privately?"

Never taking his eyes from his drink, he nodded. "Very well."

Hell, that was easier than I thought.

When we reached the doorway to the main room, Viktor rested his hand against my back and led me to the left. "Let's go away from prying ears. Christian has a tendency to eavesdrop. That's why I know when I return to my seat, there will be a fresh glass of vodka waiting for me. Isn't that right, Christian?" He ended with a chuckle.

"Did they name this club after the drinks?"

"It used to be a Sensor club," he said. "Everyone was allowed in, but they were the ones who ran the place. They would spike all the drinks and charge extra for the emotional experience."

"I'm glad I didn't order anything."

We entered a small room, and he closed the door behind him. "Unfortunately, they didn't think it through. What happens when you spike the drinks of hundreds of customers?"

I collapsed in the oversized brown chair. "Lots of fights, I'm guessing."

"Precisely. That is why most clubs no longer spike the drinks unless they're a specialty, and even those are too mild to have any lasting effect. Owners are very particular about the dose and what kind of emotional imprint they're selling." He took a seat in front of me, nothing between us. Viktor waved his hand. "You can speak freely; this room is soundproof."

My stomach knotted when I realized I had to kick off this impromptu meeting. I gathered my thoughts and relaxed my shoulders, hoping he wouldn't think I was a groveling vulture. "With everything that's happened tonight, I thought we could discuss my position with Keystone."

"Fair enough. As it stands, you have no position with Keystone." Viktor stroked his silver-and-grey beard, his rough voice softening around the edges. "I appreciate all that you have done, but I'm sorry. I have not changed my mind."

"Did Christian say something to you? Because—"

"Nyet. He said nothing. I suspect he has acknowledged the debt he owes you for finding him, and that is a valuable reward. However, given the circumstances, I would like to offer you one favor. It cannot be for a position in my house, but if you ever need money or help, you can call on me for that favor."

I swallowed hard in disbelief. "There's nothing I can say to change your mind?"

He pressed his lips together tightly and shook his head.

I stood up quickly before the sting of tears caused me to blink in front of him. My life was spiraling down a long stairwell into the unknown. I'd thought Viktor would be impressed with what I'd done, especially since it was after he'd evicted me.

"I get it," I said, nearing the door. "I just thought it couldn't hurt to ask."

He eased up behind me and patted my shoulder. "I wish you well, Raven Black. It is my desire that we remain allies; I would like to see you stay on the good side of the law. You understand there is nothing personal about my decision. I wanted this to work out, but my team always comes first."

My lip quivered unexpectedly. Luckily, my back was to him, and I left the room and hurried into the bar. Each member of Keystone watched expectantly, and when their eyes darted behind me, they got their answer in Viktor's expression. Even Niko must have sensed a change in the energy swirling around us.

Wyatt escaped to talk to a pretty blonde, and Blue followed Claude into the game room.

I hopped onto the barstool next to Niko. "Well, that was awkward."

"I was certain he would invite you back in. I'm sorry."

"No sweat off my back."

Niko placed his hand over mine, his crystal eyes almost invisible beneath the colored lights. "You needn't lie; I can read your energy."

If that were true, I felt about as naked as a girl could get in front of him. It made me want to shield my light, even though it wouldn't make a difference. I hadn't expected how deeply the rejection would affect me, and it wasn't until then that I realized how much I really wanted to be a part of Keystone.

I put my hands in my lap and pulled the ends of my sleeves down to cover them. "Will you still talk to me, or is that against the rules?"

"Apologies, Raven. I must go."

Niko hopped out of his seat and stalked through the bar so fast that my jaw slackened. It was hard to pretend it didn't hurt, because it did. Maybe I was outgrowing Cognito and needed to find a new place to call home. At least I had money in my pocket.

Which wasn't a whole lot, especially after I'd wasted it on clothes that I'd never see again. The only items in my bag were the ones I'd taken to the mansion in the first place. A girl couldn't exactly lug four trunks of clothes around the city.

Before leaving the club, I needed to find Christian. Viktor was going to have either him or someone else scrub my memory, and the idea terrified me. I didn't trust Vampires, and what if he erased everything? There were too many good memories in my life that I didn't want to risk losing.

Christian was the sort of man who could blend in with a crowd, but not so much tonight with his tight-fitting shirt and jeans. The casual ensemble somehow made his beard and dark eyes stand out all the more. After scanning the bar and finding no sign of him, I searched for someone who might know his whereabouts.

When I rounded the bar, Wyatt bumped into me, beer sloshing out of his glass and onto the floor.

"Where's Christian?" I yelled over the music.

"Room seven," he said, jerking his thumb toward the private rooms.

"How do you know?"

Wyatt licked some of the spilled beer off his hand. "Because that's where he always goes when we come here. Hope we run into each other again, Nancy Drew."

He waggled his eyebrows and rejoined the blonde, whose breasts were battling against a bra that was a size too small.

I entered the private hallways on the right of the restrooms and searched until I found the room. The door wasn't locked, so that meant he wasn't in an important Vampire meeting discussing their superiority over all other Breeds. Christian was probably brooding over the fact that I'd called in the cavalry to save him. Even though I'd done him a good turn, the man probably would have chosen to rot in that tomb for fifty years rather than have everyone on the team see him like that. Sometimes one stupid mistake can make you look like an incompetent fool.

God knows I was feeling some of that myself.

When I opened the door just a crack and peered into the room, I froze like a flower dipped in liquid nitrogen. Christian's shirt hung around his neck like an afterthought, as if he'd attempted to take it off and lost all motivation.

A dark woman beneath him had her skirt pulled over her hips, her body flush against a low bar on the left. She gripped the edge—head turned away from me, *thank God*. An empty bottle of wine lay beside her, precariously close to the edge.

Christian had shucked off his jeans below the waist, just low enough for him to get down to business. His right palm was flat against her back, and the other rested on the bar.

She moaned, gasped, and he kept a steady and controlled rhythm. His body was magnificent—I'd imagined him gaunt and full of warts, because Vampires shouldn't be attractive. They should be dastardly creatures who are pallid and bony, like I'd seen in all the movies. I stared at the rogue whiskers that grew along his jaw, wondering what it would feel like to have them scratching against my skin. His rigid stance and slow movement accentuated his muscles, tightening and contracting with every thrust of his hips. I glimpsed enough of him that it made me swallow, and he suddenly covered her with his body, resting his forearms on the bar.

His pace quickened, and my eyes skated down to admire the profile of his ass. A coil of need tightened within me, and I found myself unable to control the rapid pace of my heart. Christian was a canvas of slender muscle all the way to his strong hands. His hair was no longer neatly groomed but disheveled from a woman's touch.

The fact that he was roguishly handsome made me hate him even more.

"Do you like watching, lass?" he asked in a growly voice, his head turned away.

I wasn't oblivious to the fact that he knew someone had walked in on him, but I was curious how he knew it was me.

Christian turned his head, and I quickly looked away before he could charm me into doing something I'd later regret. He said nothing, and his gaze nailed me to the floor as his body responded to someone watching him, his rhythm becoming more frenetic. The girl beneath him cried out, and for just a brief second, I imagined myself changing places with her.

It seemed like ages since a man had made me feel that way. I shifted my thoughts to distract myself from thinking about Christian in a sexual way. Cleaning a toilet, the smell of sauerkraut, men in lederhosen…

"You got what you wanted, Christian. You're solo from here on out."

"Not at the moment," he said with a dark smirk.

I turned away, facing the doorjamb, but I could see him out of the corner of my eye through the crack in the door. I lowered my voice to a whisper so the girl wouldn't hear. "I'm calling on that favor tonight."

"Stay there, lass," he murmured to his companion.

Christian appeared at the door, and the crack revealed the left side of his body from his eye to the flap of his unzipped jeans, which he'd attempted to pull up. He smelled like sex. "What's the favor?"

"I don't want Viktor to scrub my memory. If he asks you, tell him you did it. If he asks someone else, then make sure they don't come near me."

"And you trust me with that kind of request?"

"I have no alternative. So?"

"Aye. I'll not take your memories. If this favor will remove me from your debt, I'll make sure of it." He stroked the vein in his neck, and his fangs descended. "Care for a drink, precious?"

I jerked the doorknob and slammed the door.

Why did seeing him with another woman have an effect on me? A sickly mixture of desire and hatred. Christian was worlds apart from the kind of man I found attractive—not only physically, but also personality-wise. The things he said when he opened his mouth should have instantly turned me off, but I found myself even more curious about him. In many ways, he was like every other Vampire I'd staked. But he'd also carried me to his car and covered me with his jacket. Ripping his shirt to make a tourniquet had been necessary to stop the bleeding, but why had he taken the extra measure to keep me warm? He'd also carried me to his bed but made no sexual advances even though I was drenched in blood like some kind of Popsicle stick for Vampires. Maybe I was more curious to know if he really hated me as much as he professed.

The sooner I forgot about him, the better.

I made a beeline for the front exit, passing by a table of men on the right who caught my attention. I was the kind of girl who noticed things—especially someone watching my every move.

It was Cyrus, the man who'd attacked Niko and me in the alley with his goons. He raised his glass and gave me a sardonic smile. When I glowered at him, his table erupted with laughter and he took a slow sip, resuming conversation as if I were inconsequential.

Outside, the streetlight cast a spell on the falling mist, the ethereal glow giving the appearance of a thin veil between two worlds. I pulled my hood over my head and circled around the right side of the building where I'd hidden my duffel bag in the alley. It took more than rejection to kill my spirit, but it was wounded. What did it take to get a leg up in life? The more I thought about my situation, the angrier I got.

"Let me go!" a young man shrieked.

I heard the familiar sound of physical blows—a skirmish up ahead. As I drew closer to the Dumpster, my heart thumped wildly. A bald-headed guy with rolls of skin behind his neck was straddling a man who might have been my age. With immortals, you could never tell. I didn't look over twenty-five, and that was the age I'd forever remain even when I was three thousand. Sometimes you could sense a person's true age in their eyes, and other times it had to do with how submissive and fearful they were in dangerous situations. This kid was new, and I picked up on his Mage energy. He was flaring, perhaps hoping that would lead someone to help him.

All it would do was attract the wrong kind of attention in a dark alley.

Like the juicer on top of him, gripping his hands and drawing out his energy for a high.

The young man's head bobbed in my direction, his eyes glazed over, his nose a bloody mess.

Something came over me like I'd never felt before, even when taking out a lowlife. I felt rage.

Pure. Raw. Rage.

As I stood witness to the evil that thrived in our world, I wanted to kill every corrupt Breed in Cognito.

I wanted to be the Shadow for real.

Chapter 20

As I approached the two men, I drew my push dagger and then sliced it across the juicer's back. "Get up, you filthy bastard."

He roared and launched to his feet, raking me over with his heavy-lidded eyes.

Men like him deserved to die—deserved to suffer as their victims had. Why had I wasted time with only the most nefarious men when corruption came in lesser degrees? These men should be stamped out before they hurt more innocents.

He was high on Mage light, and that made him especially dangerous. I'd never been a fighter; I just knew how to move fast and get the job done. Still, the possibility of failure hovered as I took note of the openness of the alley, shifting my stance in search of a good angle so the Mage wouldn't flash out of my grasp.

Which he did.

The juicer flashed beside me and put me in a headlock, seizing my wrist with his other hand. He squeezed until a sharp pain radiated through the bones in my wrist, but I refused to drop my dagger. I adjusted my grip on the handle and then rotated my hand in a circle until the blade slashed his arm. With nothing to stanch the bleeding, rivulets of blood ran down his arm, causing him to loosen his bruising grip on my wrist. I bit into his other arm and stomped my foot, seeking his instep with the heel of my boot in hopes he'd let go of my neck.

Tiny pinpoints of light flashed around me like pulsing stars.

We struggled, and when my blade pierced through his fleshy

thigh, he let go. I staggered forward—gasping for air—and just as I pivoted on my heel, he struck me in the face with a closed fist.

Blood filled my mouth, the metallic taste triggering my fangs to descend. I quickly concealed them, relying on the element of surprise when he got close enough. All I could do was stand my ground and wait for him to advance.

The juicer paced around me with cool confidence despite a slight limp from the deep puncture wound on his right thigh. He reminded me of a cowboy getting ready for a gunfight.

"You're not exactly seasoned," he said. "Didn't your Creator teach you how to defend yourself?"

I wasn't concealing my energy, so he knew what I was.

Or *thought* he knew.

He flicked a glance at my dagger, and I tightened my grip on the T-shaped handle, keeping it close to my body. When he flashed at me the second time, I spun around—anticipating his attack from behind—and sank the blade into his chest. It wasn't a stunner, so it wouldn't paralyze him, but it would be painful enough to slow him down. Or so I thought. He pulled out the blade and tossed it across the alley, then gripped my neck with both hands.

Two long blades crossed in front of his throat from someone standing behind him—someone I couldn't see.

"Let her go or I'll slice off your head two ways," I heard Niko say.

The man held his hands up, surrendering.

Niko kept his swords crossed, the sharp blades flush against the man's neck. "I'm going to turn around, and you're going to turn with me. Once you're facing the street, I want you to walk. If you look back, I'll show no mercy. Is that clear?"

A small trickle of blood trailed down the man's neck, and his eyes widened in terror. "Yes," he said, his voice quavering.

I glanced behind me at the empty space where the victim had once been. He had already fled the scene. When Niko turned and lowered his weapons, the man slowly staggered out of sight.

Niko's dark hood obscured most of his face, giving him a formidable appearance with his stature, his sharp instruments in hand. He waited quietly while I walked around him and collected my dagger.

"Would you have known if he turned around?" I asked.

He tucked the blades into their scabbards. "I would have seen a flicker in his color, but they never turn around."

"How could you just let him go? He was a juicer. If I hadn't caught him, he might have killed the other guy… and you just let him walk."

"Is there a ladder in sight?"

I searched the shadows. "Behind you."

"Follow me."

We reached the roof, and a damp wind made me shiver. This was my sanctuary. Any high place made it feel as though all the miseries of life were beneath me and the heavens were within reach.

I approached the edge and straddled it, one leg hanging over.

Niko cautiously followed, kicking his foot out until it met with the ledge. He used his hands to feel the width, which was plenty wide enough to sit on. He sat with both feet on the roof and then drew his hood back. The wind picked up his long hair, making him look like a fictional hero in a comic book.

"I let him go because people deserve second chances. The rogues who wander the streets aren't all as far gone as you believe; they've begun their journey down the wrong path, but who knows where they'll end up?"

"He's just going to victimize someone else."

Niko rested his forearms on his knees, his crystal eyes looking ahead. "Can you kill them all? The higher authority won't arrest juicers; there aren't enough prisons to keep them in, so they have to concentrate on capturing the most nefarious men they can. Maybe your Creator didn't explain how it works, but the growing human population keeps us from acquiring new land, and the higher authority doesn't want to use up all that valuable property for prisons. Locking up immortals for what is deemed a lesser crime solves nothing. There are some things we simply have to turn a blind eye to."

"I can't."

"Then stop the crime at hand, but don't become the executioner. Juicing is the equivalent of theft, and if someone broke into your home and stole a television because they have an addiction they can't control, do you feel it's just to take their head?"

"Maybe it depends on how big the TV is."

Niko smiled and drew in a deep breath. "Winter's coming. I can feel it on the tip of my tongue. Maybe you should think about finding a way to earn an honest living. It will put shelter over your head and give you honor."

"And who's going to hire an illegal rogue? Anyhow, the Breed world is for people with specific talents. I don't mean just the business owners and finance guys, but everyone else can use their gifts to barter, train, track, or advise. There's no honor in mopping floors."

He tipped his head to the side. "Have you considered approaching the Mageri and coming clean?"

I huffed out a laugh. "I'm illegal, and I'm also a crossbreed. Accepting me isn't the issue so much as the possibility that they might kill me after discovering what I've been doing. They'll think I'm a liability. I've heard stories about how they've put down new Learners who turned rogue before becoming independent from their Creators. They scare me."

Niko turned to face me, gingerly hanging his left leg over the wall. "Throw yourself upon their mercy. Trust that they will make good judgment and assign a Ghuardian to mentor you."

A Ghuardian was a person assigned by the Mageri to train a Mage who was without a Creator. The name was old and spelled differently since it had a unique meaning among them.

I shook my head. "I can't trust anyone with my life. No one wants me, Niko. Not unless they have a hidden agenda. I can't put my life in the hands of someone who doesn't value it."

"Perhaps you're looking at this all wrong. You're waiting to be chosen by fate, by life, by others." He reached out and touched my forehead, then trailed his fingertips down my brow, nose, mouth, and chin—seeing my face with his hand. "But it's you who needs to do the choosing in life. You won't always make the right choice, but that's how we grow." He lowered his arm and waited for a reply.

"I did. I asked Viktor, and he turned me away."

Niko inclined his head. "You give up so easily. If you want to be a part of Keystone, then you must do something to work *with* us, not against. He's not just looking for raw talent; he needs to know you have integrity. Show him you're a team player who doesn't need to always be the hero."

If anyone else but Niko had said that to me, I might have tossed them off the roof. Instead, I stared down at the streetlights.

He gripped the ledge with his hands. "You tasted a different life with Keystone, and now you want it."

"Yeah," I whispered. No sense in denying the truth.

"It's good to want things. Just make sure you understand what it is you're really seeking. Darius was once a young Mage who was given more land than most young Learners. Maybe he misunderstood the gesture and assumed his Creator was impressed by material things, and that's why he began extorting men for money. After he was stripped of his possessions—including the land—he probably felt like an inferior man. Years later, he can purchase any property he desires except for the one that matters. I'm certain his Creator shamed him for allowing that gift to slip through his irresponsible fingers."

"He's an evil man who kills humans. You can't justify that."

Niko sat up straight, his eyes seeming to look at mine. "That is true. But we're not born evil. His desire to reclaim what he lost blinded him from making the right choices. Sometimes what we desire the most can change who we are, and it's up to us to decide if that's for better or worse. You must learn to control those desires so that you're always on the right path, even if that means never attaining or holding on to the thing you want most."

Niko's words resonated in my head, and I considered the meaning. It was hard to ignore advice from someone as old as him, especially when he had nothing to gain from giving it freely.

"You *told* me to speak to Viktor, but now you're saying I shouldn't want to join Keystone?"

He swung his leg back onto the roof. "What I mean is that you can desire something without letting it be the force of every wrong decision to obtain it. If you want to be a member of Keystone, make sure you want it for the right reasons. But consider what you'll do to reach that goal."

The wind lifted my hair. "Darius has a chance of getting his land back if he keeps doing what he's doing. Even if it's wrong, he's got a better shot than if he'd done nothing at all."

"Look at what kind of man that's made him into. Just imagine an alternate universe where he had made different decisions. Are you so sure he would have never reacquired it? Sometimes we have to relinquish those desires because we attach them to goals of no importance. Ambition can destroy you if you don't learn to balance it with sacrifice." Niko stood up and reached out for my hand. "Now put your big-girl panties on and make a choice."

I reached for his hand, and he helped me up. "Big-girl panties?"

He laughed as we returned to the ladder. "Did I say that right? It can be a struggle to keep up with language when it changes so frequently. English isn't my native tongue, but I've always found it colorful."

"Thanks, Niko. You know... for not giving up on me." I hesitated, still holding his hand. "Can I hug you?"

A blush tinted his brown cheeks.

I let go of his hand. "Sorry, that was a little weird."

"Apologies. I'm usually not asked. People give hugs freely, or haven't you heard?"

When he drew me into his arms, I wanted to weep against his shoulder like a child. It had been so long since anyone had hugged me—not since my father. I stepped back before he sensed my anguish over such a benign gesture.

Niko took my arm and we continued our leisurely stroll toward the ladder. "I was once as lost as you. Sometimes we have to be lost in order to find ourselves."

"Viktor saved you?"

"No. It was long ago. I'll walk you somewhere—a hotel."

I stopped at the ledge. "I'm not leaving just yet. There's something I need to do first."

He bowed. "As you wish."

When I saw he wasn't following, I stopped at the top of the ladder. "You're staying up here? Is it because of those guys in the bar?"

"It's a night of celebration. Let Viktor know where I am. I'll rejoin them when they're ready to leave. It's a nice evening, and I like the idea of sitting under the stars."

I glanced up at heavy clouds aglow from the city lights. "There aren't any stars."

He smiled and looked skyward. "Clouds don't make stars disappear; they only hide the brilliance of their light."

"Stop being so profound. We might have to start writing those in fortune cookies and open up a store."

Niko bowed, amusement dancing in his eyes when he looked up at me. "See you later, alligator."

I smirked. "After a while, crocodile."

I strutted through Flavors with purpose, grateful that Niko had shown up when he had. He didn't just save me from a Mage who threatened to overpower me and juice my life, but he saved me from myself.

When I reached Viktor's table, I sat in the vacant seat across from him. Claude was throwing darts, missing almost every one.

After a few beats, Blue and Gem stood up to leave, tapping Claude on the shoulder and coaxing him to follow. Aware that a Vampire could be listening in, I chose my words carefully so as not to mention Keystone.

"I'm collecting my favor."

Viktor's head jerked back in surprise. He threaded his fingers through his hair and then stroked his beard. "Continue."

"What we discussed earlier? I'm okay with it, and I'm not

about to beat a dead horse. I'm in need of some basic training to sharpen my skills, and it's not something I can do on my own."

When he shook his head, a long section of his hair fell over his face. "I cannot. It's too much—"

"Only for a week," I insisted. "That's all I'm asking for. One week. This is probably the easiest favor you could hope for, all things considered. You don't know what I might have asked you for down the road. Give me seven days, and then you can scrub my memory."

Viktor raised his drink and grimaced after polishing it off. He was dressed in a knit sweater jacket with large buttons up the front. It was loose with a wide collar, and the sleeves were pushed up to his elbows. The laid-back style suited him—like a distinguished gentleman you might find sitting before a fire and drinking a glass of brandy while reading Dickens. Despite his silver-and-dark-grey hair, Viktor wasn't old. He looked like a robust man in his late forties or early fifties who'd lived a hard life, but that was how Shifters aged.

"I cannot send a trainer into the city. You realize the dangers," he said.

"That's not a problem. I'll splurge on a cab. I also have no aversion to walking, especially when the weather is nice. The same training as before, except I'd like to set the hours without condition. I've only got seven days, so I need to make every second count. Do we have a deal?"

A chuckle settled in his chest. "You strike a hard bargain. My only concern is whether or not I am training my future foe."

"You can't pick and choose the favor I ask. You're in my debt. Are you rescinding your offer?"

Viktor waved his hand. "Nyet. I do not have a crystal ball, but apparently I have brass ones to do this kind of favor. I accept." He leaned forward and shook his finger. "There will be no extensions. When the session ends, you must leave the property. I do not wish for you to speak to others in the house or make yourself comfortable. If you don't show up, you will not gain back that day.

It is lost. If my trainers are busy with other matters, you also lose that day."

"But that's not right."

"Let me finish. Don't be so dramatic." Viktor tried to drink from his empty glass and then just licked the rim. "Unless there is no alternative, I will make sure they are available to you."

This turned out to be easier than I thought it would. "By the way, Niko's on the roof. He wants you to call him down when you're ready to leave."

Viktor knitted his brows. "That is unlike him not to join us."

I tapped my palms on the table and decided I better make my exit before he changed his mind. "Well, I don't want to take up your time. Tell everyone I'll be coming by in the morning so they know to buzz me in."

In my periphery, I spotted Christian entering the game room. *Hmm, maybe I'll hang out for a few minutes longer*, I thought. I was curious to see his reaction when he found out he wasn't rid of me just yet.

I slinked across the room to the bar and sat on the stool, turning so I could watch over my left shoulder.

Christian strolled up to the table when Viktor crooked a finger at him.

"Hope he isn't with you," someone said.

A guy crossed my line of vision and sat in the chair next to me so that we were facing each other. He let out a pulse of energy to signal he was a Mage. I flared back to show interest. Why not? He looked like a movie star with his hair spiked in different directions, a smooth shave, sparkling hazel eyes, and a thin leather jacket.

He did that sexy thing men sometimes do where they trace their thumb across their bottom lip. "I know this sounds cliché, but I happen to come here a lot, and I haven't seen you before. I'd definitely remember those eyes. Did you just move here?"

Viktor was deep in conversation, but Christian had his head tilted in a peculiar manner, his gaze darting off to the side instead of looking at Viktor.

I swung my eyes back to the man. "I'm local; this is just my first time in here."

"Are you independent from your Creator?"

"That's an affirmative," I said, wishing he'd offer to buy me a beer.

"What's your name? I'm Kiernan."

"Raven."

He reached out and lifted the ends of my hair. "Now that's a fitting name. You have pretty eyes, Raven. I'm sure you catch hell for it in most places, but that's what makes you stand out. You caught *my* attention."

Kiernan let go and lifted two fingers at the bartender. Two longnecks appeared, frosty vapor coming from the freshly popped lids.

I guzzled down a few swallows and felt my cheeks flush from the unexpected compliment.

He leaned in, his voice smooth and sexy. "Careful now, I'm smitten about a girl who blushes."

Our bottles clinked, and he took a long sip, his eyes centered on mine.

Viktor must have broken the news, because a disgruntled look was splashed all over Christian's face. He leaned back, his arms hanging at his sides like dead limbs.

When he locked eyes with me, I raised my bottle and drank to our weeklong friendship. Viktor continued talking, drawing Christian's attention away.

"You're not into those Vamps, are you?" Kiernan asked.

Christian's head swung around, and his volcanic gaze could have set the bar on fire.

I hopped off the stool and touched Kiernan's arm. "Not a chance. Did you know Vampires have exceptionally small penises? It's true. All the women they sleep with are charmed into believing the sex was great."

Kiernan rocked with laughter and stood up, encasing me in his arms. His mouth brushed against my ear, our bodies flush. "You're my kind of girl."

I shivered in places I didn't know I could.

A hard tap sounded on the bar behind me as a glass knocked against the wood, and a rush of air ruffled my hair.

"I'm sorry, I don't think I've had the pleasure of meeting your friend," Christian said in a silken voice.

I drew back from Kiernan, still feeling his body against mine. He cupped my cheek and stroked the pad of his thumb against it, and there I stood—between two men.

Christian rested his elbow on the bar so he was more in my line of view.

"This is Kiernan, and we're busy," I said.

Kiernan was a smart man not to look up at Christian, who could easily compel him to walk away. "Is there a problem?" he asked.

Christian squeezed his bottle until it cracked but stopped shy of breaking it. "Not yet, provided you keep your nose out of her business."

I jerked my head around. "Maybe I like his nose in my business."

Kiernan moved me aside to confront Christian. "I think she's capable of making her own decisions, so I'm going to ask you one more time. Is there a problem, Vampire? Because the way I see it, your Breed needs to stick to its own kind."

My fangs involuntarily slid out, and I quickly shut my mouth before Kiernan noticed. Unfortunately, it didn't slip past Christian, and a look of satisfaction crossed his face.

He cocked his head to the side and gave the Mage a tight grin. "Kiernan, is it? I'd offer to buy you a drink, but it seems your mouth is full at the moment with your foot wedged in so tightly."

"Enlighten me."

Tension crackled, and Kiernan gave me a lingering look that made my heart accelerate.

Christian chuckled darkly. "Maybe you should ask her to smile."

Kiernan gripped my arm lightly. "What's he talking about?"

When I opened my mouth to answer, I forgot to retract my

fangs. Kiernan's icy stare was enough to freeze my blood, and he let go as if he'd grabbed hold of a viper.

"I should have known those were contacts. You shouldn't lie about your fucking Breed. You Vamps are nothing but filthy liars," he said, grabbing his drink and moving away.

"Wait…" When I moved to follow him, Christian seized my wrist. "Get away from me! You're the most insensitive man I've ever met."

He stood up straight and blocked my escape. "Is that so? Because from my vantage point, I was saving you from getting mixed up with some dope in a faux-leather jacket."

"That's pretty high-and-mighty coming from a man who has sex with random women in a bar. I won't even eat a hot dog served in a bar and you're sticking yours in the first bun you see. Couldn't satisfy her? Is that why you're hanging around in my zip code with all this free time?"

"You're the most stubborn, mouthy, bitter woman I've ever met and definitely *not* my type."

I smiled warmly. "Thank God for that. I don't want anything in common with a woman who'd lift her skirt in a back room for a man wearing a T-shirt advertising cigarettes."

He wrapped his hand around my nape. "Do you want to know why I really sent that blundering idiot on his merry way?"

"He shaves?"

Christian leaned in close. "He didn't once bother to ask why your lip was swollen and cut, not even when he was stroking your cheek. But that's the first thing I noticed when you strutted across the bar. Do you want to know what kind of man flirts with a woman sporting injuries on her face?"

"Are you trying to be the hero in this situation?"

"It can hardly be helped when there's a damsel in distress," he said, mocking me.

"You're not a knight in shining armor; you're someone's confession."

A smile hovered on his lips, and he lowered his arm. "I can

hardly disagree when the ladies are crying out for the Lord in my presence."

I brushed an invisible piece of lint off his shirt. "You have to do whatever I say for the next seven days, and we start bright and early tomorrow morning. Be sure you get a good night's sleep and eat your Wheaties. And why don't you take a shower when you get home. You smell like bad sex."

He took my hand and gently kissed my knuckles. "Have fun in your cardboard box this evening. I'll be thinking of you while someone is savoring my hot dog with relish."

Chapter 21

EARLY THE NEXT MORNING, I arrived at the mansion with my bag in hand. Viktor escorted me down to the gym and once again advised me against getting too comfortable. I wasn't sure if he thought I was going to rope myself to a statue, but I knew where he was coming from.

I dropped my bag on the gym floor and glanced over at Niko, who was sitting Indian style in the center of the room. His hair was pulled back into a long, thin braid, and all he had on was a pair of black sweats.

"Come sit with me," he said, his posture straight, his face serene. "And remove your shoes."

After tossing my sneakers next to my bag and peeling off my socks, I crossed the room and sat down in front of him. I noticed a small hole in my charcoal leggings and wondered if it was possible for me to own an article of clothing that wasn't stained or ripped.

He smiled. "You chose not to sit like me."

"How did you know?" I glanced at my right leg extended out and the left tucked beneath me.

"I pay attention. There is no right or wrong in your actions; they only tell me things."

"You should have seen my actions last night. A Mage was hitting on me until he got a good look at my fangs."

Niko frowned. "His loss if he couldn't see how beautiful your light is. You're different than most, you know. I'm not sure if that's because you're a halfy or—"

"A halfy?" I leaned back on my left hand. "Did you just make that up?"

"Crossbreed sounds like an experiment."

"How do you like Mampire? Or maybe a Vage?" I said with a snicker. "Crossbreed isn't offensive; it's what I am."

He positioned his hands so that one was cupping the other, and I wondered if I'd interrupted his meditation. "Tell me why you embrace your Mage side more than the Vampire."

I reached over my shoulder and scratched my back. "Um… I don't know."

"Yes you do."

I waited for a beat before answering. "There's not much to tell. My Vampire maker didn't take me under his wing."

There was more to the story than that. My maker deceived me—made me believe that I was special and he wanted a friend he could talk to as easily as he could with me. But he abandoned me when I needed him the most. I'd never talked about it with anyone, and I wasn't sure when I'd be ready to. I had given up everything—the only life I'd known—and in the end, it was for nothing. Discarded, I ended up in the wrong hands, and that was the second half of my tragic tale.

"You feel betrayed," he said. "Sorry, it's in your color."

"No offense, Niko, but I really don't want this to become a therapy session. I'm taking advantage of an opportunity to improve my skills. Fighting, Mage gifts—all of it. I've never had anyone teach me the way they're supposed to, so there's a lot I don't know."

"Such as healing from sunlight. But that I can't teach you without the sun."

I grinned. "If you can't see, why do you need sunlight to explain how the process works? Walk me through it as if we were sitting on the beach."

"I'd rather do this together because if you inadvertently draw too much, I'll be there to help. If you try it alone, I cannot guarantee your safety."

I wrung my hands, crestfallen. If he didn't at least explain the process, I might never find out how it's done. "I've only got seven days. I don't have time to wait for the weather to clear up."

Niko inclined his head and then held out his hand, palm facing up. I placed my hand over his, watching apprehensively.

"Sunlight holds more power than anything you can imagine," he began. "You can draw healing light from a Mage, and it requires concentration to filter it from regular light. But usually what happens is another Mage will be the one to offer it, so there is nothing you need to do on your part. See?"

I glanced down at the luminescent tendrils of blue light threading between our fingertips. A small taste of healing light entered my body, mending my cut lip.

Niko withdrew his hand. "If you had any superficial wounds, then that would be enough to heal them. It is preferable to draw healing light from the sun because it's not addictive the way Mage light is. But you should never pull sunlight." Niko worried his bottom lip, his eyes searching. "It's already touching your fingertips, crawling against your skin, wanting inside. You have control when the exchange begins, but you need to filter it, creating a channel so narrow that only the smallest drop can get in. Have you ever put a strong magnet against a refrigerator?"

"Yes."

"It snaps right to it. That's what happens when you let the light in. It's quick, powerful, and unstoppable. But you can slow down magnets if you know what's coming—brace yourself, tense your muscles, concentrate, and draw back when you feel the connection happening."

It was beginning to make sense. "So what you're saying is to pretend like sunshine is water in a faucet and the handle is out of control—something I have to fight against to make sure only a drop gets out."

"You got it. You'll know the moment the channel is open; it'll rush through you like nothing you've felt before. Too much will knock you out for days. Many young Learners fear the sun after their first failed attempt. Those who do it improperly can actually kill themselves."

I put on my science hat. "But the sun is everywhere. Even when it's hidden behind a cloud, light is all around us. Why do we have to wait for a sunny day?"

"Because it's indirect, filtered light. It is true the energy is still there, but it's not what a Mage requires. I can only explain what I know. We have no windows in here, so you'll have to tell me if there's a day of sunshine for us to practice with."

"I don't think I can even remember what the sun looks like." I sighed glumly. "The rain and fog are suffocating."

He rose to his feet. "Stand up."

When I did, I balled my hands into fists. Niko was the kind of guy who liked the element of surprise—that much I'd learned about him.

His expression relaxed. "If you thought I was going to attack, you should have struck me first instead of bracing for the attack. I'm going to show you how a Mage fights, and then we'll test what you're capable of doing with your energy. You said you can't flash, so perhaps no one has ever shown you how. It's possible that your gifts are limited because you're mixed, but that's what we'll focus on today."

"I want to train with you for as long as possible."

"And Christian?"

I snorted. "All I can say is it's a good thing I never joined Keystone and had to partner up with him. Christian is a male slut."

Niko lowered his head to shield his amusement. "Christian seeks comfort in the external."

"You should have seen where he was seeking it last night. He doesn't seem to have standards. Are women nothing more to him than a wall socket to stick his plug in? I'm not exactly sitting around waiting for Prince Charming, but you should at least have feelings for someone you share your bed with."

Niko paced around me. "Perhaps some men lower the bar because they're afraid to jump. I'm not to discuss personal matters about the team with you, so let's rumble."

Eight hours with Niko taught me two things, and one of them was that I had as much strength in my arms as Olive Oyl. He suggested that I climb escape ladders without using my legs to build up strength or find a free gym in the area and work out on their equipment. I was relying too much on cornering people in tight spaces so that I could either drain their energy or their blood.

The second thing I learned was that I could flash like a real Mage.

Sort of.

He demonstrated how to channel energy and use it in a burst of motion, moving from one place to the next with impossible speed. The first time it happened, I fell to my knees and shrieked with excitement, elated that I was capable of escaping and maneuvering like any other Mage.

Flashing used up energy, like draining a battery, and maybe I had a weaker battery than others. But it was still exhilarating to know that I had unfound talents. He also reminded me that sometimes it took years for hidden gifts to surface.

When he left to shower, I guzzled down two bottles of water and rested on a thin mat, staring at one of the light fixtures on the ceiling. I couldn't imagine a favor more valuable than this except money, and money doesn't last as long as knowledge.

The door opened, and I listened to the sound of footsteps approaching. I turned my head and stared at Christian's black boots.

"I followed the smell of pungent sweat and the trail led me to you."

I dragged my gaze up to his. "I'm not sure I need you anymore."

His brows arched. "Is that so? Because there's something I've been vexed about."

I sat up and swept my hair back. "And what's that?"

Christian squatted in front of me, his arms resting on his knees. "You said that Vampires were easiest to kill, but the number of bodies we have on file doesn't match up with your impressive claim. And we've never traced a Vampire murder to the *Shadow*."

"So? You can't do math."

Christian stroked his chin, pinching his whiskers between his fingers. "Tell me exactly how you killed the Vampires. You're a bright little battery using that Mage gift to pluck the light from another Mage, but that doesn't work on Vampires."

Was he serious? "I stake them."

He crunched on a piece of candy he had in his mouth. "You… stake them. You don't set them aflame or sever their heads by chance, do you?"

"Do I look deranged?"

One eyebrow arched. "You see, I've been giving it a lot of thought. I couldn't imagine you committing such a gruesome and messy act, and we don't have anything on record of Vampires burned to death in bathrooms. Most killers stick to a pattern, and if you were cutting off heads, you would have done the same with every Mage you met instead of pulling their light."

"I'm not a killer," I bit out.

He stood up and waved his hand. "Semantics. It's become clear to me that you know absolutely nothing about what you are. Your ignorance is your greatest vulnerability—one that others will be quick to exploit." He paced a few steps and turned. "You see, a Vampire doesn't die by impalement wood alone."

"Through the heart he does." I stood up and anchored my hands on my hips. "If you stop the heart, that's the end of the line."

"One would think," he said, raising his index finger. "Did you know that you can stake a Vampire through the brain and he can still regenerate once it's removed? Impalement only paralyzes its victim; it doesn't kill—regardless of where you put it."

Sheer horror swept over me.

My God, all the Vampires I'd left behind and assumed were dead! That meant they were probably out there looking for me, and I wasn't exactly difficult to spot.

Christian played with a long silver chain around his neck. "Looks like you better sleep with one eye open from now on. If Vampires were that easy to kill, there'd be none of us left. Many Breeds fabricated myths among humans so they wouldn't know truth from fiction. Crucifixes, silver, holy water—all the lies saved us from certain death."

"As much as I'm sure you'd like to demonstrate this on me, it's not going to happen."

He chuckled and lifted his chin. "I was curious about how you fought in hand-to-hand combat, so I slipped in when you were wrestling Niko. Feck me, it's a wonder you're still alive with those amateur moves."

"I wasn't fighting Niko as I normally would," I said, holding out my arms. "Besides, these aren't my usual surroundings. Normally I lure them to a confined space, and most of them aren't skilled ninjas like Niko. Half the time, I get them when they're drunk, so their reflexes are impaired."

Christian folded his arms. "So how do you take a man down?"

I shrugged. "Usually I do a scissor move with my legs and asphyxiate them."

He lowered his arms and strolled around me. "So... you can put a man's head between your legs until he passes out?" Christian leaned in close to my ear and lowered his voice. "That's not something I'd brag about, lass."

"I guess now I need to cut off their heads." My stomach churned at the idea.

Christian pinched my chin and looked me sternly in the eyes. "Are you afflicted in some way? Because I'm not here to teach you how to kill your own kind. Yes, your *own* kind. You may not like what you are, but you can't deny it. You can't pretend it isn't there. Your fangs came out last night because your Vampire nature was reacting to his insult. Vampire blood courses through your veins; it's the very essence of who you are." The sharp edge in his Irish accent softened, his words becoming tender. "You can't deny your instincts. Kiss me."

I drew forward as if pulled by invisible strings, wanting nothing more than his lips against mine, the feel of his arms encircling my midriff and pulling me in tight, his rough whiskers against my jaw as he kissed his way down to the base of my throat.

Our lips brushed together as I stood on my tiptoes, my palms on his chest, my lips parting.

Christian drew back and shook his head.

I blinked a few times, feeling a sudden disconnect. "Did you just charm me?"

He stuttered over his words. "I-I had to test you. If I'm going to scrub your memory in a week's time, I need to make sure it works on you."

A Vampire had once charmed me into a back room to make out with him, which I'd done. But they can only charm you into doing something you're willing to do, even if only a small part of you wants it. At least that was what I'd heard. Unfortunately for him, an even larger part of me wanted him dead.

I pointed my finger at him. "Don't do that again. If you want to know what I can do, then just ask me."

"Well, I'm not here to train you how to fight," he reiterated. "I'm too strong, and I'd break your bones. Vampires don't need skill to win; only proximity." He swaggered off and glanced over his shoulder. "Well, either stand there like a marble statue, or come walk with me."

I fell in step beside him and we began to take laps around the room.

He put his hands in his pockets. "Someone put me in that coffin because I let my guard down. Never get too comfortable, no matter how safe you think you are. It's the one mistake we all make, time and time again. I hope someday I run into that bag of shite so I can return the favor."

"What's your point?"

"No one's perfect, and that includes Niko. We all have our weaknesses, not just personally, but because of what Breed we are. We also have our strengths—our gifts—and you need to embrace those, even if they're a part of you that you despise. Vampires have unmatched hearing, but thank the heavenly angels we can tune out all the noise. How unfortunate you didn't acquire our ears." Christian stopped and placed his back against the wall, hands in his pockets, one knee bent and his foot flat on the wall. "How often do you use your Vampire eyes at night to see what's around you? Do you ever taste information from the victims you drain?"

"That's how I knew how evil they were."

"Have you ever charmed anyone?"

"No. And I've stared into many people's eyes and told them where they can go, and not one of them got out of their chair."

Christian tossed his head back and laughed. Small lines appeared at the corner of his eyes, and his white teeth—absent of the hidden fangs—were attractive. Laughter changed the man—made him appear almost human. When he settled down, his wild hair fell across his forehead, a few wisps covering his left eye. "Come here, lass."

I took a step forward and he seized my wrist, yanking me flush against him.

"Worry not," he said, looking down at me. "You should at least try it once."

"Charming?"

"Aye. Center your eyes on mine and reel me in."

"I don't know how to do that."

"The magnetic draw is unmistakable, and it grows stronger with each passing second. You'll know when you have it. Hold my gaze, Raven."

I drew in a breath and disappeared into his obsidian eyes, so bottomless that I could have fallen into their depths. I focused, trying to feel a connection forming. He didn't blink, and it made me wonder if maybe eye color had nothing to do with it. "Kiss me," I whispered.

"Are you sure about that?"

I turned away, embarrassed I'd fallen for his joke.

Christian laughed, following behind me. "You could have asked me any question in the world. I was halfway expecting you'd order me to fall on a stake, or embrace a life of celibacy. I have to admit I'm intrigued."

With lightning speed, I spun around and kissed him hard. Our lips clumsily bumped together, and he didn't initially react, keeping his emotions leashed as I cupped my hands around his neck. His lips were pliant, and he tasted of something dark and decadent. My fangs involuntarily pushed out, and he suddenly embraced me in a crushing hold, kissing me back.

I craved more. I needed more.

When his tongue grazed the pointy tip of my fang, I realized he was right. My Vampire instincts were primal, and suddenly I wanted to feel his tongue across my artery.

With the grace of a panther, he broke the kiss and took a step back, eyes locked on mine like a predator. "Why did you do that?" he asked on a breath.

I touched my bottom lip, my voice unsteady. "Since we're not going to be partners anymore, I wanted to know."

"Know what?"

I retracted my fangs. "I think our session's done. Niko can give me what I need from here on out."

As I strode past him, my chin high, he reached out and ensnared my arm, turning me around and pinning me against the wall.

His mouth was on mine—his moves so raw that it startled me. I'd never felt this kind of unbridled desire, each kiss he delivered making all others pale in comparison. When his thumbs hooked over the waistband of my leggings, I thought he was going to slide them down.

I wanted him to.

"Are you sure Niko can give you *everything* you need?" he growled against my lips.

The open collar of his shirt exposed his chest and neck, and the compulsion to taste his skin overpowered all sense of reason. My heart skipped like a stone as he dragged his mouth away, his soft whiskers scratching along my jaw.

When the tip of his fangs grazed across the sensitive skin above my artery, every muscle in my body locked. Dark hunger flooded my veins as if my blood were alive and whispering secrets with every beat of my heart. The sharp points of his teeth pressed at my tender flesh—beckoning to go deeper. Christian Poe reduced me to a pile of ash within his molten touch.

What am I doing? Is this really happening?

Energy poured through my body, turning my hands into weapons. Vampires were unlike other Breeds in that Mage energy had no effect on them, and we could touch them without inflicting pain. Their body was able to absorb it without the destructive power.

As ignorant as I was about some of my abilities, I knew this energy was sexual. It was the kind of energy that could only be exchanged with another Mage—something I'd heard about but never done.

Christian's mouth latched onto my neck, and he thrust his hips forward. There was no concealing his arousal as it pressed against me like granite, awakening my desire to be touched by a man.

"Your skin tastes like the Dead Sea," he whispered against my neck.

I tried not to think about Christian's words of seduction, but they kept repeating in my head until I erupted with laughter.

"Are you touched?" He backed up a step, wiping his mouth.

I waved my hand, regaining my composure as tears rolled down my cheeks. "I'm sorry. It's just that I've never had a man say that to me before." A loud snort at the end of my laugh embarrassed me enough to settle down.

"We'll resume our lesson tomorrow," he said.

I lifted my shoes with two fingers and strode toward him. "Is that what you're calling it these days?"

All that passion from moments earlier dissipated from his expression. "I think I've figured out your problem. You just need a good shag. Perhaps that's something you should remedy."

"I thought that's what I was trying to do last night at the bar until *someone* interrupted. Jealous?"

His eyes narrowed. "Jealousy isn't in my vocabulary."

"Nor is a razor. If you weren't such a petulant Vampire, you might have a chance at pairing up with a decent woman. Maybe you should think about brushing up on your sweet talk."

"You're covered in sweat," he protested. "It was like licking a pillar of salt."

"At least I don't have to charm someone to sleep with me."

That silenced him, and I gathered my things and climbed the stairs.

"I don't charm anyone," he barked at me from behind. "Do you really think I have to do that?"

I pushed open the door and strode down the hall. "After what I saw down there, it wouldn't surprise me."

Christian gripped my arm and stopped me in my tracks. "Deny your attraction to me. Tell me you didn't want that to happen back there."

I averted my eyes.

"That's right," he said in a quiet voice. "You lust for a Vampire, and that scares the feck out of you. Imagine the holy mortifying shame of it."

"Christian, this week isn't going to be about your crusade to lure me to the dark side and prove why Vampires are superior to all other Breeds. My distaste for Vampires offends you, and that's why you're cursing my immortal soul one minute and putting your mouth on my vein the next. I'm not like you, no matter how you slice it. I'm only half of what you are. At the end of the day, you don't really care what happens to me, so why should you care how I live my life? I'll see you tomorrow, and let's work more on knowledge. If you're too afraid you'll break me in a fight, then you can just answer all my questions."

I strode away, listening to him crack his knuckles.

"You're on," he called out. "Tomorrow morning—bright and early—we'll fight if that's what you want. Don't forget to shower, because I'll be spending all day with my head between your legs so you can demonstrate that trademark move of yours."

What a shame I no longer menstruated.

Chapter 22

WHY DID I CARE SO much about what Christian thought about me? After all, he was just a Vampire, and you couldn't trust a fang as far as you could throw him. They were secret-stealers by nature—most turning it into a profession of blackmail. Nevertheless, I spent that entire evening thinking about what he'd said. I wanted to hate him like I hated all the others. His banter might have rubbed most people the wrong way, but I had to admit there was a familiar comfort to it. It matched my own personality, and maybe I didn't want to see similarities between us.

While his delivery had been boorish, Christian had a point about ignoring my Vampire nature. There was no excuse for ignorance. How humiliating to think I'd been going around staking Vampires through the heart, believing that was enough to kill them.

Contrary to human beliefs, Vampires have beating hearts, warm skin, and bleed like everyone else. So stopping the heart sounded good enough to me.

It was a wonder I wasn't dead. Immortals held grudges for a long time, and I'd been walking right into the lion's den—revisiting those same locations where I'd staked those men.

After leaving Keystone, I took a cab into the city and spent hours in Ruby's diner, eating four servings of hot apple pie and drinking six cups of coffee before heading out. I couldn't stop thinking about Christian's roguish grin, the way his lips warmed against mine, the press of his hard body… it made me wonder.

Was I attracted to him, or was I just curious about my Vampire nature?

Maybe I just needed to get laid.

In any case, it was a good thing Viktor hadn't hired me. That kiss had stoked the embers of an unnatural lust for a certain Vampire—desires that went against everything I believed in. I thought kissing him would convince me that the attraction wasn't real, but I was wrong.

Why did I have to throw myself at a man who looks at women like disposable utensils? my inner voice nagged.

Despite that little blunder, I took advantage of the opportunity to brush up on my knowledge and fighting skills.

Six days of training passed too quickly. Niko did his best to refine my techniques and help me learn the limitations of my Mage abilities. Learning to fight like him in a week—let alone a century—was impossible. So we focused on using weapons more skillfully, how to defend myself from common maneuvers, and the basics of Mage gifts, such as telling time and sensing direction. He warned me not to deprive myself of food. Even if the Vampire side of me didn't require it, the Mage in me needed sustenance to convert into energy.

I also had to be cautious about flashing too often since it would weaken me in a fight if I relied on it too much. My energy was dimmer than most, either because it was innate or had been suppressed after years of nonuse. Probably the former since being a crossbreed meant some of my gifts were altered, but since I had more abilities than most, that made up for any shortcomings.

I'd never met anyone quite like Niko. No wonder those men had to rush him so unexpectedly. Niko was perceptive and would have sensed them had they approached at a normal pace.

As for Christian's sessions, they involved no physical training. I didn't want to be locked in his arms and pinned beneath him after what had happened between us. He enlightened me on Breed facts in his imperious manner, but I didn't spend as much time with him as I did with Niko. Christian's antagonistic remarks left no doubt that he was only there on Viktor's orders.

But the tension between us had more to do with that awkward kiss. It became a veil of shame, making our conversations stilted and rushed.

It was the night before my final day, and while I'd contemplated Niko's advice about choosing the right path, it didn't help me with figuring out what to do with my life. A career as a personal bodyguard skipped through my head a few times, but who was going to hire a woman who wasn't legal with the Mageri? On top of that, I'd have to lie and tell them I was a Mage, and it wouldn't be long before they figured out the truth.

In times like these, I always returned to the one place that centered me.

Home.

A home I'd readily abandoned when I was young and wild and thought I knew everything. After high school, my father had offered me a job at his garage, but I was delusional and thought a mall job would give me a normal life. Maybe it was just being around people who lived in a perfect world that made it seem possible for me to be a part of it.

My daddy was a mechanic and former Marine. But I knew him best for being a biker with a grey mustache, long goatee, tattoos, scars, weathered hands, blue eyes, and long hair pulled back in a ponytail. He drove a couple of Harleys, loved to watch TV, and drank a lot of orange soda. He was just the sort of guy you'd expect to see spending his nights at the bar, but Crush was a recovering alcoholic and stayed away from that scene. He got his nickname because of all the sodas he drank after he kicked the habit and joined Alcoholics Anonymous.

He wasn't an angry drunk, but he almost lost custody of me when I was nine after the police arrested him for driving under the influence. I was thrust upon him at an early age after my mother died, and he wasn't prepared to be a full-time father. My parents didn't live together; Crush had a special relationship with my mom, but his drinking might have kept them from something more permanent. Regardless, my mother had never denied me knowing my father, and for that I was thankful.

After he got clean and sober, we built so many great memories together. He didn't become a different man, just a better one.

If only time machines existed. Just thinking about those nights when I'd stormed out the door and told him I hated him for making me live in a trailer park made me sick with regret. It was one of those asinine things that most kids say to their parents, but I never got the chance to make it right. Crush was a hardworking man who kept me out of the foster care system after my mom died. I learned street smarts from him. He taught me to be a strong woman who could think for myself, but I never realized the sacrifices he'd made.

That epiphany only came *after* I'd become immortal, and by then it was too late since I'd had to cut ties with my human life.

I knew all his hangouts, so I never worried about running into him. Aside from that, Crush was the kind of guy who worked long days and came home to watch any comedy show on TV he could find.

I missed his laugh.

Maybe that was why I still crept over to the trailer on occasion, climbed the tree in the back, and then lay on the roof with my ear pressed against it. My love for heights began with that trailer. I'd spent many nights as a little girl sitting on top of it, pretending it was my castle.

At night I could hear him in there, popping the lid off his orange soda and belting out a laugh at something on TV. Sometimes when it grew quiet, I wondered if it was because he'd fallen asleep or because he was lost in his thoughts.

Did he ever think of me?

The worst part about it all was that I had no idea if someone had given him my cremated remains. Did a grave exist with my name on it? Had my Mage Creator hired someone to scrub his memory of me? There were so many questions I'd never have the answer to, and I wasn't sure if I wanted them.

"I miss you, Daddy."

Mist coated my face, and I stared bleary-eyed at the low clouds drifting overhead. My Vampire eyes could pick up the subtle shifting of light behind the darkness that hinted dawn was fast approaching.

"I think of you all the time," I said quietly, tears gathering at the corners of my eyes. "I'm so sorry for everything. You were a great father, and I don't think I ever told you that."

Crush wasn't a sensitive man, but he bought me a bunny on my eleventh birthday, even though he was allergic. Any guy who buys his little girl a bunny is a good man in my book.

I wiped my face with the heels of my hands and sat up, my back stiff from lying on a hard roof for the past nine hours.

This place felt so familiar, as if I could walk in the door and pretend nothing had ever happened. But knowing about our world would endanger his life. Aside from that, what would he think about his daughter becoming a monster? Part Mage, part Vampire, and complete killer. I wanted him to remember me as the little girl in crooked pigtails, because Crush didn't know how to do hair.

After saying good-bye, I hurried down the road toward the gas station off the main road. I closed my eyes, imagining the sky turning an indigo blue before the pale-orange light bled into the horizon. Instead, morning greeted me with rolling fog on the tree line to my right and thunder rumbling in the distance.

It only took the cab driver ten minutes to arrive—impressive considering we were on the outskirts of the city. I tossed my duffel bag on the floor and got in, my clothes damp, my throat parched.

After giving the driver directions, I hugged my midsection, shivering from the cold air. My eyes closed as thoughts of my father stayed on my mind. When I was first offered immortality by my Vampire maker, I thought I'd hit the jackpot. But after a few years of living the life, immortality frightened me. Someday I'd be thousands of years old, and my father would be nothing but a distant memory. Would I still remember the sound of his laugh?

The car slowed, and the back doors suddenly opened. Someone slid next to me on the right, and when I turned, I saw another man getting in on the opposite side.

Confused, I knocked on the plastic divider between the front and backseat to alert the driver. Maybe he hadn't switched the light off.

"Darius wants to speak with you," one of the men said.

My heart thumped against my chest, and I turned to look at him. He calmly sat in his seat, eyes forward, making no aggressive moves to restrain me.

"Maybe I don't want to speak with him."

They both had on sunglasses, and the one on the right looked more the part of an FBI agent. "That's your choice. You can either go willingly, or we can do this the hard way, but you *are* going."

"Fine."

I sat back and crossed my foot over my knee, casually tapping my fingers on my boot.

When the driver sped up, I heaved a reluctant sigh, reclining my head against the seat. Had I tried to escape, they would have restrained me, so I played it cool until I found an opportunity to do something about my situation. Not long after we entered the city, the pedestrians had become a distraction to the man on my left. Each time we stopped at an intersection, his head would turn away.

I glanced up at the goon to my right and blew a soft breath on his neck. He shivered and looked down at me, his lips pressed tight.

"Ever had a threesome in the back of a cab?" I whispered.

His eyes were concealed, but when his lips parted, that was the answer I needed.

With lightning speed, I pulled a blade from the heel of my boot and jammed it in his leg. I turned left and reached into his friend's jacket in search of weapons. The cab swerved, and the man tried to throw me off, his friend still paralyzed from the stunner I'd left in his thigh.

He slammed me against the divider and reached inside his jacket. I grabbed his arm and wrenched it away, punching him in the throat with my free hand. He swung his right arm and hit me in the shoulder instead of the face. I grabbed hold of his weapon—a long dagger—which I held to his throat.

"Is this a stunner?" I asked, removing his sunglasses. "Let's find out, shall we?"

The cab was going at breakneck speed. If the driver had stopped, I would have gotten out and fled.

I pressed the sharp tip of the blade into the man's neck until blood crawled down onto his shirt. His eyes bulged, and his trembling movement confirmed that this was no blade infused with magic.

But daggers could still do some serious damage, and he didn't seem like the kind of man with a high tolerance for pain.

"Okay, okay," he said, raising his arms.

"Tell your friend to pull over."

When he suddenly glanced out the window, it made me look.

The next thing I knew, the guy behind me grabbed my arms and held them back, forcing me to drop the knife.

The guy on my left had my push dagger in his right hand. He must have pulled it from his friend's leg when I wasn't paying attention.

Sneaky bastard!

My fangs punched out, and I lunged for the man's bloody neck.

He recoiled, shoving me back. "Holy Christ! What the hell *is* that?"

Cuffs clicked around my wrists. "We could have done this the easy way," the guy on the right said, bearing his weight down on me.

The closer my head got to the other man's leg, the more I tried to reach to bite him. He all but stood up on his seat, climbing over me to the other side of the cramped cab.

"Scoot over!" he barked at his friend.

He shoved me against the left door, leaving me in an awkward position, my arms bound.

They unzipped my duffel bag, and he said, "Hold her down."

When the big guy put his weight across my hips, holding my head against the door with his hand, I thrashed beneath him like a feral animal. My hips screamed in pain, and something felt ready to snap.

They tied a strip of fabric around my head so that it went between my teeth. Two of my sharpest weapons snagged in the tight weave of a red T-shirt. I could have fought, but what was the point? I'd spend the rest of my life looking over my shoulder, and I had no one to protect me. I had to look at this as an opportunity I might never have again—to face the man who wanted me dead.

Beneath the one guy's crushing weight, the lack of oxygen made me light-headed. I should have never assumed the men had accidentally gotten into the cab. That was my human nature still kicking and alive. Humans rationalized dangerous situations, afraid to react when it might be a misunderstanding.

And now two hundred and fifty pounds of misunderstanding was squeezing the life out of me in the backseat of a taxicab.

Christian entered the interior balcony that overlooked Keystone. A heavy mist thickened the air, and had there been a hint of sunshine, he was certain a rainbow would have appeared. He placed his forearms on the stone railing and leaned forward, his gaze chasing a wild rabbit that was scurrying across the lawn. It wasn't common to see them out in the daytime since they burrowed low to hide from the hawks.

Maybe the rabbit saw him and recognized Christian for what he was: a predator. A dark soul with black eyes and the instincts of a hunter.

Killing was a Vampire's nature—a melody in their blood they could either dance to or ignore. In the early years, Vampires needed that coping mechanism for survival, removing the remorse they would inevitably feel after draining their victims. But this was no longer the Middle Ages; Vampires had long since become civilized in terms of controlling their blood addiction. A youngling's first years were the most difficult, so their maker needed patience to guide them through the bloodlust. A Vampire occasionally drank blood to uncover information about people, so it was imperative that they learn to control their urges.

Raven reminded him a lot of himself in the early years. His maker had tried to temper his anger, but Christian was bitter from the mistreatment he'd endured in his human life. The land of opportunity had turned out to be a cesspool filled with poverty and greed. America attracted aristocrats who saw an opportunity to elevate themselves by ensuring the lower class stayed right where they were. Had his maker not been a patient man, there was no telling where Christian would be now.

His thoughts drifted to Raven. A rogue stood no chance at long-term survival, and those that did were the men Keystone hunted.

"What are you doing out here?" Blue asked.

Christian nodded, his gaze fixed on a white cat who seemed to be searching for the rabbit.

Blue leaned on the railing to his left, her hair pulled up in a messy bun. "It's a little warmer today. I think the sun's angry at the clouds."

"They can keep bickering for all I care," he said. Christian's pupils were fully dilated, which made his eyes permanently black. Over the years, he'd learned to endure the discomfort of bright lights, so sunglasses and cloudy days were a godsend.

"Today's her last day," she continued. "I wonder if Viktor's having regrets about granting her a favor like this. Someday we might be hunting her, but here we are, showing her the best way to kill us."

"I don't think that'll be a problem. Raven only hunts criminals."

Blue swiped a loose strand of hair away from her face. "I've never met a rogue with principles. Have you? Time and experience will wear her down. At least she won't remember us after you scrub her memory, but what if you miss something and she starts to remember? Maybe you should just clear it all to be on the safe side. The last thing we need is another enemy."

"Aye," he said, recollecting his promise to Raven. A promise that could one day unravel Keystone.

Blue turned around and pushed herself up so she was sitting on the ledge, facing away from the property. "You're moody today. Don't think I haven't noticed that you've spent all week on the first floor, probably eavesdropping on Niko and Raven. Am I right? But not today. Instead, you're up here brooding. If I didn't know better, I'd say she grew on you a little."

"Ah, shut your beak." He turned his head and gave her a crooked smile. "It's only been a fortnight since the little tornado swept into our lives, leaving a path of destruction. The sooner she moves on, the better. And don't think you can rile me up, lass. Women just love to insinuate." Christian stood up and tucked his hands in his pockets. "Viktor made a mistake thinking he could dust her off and make her shiny as new."

Blue crossed her feet at the ankles, her eyes drawn upward. "Isn't that how he found all of us?"

"He's got a good thing here now. He shouldn't worry so much about bringing in new blood. Seven is a magical number. The seven wonders, seven samurai…"

"Seven deadly sins," she added. Blue settled her doe eyes on him. They sparkled like sapphires rimmed in black, so stunning against her brown features. She was more down to earth than Gem—didn't talk as often and was always trying to please Viktor. "You just don't want a partner. That's not how it works, Christian. You can't drive away every new person he brings in just because you'd rather work alone. It's not your place to choose your partner; that's Viktor's decision."

"Would you be saying this if he'd paired you with Shepherd instead of Niko? I'll not be matched up with a lunatic. Viktor knows my position."

"That's blackmail."

He folded his arms, his voice rising an octave. "And how do you see that?"

Blue hopped off the ledge and dusted off her hands. "Because threatening to leave if he doesn't find the right match could force him to make different choices. Keystone doesn't revolve around Christian Poe."

He grunted and swaggered toward the door. Blue was colder to him than she was with the rest of the house, just as many were around Vampires. "Don't pretend like you didn't try to convince him otherwise when he invited a Vampire into the mix."

With his Vampire hearing, he caught the sound of her heart skipping a beat and a slight intake of breath.

"Who told you a thing like that?" she asked.

He turned dramatically and bowed. "You did. Just now."

Blue squared her shoulders, not revealing her obvious disdain for his abilities. "Then perhaps you should have a little compassion for the next person, given you know what it feels like to be the outcast. We're guarded around you, that's all. It's nothing personal, I—"

"Don't trust my kind," he finished in a flat tone.

Her shoulders sagged. "I haven't always approved of Viktor's choices, but I've never tried to force his hand. I trust him with my life. Do you want to know what really took me by surprise? When he didn't invite Raven back for another chance after she led us to you. She impressed him, but something tells me that you had an influence on his decision, forcing him to choose between someone he trusts and a rogue with potential." Blue turned her back on him, loosening her hair from the bun. "Careful what you do with that power, Christian. Someday Viktor might lose his trust in you because of it."

Blue strode out the door and left him alone.

"Women," he murmured, stalking in the opposite direction.

He picked up a few wrappers and matchsticks along the way, tossing them into the nearest wastebasket. Shepherd smoked and threw his bloody matches all over the place. Christian had half a mind to glue each one he found to Shepherd's bedroom door.

He descended the stairs until he reached the ground floor. It seemed unusually quiet as he approached the stairwell to the underground gym. Christian hadn't expected to warm up to the little scavenger, but as he reflected upon the past two weeks, he realized that he was going to miss their sarcastic repartee. He'd never much cared for a woman who spoke profanities—although she wasn't excessive with them—but Raven was different than most of the women he'd known. She was confident, strong, and clever. She didn't let personal feelings get in the way of what she wanted, and she had better survival skills than some of the most qualified bodyguards he'd met. Christian didn't look at her as an object of affection, but an equal.

Or at least he *had*, until their kiss.

While her leaping into his arms had taken him by surprise, it wasn't nearly as startling as his reaction to her walking away. True, a little ego was involved, and when he sensed her indifferent response, he impulsively wanted to do something that would leave her breathless. But the moment he'd felt her body flush against his—Mother of God, the woman hadn't a clue that her kiss could set Hell on fire.

And Christian had kissed many women—enough that he often preferred to get down to business rather than wasting time on all the licking and sucking.

He'd thought about their kiss often, rewinding to the moment when she'd turned and their lips met, remembering how stunned he'd been since she had professed nothing but hate for Vampires. Raven had a decadent taste, soft skin, and she knew exactly what to do with those lips. She kissed him as though she were starving for him.

While they both tried to pretend it had never happened, it made their training sessions brutally uncomfortable for him. She avoided eye contact and held back on some of her usual quips. Was she ashamed? It made him even more adamant about getting her out of the house.

He entered the training facility and scanned the empty room. Niko looked like a statue in the center, sitting on the floor with his eyes closed.

Christian rocked on his heels. "Let me guess, she decided to skip the afternoon session."

Niko retained his perfect posture. "She never showed up."

Christian cocked his head and gave him a peevish glance. "Don't be daft. Of course she showed up."

Niko drew in a deep breath and rose to his feet, stretching his neck and arms. "Viktor won't allow her to make up for the time lost. It appears we've seen the last of Raven Black."

Christian seized Niko's arm when he walked by him. "You're telling me she didn't show up all day? Not even a phone call?"

"That's exactly what I'm telling you."

"And you don't find that the least bit suspicious?"

Niko pulled out of his grasp and straightened his black T-shirt. "She's not a predictable woman. Maybe she's afraid of your scrubbing her memory, so she decided to leave town. I've spent hours considering different scenarios, and that's the most logical conclusion. What more could she gain in one day? She knew she wasn't going to leave this house with her memory intact."

Christian bit his lip because he knew otherwise. "What other reasons did you come up with?"

"That she instigated a fight to test out some of her new tricks. If she lost the battle, we may never find out what happened to her. If she won, then she's probably ill after drinking too much of his blood or stealing his light. Perhaps the real reason is that she's not willing to accept the finality of this decision. The last day would serve as a reminder that she will not become a member of Keystone, and that is what concerns me the most."

"Why do you say that? She has a few coins in her pocket now; she can afford a place to sleep."

"This place was more than a roof over her head, Christian. Keystone was her salvation. When you strip away a man's hope, you don't know what he's capable of becoming. All we can do is pray for her."

Christian snorted. "Pray to whom? The Mage gods? The Vampire gods? What god created us?"

"The fates created us. The power that's behind all the mysteries. Some things are too magnificent for us to see."

"Like the middle finger I'm flashing at you?"

Niko smirked. "I don't need to see your finger to know your intention."

Christian shut down his feelings and locked them up in a tight little box. "I told you not to do that with me. I don't use my gifts on you, and I'd appreciate the same courtesy."

"Apologies. Some things are difficult to ignore."

Christian put his arm around Niko. "Well, no sense in wasting the day away. Let's have a pint and do some celebrating."

Chapter 23

WHEN WE ARRIVED AT DARIUS'S property, I gritted my teeth and held my chin high. I refused to let him see me as a defeated woman. Superficial wounds and handcuffs aside, Darius was going to learn he was no match for a woman like me.

The guards had removed my gag when, after they'd placed a shirt over my head to blindfold me, I made heaving motions as if I were going to vomit. Hopefully they'd fall for it—I needed to get that strip of fabric away from my mouth. Words were the only weapon I had, and I'd be damned if they were going to deliver me like a prisoner of war.

They guided me from the cab, and we ascended the outside steps to his building. When we entered an open room, they removed my blindfold. I didn't have time to survey my surroundings as they led me to the left. It felt like a death march by the way the guards flanked me, keeping a secure hold of my arms with me one step ahead.

When the smaller guy opened a door on the right, a gust of air swept my hair back. Everything moved in slow motion, including my heartbeat, as I marched at a determined pace toward Darius, who stood at the far end of the dimly lit hall.

Our footsteps sounded like a stampede against the cement floor. Darius didn't seem to have a clue about interior decorating. This place had a nightmarish quality to it, as if those white walls were closing in on me.

Darius inclined his head, and a smile touched his lips. One

of the men yanked me to the right and shoved me into an empty room.

When I saw the lone chair in the center and a fireplace on the left with a fire going, I backed as far away from them as I could get.

"You said he wanted to speak with me!" I shouted. "Darius!"

"Oh, you'll get to talk to him," the big guy said, closing the door. "Just as soon as we're done asking you a few questions." He nodded at his partner. "Tie her up."

The smaller guy was afraid of my fangs, and knowing this, I forced them out and smiled at him. He came at me, arms wide, and I sidled to the left. There wasn't a single piece of furniture in the room aside from the chair, so that left me with no weapons.

Except for the two in my mouth.

I stood close to the wall and bent my leg to anchor my foot against it, bracing myself to launch at him. His eyes widened when he drew nearer.

"Move it along, Kevin. We don't have all day."

"Then why don't you get over here," Kevin bit out.

His hands moved close together, and I could see his plan of attack was to grab hold of my neck. He took one tiny step forward and lunged.

I dropped my foot, and instead of attacking him, I channeled my Mage energy and spun multiple times to the right. I flashed across the room, stepped up onto the chair, and drop-kicked the big guy right in the chest.

He wheezed as the air slammed out of him, and I crashed to the floor at the same time he hit the wall. The landing hurt since my hands were still cuffed. Ignoring the pain, I was scrambling toward the door to open it when Kevin grabbed me in a viselike grip, dragging me backward.

I kept my legs stiff, refusing to sit when he tried to move me by force. The air and blood cut off from my head, making my limbs weak.

"Get up, Declan! I can't hold her for long," Kevin shouted.

Declan crawled to his feet, one hand on his chest, and stalked forward. With brute force, he kicked my legs out from beneath me and shoved me to a seated position. Then he sat on my lap to keep me still while Kevin wrapped a tight cord around my body, strapping me to the chair before I could sink my teeth into Declan's back. Both of my ankles were tied to the chair legs, but those bindings didn't feel as secure.

When Declan finally stood up, he wiped his brow and strode to the fireplace. A log snapped as he gripped the handle of an iron poker and withdrew it from the flames. The metal had a dull glow that made me straighten up in my chair.

"I have a few questions to ask, and you're going to cooperate, aren't you?"

I won't die from this. I won't die from this, I kept repeating in my head.

He loomed over me with the hot tool. "Who do you work for?"

"I'm self-employed."

I clenched my teeth when the poker neared my face.

Declan scanned my body. "Too bad you're wearing that sweatshirt. All that clothing doesn't leave me with many options of where to put this."

He flicked a glance at the man behind me, who gripped my hair and held my head back.

When the tip of the poker seared my neck, I jerked violently.

He lowered the torture device and glanced at his friend. "You're going to need to hold her head tighter."

Kevin's hand covered my forehead, and I found myself unable to look away. "Don't you burn me with that," he warned Declan.

"I'm not telling you anything," I snarled. "The only person I want to speak with is Darius, so call him in here."

He bent down, holding the rod close enough that I could feel the heat. "*Who* do you work for?"

"No one. I'm a rogue. Why would I be walking around with a duffel bag full of dirty clothes if I had a job?"

"Wrong answer."

He lowered the flat end of the poker until it branded my left cheek. I screamed, slipping into a primal state of survival. The pain was unfathomable—sharp and real, pulling me right into the moment. My eyes watered, and my skin pulsed with searing pain that intensified with each passing second. He stood up, watching me writhe and bare my teeth like an animal caught in a trap. Tears were streaming down my face, reawakening the fresh pain that continued to burn as if he had never removed the iron.

Oh God, I can't survive this. Now I knew why men cried for their mothers when dying on the battlefield. I just wanted someone to make it stop, to get me out of there.

Kevin let go, and as I sat there and sobbed, I became incensed that these two men were standing there watching me and laughing. I jolted forward, tipping the chair and sinking my fangs into Declan's thigh. The momentum tore my teeth down his pants, cutting through his flesh in the process.

He bellowed in pain, but I barely heard it over my own roar. When I hit the ground, Declan stumbled backward, almost losing his footing. If he kicked me in the legs, I didn't feel it. I wriggled my body, trying desperately to loosen the ropes—the smell of burning flesh sending me over the edge.

"Dammit, pick her up!" Declan shouted.

Kevin wasn't a threat to me; he was more of an annoyance. Men who couldn't think for themselves would spend the rest of their lives as followers. Declan... Well, he had officially penned his name in my book of people I wanted to destroy.

They righted my chair, and my chest heaved as I tried to capture a satisfying breath. The taste of his blood in my mouth made my stomach twist into painful knots.

The door opened, and Darius entered the room. "What's going on in here? What have you done?"

My black hair curtained my face, and I was beginning to feel the pattern of the burn that started at the corner of my mouth and stretched across my cheek to my eye.

I finally looked like the monster I'd become.

"Get out," he said, snapping his fingers. "Both of you."

Some of my hair blew forward as I breathed steadily, in and out through my nose. I must have sounded like a fire-breathing dragon. I was vaguely aware of the pain around my wrists from the handcuffs pinching my skin. My teeth were clenched, muscles tight, and shoulders hunched. Rage funneled through me in the form of energy, and I focused on leveling it down before it spiraled out of control and caused me to black out. That was the first lesson every Mage learned whether someone taught them or not: control your energy before it controls you.

Darius tilted my head back and threaded my hair away from my face. "I instructed them to rough you up. This was certainly uncalled for." He grimaced when he got a close look at my face. "That's going to take a while to heal on its own. It's a good thing they didn't have any liquid fire."

The statement hung in the air like a thinly veiled threat.

Darius plucked a handkerchief from his suit pocket and shook it out. He knelt before me and wiped Declan's blood from my mouth. "Who is protecting you now? Why should you protect them?"

"I don't protect anyone."

"Who is Houdini?"

I furrowed my brow. "I don't know."

"Who was the man you were sitting with in the pastry shop? I want to know who lives in that house and what they know about me. My men followed you there, and something tells me your friends know my business. I don't like *anyone* knowing my business. Are we clear about that?" A ridiculously long moment of silence stretched between us, as if he actually expected me to answer. "As much as I'd like to untie you so we can speak as equals, I don't think cooperating is what you have in mind."

I steadied my eyes on the iron poker.

"We haven't been formally introduced, Miss Black. I'm Darius Bane."

"Delighted," I ground out.

He folded up the bloody handkerchief and tossed it into the fire. "Are they worth giving up your life for them? You can't mean that much to them if you're wandering the streets alone. Have you heard of the Shadow? If you're who I think you are, I'd rather have someone like you on my side." He stood up. "Let me get a chair so we can talk."

When he left the room, I searched for a way out. *I can always throw myself into the flames to burn the ropes*, I mused.

Darius returned with a wooden chair. He closed the door behind him and sat down in front of me, his fingers steepled. "Who is Keystone?"

I shook my head.

"That's the name I heard when you were screaming."

Oh shit.

Those moments had been a blur, and I couldn't be sure of what I'd said. What did it matter anyhow? I didn't have any loyalty to Keystone.

"I'm not with them," I said. "He owes me a favor, so they're giving me pointers on how to protect myself on the streets."

Darius sat back and ran his fingers through his curly hair. "Tell them you want a refund on your favor. I don't see that it's helped much, do you?"

I averted my eyes.

Darius leaned forward again, his eyes narrowing and forming wrinkles at the corners. "What has Keystone truly given you? Their loyalty? Their unwavering protection? It looks as if they have more important things on their agenda than protecting a scavenger. Groups like that will never elevate you to a better position. I've spent my entire life working to amass a fortune; all it takes is a little vision and good partners I can trust. It just so happens I'm missing my right-hand man. You wouldn't know anything about that, would you?"

I shook my head.

"If he's missing, then he wasn't qualified for the position. You could fill those shoes, Raven. I can offer you a place where people will respect you and follow your lead."

I tilted my head back and settled my eyes on his. "You're offering me a job?"

"I'm offering you much more than that. I can give you a place at my side, and our empire will prosper. Choose the right opportunities, because you don't always get a second chance. I can protect you from men who would harm you," he suggested, his gaze fixed on my burn. "If there are people you love, then you already realize how your very existence puts them in danger. I can offer them my protection as well."

"I don't have anyone."

His brows arched. "Oh? I'm curious why my driver had to venture all the way out to that gas station this morning. That's a desolate side of town. The only notable place in the area is a human trailer park just down the street. You strike me as recently made, and I'm sure it's not been easy to let go of your human life. I've seen it all too often. According to my men, that wasn't your usual spot. Sometimes the biggest flaws a man can have are right under his nose."

My skin went ashen. Darius didn't know who was in that park, but it wouldn't take him long to find out. It was another indirect threat, and this time I gave him my full attention.

"That's what I do, Raven. I offer people my protection."

"You extort men for money. *You're* the one they need protection from."

He chuckled and rubbed his cheek. "Aren't we all our own worst enemy? This isn't about good and evil; it's about right and wrong. I know what it's like to have nothing and for people to see me as nothing. These so-called laws stripped away everything my Creator had given me, so I've spent my life rebuilding what was wrongfully taken."

"You kill humans."

He crossed an ankle over his knee and regarded me for a moment. Darius was a well-groomed man, someone I could easily imagine sipping champagne on a veranda while an ocean breeze blew back his dark, curly hair. "These mortals will perish like flies, and that's something you'll realize in the coming years. Once you understand how long your life will be, you'll no longer dwell on moralities. You have to preserve your wealth and secure your future. Why do you think immortals focus so much on money and property? You can't live on the streets forever. Ten years? Maybe.

But what regrets will you have in two thousand years when you're wandering around in search of a place to sleep for the night? Prepare for the unexpected changes that will come, and you will be in a better position to survive."

My head was spinning. "What do you want with Keystone?"

"If you've told anyone about me, you've compromised everything I've worked hard to achieve. I could throw you in an abandoned well or cut off your head, but you have connections to this group, and that makes you valuable. We can work together."

I barked out a laugh. "You just threatened to kill me. What makes you think I would trust you?"

Darius shrugged. "I threaten to kill everyone. A rogue like you will never understand the baneful influence an organization like that is to entrepreneurs like me. It doesn't take a genius to figure out what they do, and by the looks of the property, I'd say they have powerful connections. You know more about them than anyone else, and I don't sense you're as loyal to Keystone as you pretend to be. This isn't about honor, Miss Black. It's about survival. Your survival."

"I don't have any information that's useful. They didn't tell me their secrets, and there's nothing you haven't already figured out."

Darius leaned forward, his voice softening. "I don't want you to give me information. I want you to kill them."

My heart skipped a beat.

"I know you can do it," he continued. "You've shown me the weak spots in my security. If this Keystone group is allowing you into their home, then they trust you on some level. Trust is an Achilles' heel."

"They're not inviting me to any weddings."

He sat back, his expression pensive. "On second thought, I'm beginning to have doubts that you can pull off something this big. Perhaps it's too much. What a shame, because I'm eager to share my fortune with a capable partner."

I thought about it. "The mansion is huge, and most of them stay in separate areas during the day. It wouldn't be hard to take them out one at a time without alerting the others."

"You're just a street scavenger, and I'm not sure if money is motivation enough for someone like you."

I huffed quietly. "What do I care what happens to them? They made a joke out of me. And you're right; money isn't what I'm after. I'm not saying I won't take it, but I'd rather have someone who respects what I can bring to the table."

A smile touched his lips. "Before you think about betraying me, just remember that I know the places you frequent and the people you interact with. I'll eventually find the one person who matters. I can make your life hell before I eventually kill you, or I can be your mentor." He reached out and moved a few strands of hair away from the burn. "Would you rather have more misery, or do you want a chance to become someone that people respect and fear? Work for me and I'll furnish you with nice clothes, a home—anything your heart desires. No more sleeping in alleys or eating cold apple pie at an empty table in a diner."

It was then that I realized Darius had been spying on me for the past week. He probably knew all my hangouts, where I slept, and the people I came in contact with. I flinched when another sharp wave of pain lanced my cheek, reminding me that I wasn't going to escape.

"Your fate is in your own hands, Miss Black. Make the right choice and you'll prosper for many years to come. Be loyal to yourself first and claim what's rightfully yours in this world."

"Untie me," I said, holding his gaze.

"If I let you go, what is your intention?"

"To kill every last member of Keystone."

Chapter 24

Every promise I'd made to Darius was a lie.

He'd tempted me with money and power, and had I been a weaker woman, I might have accepted. But men like him didn't take on equal partners. They manipulated people to get what they wanted.

Darius might not have trusted me, but he was consumed with the fear that an organization like Keystone knew about what he'd been doing and that they had connections to the higher authority. I was his only chance, and after seducing me with promises and indirect threats, he seemed certain I wouldn't betray him—especially with the incentives he offered. We spent an hour laying out plans, but he didn't seem willing to send his men in with me. Either he didn't want to risk losing the few people who were loyal to him, or he was afraid that if someone captured them, they would give up incriminating information on him.

I had until midnight to complete the mission. At first, he wanted me to bring their heads as proof. I finally convinced him that taking a cab with a bunch of severed heads might attract attention.

The plan didn't matter. I would have agreed to dance naked in moonlight, wielding a battle-axe while singing show tunes if it meant getting the hell out of that house.

He let me keep two daggers but held my other weapons along with my bag.

Then he made a final proposal: "If you fail or turn your back on me, I will hunt you to the ends of the earth. Before you die,

I will force you to witness the deaths of everyone you've ever cared about, starting with that sweet old lady in the diner. If you succeed, you will return to my house and confirm the body count. I'll send two of my weakest guards to verify your claim. If they don't return, our deal is off. Succeed at this mission and you'll have my unwavering trust. I'll reward you with the highest rank in my house and pay you handsomely for your partnership. We can do many great things together."

One of his men had dropped me off down the road from the Keystone estate before turning around. Because Keystone was located in an area with a primary road and no neighborhoods, an unfamiliar vehicle parked on the road would draw attention. I told Darius that in order to execute our plan, I needed his cooperation and to keep his men away. Aside from that, he didn't want to send them in until he heard back from me.

I drew the hood over my face to protect myself from the light breeze and sprinkles of rain that reawakened the pain in my face. There was a lot of open country out here—no sidewalks or houses near the road. The only things indicative of there being property in the area were iron fences, stone walls, and hedges that marked certain territories. Much of it was untouched—just rolling hills of green, overgrown trees, and wild animals.

I reached the private road on the left and approached the gates. After I pressed the button to request access, the gates opened. I trudged up the paved road, dreading what was to come.

It was late afternoon, and pockets of fog appeared to be lifting. Not that I could see sunlight, but Niko's comment about the stars always being there reminded me that somewhere high above those dark clouds was a blue sky and warm sun.

I reached the door, and the knob turned easily. With my head down, I made my way through the house toward Viktor's office. My shoes were quiet against the stone stairwells, but not quiet enough.

"And where do you think you're going, lass?" Christian asked from below.

I ascended another flight, hearing him catch up with me.

"Are you deaf, woman?"

"You sound drunk."

"Just a pint or two. We're celebrating, you know."

When I reached the second floor, I turned left down a long hall with lanterns hanging from the ceiling. There weren't any windows, and despite the arched ceiling, the walls closed in on me.

"Going to say your good-byes to Viktor? Well, doesn't that warm the cockles of my heart," he said dramatically.

I rapped my knuckles against the door, and Christian eased up beside me, leaning his shoulder against the wall. "You have a peculiar smell about you."

My hood shielded my face, and I had my arms crossed defensively. "I'm not here to talk to you."

"Well, that's a shame."

"Come in," Viktor said.

When I entered the room, I felt Christian behind me, so I stopped, blocking him in the doorway. "I need to speak to you alone," I said to Viktor.

Because of my hood, I couldn't see Viktor, but it sounded as though he was setting something down on his desk, maybe a book.

"It is unfortunate that you wasted your last day. If you came to ask for an extension, then the answer is no. We had an agreement, and I always stay true to my word."

"It's not about that. Tell Christian to leave."

A quiet exchange passed between the two men—maybe a nod of the head or hand gesture. In any case, Christian left the room and closed the door behind me.

Viktor's chair creaked as he rose to his feet and crossed the room. I took a few steps forward to meet him in the middle.

"What is this about? If you are asking me not to have Christian scrub your memory—"

"Darius sent me to kill you."

After a pregnant pause, he quietly chuckled. "And here you are. What kind of joke is this?"

I pulled back my hood and reduced the space between us. His eyes widened when he saw the raw wound across my face. Viktor actually backed up a step, flicking a glance at his desk. He probably kept a weapon in those drawers.

"I'm not here to kill you, Viktor. I came with an opportunity to attack Darius. This might be the only chance you'll get in the near future."

He folded his arms. "And how do I know you speak the truth? That scar on your face leads me to believe—"

The door crashed open, and I spun on my heel.

Christian strode toward me, his eyes narrowing. When his brows sloped down, I fell back a step, ready to flash out of his grasp if he tried to deliver a crushing blow with his powerful fists. When he didn't stop, I gathered up my energy and flashed around him, but he reached out and hooked his arm around me. Christian gripped my chin between two fingers and turned my head to the side.

"Who did this to your face?"

Viktor raised his voice. "Christian, leave us."

I tried to wriggle free, but his grip was tight. His obsidian eyes settled on mine, and I looked away before he could think about charming me.

"Christian!" Viktor bellowed.

Christian suddenly let go and charged toward the door, slamming it shut. "I'm not moving one inch until I find out who put that mark on her face," he said with tempered rage. He kicked his foot like a mule and left a crack in the door.

Butterflies circled in my stomach.

"Let us hear what she has to say," Viktor said.

The room grew uncomfortably warm, and I pushed up my sleeves. "I have until midnight to finish the job. This isn't something I can run from. He threatened to hunt me down and kill everyone I know—innocent people. He wants me to return when I finish so he can send in two men to confirm everyone's dead."

"And what did he offer you?"

I swallowed, my throat dry.

Viktor stroked his beard. "He wouldn't have set you free on a promise of letting you live. That's not enough motivation to assure him you won't run."

"He offered me money and a position working as a partner."

"A *partner*," Viktor repeated. "That's a generous offer."

"He thinks I'll either complete the assignment or flee, but he won't expect what I have planned."

"And what do you propose?"

"Attack him when he's least expecting it. Tonight. His mind will be so preoccupied with what I'm doing here that he's not going to think for a second that I'd actually return and raid his home. He doesn't think I have a strong enough alliance with you, and maybe I don't. That's what I'm here to find out. He lives in an old brownstone building on the east side, and I happen to know they have underground tunnels that lead to some of the basements. Wyatt probably knows about them from his research, but I once heard two guys who were planning a robbery talking about it. The tunnels were built around the turn of the twentieth century as an escape route from humans. I guess they were afraid if humans discovered them, they'd burn the buildings or something. Anyhow, every basement has one, although some might be sealed off. He said most people had just forgotten about them over the years, especially as properties changed hands. The entrance looks like a storm drain."

Viktor waved his hands and circled around his desk, taking a seat. "Wait a minute. You are suggesting we raid his home and fight who knows how many guards?"

"He has exactly four in the house, excluding a personal secretary who only works days. Is that too many for you?"

Christian crossed the room like a slow-moving shadow, his eyes still on my face. He stood in front of the desk, gripping the edge and facing toward me. "And how do you know so much?"

I lifted my chin. "Darius likes to talk, and he had no problem telling me about how he'd outgrown that little building—that it was too small and he was always running into his guards. He wants more security but doesn't have the room. I offered him my protection since I'm worth at least four of his guards."

"Was this before or after he burned your face?" His knuckles whitened as he squeezed the edge of the desk.

"Darius didn't do this to me; one of his men did."

Christian lowered his head until all I could see was his scruffy beard and dark hair.

"I'm begging you, Viktor. This isn't a trap. I'm here because… Darius is going to kill my father. Please…" Tears stung my eyes, and I quickly wiped them away before they reawakened the searing pain on my face. "Please don't let him kill my father. I can't do this alone."

Viktor shaded his eyes and fell silent.

I advanced a step. "I want Darius gone, and so do you. There's enough evidence to support any action you take. You have motive, and you also have that Mage buried in the cemetery that the higher authority could question. Whether you turn me away or not, he's still coming after Keystone."

Viktor flashed me a stony glance. "And what does he know about Keystone?"

I looked between him and Christian. "I told him."

Viktor sat back. "Yes. You *told* him."

Christian spun around to face Viktor, waving his arm at me. "*Of course* she told him. Just look at her! He burned off half her fecking face. What do you think a man will say when he's put to the fire?"

"You would have said nothing," Viktor replied.

I pointed at Christian. "But he's a loyal member of Keystone; I'm not."

Viktor laced his fingers together, resting his chin over them. "Your motives are self-driven. How can I trust you?"

I shook my head in disbelief. "You can't throw me out and still expect my loyalty. If you're not convinced, have Christian charm the truth out of me and you'll see that I'm not lying. After tonight, Darius is going to be on the defense. He employs several men who rotate their duties, but there are only four in his house at the moment. Consider that. He's also talking about moving, and if that happens, you'll have lost your chance. Maybe you just have to trust me."

Christian kept his palms on the desk, his tone more calm. "We should do this, Viktor. Now that he knows we're after him, he'll be doing whatever he can to protect himself. I think it's time we show this weak battery who's boss."

Viktor abruptly stood up. "Very well. I have been contemplating our attack, but you have forced my hand with this new information. I have enough evidence to supply motive, but nothing to link him to the crimes. The laws are not going to support a capture without proof, and there is too much red tape. Gather up the team. We're taking him down. I want you to scout the area and make sure we have a clear exit. And get Niko to heal her."

"No," I blurted out.

They both stared at me slack-jawed.

"Are you mad?" Christian said. "Without sunlight, it'll take weeks before that heals up entirely, and you're not even sure what your limitations are."

He was right. Without Mage light, wounds healed naturally. Broken bones usually had to be set to seal together properly. What did it matter? Maybe after all the screwups, this was what I had coming.

"Let me worry about myself," I said, turning away. "Viktor, call me when you're ready. I don't want to face the house just yet."

I pulled my hood over my head and hurried down the hall. Footsteps closed in from behind, and the next thing I knew, Christian pinned me to a wall.

"What's wrong with you? Are you a masochist?"

I shoved him. "Go drink your beer and finish celebrating my eviction."

His lips thinned, and he flattened his palms on the wall behind me, caging me like a bird. His gaze was penetrating and his voice baleful, sending a chill up my spine. "We've had our differences, and I don't particularly care for the way you live your life. That aside, I'm not the kind of man who takes kindly to seeing a woman tortured. You can think whatever you want about me, precious, but I promise you this: I'll crush the man who did that to your face."

My blood heated like fire. "Let me take care of my own business."

"Do that. You can take Darius and stretch him on the rack if you like, but the coward who did this..." Christian moved the hood away from my face, his voice falling to a whisper, his fangs sliding out. "That one's mine."

After slithering away from Christian's grasp, I hurried down the stairs, turning my head away as Shepherd walked toward me, his phone in hand. In a mansion this enormous, it was probably just easier to text everyone a message than yell out.

Why did I have to kiss Christian Poe? Had he not kissed me back, I might have gotten over it. Now I couldn't even look at him without having childish fantasies about rushing into his arms. So hearing his promise to kill Declan had incited unexpected emotions in me, made me feel protected. I hadn't felt the shielding comfort of someone looking out for me in a painfully long time. Maybe that was why Keystone was such an attractive proposition. It was security—a place to call home.

After emerging from the back door, I crossed the open grounds and crested a hill. This part of Cognito was magical—a place I never knew existed, as if someone had plucked locations from a fairy tale and placed them in the real world. I fell to my knees, uncertain if I'd made the right decision. What if my going after Darius would cost my father his life?

"What do I do?"

A mystical glow illuminated the landscape when the sun found a breach in the clouds. An orange shower of light descended from the heavens, sliding in my direction until it engulfed me. The grass glistened, and the air grew heavy with the sudden heat. It seemed as though I hadn't seen the sun in a lifetime. I'd forgotten how pure it felt, how extraordinarily powerful.

I opened my hands, sunlight drenching my fingertips. Without a second thought, I concentrated on opening the channel, fighting the immense energy that was surging against my palms. Too much at once could either kill me or knock me out for days, but if I could extract just enough...

My skin prickled, the energy sifting in and working its way through my body. I closed my eyes when the heat flooded my face, mending the skin and healing the raw burns. It tickled for a brief moment before the pain vanished as if it had never been.

When I opened my eyes, I shut off the connection and gazed down at my hands, tears splashing onto my palms as I wept like a child.

I'd never really accepted my life as an immortal, not since the day I became Breed. No one forced me into this world; I'd chosen it of my own free will. But when things didn't go as expected from day one, I felt cast aside by my maker, by God or whoever was running the show. I grew resentful of the immortals around me who flaunted their wealth and happiness. I'd contemplated suicide in the darkest times when all hope was lost and my days were filled with sorrow. It took me a long time to redirect that anger and find a purpose, but I still hated what I'd become. Killing made me feel brighter in this world, but in the process, I'd been poisoning myself with dark light and tainted blood.

Now, for the first time, I glimpsed a future with many lifetimes. Healing myself restored something I'd lost years ago—something I hadn't realized I needed until just now. Hope. I wanted to be excited about what each day brought, and that wasn't going to happen as long as I was holding on to all that rage and resentment. It wasn't completely gone, but maybe just enough that I could start over.

The sun moved swiftly behind a cloud, and a blanket of shadows spread across the land, cooling the temperature and dulling the colors.

Nothing good ever lasted in my life—that was why I'd always chosen to live for the moment and not the future.

I rose to my feet and returned to the mansion, armed with a sense of purpose. Lives were at stake, and running was not an option.

"Viktor!" I charged up the stairs, skipping every other step. "Viktor!"

When I reached the second floor, I found everyone gathered in the open area, deep in discussion. Claude rose from a sitting chair, and Niko looked around as if he were watching an energy show.

Gem scanned my face and then whipped her head around to Christian. "I thought you said she was badly—"

He covered her mouth, his eyes locked on mine, staring in disbelief.

I flipped my hood off and shook out my hair. "My father's in danger. If Darius means to blackmail me, he's going to send one of his men to the trailer park to find out who I've been visiting. I can't go after Darius until I know my father's safe, and if that's not something you can give me, then we'll have to part ways."

Viktor furrowed his brow. "He might not."

"I can't take that chance." I waved my hand at the group. "And spare me the lecture about cutting human ties and letting destiny do its thing. If you were in my shoes, you'd do the same. You can make me give up my family, but you can't make me stop loving them."

Blue reached in her pocket and pulled out a short necklace with a long silver spike. She latched it around her neck and looked at Viktor. "I'll go."

He nodded.

Relief swam through me, and I gave her the address and the best way to find it. You couldn't miss his motorcycles out front.

With a graceful turn, Blue ran down a long hall toward an open window. In a fluid motion, her clothes fell away and large wings extended as she gracefully shifted into a grey falcon. She angled her body as she neared the open window and then disappeared.

I released a breath I'd been holding. "What did she put around her neck?"

Gem sat down on a small end table. "It's one of those stunner spike thingies. There aren't many like those around. When they used to make stunners, they mostly used daggers. Spikes and arrowheads weren't as common because people lost them all the time. It's easy for her to carry since it stays on her animal."

"What if there's more than one Mage?"

Shepherd smirked from his seated position in a curved-back chair. He continued sharpening his knife against a thin rod, the same knife he probably used to shave his head. "Blue can take care of herself."

I imagined a beguiling and very naked woman approaching Darius's guards, concealing the spike in the palm of her hand. That would be like shooting fish in a barrel.

Viktor headed toward the staircase. "I want everyone dressed and weapons ready in fifteen minutes. Meet me downstairs at the table, and we'll devise a plan."

Gem strutted toward me and hooked her arm in mine. "Let's get you changed into something a little more appropriate than a ratty old sweatshirt."

Christian reached out and clasped Shepherd's hand, pulling him to his feet. "Gird your loins, men. We're going into battle."

Chapter 25

While I was perfectly content going on a raid in my jeans, Gem pointed out the bloodstains and insisted it was bad luck.

Given Gem was about four inches shorter than me, and I was a mean five-eight, borrowing her clothes was out of the question. The clothes I'd left behind were still in the armoire, and when she pulled out a black dress, I regarded her with a patient smile.

"This isn't a cocktail party," I said, tossing it on the bed.

Her wavy hair bobbed when she tilted her head to the side. "A dress is less restrictive if you have to flash."

I gave her knee-high boots a pointed stare. "What about those?"

"I can run in anything," she said with a playful smirk.

Not everyone could pull off tall boots and a black romper. I admired her confidence.

After I threw on a pair of dark jeans and a formfitting shirt with long sleeves, we rushed downstairs where the van was waiting. It was after dark, and once Christian had checked the area to make sure it was clear, we headed into the city.

The van bounced around, and I gripped the bench to keep from flailing about since we didn't have on seat belts. There were no regular seats, only narrow benches on either side. Viktor drove, Shepherd rode shotgun, and the rest of us were holding on to our butts during sharp turns.

Wyatt tapped his boots on the cheap carpet. "I'm not going

anywhere near you guys, just so you know. Don't even think about following me."

"We know," Gem said with an exaggerated tilt of her head.

I looked across the van at him. "Why not?"

He lifted his eyes. "Do you really need to ask? I don't like to be anywhere in the vicinity of a murder scene, especially when it's happening. I'm just here to search for evidence. You keep those freshies away from me. That's a therapy session I ain't got time for."

Christian sat to the right of Wyatt, and he'd been staring at my legs since we left Keystone.

I tipped my head to the side. "What?"

"Where's your lucky dress?"

"Where's yours?"

Claude put his arm around me. "Tone it down, Christian. Let's not turn on each other before we even get there."

Christian folded his arms. "That's grand coming from a big house cat who flipped his switch on our last raid."

"That wasn't my fault," Claude growled. "He hit Gem."

Gem stood up and crossed the van, taking a seat in Claude's lap and wrapping her arm around his right shoulder. "Don't worry about me; I'm a Mage, remember?"

"That doesn't mean I like seeing a female get hurt."

She giggled. "I'm the lookout girl tonight, so you don't have to worry about me. Just stay calm. We can't control you when your switch is flipped—it's chaos. And the last time, we were supposed to catch the guy, not kill him."

Gem poked at his teeth where his fangs would be if they were out, and I realized he must have bitten a Mage and sentenced him to death.

I couldn't tell what direction we were heading. Viktor's plan was to park a few blocks away from Darius's house, just in case his men were scattered to report suspicious activity. I had drawn a layout of the building from what I'd seen, and I had to describe it to Niko, including furniture placement and any steps I remembered. There were numerous floors I hadn't seen, so that raised concern.

Wyatt showed everyone the blueprint, but I noticed that it had been renovated from the original design.

Wyatt chuckled privately, his eyes downcast.

Christian glared and elbowed him in the ribs. "Mind sharing the joke?"

"An architect was checking out the land next door to Keystone. It looks like someone's buying it."

Niko leaned forward from his seat on my left. "That land has been up for sale for years. No one can afford the price they set."

"Well, someone did. Any guesses on who it is?"

Shepherd peered around from the passenger seat. "Hell to the no."

Gem looked between them. "Who is it?"

"My bet's on Darius," Christian said.

Shepherd cursed under his breath. "If he's the new neighbor, I'm torching his lawn."

A few of us chuckled.

"Who owns it?" I asked.

Christian stroked his beard. "Someone who wants to make a lot of money. That's prime real estate up there."

Gem squeaked when the van hit a bump.

I glanced around. "We're dressed like we're going to a funeral."

"Are you trying to jinx us? Jaysus wept."

"I'm just pointing out the obvious. If we pile out of the van looking like this, someone's going to think we're up to something. No one ever goes to these things in polka dots?"

Niko barked out a laugh. "I wouldn't know the difference."

"Maybe we should shut off the circuit breakers when we get inside," I suggested. "Throw those goons in the dark."

"What good would that do?" Wyatt asked. "Do I look like I can see in the dark?"

I tapped my finger against my temple. "Think about it. Four of us in this van are undetectable to a Mage. Gem, Niko, and I can conceal our energy, and nobody can sense Christian. We're not as helpless as they are. Claude can sniff out a Twinkie within a five-mile radius, Christian and I can see in the dark, and Niko doesn't need light. We'd have more of an advantage than they would. You can take a pen light."

"That's not a bad idea," Viktor said over his shoulder. "Scan the outside of the building for the circuit breakers, and if we find nothing, then check the basement."

"*If* we get in," Wyatt said, giving me a skeptical glance.

I unknotted a small tangle in my hair. "Look, if there's no secret passageway, we'll bust through the windows. No big deal. The only place they'll have to go is the roof or out the back door."

"Unless they have fire escapes," Wyatt added.

Shepherd glared at him. "Why do you always have to be the wet blanket?"

Viktor parked the van, and we climbed out the rear door. When Claude jumped out, the van practically bounced with relief.

"Pair up," Viktor said.

Christian stepped out and breezed by me. "I go solo."

Viktor pointed at Shepherd. "You're with Raven. Keep an eye on her."

The team scattered in different directions, some walking up the dark street and others skulking in the shadows. Shepherd and I stopped by a square-shaped manhole cover in an alley that I recognized as one leading to the underground tunnels. Most of the street covers had been sealed up over the years, but usually the ones that were forgotten were located in alleyways.

Shepherd set down a cloth tool bag and tire iron. The manhole was large enough that I could easily slip through, but I made a skeptical appraisal of Shepherd's V-shaped body and broad shoulders.

He ran his hand around the square cover. "It's not bolted."

"Hurry up," I whispered.

He glared. "Feel free to lend a hand. This thing weighs more than you."

Shepherd used the tire iron to pry open the lid and drag it aside. Then he rose to his feet and gaped down at the black hole. "I'm not sure I can fit in there."

I clapped my hand on his shoulder. "Of course you can. I'll go first, and if you get stuck, I'll just tug on your legs until something pops."

"Get in before I change my mind."

I sat on the edge with my legs hanging down, pushing away thoughts of flesh-eating monsters that would devour me. I lowered myself, gripping the edge and then dropping to the lower level.

Grit and dust covered the concrete floor, and when I switched on my flashlight, it revealed a dark tunnel with a curved ceiling. A few rats screeched and scurried into the shadows.

Shepherd sat down with his legs dangling, and when he tried to lower himself, he got stuck. After a few curse words, he slipped one arm through the hole and then hung suspended for a brief moment before he fell onto his back. Sweat glistened on his forehead, and he stared warily at the tiny eyes glowing in the darkness before scrambling to his feet.

"Don't you need the tire iron?"

"Not from inside," he said, glancing at our surroundings. "I don't feel good about this tunnel situation."

"It's not so bad. A few drapes, a pretty vase…"

He ran his hand across his bristly hair. "You don't need to tell me if anyone's coming at us. I can usually feel the emotional spike. Sharpen your light and rely on your senses. If anyone approaches, use your night vision to see if they're armed. Got it?"

"Where's Wyatt? I thought you two always partnered up."

"He's probably with Christian. Wyatt doesn't carry weapons. That's not his job when we go on these assignments. He stays out of the action, so he needs the most protection."

We moved north, my flashlight flooding the ground ahead of us. "Maybe Viktor should have partnered them to begin with."

Shepherd spat out a curse when he stepped over a rat. "Wyatt and I work together searching through evidence. Mostly I just protect his ass until he gets the job done, but sometimes he needs me to pick up emotional imprints on documents to find out what's important."

Shepherd had packed a knife but no guns since they would

draw attention in the city. A guy like Shepherd didn't need a weapon with arms like those.

"How do you know we're going the right way?" he asked.

"I have a good sense of direction. After a few years living on the streets, I got into a habit of counting my steps, and I know how many it takes to cross a street or pass a building. Right now we're passing the bookstore. I know where we're going and how far it is from here, so it shouldn't be a problem."

"Ah. So you're like a little Rain Man."

I smiled and looked up at him. "I think this is the first time I've heard you utter more than two sentences. You're a quiet guy."

"Don't have much to say."

I shone the light in his face. "Really? Because usually those are the people with the most going on in their head."

He winced and knocked my hand away. "Get that light off me."

Even though I tried to play it off like he didn't scare me, Shepherd was an intimidating man. He reminded me of some of the tough guys my father used to hang around with at the biker bars, and not all of them were teddy bears. Some of those men had done hard time and were broken beyond repair—to the point where doing bad things gave them a thrill. It made me wonder how a Sensor—who could feel people's fear, love, anger, and sorrow—could be so apathetic.

I increased the distance between us, keeping my hand on the dagger strapped to my thigh. For all I knew, Viktor had given him a special order to dispose of me when this was all finished.

"This is it," I whispered, looking up at a pocket of light that seeped through a small hole in the cover above us.

Shepherd lifted his hands and touched it. "I don't sense anyone in there." He set his wrench on the floor and then reached up, pressing his palms against the rectangle. "Moment of truth."

I held my breath, praying it hadn't been sealed from inside. From what I'd overheard, many of the building owners didn't know the tunnels existed, or if they did, assumed they were for drainage.

He pounded at it a few times before exerting all his strength pushing it up. The metal scraped, and then one side popped up. He carefully balanced it in his hands so as not to make more noise than necessary. After a few solid pats with the palm of his hand, the other side lifted up. This one wasn't as heavy-duty as the one on the street. Shepherd stood on his tiptoes and carefully moved the lid out of sight.

"I can't reach that," I whispered.

Didn't matter, because Shepherd must have been the master champion of pull-ups. He lifted himself with ease, squeezing one arm in first before wiggling his way through. I held on to his legs, boosting him up so he wouldn't get lodged in the opening. After a second, he reached down with one arm and I took it. I was moving from one dark place to the next, and halfway out, he let go so I could crawl the rest of the way. I shone my small flashlight around the dark basement. Large dusty boxes and pieces of junk were stacked in corners, and wooden beams supported the ceilings.

Shepherd walked the length of the room in search of the circuit breakers. He almost passed a box and then did a backstep.

"What is it?" I whispered, shining my light on the wall.

He shook his head. "Security alarms."

I snorted. "Does he think calling humans to save the day is a good idea if a Mage breaks in?"

"I doubt it goes to one of them. There might be a private group set up with Breed, but it probably came with the building. Either way, it's a noisemaker, so snip snip."

While he took care of that, I tested the air in search of Mage energy. Most let their shields down in private places, so their energy pulsed and quivered. I didn't sense anything in the immediate area.

After Shepherd finished messing with the security box, he found the circuit breakers. "Get ready," he said. "When the lights go out, someone's coming down. Hide behind that beam."

When Shepherd switched off the breakers, I turned off my flashlight and waited in darkness. Gem was the lookout girl on the street, and Niko had climbed onto the roof with Viktor. I wasn't sure where everyone else had gone, but our job was to get in and kill the lights. That was Keystone's signal to enter.

The basement door opened, and Shepherd slipped out of sight. My Vampire eyes allowed me to see somewhat, although not as well as I would have liked.

My heart raced as someone approached with clumsy steps, his shoes scraping against the floor and the smell of his cologne wafting over.

"Dammit," he murmured. "Where's a flashlight when you need one?"

He moved into sight, his hand running along the wall. Shepherd crept toward him, cocking his head as if he were using sonar to detect where the Mage was in proximity to him.

Even though I could see, I gave this one to Shepherd. Did a guy like that really need backup? Part of me wanted to watch him in action and see if a Sensor—who didn't have any gifts of strength or speed—could take on a Mage.

"Hurry up!" a voice shouted from the top of the stairs.

Shepherd's eyes turned in that direction, and they were wide. We'd expected one to come down while the other guards scrambled in the darkness to secure the doors.

That was what smart guards would have done.

But this added an additional layer of fuckery to the situation. If the guy at the top of the stairs sensed something was amiss, he'd alert the house and lock us in. Hopefully Viktor and the others had found a way inside.

I moved stealthily toward the staircase.

"Jim?" the man called out.

"Christ on a cracker, give me a second, will ya?" the man by the breakers yelled back.

I neared the stairs, assessing the man who stood in the doorway. He didn't look especially strong, and I didn't see a weapon in his hands.

When a metal tool hit the floor behind me, he took a step back. "Jim?"

Before he could slam the door, I rushed up the stairs and drove a stunner into his chest—the only stunner I had brought with me.

He fell like a sack of potatoes, and I closed the door and slid him down the steps before someone heard the ruckus.

Shepherd hustled toward me, his hands reaching out blindly in the darkness.

"Watch your step!" I hissed.

He halted in his tracks, just inches from the body slumped at the bottom of the stairs. Shepherd took a few baby steps until his foot nudged the Mage's thigh. I tensed when I considered he might finish off the Mage, but Shepherd stepped over the paralyzed man, climbing the stairs until he bumped into me.

"That leaves only two more," he said quietly. "Right?"

I swallowed the lump in my throat. Viktor would have never agreed to this if I'd told him I was uncertain how many guards there were in the house. Darius mentioned four in conversation, but he could have been lying.

Shepherd reached for the doorknob and opened the door. "Did you finish him off?" he whispered.

Finish, as in beheaded.

"Hell no," I whispered back. "I'm going to leave my dagger in his chest and pick it up on the way out. You might be able to use him for questioning."

Shepherd's jaw set.

I flounced into the adjoining room. Sure, I could have popped his core light and killed him the easy way, but time was ticking, and killing a guy for blocking a doorway didn't seem like a necessity.

The kitchen was bereft of color or other decorative items one might find, like fruit bowls or sugar canisters. Light trickled in from a window by the side door, illuminating the white tile and matching cabinets. Shepherd moved quietly to the left and turned the lock.

Christian filled the doorway, leaning against the doorjamb on his left arm, one foot crossed in front of the other, his other fist anchored against his hip as if he'd been collecting dust for hours.

Just outside the kitchen was the entrance of the house—front door to the left and a hall and enclosed stairwell to the right. I knew there was a hall on the other side of the living room, so I nudged Shepherd and pointed in that direction. "Check out the rooms on the other side."

Christian put his arms around us, poking his head in the middle. "Lest you forget, I can hear a sight better than you. Everyone's upstairs. Bottom floor's empty."

I shrugged him off and headed up the steps, gripping my only remaining weapon: a push dagger. Most of my good stunners were in my bag, which was either somewhere in this house or in an incinerator. We ascended the steps, and Shepherd brandished a knife and jogged past us.

"He likes to be the hero," Christian said quietly.

"And what about you?"

"I approach battle like sex."

I snorted. "Infrequently?"

He took an extra step so he was ahead of me. "When you get wrapped up in emotions, you make mistakes. There's never a reason to hurry. Take your time, assess the situation, and you'll always come out on top. Men who get excited and hurry never do the job right."

We reached the second floor and realized there wasn't a door. It was pitch-black, and I could barely make anything out. It looked like someone had remodeled the inside to resemble an office building, with a long hall and several doors. It made it impossible to hide, let alone flee if someone attacked us. We turned left and approached an intersecting hall that led to the right, cutting across the building.

Christian held his arm in front of me and placed his index finger against his lips. Shepherd kept going straight, his hand brushing against the wall as he attempted to maneuver through the dark. I suspected he was also using his Sensor abilities to read emotional imprints.

Christian and I neared the middle hall that Shepherd had passed, and as soon as we turned right, we noticed a Mage on the other side, leaning against a door.

I'd never seen a Vampire shadow walk up close, but watching Christian float through the darkness without making a sound was breathtaking. One minute he was by my side, and the next, in front of the Mage.

Shepherd barked out a curse, and a fight erupted in a nearby room. The Mage in front of Christian started to move, but Christian struck him in the head with a powerful blow.

I ran back to the stairs and charged up to the third level, my heart pounding with adrenaline. As I emerged from the stairwell, a Mage on the left was barreling toward me like a tornado, his fists pumping in the air. Because he couldn't see in the dark, he wasn't using his Mage energy and his pace was unsteady. I jumped when a gunshot went off on a floor above.

The Mage drew a gun, and I wondered why Darius felt safe arming his men with such ineffective weapons. I flattened my back against the wall, deciding not to waste my efforts on this idiot when my real target was Darius.

After he passed me and vanished down the stairs, I opened the door to a middle room and shone my light in, not caring if anyone spotted me. When I saw it was empty, I crossed to the door on the opposite side. This place felt more like a maze than a home. Who could live like this? Darius made such a fuss about land and property, yet his own home felt more like a prison or a mental institution. If there were windows, they only existed in the outer rooms, which were all closed off.

As soon as I stepped into the hall and turned right, I ran into someone.

Wyatt stumbled backward, his eyes wide. A small penlight fell out of his hand and tapped noisily across the floor.

"It's me," I whispered. "Raven."

Wyatt heaved a sigh and quietly said, "You scared the crazy out of me."

I watched as he bent down to pick up his flashlight. "I thought Christian was supposed to be protecting you?"

He pulled off his hat and stuffed it halfway into his back pocket. "If that man were a sock, he'd be the one that goes missing."

"Well, I saw him downstairs. Is there anyone else on this floor?"

He shrugged. "I came in through the fire escape. You didn't hear the window break?"

"No, that must have been when the gunshots were going off."

He peered over his shoulder at Viktor, who stepped out from an open door. "I need to find his office. Have you seen it? Anything with filing cabinets or a desk."

I shook my head, and we parted ways. Since Viktor and Wyatt had this floor covered, I circled back to the stairs. If Darius was in the building, he was probably hiding as close to the roof as he could get.

A commotion sounded from above, and I ran up the steps, my light moving erratically across the walls with every swing of my arm. More shots fired, and I stumbled out of the stairwell, spinning in confusion when I didn't run into a wall. Instead of narrow hallways, the entire floor was wide open, separated by accent walls in the center that went toward the back.

A light flashed with the crack of a gunshot, and a sharp sound whizzed by my ear. I dropped my flashlight and shrieked, then raced across the open living room.

Claude roared, and when I reached the other side, I glimpsed him fighting a Mage who was armed with a dagger. Claude didn't need a weapon. He had venomous fangs, and before they moved out of my line of vision, I saw him dive in for a bite like a savage animal.

Another shot was fired and grazed my arm. I flashed into a dark corner, grimacing in pain and trying to get a sense of the layout. There were several couches, two coffee tables, and a wall with a stone fireplace on the center wall to the right. I grabbed a vase and flung it across the room at the Mage, hoping he'd stop shooting long enough for me to do something.

Still armed with my dagger, I flashed toward him but tripped over an area rug. I rolled hard across the floor, close enough to him that I swiped my blade, cutting his leg. I tried to remember the moves Niko had shown me. Punching him in the testicles wasn't one of them, but it always got the ball rolling in the right direction, so to speak.

He had the perfect opportunity to shoot me point-blank, but he cursed and dropped the gun, attempting to grab my wrist and disarm me. He was probably more concerned I had a stunner, and as we wrestled, he accidentally kicked the gun away with the heel of his shoe and sent it flying beneath the couch.

"Hold her still!" someone shouted.

When I heard the first shot, I scrambled out of sight. My flashlight was on the floor, aimed at the empty fireplace, but it illuminated the room just enough to allow me to see more clearly.

With a second gunman coming at me, I raced toward the stairwell, and just as he began firing, something slammed against my back and pinned me to the wall. At least seven more shots went off, making me shrink where I stood. A few of them struck the wall on either side of me. Suffocated and confused, I spun around and realized Christian was shielding me from the attack—using his body like a cage, his forearms pressed firmly against the wall, his head low. He was taking bullets for me. One right after the other until clicks sounded from an empty cartridge.

"Dammit," the man hissed.

I looked up at Christian with wide eyes. It took me a second to process that he had just saved me from being turned into swiss cheese. I released a shaky breath, my eyes fixed on the blood oozing from his right arm, neck, and God knows where else. With a trembling hand, I touched my chest and stomach, searching for injuries that weren't there. The bullets must have lodged inside him, perhaps ricocheting off his bones.

He eased back a little and grimaced.

"Why did you do that?" I whispered.

Christian lightly shrugged. "Old habits die hard."

He stepped aside, appraising the gunman. It was then that I recognized Declan—the man who had tortured me with a hot iron.

"That one's mine," I said through clenched teeth.

A dark look flickered in Christian's eyes. "I just took a Hail Mary of bullets for you—twelve to be exact. You're fresh out of weapons, and you want to go for the big arseface who's twice your size?"

"That's the man who burned my face."

I thought Christian would stand aside with a sweep of his arm and let me get my revenge, but his fangs descended, and I'd never seen him more menacing than in that moment.

Christian inclined his head and dramatically turned, stalking toward the man who'd just loaded another clip. He fired at Christian, each shot resounding in my head and making me jump.

Bang.

Bang.

Bang.

Christian walked coolly toward him and then snapped the man's wrist, the gun falling to the floor. Declan wailed in pain, unable to escape the Vampire's iron grip.

Christian seized the man by the throat and lifted him off the ground for a few breathless seconds. The second Mage took off as soon as he realized they were up against a Vampire.

"So you're the one who likes to torture women."

Christian spoke in a calm voice, one that told me he was charming the man. "Do me a favor and light a nice warm fire. I want the flames high, and be sure to place the same instrument in there as you used on Raven. You and I are going to have some fun. You'd like that, wouldn't you?"

The man coughed for air when Christian set him down. He turned toward the fireplace and put a log on the grate.

I dragged my eyes away from him and stared daggers at Christian.

He chuckled, his voice throatier than before. "Worry not, lass. Sometimes you have to lie to get them to cooperate."

I picked up the flashlight and shone it on him. "You're still bleeding."

He glanced down. "Aye. It's slower to heal the more blood we lose. There's only one thing that'll speed it along." He lifted his gaze to my neck, and I stepped back.

"Then slurp on *him*," I suggested, nodding at Declan.

Christian gave me a crooked smile. "I have other plans for that one. Besides, it doesn't work as well unless it's from a Vampire."

"I'm not letting you drink my blood."

He clapped a hand on my shoulder, his voice raspy. "That's all right. You're only half Vampire anyhow, so it probably wouldn't work. Never you mind. The bullets left over will work themselves out... eventually," he said, laying on the guilt.

Christian took a seat on a small stool while the Mage stoked the fire.

Claude rounded the corner, blood staining his mouth. He looked like a fallen angel with his beautiful features and savage eyes. He flared his nostrils and surveyed the scene before disappearing to search the outer rooms.

I thought about those split seconds when Christian reacted like a bodyguard—my bodyguard—shielding me from an onslaught of bullets. Was I overreacting? He could have just let the Mage take me out, and that was exactly what I'd expected from a man like Poe.

But why didn't he?

I drifted toward him, a rattling sound coming from his chest each time he drew in a deep breath.

One swallow of blood; it seemed like such a little thing. Still standing, I straddled his legs and cupped his face in my hands. Christian's eyes rose to meet mine. His shoulders were hard beneath my fingertips, and before one of us said something that would change my mind, I bent over and turned my head away, feeling the brush of his short beard against my neck.

His breath heated my skin in the place his lips touched.

"I can't do this," he whispered unconvincingly.

"Take what you need."

His fangs grazed along my neck, inviting and deadly. My heart slowed down, beating strong, and something flickered between us—a sharp desire that made me lean into him. His hand briefly slid between my legs before he pushed me back.

Christian's dark gaze fixed on my bleeding arm, and he lifted it, placing his mouth on the wound and gulping down the blood. This felt way less erotic, and all that sexual tension that had sparked up between us melted away as I watched him licking my arm.

"I'm not an ice cream cone," I said. "Hurry up."

"It's not as pleasant this way," he snapped.

"I offered you my neck. Doesn't it all taste the same?"

He licked the corner of his mouth. "Maybe I prefer to draw the blood out and not have it gush into the back of my throat like from a stuck pig."

"I could always pour it into a glass. Or would you prefer a baby bottle so you can suck on the nipple and draw it out?"

He lapped at another stream, his voice a murmur. "This is a truly scintillating conversation. If you don't mind, a little peace and quiet would be appreciated."

Watching him drink my blood should have repulsed me, and in some ways it did, but it also made me think of moments ago when his lips were pressed to my jugular and a spike of need went through me. Was the Vampire in me really a separate entity, waving her arms and begging for someone to take her vein?

It made me want to smack her.

His eyes darted up, and I had the strangest feeling come over me—as if he'd seen me naked.

He let go and wiped his mouth with the back of his hand. "You really don't like Vampires, do you? I can taste it in your blood. Is it because you're afraid of what I can do that you can't?"

"No, it's because Vampires think everyone is inferior to them."

"You're marvelous at hiding pain," he said, nodding at my arm. "The bullet struck a nerve."

"What else can you tell?" I asked, my voice unsteady. I hadn't given much thought to what he might learn from me by drinking my blood.

He stood up and arched his back. "I think we better tidy up."

A pinging noise sounded when one of the bullets popped out of his chest and onto the floor.

"That's disgusting."

He stepped closer and stroked my cheek with the back of his hand. "You can't fool me, precious. You're curious enough about blood sharing that you would have preferred me to drink from your neck." He leaned forward, his lips against my ear, his words a soft whisper. "Deny it."

I shoved him back when another bullet clinked against the floor. "Not everyone thinks you're the Adonis of the modern era. Are you done playing with your food, or can I finish off that Mage?"

All emotion erased from his expression, and he inclined his head. "You need to make yourself absent now. What I'm about to do to that man will give you waking nightmares for the rest of your life."

I shuddered at the black look he gave me and hurried away. Before entering the stairwell, I glanced over my shoulder and saw Christian turning to face the fire, watching the Mage place an iron poker into the flames.

When I reached the third level, a blanket of darkness surrounded me, forcing me to sharpen my Vampire eyes. I slowed my pace, opening each door I passed and searching the dark corners. Most of the rooms were empty, but some had sitting chairs and other casual furniture. Two were garishly decorated—stuffed full of abstract paintings, silver candleholders, and zebra-print sofas. If that was where he seduced his women, no wonder he was single.

I stopped in my tracks when I noticed a faint light seeping through the edge of a bookcase. Not bright enough for the human eye to detect, but enough that it made me go in and check it out. There were hinges on the left side, so I thought about it like a door, assuming something functioned as a lever. In the place a doorknob might be, I noticed a dragon-shaped bookend. I pulled the head and heard a click.

The heavy case quietly pushed open, and I entered a small room. Pale light skimmed across the floor from another bookshelf to my right, and that was when I realized that someone had done a masterful job at constructing a secret room within a secret room. I drew in a deep breath of stale air, looking around at the two sitting chairs, thin carpet, and wood paneling.

Unarmed, I searched for something sharp or heavy. The only items that fit the bill were a pair of toenail clippers and a floor vase that looked heavier than a small cow.

Didn't matter. Whoever was in that room was about to die.

Chapter 26

I surged into the secret room, coming face-to-face with an empty leather chair. The light hurt my eyes, and I noticed my shadow stretched in front of me to the right, joined by another. I turned, taking a few steps back from Darius, who stood beside a tall floor lamp. The door quietly closed, leaving us alone in this confined space.

"What treachery is this?" he asked calmly, quietly. "We had an arrangement. How dare you bring them here… to my home!"

Darius had on gym attire: black pants, no shirt, and white gauze or cotton wrapped around his hands. By the looks of the sweat still dripping from his hair, we'd definitely taken him by surprise. My eyes flicked up to a longsword on the wall behind the lamp.

Darius kept his eyes steady on mine. "You foolish child. You could have had everything."

"If you wanted to know what an imbecile looks like, all you had to do was look in the mirror. Oh, it doesn't seem like you have any here in your hidey-hole. You're a courageous man, Darius. Truly."

He advanced, forcing me to step back. "I value my life. It doesn't look like you can say the same."

"You got that right. I'm here because it's not just my life I value, but the people you threatened to harm."

I flashed around him, but he caught me by the waist. Darius flung me against the wall, and I fell hard on my back. When he came at me, I kicked his leg and he stumbled, giving me enough time to scramble to my feet. The few maneuvers Niko had taught me were defensive tactics for escaping, and when Darius seized my wrists, I had reason to test their effectiveness.

I twisted my arms and broke his grasp, then kicked him in the stomach. Before I could withdraw my leg, he grabbed it tightly and swung my entire body around. When he let go of my leg, I crashed into the chair, scooting it several feet across the floor before landing on my side.

Darius fell over me, striking my face twice before I shielded myself from the attack with my arms. I tried to buck his weight, but it was useless. I had the wind knocked out of me, but I was in survival mode and not ready to give up the fight. When he made the mistake of resting his left arm against the floor to prop himself up, I lurched forward and sank my fangs into his fleshy bicep.

He shoved my head away, scrambling backward to put distance between us.

I stood up and tested my jaw to make sure it wasn't broken. "Why do men like you exist?"

He swiped the blood trickling down his arm and sneered. "And what makes you so superior? A congenial smile?"

I withdrew the sword from the wall and sliced the air between us. "Nope. But I'm really awesome at playing piñata. Never tried it with a sword."

He crawled backward on his elbows until he reached the far wall. Darius lifted the tufted chair, using it as a shield.

"Are you kidding me?" I shouted.

It wasn't a large room—maybe twelve feet one way and twenty the other. Acting on impulse, I swung the sword and struck the lampshade. The bulb shattered, throwing us into darkness.

I held my breath, moving aside as I waited for my eyes to adjust. With my Mage light concealed, the only way he'd know my location was by sound.

Grainy images slowly came into focus. Darius held the chair, his arms trembling from the weight of it.

He suddenly tossed the chair at me and I dodged it with ease. Darius squatted on the floor, his eyes drawn upward and head cocked to the side. I squeezed the grip of the sword, angling the blade over my left shoulder.

My heart skipped a beat when the door cracked open, and we both turned to look. Before I could see who was coming in, Darius charged at the door, slamming it partially shut as someone roared in pain. A penlight toppled onto the floor, spraying a narrow stream of light across the room in a cartwheel of motion.

"Son of a ghost!"

The door surged open, and Wyatt stumbled into the room. Darius threw a burst of energy into him, and Wyatt's feet came off the ground as he absorbed what could have been a thousand-volt shock of electricity.

I ran forward and swung my sword, but Darius ducked out of the way. It sliced against the open door, wedging deep into the wood. I tugged, but I couldn't dislodge it fast enough.

Darius exploded into action, charging toward me and slamming his hand into my chest before I could free the sword. He was testing to see if Mage energy affected me.

My feet came off the ground, and I hurtled backward in the short space until my back hit the wall with a sickening thud. I toppled over to the floor, clutching my chest and wheezing for breath. The energy blast hadn't put a dent in me, but he'd hit me rather hard with his palms.

Darius pivoted around, gripped the sword, and wrenched it out of the wood. My eyes widened when the flashlight glinted on the metal as it sliced through the air. I rolled across the floor, the tip of his sword nicking my arm, right below the gunshot wound.

I surged to my feet and flashed around him, going for the metal penlight on the floor. The beam of light spun about the room as I raised my arm and drove it into his back with all the force I could muster. One might believe a penlight could never penetrate skin, but that would be a misconception.

Darius roared in pain.

He flung his sword backward and let go. I turned to watch the tip of it stab the floor right between Wyatt's legs, just inches from his...

Wyatt shrieked, holding his crotch as the sword bowed back and forth. "I don't get paid enough for this shit. You hear that, Viktor?" he shouted. "I want a raise!"

Darius fell to his knees, desperately trying to grasp for the light, which was centered out of his reach.

I sauntered over to Wyatt and pulled the sword out from the wood. As I approached Darius, I smirked when a thought crossed my mind. "I guess the pen really is mightier than the sword." With my fingers around the grip of my blade, I circled him, aiming for his neck. "Can't win 'em all."

He was still reeling from the pain in his back—the light beaming onto Wyatt's face and climbing up the wall as Darius hunched over, trying to reach for it. "I'll give you money."

"If I wanted your money, I wouldn't have brought backup. Don't you think?"

I'd never done this before—beheaded a man. I knew immortals saw it as a necessary means to an end, but the image was strikingly gruesome. I leveled the blade across his neck and drew back like a batter about to hit a home run.

"Wait! Raven, wait," Wyatt sputtered, still struggling from his injuries. "We have evidence."

I glanced over my shoulder. "So?"

Shepherd filled the doorway, a file in one hand and a slim cord in the other. "You don't have to kill him. We've got everything we need to take this son of a bitch down."

Seeing the relief on Darius's face filled me with inexplicable rage.

Shepherd stepped forward and shouted, "Don't do it!"

I'd positioned the blade against Darius's neck, power surging through me.

Wyatt tried to stand but fell over. He gripped Shepherd's ankle. "Get me out of here. I can't be around to watch this."

I stared at Darius long and hard, contemplating in those seconds which choice was the right one. When I thought about sending him to Breed jail so they could execute him for his offenses, an unexpected feeling of satisfaction swept over me. A quick death seemed far too merciful compared to the humiliation of jail, court, and then facing his peers as a broken man.

"I never thought I'd say this, but cuff him."

Shepherd didn't just cuff him, he hog-tied the man so he wouldn't be able to use his Mage energy. When Shepherd finished, he assessed Wyatt's injuries and discovered a few broken ribs from when Darius had slammed the door on him.

"Sit down," Shepherd ordered me, setting the leather chair upright. He tore the bottom off Wyatt's shirt and held it between his teeth. "Looks like a clean shot. Didn't hit a major artery. That gash is a problem." He skillfully wrapped the cloth around my arm and tied it tight.

"You're good at this," I said, noticing how he doctored my wounds as if he'd done it a million times before.

Viktor entered the room with a flashlight. "Shepherd, take the vermin out of here. I've made a call to the higher authority; they're sending in Regulators for an official investigation."

Shepherd stood up, clearly exhausted, but he didn't rest for a moment before dragging Darius out of the room by his feet.

I looked myself over for other injuries but only noticed a few bumps and bruises. I'd never taken on anyone who was armed with a sword, so I was lucky to have made it out alive and with all my limbs intact.

Viktor knelt in front of Wyatt and patted his leg. "You did a good job finding those documents. Selfish men always make stupid mistakes, like keeping records of the money transactions from the people they're extorting. It makes them feel accomplished to look at the numbers and add to them."

Wyatt clutched his chest and grimaced. "And making a list of their victims so they can cross out the ones they disposed of. Why is it that most of the guys we catch get caught because they did the most inane things?"

"You found them," Claude said, making his way into the room.

Wyatt lazily looked up. "The trick doors automatically close. I just happened to walk by when I heard someone yell. It took me a minute to figure out how to open that blasted thing."

Viktor rose to his feet. "Where's Christian?"

A loud scream came from upstairs, and we all simultaneously looked at the ceiling.

"He's, um… indisposed," I said.

Claude's piercing yellow eyes locked on my blood-soaked bandage. I tensed when his fangs descended and a creature who was my mortal enemy approached me. One bite with all four canines was all it would take to end my life.

"Come here, female," he said, lifting me into his arms.

His purr was hypnotic, resonating in his chest and calming me almost immediately. I pressed my ear against him, curious about the bizarre reaction it elicited.

I heard Gem giggle. "Someone made a new friend."

Claude turned around, clutching me tighter.

Gem put her hands on her hips and erupted with laughter when she looked at Wyatt. "I *love* the crop top look. I just happen to know a fabulous Relic who's looking for a new friend."

He stared daggers at her.

A little embarrassed by the coddling, I drew back from Claude. "Why are you purring?"

He looked between Gem and me. "My girls are safe."

I'd never been anyone's girl, but the inclusive sentiment—sincere or not—kept me from sliding out of his arms and walking out the door. I had no excuse to lie in his arms like some helpless woman. My legs weren't injured, and I was perfectly capable of helping the men clean up.

But damn if I didn't let that Chitah carry me all the way out to the van.

Niko had his work cut out for him. Wyatt's ribs were so bad that he couldn't tolerate the constant pain whenever he took a breath, so Niko used his healing light to mend those breaks. Wyatt periodically gripped his crotch as if checking to make sure the boys were still there after his close encounter with the sword. Viktor had been shot three times, but he'd shifted into his wolf during the fight and then back. Exhausted, he sat in the passenger seat and napped while Claude took the helm and drove us back to Keystone.

No one stayed behind to give a statement. Viktor said the Regulators were given specific orders to collect the evidence left on the coffee table downstairs and document the scene. His contact with the higher authority would take care of the rest. Christian stayed behind for other reasons.

It was the first confrontation I'd ever walked away from victorious where I didn't want to vomit because I'd ingested blood or dark light.

The van hit a big bump, and everyone shouted and groaned at Claude's driving.

Niko wrapped his hands around my arm, gathering up his energy and forcing it into me with a snap of light. He leaned against the van, breathing heavily as if he'd run a marathon.

"Thanks, Niko. You didn't have to."

He laughed. "Women."

I rubbed my hand over the healed skin. "Why were they all armed with guns instead of stunners?"

"Guns work on everyone," Niko said. "It's a quick weapon that will either immobilize a man or slow him down. Then they can figure out what Breed they're dealing with and how to capture or kill them."

With the loud motor going and everyone half-asleep, I looked up at Niko and lowered my voice. "I think it's pretty shitty that they put the best warrior on roof patrol."

A smile touched his lips, and he inclined his head.

Maybe Viktor chose the best man to guard the roof in case Darius or his men fled the scene, but I couldn't help but think how spectacular Niko would have been, hunting and fighting those men in the dark hallways.

My body jerked when something heavy crashed on top of the van.

Gem looked up. "Why do you always have to do that?"

The back door swung open, Christian hanging on the edge. He reached for the roof and slung my duffel bag onto the floor. "I tripped over this in a hallway," he said, casually stepping inside and closing the door behind him. "You shouldn't leave behind things at the scene of the crime... like evidence."

"What took you so long?" she asked.

He waggled his brows. "I never turn down a free drink. What's wrong with Spooky?"

Gem glanced over at Wyatt, who was fast asleep on the bench across from us, his head practically in Shepherd's lap. "He almost got a vasectomy."

"Shame I missed that." Christian tossed me my dagger, and I almost shot out of my seat. "You left that upstairs."

"I had another in the basement."

"Don't worry about that," Shepherd said, arms folded. "Viktor's guy returns weapons left behind."

I glanced up at Niko, who had his eyes closed. Since the bench was long enough to lie on, I stood up and told him to rest. He curled up on his side, utterly exhausted, with one foot on the floor to keep him from rolling off the bench.

I moved toward the back doors, stepped over Christian's legs, and sat on the edge of the bench, putting Niko's other foot in my lap. It was a roomy van, absent of any windows.

I leaned against the door. "If your group gets any bigger, you're going to need a boat."

Christian wiped a smudge of blood off his wrist. "We'll just strap them on the front like a hood ornament."

He groomed his beard, acting as if we'd just left a fancy restaurant instead of a bloodbath. I wanted to ask him what he did to the Mage, but something told me I didn't want to know all the details. The look of gratification on his face was answer enough. Christian was a paradox—on one hand making remarks about my unethical behavior and knowing myself, and yet he relished his own kills.

Which just reaffirmed my belief that you can't trust a Vampire.

Sirens wailed behind us, and the van slowed to a stop.

"Oh for feck's sake," Christian spat. "I hope you have an extra set of plates for the van; he's going to call it in."

Claude rolled the window down, and I had to laugh at how ridiculously suspicious this looked.

"Is there a problem, Officer?"

Shepherd snorted.

A flashlight shone on Claude's face. Viktor roused from his sleep and sat up but didn't speak. Perhaps he thought someone with a Russian accent would appear suspicious to a cop.

"Your taillight's out," the human said.

Claude rested his arm on the van door. "Is that illegal?"

"I need to see your license and registration."

"This is bullshit," Shepherd muttered quietly.

Gem made a facial gesture that told him to shut up. The cop hadn't aimed his light in the back and didn't seem to know there was a vanload of immortals.

"Step out of the van," the cop said.

When Claude got out, Christian turned around, facing the rear.

The back doors popped open, and the officer shone his light in Christian's face. Then he aimed it to the left, and Wyatt lifted his head from Shepherd's lap, wiping the drool from the side of his mouth. His cropped shirt exposed his belly, and I barked out a laugh at the cop's bewildered expression.

His light beamed in my face and I winced, holding up my bloodstained arm to shield my eyes.

Christian leaned to the side, blocking the cop's line of vision. "Guard, let's you and I take a long walk." He slowly got out, keeping his eyes on the officer, who looked entranced.

Gem took a seat across from me. "This should be interesting."

"Is he going to kill him?"

Wyatt laughed. "If he's lucky. The last time Christian took a cop for a walk, the poor guy came back believing that we were fairy godmothers on our way to a ball. I bet they locked him up in a padded room."

Claude returned to the driver's seat and started up the engine.

After a brief minute or two, Shepherd got up and slammed the rear doors. "Nobody's got time for that. Let's go." He knocked on the door twice, and Claude hit the gas.

Chapter 27

As soon as we entered the mansion, the Keystone group howled victoriously. Several headed for the dining room to open a few bottles of wine while the rest of the team changed out of their bloody clothes. I took advantage of the last shower I might have for a while, taking a final look at the room that was once mine. Since my clothes were stained with blood, I stuffed them back into my bag and put on a loose pair of jeans and a long-sleeved grey shirt. After my last cab ride, I decided to walk back to the city. As long as it didn't rain, it would be a nice evening for that.

I hefted my duffel bag and slung it over my shoulder, taking a leisurely stroll down the stone steps, my fingers running along the banister and tracing the grooves of a corner statue. My shadow ran away from me each time I distanced myself from a hanging lantern.

When I saw Blue crossing the room in front of the stairs, I dropped my bag and ran down to the first level. "Blue! My father..."

She turned on her heel and touched my arm. "He's fine. Darius didn't send out his men to search the area. The only thing I saw moving for miles were a few rabbits and a teenager sneaking out."

My shoulders sagged, and I collapsed on the step behind me. I don't know what I would have done if anything had happened to him. I never meant to put him in danger with my late-night visits. I rubbed my eyes with trembling hands, trying to hide my emotions.

Blue's floor-length red dress looked antique, with long sleeves that widened at the cuff and a hood in the back. It was very plain and a deep rose color. It swished as she turned and sat to my left.

"Were you two close?" she asked.

He was my world, I thought to myself. But that was not what I said. "It wasn't the typical father-daughter relationship. I didn't appreciate him as much as I should have."

"Memories should be cherished, not looked upon with regret."

I tucked my unkempt hair behind my ears. "It's hard to think of my father as a memory when he's still alive."

She nudged me with her shoulder. "It gets easier with time."

I laced my fingers together. "So, you're a bird?"

She laughed and stared at the tips of her shoes. "My animal is a peregrine falcon. It's not as formidable as a bear or panther, but she allows me to go virtually anywhere undetected. She can rest on windowsills, fly through subways, and travel across the city faster than a cab could get you there. Most people don't pay attention to birds, so we make good trackers and spies."

"Don't you lose a lot of your clothes when you shift?"

"Not really. I plan most of my shifts and always choose a spot to leave my things where no one will find them. But the earrings sometimes get lost. No big deal. There are plenty more where they came from."

I hadn't connected the dots until just then. The feather in the earrings I'd seen her wearing must have belonged to her animal.

"You did a good thing tonight, Raven. To be honest, I didn't expect that from you. Darius has money and power, and his offer must have been tempting. That's a lot more than Viktor offered you. I've known people who switched sides for less."

"Darius only wanted to use me for his own gain. I'm nobody's lackey. If he hadn't done it right away, he would have eventually tried to get rid of me like he probably does with anyone who stands in the way of getting what he wants." I stood up and lifted my bag off the floor. "Thanks for looking out for my father. I guess maybe I owe you."

She stood up and lightly tugged a lock of my hair. "It wasn't a favor."

I looked on wistfully as Blue headed off toward the dining room, where bursts of laughter echoed through the dark hall.

"Raven, can I speak with you before you go?" Viktor asked, standing in the open doorway of a room to the right of the stairs.

The front door opened, and Christian strode in with an arsenal of attitude. He flipped off his trench coat and draped it over one of the wings of the statue next to me, pretending I wasn't there.

"I should give you a thick ear for leaving me behind like that, but I'm beginning to see my place in this house."

Viktor folded his arms. "Let's not be dramatic."

"I'd like to speak with you, Viktor. *Alone.*" Christian flashed an enigmatic look at me.

"It will have to wait. I need to discuss something with Raven before she leaves."

"It'll just take a moment of your time."

Viktor's hand flew up. "Let's not spoil the festivities. Unless someone is dying, it can wait."

I followed Viktor into the dark room, and he struck a match, lighting a small candle on the table to my right.

"Sit down," he said, closing the door. "This won't take long."

"You should really think about solar-powered lights. Did you know hardware stores sell lanterns that are rechargeable?"

He chuckled and moved the candle to the center of the table. "You young ones and all your inventions. There is something that natural light brings to a conversation that artificial cannot."

"An inability to read people's facial expressions?"

The candle stopped flickering and finally stretched into a slender body of light.

Viktor tucked his cheek against his fist. "What are your plans?"

"To leave the city."

His brows furrowed. "Why would you leave?"

Maybe I was just tired, but I had to clear my throat before I replied. "There's nothing left for me here but enemies."

"There is more to your story than that."

I placed my hands flat on the table, watching the way the candlelight illuminated my skin with gold accents. "I always believed that the custom of leaving behind your human family was pointless, so I kept visiting my father."

Viktor's eyes narrowed and he lowered his arm.

"No, it's not like that," I quickly said. "He doesn't know I'm alive. I just kept going back home so I could reminisce, I guess. It just felt good to be able to see his shadow moving around inside. Listening to the sound of his voice made me feel normal again—made me forget what I was, even if it was just for an hour. I've been putting him in danger all along, and I can't do that anymore." Tears gathered in my eyes, and I looked down.

It devastated me to sever that last thread—to say good-bye and close the door on the possibility of ever returning to my old life.

"I understand how you must feel," he began. "You are finally accepting your true death from that life. It must pain you beyond measure to turn your father into a memory, but we make sacrifices in order to protect those we love. That is why I asked you to leave. Each member of Keystone is family to me, and I would never put them in unnecessary danger."

"I'm sorry for that. I just didn't know how quickly I'd talk after someone put a fiery metal rod against my face." I rubbed my cheek, remembering the scorching agony. "I would have never been loyal to Keystone."

Viktor leaned forward. "Your actions belie your words of self-doubt. Not many people have as much conviction as you do, even if it's misdirected. There are times in life that we have to trust our instincts, and mine are telling me that you should stay."

I sat back, dumbfounded. "You're not serious."

"Finding Christian wasn't enough to change my mind. Loyalty is the glue that holds this team together, and you proved that tonight. When I saw you heading out the door, I realized that you hadn't done this to get back in." Viktor's eyes were reflective as he gazed at the candle, the lines etched in his face more visible. "It is my dream to someday see more groups like this one. There is too much crime and not enough effort to clean things up. You cannot imagine how many people are illegally making Vampires, but maybe you can, seeing as you're half. The population is growing, and it must be controlled. The black market is good money for those who do not want to earn a living the honest way."

"You kicked me out. I gave up information about Keystone."

"Why are you trying so hard to convince me otherwise? Do not squander your immortality. I cannot promise you riches or a chance to rise to a higher position; everyone here is an equal. All I can offer is a sense of justice in your life. This is an imperfect group of individuals, but we find balance." He rested his elbows on the table, his hands moving while he talked. "I cannot send Wyatt to fight because that's not what I hired him for. What can I do? I pair him up with a capable man who is not only skilled in combat but also has medical experience. Shepherd is impulsive and aggressive, and Wyatt's intelligence and quick thinking evens out their weaknesses. You see? I had my doubts when you went behind my back. That kind of influence is what could tear this group apart. But you have also shown growth and the potential to learn from your mistakes. What say you?"

I blew out a breath, and the candle shivered. "I wasn't expecting this at all."

"Perhaps you need a moment to think about my offer."

"Christian will leave if I stay. Am I worth losing someone you trust?"

"I have no control over free will." When Viktor rose to his feet, the chair noisily scraped against the floor. "I'll be in the dining room. Join us when you have come to a decision. You are welcome to stay for drinks no matter your choice."

He walked briskly toward the door and left it ajar on his way out.

I'd never felt so many conflicting emotions. This was an important decision that could change my life, and I needed to consider if this was something I actually *wanted* to do.

After a few moments, I blew out the candle and returned to the entrance room, where I stood in front of a window that overlooked the estate. The only thing I could see was darkness and my own reflection.

A grating sound caught my attention, and I turned to see Gem speedily approaching from the long hall on my left. She had on a pair of roller skates—the old ones with a wheel on each corner. Her arms swung back and forth as she breezed by me and giggled. "You'd better hurry up before they drink all the wine!"

A few strands of my hair floated in front of my face from the gust of wind left behind, and I thought how amusing it was that a Mage—who could flash at incredible speeds—would put on a pair of skates to get around a big mansion. Gem had a youthful heart, and it made me curious how she ended up in a place like this.

"Did he offer you the position?" Christian asked.

I watched his reflection in the window approach me from behind, but I didn't turn around. "Yes."

"And?"

"I'm thinking about it."

He tilted his head to the side. "You're an odd woman. One minute you're ready to cut a man's throat for the job, and the next you're having second thoughts."

"Can I have a moment to think?"

Frustrated, I stepped around him and hurried up the stairs. The last thing I wanted was a Vampire needling me when I had an important decision to make, and I didn't want him to say anything that would influence me either way. Viktor might want me, but would the rest give me a second chance if I were responsible for someone quitting? How would Christian leaving change the dynamic of the house?

I opened a set of french doors and stepped onto a small balcony that overlooked the estate. The railing was circular, large enough to accommodate a party of three. When I glanced up, the moon was shining bright, missing only a sliver from her edge. It was enough light to frost the tips of the trees. Most of the land in front of the house was a meadow, with only a few clusters of trees at a safe distance. It made sense not to have anything that would allow intruders to climb into the building. I had a breathtaking view of the road that led to the main gates, and the dense forest that surrounded Keystone from a distance.

"Looks like the rain finally cleared up," Christian said, leaning on the balcony to my left. "That's how I know Mother Nature is a woman. She changes her mind that fast." He snapped his fingers.

"Did you come here to impart your words of wisdom?"

He snorted. "Do I look like a fortune cookie? I just came up here to make sure you didn't jump. That would be another mess of yours I'd have to clean up."

I snickered. "If I wanted to kill myself, I would have gone to the roof and aimed for the courtyard pool when it was empty."

"I would have left you there for a week until your corpse festered."

"It's hard to believe you're single." I turned around, my elbows on the railing.

Christian stepped over my legs in a straddle and placed his hands on the rail behind me so we were inches apart. "Made up your mind?"

"Back at the cemetery, I realized how much they care about you. If you leave, they'll despise me. It might not be worth it."

He tilted his head to the side, lowering his eyes. It was a submissive gesture I'd seen Vampires do when they wanted your trust. "If you stay, I'll stay."

"And if I go?"

His eyes lifted to mine. "Let's stay, precious."

A gentle breeze cooled my hair, ruffling it over my shoulders. "We might end up killing each other."

Christian's smile widened, and it was a handsome grin. "Aye, but I'm rather fond of working with someone who can't stand me. Never a dull moment."

I lingered on his wolfish brows that sloped down and how beautiful his skin was up close—not alabaster and dull, but a natural beige with warm undertones that glowed with health and vitality. "I don't hate you, Christian. I think that's what scares me the most. That's why we need a clean slate."

He pursed his lips in thought. "And what do you propose?"

"If I stay, you still owe me a favor."

He leaned in close. "I'm not washing your knickers, if that's what you have in mind."

"I want you to scrub my memory of our kiss."

Christian blinked rapidly and jerked back. "Pardon?"

"I won't be able to work with you as long as I can remember us locking lips. It doesn't seem to bother you, but it changed things. I don't want to partner with someone that—"

"That you feel something for?"

When I stood up straight, he stepped back. "That's not what it's about. I have my reasons, and it shouldn't make a difference to you either way. If you erase it and this conversation, we'll be good. I don't work well with distractions."

"Maybe you just don't want to admit you feel something for a Vampire."

"It shouldn't matter to you *what* I feel."

He put his hands in his pockets and rocked on his heels. "I don't hate you any more than you hate me. You and I are cut from the same cloth, and that's why all the friction. That's not an admission I like you either—I don't have love for anyone. My heart is too black to feel such a whimsical emotion. If I can put the memory out of my mind, why can't you?"

"Yes or no?"

Christian lifted my chin with the crook of his finger. "Aye, I'll do it."

"Don't go poking around in there erasing other stuff. Just the kiss and this conversation. I don't ever want to find out about it. Don't joke about it or allude to it; just pretend it never happened. Give me a chance to do my job."

Maybe it was just a kiss to him, but I hadn't been able to put it out of my mind since. It hadn't been such a big deal at the time because Viktor had already thrown me out. But things were different now—I was different. I'd never be able to partner with him as long as we had this memory lingering between us like a sticky cobweb.

When Christian gazed deep into my eyes, a sweet rapture pulled me closer until the entire world blackened and all I could see was him.

"I've never met a woman quite like you," he said on a soft

breath. "And I don't know if that's a compliment or an insult. How old are you?"

"Timeless."

"Hmm. You're going to be a handful in a few hundred years. Hold still, lass," he said, his voice smooth and velvety. "This won't hurt a bit."

"Christian?"

"Yes?"

"Why do you call me precious?"

He drew closer, his hand curving around my nape. His tone was smooth and innocuous. "You don't read much, do you? The idea came to me when you were trying to steal my onion rings. There's an interesting book about a shiny little ring that drives men mad."

Our lips almost touched. "Be sure to erase that too."

"Aye, precious."

Chapter 28

AFTER STROLLING THROUGH THE MANSION and deliberating Viktor's offer, I finally headed down to the dining room with my bag in hand. I passed the empty booths and turned left, confronted by the expectant eyes of everyone in the house.

The crystal glasses on the table glimmered beneath light that emanated from the candles on the iron chandelier and lanterns alongside the wall. Several bottles of wine were open, some empty, and the ambiance in the room had an Old World feel, as if I'd stepped back in time. Viktor had made a fair observation about natural light; it was like a living organism that could affect your mood and frame of thought, making you feel more present.

Christian swallowed his entire glass of red wine and sat back.

Viktor's eyes swam down to my bag, and he rose to his feet, his glass high. "Let us make a toast to Raven and wish her a safe journey."

I dropped my things and strode forward. "No need to get up. I've considered your offer, Viktor, and…"

Everyone looked on with bated breath.

"And?" Wyatt blurted out. "I hate suspense."

"I accept."

Several of them drummed their hands against the table, creating a riotous sound of applause.

Viktor took his seat, a smile softening out all the hard lines of his features.

When I moved toward my chair and pulled it back, Niko placed his hand in the seat.

"You can't sit there."

The right side of the table got up and moved one down so that the chair to Viktor's left was empty.

"This is not a special seat," he said, wagging his finger. "Otherwise I would not have Wyatt on my right. I like to keep an eye on the new ones, so you will stay close to me."

Gem gave me a bright smile, her mouth open with excitement as she raised her glass.

"I thought you didn't drink," I pointed out.

"Grape juice."

Wyatt snorted. "She likes the berries *before* they've been devirginized."

Viktor rose from his seat and turned around, getting something at the short table behind him. Curious about Christian's expression, I risked a glance. We'd had a brief discussion earlier, but some of the details were fuzzy. I guess I had too much going on in my head to pay attention.

Wyatt looked three sheets to the wind. He removed his hat, slid it onto Shepherd's head, and then laced his fingers together while eyeballing Christian. "So how do you feel about your new partner, Mr. Poe?"

Christian draped his hand over the back of my chair. "She'll change her mind before the week's over. Not even her eyes can decide what color they want to be."

I smiled up at him. "If I have to do your laundry this week, I might have to agree." I leaned in and sniffed audibly.

Gem chortled. "It looks like Christian's met his match."

He withdrew his arm and gave me a peevish glance. When Viktor returned with a chalice in his hand, I turned to look. Christian tried to be discreet about sniffing his armpit, but I caught it out of the corner of my eye.

"This cup has been in my family for centuries," Viktor began. "And with this empty cup, we look to each other to fill it up with justice, friendship, brotherhood, and blood."

He handed the cup to Wyatt, who used the tip of a knife to prick his finger. Wyatt squeezed a couple of drops into the cup and then stuck his finger into his mouth.

"Really?" Shepherd said with derision. "You're the biggest wuss I know. Give me that."

Shepherd took the cup and knife from him, then sliced into his hand, sending a steady trickle of blood into the cup. "That's how it's done."

Wyatt pulled his finger out his mouth. "I'm hurting."

Shepherd glared at him. "Bullshit. You see this cup? You touched it, and that means I can feel what you're feeling."

"At least I won't need stitches."

Viktor snapped his fingers and pointed at Gem. Shepherd passed her the cup and knife, and they each took turns adding to the cup. When it reached Christian, his fangs punched out and he simply bit into his wrist, allowing the blood to trickle into the chalice.

When he set it in front of me, my stomach lurched. "I don't have to drink this, do I?"

Niko sputtered with laughter.

Viktor set a clean knife in front of me. "It's just symbolic."

"She can use her fangs," Christian suggested.

I picked up the knife and cut my hand, grimacing from the wound that would heal without a scar. Once I added my contribution, Viktor made a cut across his palm and squeezed his hand into a tight fist, releasing fat drops of blood to mix with our own. When he finished, he lifted the cup with his other hand.

"We are all different," he said, "but we are all the same when it comes to our purpose in life. Keystone was just an idea, but has become a beating heart because of each one of you. We are different Breeds, genders, and personalities, but as you can see, our blood is the same. Let us drink together and celebrate our victory... and our future. Now, enough with the formalities. Pour the wine!"

A few cheers sounded, and Viktor placed the glass in the center of the table as a symbol of our union. No one touched it, and I wondered what he was going to do with it.

I bent close to Christian. "Thirsty? I bet that's torture."

He circled his finger around the rim of his glass, creating a bright note that hung in the air. "Not as torturous as having to partner with a scavenger. Come to think of it, I might need that drink after all."

Hours later, I was gloriously inebriated. I quietly sat back and listened to everyone tell stories about their previous jobs, although some I had trouble following because of the uncontrollable laughter and inside jokes. Shepherd abandoning Christian with the cop was just one of many antics they played on each other. Their sense of humor delighted and frightened me all at once.

Gem skated out of the room when Wyatt turned in his chair and started talking to no one. Talking wasn't the appropriate word so much as arguing with thin air. When we had a moment alone, I asked him why—as a Gravewalker—he hadn't detected Christian at the cemetery. After all, that was his primary skill. Wyatt just gave me an impish grin and said he wanted to give the discovery a push in my favor. Maybe he was embarrassed to admit that he'd switched off his senses after assuming Christian was dead, but it was a nice thing to say.

I grabbed a bottle of wine with a few good swigs left in it and journeyed upstairs to my room.

My room.

I finally had a nest—a place to call home. A retreat where I could have privacy, feel safe, and not have to worry about where I was going to sleep on a rainy or wintry evening. But tonight wasn't for sleeping, so I crawled out my window and onto the roof, balancing along the peak and nearly tripping when I spotted Gem in the courtyard pool, floating in the water. Not in her skates, of course, but she'd changed into a white gown. She looked like Ophelia down there—not swimming, just floating peacefully with the soft glow of green lights below her.

I crossed to the other side of the roof where it wasn't so steep and sat down next to a window facing east. The stars burned through the night like pinholes in the curtain of darkness. Somehow the air felt cleaner, cooler, and the world opened up to a vast universe. Had it always been so beautiful?

My heart quickened when the window suddenly opened and Niko poked his head out.

He squinted at me and then smiled. "Mind if I join you? I thought I heard someone walking up here."

"Sure. Just be careful. It's slippery, and the roof is slanted," I said, my words slurring.

Niko stepped behind me and sat to my left, a pleasant breeze blowing his hair behind his shoulders.

I took another swig of wine and handed it to him. Niko held the bottle and drank a mouthful before handing it back to me.

"I bet you're not as drunk as I am," I said, setting the bottle on the window ledge.

He lay back and stared at the sky. "I feel drunk beneath all these stars."

I eased back next to him. "How is it you can see stars? Are you sure you're blind?" I said with a snort.

"I'm quite certain. I've been thinking how strange it is that people have ridiculed you for your eyes. Why is color so important to those who see?"

"Because aside from gender, color is the easiest way to divide people."

"I've experienced quite a lot of prejudice in my lifetime because of my heritage, but I'm trying to imagine how eye color can be important. Eyes are so small. It's not as if your head is purple."

I laughed. "Maybe you *are* drunker than I am."

He made a soft sound, still staring upward. A shooting star quietly skated across the sky.

"So what do they look like?" I asked. "The stars, I mean."

His voice was loose and relaxed. "I can't compare it to what you see. Light is energy, and all that energy is flickering and shining above us. Maybe shining isn't the right word, but it's everywhere. Did you know most of those stars died long ago? Their light still shines. I never knew such things when I was young; not until I became a Mage did the universe open up to me."

"How do you fight people who have weapons?"

His brows drew down. "Good question. Some of it's instinct, but weapons are an extension of their master. They absorb energy and intention, making them visible. Not always, but especially with a Mage or someone who's lost control over his emotions. I've had centuries to refine my skills, but I'm not perfect. I still trip over curbs and run into poles."

I shivered and took in the incredible view. I'd been on a million rooftops, but the only scenic views they gave were concrete streets and urban life. Moonlight glazed the tops of the trees like icing, and the sky was impossibly clear.

"So… you're okay partnering with Christian?"

I laughed. "I wouldn't go that far. You can't trust Vampires."

"Including you?"

I leaned over, my voice a loud whisper. "I'm part Mage."

"Ah. So I can trust you partway."

"Bingo." My eyes hooded when the breeze skated across my skin. "Viktor didn't leave me with a choice, but it doesn't matter. I can deal with Christian."

"You'll be the first then. He keeps to himself most of the time. It hasn't been an easy adjustment for the group, but maybe you'll bring him out of his shell."

"What am I, the turtle whisperer?"

Christian being the hermit of the house struck me as comical given his personality, but Vampires weren't exactly notorious for forming close relationships with people.

"Niko, can you keep this a secret? Me coming up here, that is. It's where I like to be alone."

He snickered. "The roof?"

"When I was a kid, I used to climb on top of our trailer and just lie there, looking up at the stars. I still remember the sound of the train in the distance, the horn blowing in long intervals. I used to dream about running away and jumping onto one of those trains. It seems silly to think about it because they probably just went through small towns, but I craved adventure. I wanted to discover the world and be someone."

"That is what all children dream." He scooted his feet up, his legs bent at the knee.

I focused on a distant star and yawned. "Then we grow up and see the real world for what it is, and it's not as magical as we first imagined. It's dark and full of pain."

He turned to face me. "So why do you still look up?"

Niko's question spiked me through the heart, and I pushed myself to a sitting position.

He sat up and put his hand on my shoulder. "What did I say? Your light changed."

After another gulp of wine, I lowered my voice, as if someone might actually hear me. "Do you think I'm evil?"

"Why would you ask me that?"

I pulled up my knees and hugged them. "All those men I've killed. Not as many as I first thought, now that I know how Vampires die, but still. I don't feel any remorse for what I've done. They didn't provoke the attack; I sought them out to punish them for their crimes."

"They weren't innocent," he pointed out.

"No, but what makes me any different from them? I've been thinking a lot about it—good and evil. Is it based on our actions, reasons, or how we feel afterward? Is killing only wrong when the victim is innocent?"

The question hung in the air for what seemed like a stretch of eternity.

Niko glanced upward, the moonlight illuminating his face. "I don't know, Raven. Maybe there is no good and evil."

"So what makes us different?"

He gazed pensively into the darkness ahead. "We're all sinners. Maybe what makes us different is that we're willing to change."

"I barely change clothes."

"You're here," he said, tapping on the roof. "Same sky, different way of looking at it. Right?"

I'd felt disconnected for a long time. So much so that I didn't even recognize my face in the mirror anymore. Keystone offered me a glimmer of hope that I might be a part of something greater, but I wondered if that was just a lie I was telling myself.

"Just be careful, Raven. This isn't the end of your journey; it's the beginning. You would be a fool to believe you've figured out your destiny. You are so young, and life will test you in more ways than you can imagine. Someday you'll look back on this time and wonder who this person was. Just when you think you've figured out who you are, the fates have a way of testing you." Niko stood up and carefully walked by me. "I'm full of spirits this evening." He gripped the top edge of the window and turned his head. "Are you coming?"

"Nah. I think I'm going to watch the sunrise. It's been a long time since I've watched one, and it looks like it's going to be a beautiful day."

"As you wish."

When he stepped inside, I glimpsed a dark shadow moving swiftly over the roof to my right. I could have sworn it was Christian, but the wine was probably playing tricks on my eyes.

I leaned back and gazed up at my future.

"Starlight, star bright…"

Acknowledgments

This book was a labor of love. Thank you to Kelly R., Teresa, Amber, Mikaela, Erin, Kelly K., and Bretaigne for your valuable contributions. Thank you, Anne, for cleaning up my messes and making my books shine. Thanks to my family for your unwavering support.

Keystone was written in 2010 as a follow-up to the Mageri series to explain where Christian Poe went. Destiny had more in store for him. Seven years later, he's ready to share his story. It was also the chance for me to fall in love with a new leading lady, Raven Black, who is every bit as complicated, loyal, and tough as I could have hoped for in a character.

I dedicate this book to all my loyal readers who are always eager for the next adventure and new characters to fall in love with. This series will contain twists.

Enjoy the ride.

Printed in Great Britain
by Amazon

78965533R00178